Cadon, Hunter

By

Rebecca Bradley

Cadon, Hunter

Published by Loom
Printed by Lightning Source International

Cover design: Loom, adapted from a fresco found in the Villa Boscoreale.

Trade paperback ISBN: 978-0-9926000-6-8

LM01

For Ellen

About the Author

Rebecca Bradley, born in Vancouver and raised mostly in Calgary, started a round-the-world trip in the 1970s that lasted twenty-odd years and gained her a family, a Ph.D. in Archaeology from Cambridge, much experience grubbing around in the Nile Valley, and a lifetime of entertaining things and places to write about.

In the meantime, she wrote the Gil Trilogy (fantasy), Temutma (horror, coauthored with Stewart Sloan), The Lateral Truth, and a slew of short stories for anthologies and her own collections. Her work has been presented on radio on the CBC in Canada, RTHK in Hong Kong, and in translation in Germany.

Rebecca now lives in thrall to cats and chickens on an acreage in British Columbia, and writes a blog for the Skeptic Ink Network.

Table of Contents

Cadon, Hunter

Prologue

The shamans would say the night was full of Watchers: below, ten thousand eyes gleaming red in the dark forest; above, five thousand eyes set like flakes of mica into the ceiling of the world.

These Watchers were the stars, and what they saw on moonless nights was a black sea where floated black mantles of land, their darkness stitched here and there with patterns of light. Some of these patterns were ancient and familiar: glittering strings of volcanoes, bold curves of coastline limned in phosphorescence, the dark-hearted outward-creeping rings of steppe and forest fires. Some were small and not so familiar, single points of flame: a fire-circle of the People, the lamp of a farming homestead high and lonely in a wrinkle of mountainside. Others were larger and even more novel, the lights of the settlements and newborn cities, where a thousand household lamps glowed inside the perimeters of torches on palisade walls.

On a certain night, the Watchers took note of a lone campfire far from all other lights, eclipsed now and then by the branches of a tree swaying above it. The youth roasting a hare in its embers was planning his next day with excitement and a touch of dread. After a while, he kicked the fire to death and climbed high into the tree with the cooked hare in hand, out of the Watchers' sight.

They shifted their attention a little to the south and east, to a scatter, smaller than many but larger than average, of hearthglows escaping the chinks of poorly built wooden dwellings. In the centre was a square patch outlined by torches, filled with reflections off the greasy hair and pale garments of many people. At the brighter end of the square, another youth was pretending to watch something unspeakable taking place on a covered platform, hidden from the view of the stars, but he was in fact devising a poem in his head.

Eastward again, far to the east, to where a jewel of light glittered at the highest point of the greatest cluster of torches anywhere on the black mantles of the land. There was a young man there, too, but he was planning nothing, devising nothing, and seeing very little, though he was perhaps the only wingless creature in the world to have such a view. He took a long pull from a golden chalice, after which the lights of the city below his window blurred and spun. Before long, he threw up, and then he drank from the chalice again.

Chapter One

The Woven Wonder

Cadon remembered feeling like this once before, while creeping towards a rock-shelter where a hillcat kept her stash of ripening kills. Then, however, he was one of five hunters, and they had the musk of the cat to give them a good feel for her degrees of hunger and heat, fear and irritation. Now he was alone, and the scents that came downwind to him from the savages' huts were either unfamiliar or unexpected, and certainly all wrong.

Crouched in cover not far from the edge of the ashgrove, he tasted the wind again. It was suspiciously clean. Furin had sworn the savages lived in these places as tightly as wasps in a nest, also that they pissed in the same rivers where they fished and shat behind their own filthy berths, where captive animals lived and shat alongside them. Perhaps these savages had tidier habits than the ones Furin had known, he reflected. Or perhaps his far-uncle had been making things up.

With a deep breath, Cadon rose from cover, each hand dangling a long loop of shells gathered on a beach of the far western ocean. Nothing came to his ears but the small noises that would be ominous only when absent: birds, tree rats, buzzing insects. Nothing man-sized moved in the shadows of the ashgrove.

"This man," he called out, "is Cadon of the Fox lineage, of the People. This man is a friend." Simple and direct. Until he was acknowledged, the detailed account of lineage would be a waste of breath. He lifted his head again to listen, and not just for sounds of savages inside the huts. The Old Man would not mind, but there was a chance the Old Woman would chide him for claiming the status of a man when the man-making was still a few days away. The Old Woman's chiding could take the form of a near miss by a lightning bolt, a falling tree, a charging boar—the annals suggested she had a capricious sense of justice, if not of humour. Cadon breathed a quick charm, just in case, and returned his attention to the huts.

Still nobody. Stymied, Cadon shifted his weight nervously from foot to foot. He was well trained in the courtesies of approaching another family of the People: arms wide open and hands full of visible gifts, a large fish, a fur, a bunch of healing flowers from deep in the forest, plus a reasonable amount of noise to announce one's arrival, and a full-voiced summary of one's lineage. Once the grannies pronounced on the exact degree of cousinship, appropriate greetings and embraces would follow. Then food. But how did one approach the savages? Furin said they did not fully understand the courtesies. Worse, he claimed they were as defensive as wolves about the miserable patches of territory they considered their own.

Still nobody. Cadon crept on towards the ashtree-shrouded huts, noting with disapproval they were badly placed for either hunting blinds or forest berths, crammed together and overloaded with the wrong kind of cover. Perhaps it was true the savages did not do much hunting.

He stopped when the peeling flank of the first hut was only an armlength away. There was a humid stench in the air under the ashtops, though the morning was still cool. What had possessed these savages, Cadon wondered, to build their hive in a marsh and sleep among the needlenoses and the gnats? He scanned the dimness under the trees, caught his breath at splashes of paleness on shadowed tree-trunks—not human heads, he realized after a very bad moment, but some of those giant wrinkled face-flowers that, for all their beauty and scent, were known to the People as a marker of unhealthy ground. More of them peered at Cadon from deeper in the ashgrove, where the sun would hardly penetrate even at noon, clots and crowds of weeping white faces battening on the ash trunks. Perhaps they accounted for his uncomfortable feeling of being watched. All his senses were telling him he was alone, but his instincts were not so sure.

There were more huts squatting among the trees than Cadon had realized at first glance. Twenty, thirty? It was sometimes hard to tell where hut left off and vegetation began. The wattle was sagging and patchy, with many holes through which someone might have watched him approach, and might be watching him even now.

Moving quietly, he muffled the shells away in a belt pouch and pulled his thrusting spear from its loop at the side of his backpack. Only then, spear at the ready, could he bring himself to peer into one of the huts. Cramped and filthy, much as in his far-uncle Furin's description. The subtle residues of a range of odours—old smoke, old sweat, animal hair, decay—came through faintly, but at last in a code he could understand. Nothing had lived here for months, but something had surely died here, at least a season ago; it was certainly in or before winter, whereas the Long Days were now approaching. The smell of death was no more than a hint of a trace. The interior was empty except for a wet spring's growth of vines and some kind of prickly shrub, rioting over the floor to about the height of Cadon's knees. He shrugged and moved on.

Although the forest seemed to be reclaiming this territory, with something like the second growth that follows a fire, Cadon could trace phantom trails among the huts, and patches of ground that had once been cleared. There were even a few rough squares like those on the river terrace outside the ashgrove, dominated by a kind of podplant with outflung runners that swarmed up the ash trunks and the decaying wattle walls. The firstfruits had been plundered by birds and tree-rats, from the look of the empty pods, but none of them had been plucked or cut from the runners in a way that implied a human hand at work.

So where had the savages gone, and why? *If* they even existed, which Cadon was beginning to doubt. His far-uncle Furin had said they did not move around like the People, but clung to one place like limpets on a rock, producing litters of many children and allowing *all* of them to live. It was the most outrageous of Furin's many stories; and now, in this lifeless place, it seemed possible that Furin himself—two-time champion storyteller at the Caucus of the People—had created the entire legend of the savages, root, trunk and branch. Maybe the huts were just some kind of bizarre forest growth, like giant hollow mushrooms.

Cadon picked his way along one of the phantom trails to a hut that looked larger and better made than the others. The roof was intact, the rifts in the wattle were smaller, and some decorative effort was visible on the mud plaster near the entrance, chevron patterns applied in red earth. They were reminiscent of the face-signs of the Red Deer lineage, but crudely done, the sort of botch-job that would cause a granny to rap the artist on the knuckles and tell him or her to get it *right*. Shaking his head critically, Cadon lifted away the woven-willow screen that blocked the entrance, allowing feeble daylight to wash inside.

Here at last were some of the peculiar objects Furin had described. There was a sleeping platform at one end of the space, more solid than the simple raised pallets the People installed in their winter base camps, and there were other constructions for which Cadon had no words. Near the other wall, an ash-filled hearth was sunk into the dirt floor, nearly strangled by creepers. Cadon drifted around the musty interior, examining—but prudently not touching—the artifacts of the savages. Nothing here was as exciting as he had hoped.

He stopped beside the sleeping platform, a wooden framework raised about knee-high off the ground, lashed together with twine and smothered in a careless heap of skins. The skins were a scruffy lot, not worth a second glance from a hunter of the People, badly cured and probably infested with fleas. He remembered his far-uncle saying that bodybugs were among the worst trials of living with the savages, along with dirty water, disgusting food, bad air, and the savages' mystifying compulsion to work long hours in the hot sun. Cadon snagged a skin on the point of his spear and held it up in the light from the entrance—poorly tanned, some kind of goat. But as he shook it off his spear with a grunt of distaste, he caught sight of the marvel it had concealed.

The colours caught him first, glimmering at him through the dust of many months and the beginnings of a patina of mould at one end. A bright, rich blue, the colour that a perfectly clear sky takes after sunset, before the coming of full darkness. A yellow that brought to Cadon's mind the short-lived flowers of a tundra summer, far to the north. A vivid red that called up autumn berries, a russet like sunrise before a storm. The pattern was complex and seemed to be part of the body of the thing itself, unlike the embroideries that women of the People applied to soft-cured hides and the leather waistbands they wove for their marriage skirts. Forgetting caution, Cadon threw aside the rest of the woefully cured skins so he could see the marvel in its entirety.

He supposed it was a coverlet, but *woven* instead of tanned; and woven not out of twisted plant fibres or leather strips, but out of coloured strands that were soft and fine. He dared to touch the thing at last, smoothing the surface tentatively with both hands, delighting in the novel texture. It was as pleasant to the touch as the sleek pelt of a mink.

It was just the sort of thing he was looking for.

He continued to stroke the coverlet while he thought it over. He had come all this way to make a fair trade with the savages, and it was not his fault they were not here. The man-making was only a few days away. Cadon had his strings of exotic shells to present to the Ones Before, and a couple of excellent pelts, but he doubted they had any chance of standing out among the gifts of the rest. Of the thirty-odd age-brothers becoming men at this Caucus, Cadon predicted that no less than eight would be presenting strings of exotic shells from the same far western beaches, and almost everybody would have one or two good furs to throw in as well. Two summers before, all five shamans had voted for an exquisitely cured bearskin offered by that fool Barik Aurochs, who was clearly not up to the honour. Rami Horse's shell-gathering had prevailed four summers ago, but his offering had been one enormous coiled monstrosity the size of a man's head, from which Rami could coax amusing noises, rather like farts. The shamans had been enchanted. Cadon's exquisite strings of little shells would suffice to make him a man, fit to be a father and to sit on the edge of council, but they would never make him a *big* man. This woven wonder was another matter.

When it came to standout gifts for the Ones Before, quality counted the most—his perfect shells had been selected with agonizing care from *thousands* on just that basis—but the shamans might also take uniqueness, originality and danger of acquisition into account. Unfortunately, no impressive animal had considerately presented itself to Cadon for killing in many months. If not for far-uncle Furin's chance remark three days ago, he would certainly have been stuck with the shells.

"About two days south of here," Furin had said as they walked along under the lee of a distinctive crag, "that's where those savages live that I told you about, poor overworked underfed buggers." And, when pressed, "South, like I just said, further south than we like to go. There's a big river flowing east-west down there, with settlements all along it as thick as teeth in a jaw, and that's where the savages live." When pressed further: "Of course you could find them, nitwit. Their stench goes for *miles*." When pressed no further, Furin had failed to raise the dangerous question of why, exactly, Cadon wanted to know how to find the savages. And during the siesta stop, after bribing his cousin Lusil to wait two hours and then tell the Fox elders he'd gone—Cadon went. He planned to use three days to find the savages, one day to make a trade, and two days to cut northeast at great speed to catch up with the rest before they reached the massif, well in time for the Caucus. And planning beyond that, he intended to enter the man-lists with a gift of stunning uniqueness and outrageous originality, something to crush the boring bearskins and ho-hum monster shells of previous man-makings, to cause this year's donors of tired old seashells and obvious pelts to feel sick with envy: something from the savages. As far as he knew, nobody had ever thought of that before.

***

Theft was not a word in Cadon's active vocabulary. He had come to trade fair gift for fair gift, and it mattered nothing that there was nobody around to keep him honest. He took the loops of shells out of his pouch and arranged them carefully and rather prettily on a table-thing made of strangely flat wood. After another glance at the woven wonder, he frowned in calculation and unwound a couple of well-cured rabbit pelts from the bentwood frame of his backpack, to add to the composition. And then, after a brief struggle with himself, he reluctantly but scrupulously added a third. The deal was done to his own satisfaction, and nobody could ever say he had tried to cheat the savages.

It was about time the deal was done, anyway. Now that he had found the perfect gift for the Ones Before, Cadon discovered how completely his curiosity about the savages had vanished, and how pressingly he wished to leave this place behind him. How could the savages have tolerated living here, encased in the tainted air rising from the ground, the squalid walls of the huts, the oppressive shade of the ashtrees? Through the doorway, face-flowers gazed at him in a hostile and calculating manner—or was one of them a *real* face? He whirled to confront it. Nothing looked back but the swollen white blooms. Yet the feeling persisted, and powerfully: the feeling of being watched, even stalked, as if the savages had really been there all the time, cunningly hidden behind every hut and in every patch of shade.

Enough of that. He took a few bites of jerky and dug out some twine to fasten the coverlet to his pack. One more gloating look at its rareness and beauty, and then he grasped the top corners and began to draw them back to meet the others. But the instant he lifted the corners, the faint scent of death strenghthened tenfold: a stink that was old, from sometime between first frost and the Short Days, but at least now he knew *where* death had happened. He leapt backwards, his hunter's instincts intervening to keep him from crying out, and to place the spear in one hand and his mace in the other without conscious impulse. Outside the hut, the bird noises serenely carried on. Inside the hut, silence.

The coverlet had hidden them. Three heads close together, chins touching a hide blanket directly underlying the woven wonder. The skulls were not yet down to bone. Hair and shreds of flesh remained, though eyes were gone, plus tongues, leaving dark caverns in the orbits and yawning mouths. *The dead will not normally harm you*, Cadon heard the grannies say in his head. He took a deep breath and pulled away the hide, exposing another layer of old stench to the humid air. And now there were four, the fourth a baby whose hairy little skull had almost merged in corruption with the breast it was pillowed on. The others were probably full-grown, though none would be considered of decent adult stature among the People, not even the male savage whose scalp bore a floss of greying hair. Skins had burst with the vapours of decay, blowflies had found their way under the hide to grandfather whole lineages of maggots, but even so the bones still lay in a dark matrix of old bodily fluids: well-dried excrement smeared from haunches to kneebones, and a black staining around shrivelled lips and throats.

Once his heart settled down, Cadon found himself properly shocked. These people having died foully on their own sleeping platform, how was it that nobody had come to clean them up and clear them away and perform their obsequies? It was simply not right. Cadon had seen death before, but unattended or unceremonious death only rarely, and this horrified him far more than the sight of the remains.

Time to leave.

Working with breathless rapidity, he folded the woven wonder and rolled it into a cylinder, wrapped it in the last of his spare hides and secured it to his backpack like an extra bedroll. What misfortune or curse, he wondered, could have made those savages ill enough to die in that loathsome fashion? Illness was known to the People—hunting wounds sometimes rotted, snakes might bite, the occasional idiot might mistake deathwort for its harmless cousins, *anyone* could take a fever or a chill—but this noxious voiding from both ends at once was something Cadon had never heard of before.

At the door, he paused. Duty was calling to him with a granny's voice, sounding as he imagined the Old Woman would sound. The Old Man, typically, was nowhere to be heard. Vainly Cadon carried on an internal debate: he did not know the degree of his cousinship to those corpses, so how could he perform any obsequies for them? Anyway, the savages were very hard to figure out. People who could build their homes in a mudhole like this might well have peculiar obsequies, which may already have been performed. Maybe the savages did not customarily wash their dead, and preferred to leave them in places like these abandoned huts. Furthermore, he argued with himself, he had no time to expose the bodies properly, and most certainly would *not* be returning to retrieve the skulls. Why start something he could not finish? But in the end, he and the Old Woman compromised. Cadon sprinkled some powder from his pouch over the corpses on the sleeping platform and gabbled the forms for farthest-cousins, as being the words least likely to offend the deceased. Then he was out the door and on the most direct route he could see towards the riverbank, not taking time to retrace his steps.

Almost immediately, he discovered that his first instinct had been correct. The savages had indeed been present all along, and all around him, cunningly hidden in the huts and the shadows. Three steps off the overgrown path, his boot crunched through a rounded stone that was not a stone, but a nearly naked skull. Another lay tangled in the podplant runners a few steps away. It appeared boars had been rooting here, though not for podplants, and assorted ribs and longbones were scattered in the undergrowth. Something that was not a face-flower grinned at him from the ruins of a collapsed hut to the left. To the right, a bony arm lay across the slate slab of a threshold. That was the last relic of the savages Cadon chose to notice. Ignoring the grannies in his head, he ran like a spooked stag through the deathly ashgrove and splashed across the shallows to the far bank of the river.

***

He did not look back as he set off on his return journey to the People. He never wanted to see a settlement of the savages again for as long as he lived. He would be happy never to hear another of Furin's stories about them. He set off towards the northeast, choosing his course with a knowledge of direction so sure and ingrained that he was hardly aware a choice was being made. Swinging along with the tireless pace that was natural to the People, he melted the miles as easily as sunlight melts the snow on a warm boulder.

Healthy young animals like Cadon do not dwell for long on the unpleasant past. The more distance he put between himself and the sorrowful huts of the savages, the better he felt. Two or three days would see him back among the People, where he belonged. Five days more would see him become a man.

Chapter Two

God and Poet

Far to the east, at the centre of the greatest of the few great cities in the world, a stone tower stood high above a tangle of teeming streets. On a moonless night, the youth who languished in its highest windows could imagine the lighted city to be a huge galley adrift on a sea of black water. By day he could look across the rooftops and palisades of Balimhavar to lush expanses of fields and terraces, orchards and villages, stretching unbroken to the ring of mountains a day's journey to the north. All of it—up to, including, and around the mountains—belonged to him. So did the people he could look down upon from his high tower, the trader-ants swarming in the streets of Balimhavar, the farmer-ants busy in the fields, the sailor-ants unloading galleys at the waterfront. He was scrawny and narrow-chested, dark-haired and still beardless, with a mouth that turned down at the corners in a contour of chronic discontent. His name was Filkamos, and he was a living god.

He sipped from the chalice that was always within reach. Then he rested his chin on the sill and tilted his head outward just far enough to get a view down the sheer face of the tower. Directly below him, a long way down, many ants bustled back and forth across the temple square. Not for the first time, he marvelled at how strange the act of walking looked from above, as if each step were a potential fall arrested by a leg swinging forward at the last moment, and then another, and another. It was undignified. Filkamos was sure that *he* would look quite different to anyone observing him from above, if any such blasphemy were ever allowed to happen.

Idly, he fingered the stone at his throat, a fine blue crystal set in a heavy gold torque, worth at least fifty of the swarming human insects he also owned. He twisted the ends of the torque until he could remove it from his neck, and weighed it musingly in his hand. The three plump girls sprawled on the cushioned dais looked hopeful, but he did not toss it to one of them. He held it on his palm, out over the sill, so he could peer at the lowering sun through the blue crystal; then he turned his hand, and let the torque fall away towards the temple square far below.

He could see it glittering all the way down, falling away from him into a rabble of heads at the near edge of the square. One inconsiderable ant slumped to the flagstones in a fashion that looked most comical from Filkamos's vantage point. The little leg did not swing forward. The round head completed the ever-threatened fall and began to make a dark puddle around itself on the stones. That was the first joke. Then dozens of those tempting round heads converged, like ants around a drop of honey, and a struggle seemed to develop—no doubt, Filkamos thought, for possession of the fatal torque. Shouts drifted up to his ears, tiny faces turned up towards his window. He could also hear the ticking of the scribes' styluses in the observers' cell behind the wall.

Grinning, Filkamos reached into a chest on the table and brought out a handful of heavy nuggets. Leaning out again, he let these fall from his fingers one by one, and watched with interest as some of the insects dropped to the flagstones in a manner similar to the first, while the rest—after a brief retreat—converged again. Some wore the dark colours of his own court troops, and these seemed now and then to be trying to force the crowds back; whether for their safety or to enable the troopers to take the nuggets for themselves, Filkamos could not quite make out. He did his best to aim at them.

On the dais, the girls pouted. Filkamos ignored them, because this new game of raining gold and death down upon the crowd in his forecourt was so much more beguiling than the thought of dalliance. Then one of the girls rolled off the dais and approached Filkamos, swaying her perfect hips. He grimaced as he heard her come up behind him and felt her press against his back, nestling his neck between her breasts. Filkamos shrugged in irritation, but the girl mistook him, and twined her arms around his neck.

"Lord in Earth," she breathed into his ear, "stop playing this foolish game. Come play with us instead."

Filkamos reached automatically for the chalice and took a gulp. "Nothing the Lord in Earth chooses to do is *foolish*," he said in gentle reproof as he set it down. Warned by his tone, the girl began to back away. Too late. Filkamos swung himself around and used the momentum to put more force behind his fist; and then, since the girl's nose was broken and she was no longer perfect, he swung her around and seated her screaming on the windowsill, and pushed. Behind the wall, one of the observers gasped, but the ticking of stylus on tablet never ceased. Filkamos leaned out in time to see the end of the girl's cartwheeling downward progress, and to note with interest that she landed in a tangle of pale limbs on another of the dark-headed ants below. This gave a whole new dimension to the game.

Filkamos turned and looked appraisingly at the two girls hunched in terror on the dais. He took a long gulp from the chalice and waited for his eyes to come back into focus. After a moment, he smiled at the girls. "Come here," he said. "You first. What was your name again?"

***

Far, far below, but still a floor above the level of the square, two portly old men were discussing a matter of great importance when the first shouts disturbed their peace.

Grandis Dreeve, the Recorder of Balimhavar, looked up in irritation. "Oh, *what* is it this time?"

His cousin, the Palace Master, rose and crossed the chamber to peer through the balustraded open arches overlooking the temple square. He recoiled at a fresh wave of shouting, then leaned out to peer upwards, and hastily pulled his head in again. After a moment, he sighed. "I sometimes wish the Lord in Earth would find less original ways to express the divine will."

"Careful, Villamar, that's the next thing to blasphemy," the Recorder piously reproved him. "Whatever the Lord in Earth chooses to do has been destined from the beginning of time. It is not our place to question his actions, only to interpret them and obey. But," and his voice changed to one of weary interest, "what is the blasted boy doing now?"

"See for yourself, Grandis," said the Palace Master, "but don't put your head out too far."

The Recorder reflectively drained his chalice before hauling himself up. Filkamos needed something to keep him busy, that was the problem, but obviously the Lord in Earth could not demean himself by doing anything normally defined as useful. The boy was no common son of the soil. He could not play at being a tailor or a butcher or a tanner, nor a scribe, nor an astrologer. As the living manifestation of the male powers pervading all that existed, he could not be risked in battle, nor taken on a hunt, nor even given a garden to cultivate. He had to be free of all duties except the divine imperative to express his own wishes, as the great weathercock of the world—every act, every whim, every impulse, pointed out the path down which a heaven-fearing people must go. And whatever mad, drugged whim the boy was indulging at the moment, the Recorder sourly told himself, the interpretation of it would keep the court diviners busy for days. What a relief it would be when the Dreeve Faction had a free hand! Sighing, he joined the Palace Master at the balustrade and watched the turmoil in the square.

"It's surprising," said the Palace Master at last, "how much damage even a small object can do when dropped from a great height."

The Recorder clucked his tongue. "Gold, isn't it? Must be the chest from Mori. I wondered about the wisdom of leaving it there for him to play with. Why isn't the spear-captain clearing the square?"

"I believe he was trying to," said the Palace Master. "He's on the ground near the archway."

They both started as something large and pale shrieked past them. The Recorder risked leaning out a little farther than before. After a few moments he said, "Villamar, make an old man happy. Tell me the Consort Chanithel was with the Lord in Earth today."

The Palace Master sighed. "I'm sorry to disappoint you, but he's hardly sent for her since the day they were conjoined. She loathes him, and I'm not sure he remembers who she is. Why?"

"Because if she *had* been with him, the damned girl would be dead now. How many playmates today?"

"The usual three, I'd suppose. So that was—*watch out!* Lords in Heaven, that was close!"

The Recorder patted the Palace Master soothingly on the back. "Don't worry, cousin, my deliverance was obviously destined from the laying of the foundations of the world, just like everything else. Look, those idiots are fleeing the square at last. I suppose girls raining from the sky are not as tempting as gold nuggets. And here comes the third bedmate—Villamar, what a pity."

"Yes, yes, poor girl."

"I meant, what a pity it's not Chanithel Hithe. Think of the trouble that would save."

"Indeed it would," the Palace Master said wistfully, "and we'd have been blameless, truly and honestly blameless. Perhaps, while the boy's in the mood to fling young women out of windows, we should—?"

"—send up the Consort?"

"Just a thought."

"No, Villamar, too obvious," the Recorder said after brief consideration, but not without regret. "We've missed the moment. The Hithe Faction would not accept the coincidence."

The Palace Master shrugged. "Right you are. Damn it, though, this is not a good time for Filkamos to be inventing novel pleasures."

"Any time chosen by the Lord in Earth is the *right* time."

"You know what I mean, Grandis. Anyway, perhaps it's the right time to put bars on his windows, and maybe a covered colonnade along the palace side of the square."

"You'd be tampering with the expression of the divine will," the Recorder chided him.

"Perhaps, but we really can't let him go on idly killing his own chattels—"

"Why not? Their lives belong to him."

"But—"

"Anyway, Villamar, think of the honour of dying in such a way. Brained by a lump of gold, fallen from the hand of a god! Too good for them, really. Well, we can think about installing some bars on the windows, but a colonnade is going too far. What we might do, though, is increase the strength of the tincture."

"Again? Already?"

"It seems the present dose is no longer sufficient."

The Palace Master looked unhappy, but he nodded. "Right again, my dear Grandis. As always." He refilled both chalices, and handed one to the Recorder. In the square, a chorus of shouts suggested the god-king had run out of girls, and was now pissing out his window.

***

Ten days' sail to the northwest, in the petty kingdom of Lazoon, another young man lay on his back in the grassy courtyard behind the temple, gazing up at the pattern made by the linden leaves against the sky. He wore the white calf-length shift of the Lazooner priesthood, and was not ill-grown for a son of upriver peasants, though he was thin as a whittled stick. His face was narrow and pleasingly symmetrical, and his ears were nicely folded back against the sides of his shaven head. He was fortunate in this, because some of the other priests looked like double-handled jugs when they removed their headdresses.

At the moment there was a piece of cloth stuffed inside each of those well-formed ears. He was trying not to be distracted by the distant wailing in the quarantine camp on the outskirts of Lazoon, where columns of smoke from the charnel fires seemed to hold the sky in place with thick black fingers. True, it was not as terrible as during the height of the plague, when the peasants carrying their dead to the charnel ground often fell dead themselves in the middle of the track, and the cries of mourning and the upthrust fingers of black smoke were as unremarkable as wet ground after rain. But it was still terrible, and already the famine that often marched with plague had begun to pick off the poorer refugees, and misery was rampant —not at all the right background for composing an ode to springtime in the new and perhaps overly complex verse-mode that Valdur was inventing for his own amusement.

In fact, he wondered if he might be making things a little too difficult for himself, not just with the intricate pattern of syllables he had set as a goal, but with his choice of subject. Perhaps he should take the cloth out of his ears and listen to what the world had become. Perhaps he would be better occupied in meditating on death, or on despair, or on the Heavenly Fathers' strange habit of piling up sorrows for their children on earth. Any normal poet might find enough material in a single one of these desperate days for a lifetime of lamentations.

But Valdur did not want to be a normal poet, and he did not want to dwell on thoughts of death, plague, or famine. More than anything in the world at that moment, he wanted to close his eyes and think of a three-syllable word with the meter ta-TA-ta to round out his verse on the trembling of linden leaves in a late spring breeze. He had got as far as closing his eyes when he felt the vibration of somebody thumping across the grass, and a shadow fell on his face.

"I'm busy," he said.

The cloth was yanked out of his ears. "Valdur, where in the name of the Heavenly Fathers have you been? The Master Speaker wanted to see you."

Groaning, Valdur sat up. "I've been right here, Zayn, exactly where I said I'd be."

Zayn, a junior cutter priest, and one of the unlucky double-handled-jug brotherhood, put a hand down to jerk Valdur to his feet. He said with justifiable annoyance, "You did not say you'd be hiding under the trees with your ears plugged. I've been here three times already, looking for you."

"Well, you've found me now. What does the dismal old farter want to see me about?"

"I said he *wanted* to see you, Valdur. He's dead now."

"*What?*"

"Yes, dead—not plague, though. A seizure of some kind while he was eating his lunch. He turned purple and tipped over and spent an hour or so rattling himself to death in his own bed, and that was the end of him. But he's not officially dead yet," Zayn corrected himself, "because the king can't declare him dead until you get there. So come on."

"Me?" Valdur stopped in his tracks, or would have done if Zayn had not been propelling him along with a firm grip on his shoulder. "What have I got to do with it?"

"You've got to take the ring off his finger. He should have passed it on to you before he died, but we couldn't find you, could we?"

"But I'm not—"

"—the new Master Speaker? Actually, you are. Congratulations. Now move, they're waiting."

Valdur blindly trampled across the edge of the late gardener's beloved pansy bed, now ragged with neglect. "But I can't be! What about Mandel?"

"Mandel died this morning in the quarantine camp. You're the senior surviving speaker priest. Don't worry, you'll be fine."

"Fine? I'll be better than fine, thank you all the same," Valdur said, beginning to recover. "I'll be wonderful. But it's a pity about Mandel and all the others. I won't pretend to grieve for the Master Speaker, though, the vicious old shit. Zayn, I'll be the youngest Master Speaker ever appointed, won't I?"

"Yes you will," Zayn said severely, "but don't swell up about it. It's a plague-time, remember? Otherwise you might have waited another ten years before getting your chance, if ever, no matter how clever you might be. And yes, we all know perfectly well how clever you are, little man. Even the old Master Speaker knew it, which is probably why he loathed you so dearly. But Valdur?"

"Yes?"

"You're going to have to behave now. You have to be responsible. Lazoon depends on you. No more running off to make poetry. No more hiding under bushes. And no more trying to mess about with the litanies."

"Some of them could use improvement."

"They're the words of the Heavenly Fathers, you fool. Even the Master Speaker cannot change them. Save your fancy wordsmithing for the trials and narrations."

They trotted down the cloister that ran alongside the temple, a bright rectangle of plaza looming ahead of them at the end of the darkness. The shortest way to the palace block was to climb the stairs at the end of the cloister and cut across the raised portico of the temple, but it was considered disrespectful to do so while a messenger was still suspended in the Doorway of Heaven. There was one there now, two days dead, a buzzing woman-shape black with flies and smelling ripely in the midday heat. Valdur grimaced, not at the familiar death-stench in particular, but at the strange logic of the sacrifices. Though he was a priest himself, it still seemed odd to him that so many poor sods who managed to survive the recent winter of calamities were apt to end up dead anyway, and horribly dead, flayed alive by the cutter priests. In these times of the Heavenly Fathers' obvious displeasure, the king was ordering a messenger to be sent skyward every few days. Valdur was glad he was not a cutter priest.

"I see only a few people in the plaza, and they're not looking. Let's risk it." Zayn caught Valdur's arm and started to pull him across the deserted portico.

Valdur let himself be tugged halfway before he shook free and planted himself in the middle of the great stage of the portico, gazing across the dusty, empty expanse of the plaza. Empty now, but soon to be packed with the peasantry. Five thousand people lived in Lazoon before the disasters, and almost as many lived there at the moment, because the losses from the plague had been made up for by refugees still straggling in from the villages. He could imagine them—all those eyes, all fixed on him. At the next sacrifice, *he,* Valdur, orphan of the horny-handed peasant Jinoon, bond-child to the temple from the age of three, would be the priest invoking the Heavenly Fathers in front of all those eyes. The people of Lazoon would hear *his* words in the trials and narrations, be made breathless by *his* enactments on the great holy days.

He laughed aloud with pure unexpected joy as he ran to catch up with Zayn. Maybe he could slip a few lines of his own poetry into the litanies without anybody noticing.

Chapter Three

Camping with the Relatives

Cadon was capable of tracking the Foxes to the massif on his own skills, but he was touched to see how considerately some pointers had been left for him, an indication his seniors were not very upset with him for going off on his own. Lusil had been instructed to tell them he was making a last-minute hunt for a more impressive man-making gift, which was true, though incomplete. Anyway, so close to the pleasures of the Caucus, the elders were inclined to be tolerant of youthful enthusiasm.

At noon he passed through the campsite the family had occupied the night before, leaving him just half a day behind. There were clear signs the Foxes had been joined by another lineage sometime the previous afternoon, and the two had made fire and travelled on together. Cadon wistfully deduced they had started the joys of the Caucus a little early. Sixty-odd people in a festive mood left a very clear collective footprint. His near-uncle Xirn's morning-after tracks, in particular, showed evidence of a *very* good time. This could mean the men would be too hung over to scold him when he caught up, whether or not they started out angry with him, which only left his mother and the grannies of the Fox family to worry about.

And, possibly, the grannies of whatever lineage was now travelling with the Foxes. He cast about for traces of their identity, hoping he'd find a sign of the Wolves, but his father's well-remembered tracks were not among those that stood out. On the other hand, one man going barefoot on this easy stretch was missing a small toe on the left foot, which could mean either Hiram Eagle or Mil Roebuck. He rather hoped it was not the latter. Cadon did not want to think about the Roebucks until he absolutely had to. He looked carefully for indications of a shaman among the tracks, remembering that Shaman Fial was travelling with the Eagles this year, but nobody seemed to be dragging a tail in the dust behind him. More likely the Roebucks, then.

He caught up by evening, a half-day short of the massif, coming down on the camp from one of the rocky hills that enclosed a broad valley. It was a pleasure to recognize the valley as a traditionally happy place, one of those where the Old Man first taught his skills to the Nine Hunters. From the hill, he could see that it was indeed the Roebucks who had made fire with the Foxes the day before, and today they had been joined by the Hillcats, and so the bivouac was bustling. Numerous forest berths had been pitched and fires made, and the smell of roasting wafted up to him. Someone had killed very handily on the day's easy march. It was a pity his stomach was a little unsettled.

The pickets were loose and genial in this auspicious valley. Even the dogpacks were in a good mood. His far-uncle Pinne Fox, out on point, ruffled his hair in greeting and sent him on with a good-natured scolding. Cadon's loan-cousin Goran Horse was on the second line, but he waved Cadon forward from a distance, and Cadon was happy to avoid being subjected to more of Goran's heart-burning. Goran was destined to return to the Horses after this Caucus, and had been moping about it for the last month. Cadon was unable to see how leaving any woman behind, much less his cousin Bintah, could occasion such misery.

Furin Fox, spotted with an armload of fuel just outside the bivouac, seemed to want to speak to Cadon very much, but Cadon was not ready to discuss his journey yet. Waving cheerily to his far-uncle, he ducked through the undergrowth on to another path and stopped to make sure his prize was still well hidden inside the camouflaging skin. He made some token noise as he approached the berths, as a courtesy to the other families sharing the camp, though the camp was hardly quiet. Inside the circle of berths, the seven-yearling boys who would become hunters at this caucus were being drilled in the Prey Dance by one of the Hillcat elders. Chattering matrons and girls were digging a firepit, dogs were barking, a few of the older men were mending arrows in the shade. Cadon started across the circle to join them.

"Here he is now," said Granny Crooshah, at the entrance to one of the berths. "Cadon Fox, you get over here." She was the sister of Cadon's dead grandmother, and second only to Granny Sullah in the pecking order of the Fox women. She was not too bad, but Cadon's heart sank as he recognized her companion. Granny Dillah Roebuck was famous among the People. For one thing, she was very old. Still healthy at the phenomenal age of fifty-five, she had lived long enough to stop bleeding, a rare achievement. She made Crooshah, an elderly forty-three, look positively youthful. Granny Dillah Roebuck was, Cadon had heard, the sort who would need to be beaten on the head with a big rock before she would consent to die. And from what he knew of her also-famous temper, she spent much of her time inviting something of the sort. Cadon had managed never to come to her attention since she'd boxed his ears for him at the caucus ten years before, the day after he became a hunter. He remembered it vividly. He put down his pack and approached the old women with a polite smile and a respectful folding of hands.

Granny Crooshah Fox returned his smile, but with a look in her eye that said, *later, sonny.* Granny Dillah Roebuck's mouth, netted about with fine lines, did not look capable of returning a smile. She was short for a woman of the People, with a slight but definite crooking of her spine. She managed to look Cadon up and down very thoroughly with her beady dark eyes, without actually acknowledging his presence. "Well-formed," she said to Granny Crooshah, "but a bit gawky with those long legs."

"He's still getting used to them," said Granny Crooshah, "and he's better than he was. You should have seen him last year."

Granny Dillah continued to stare disapprovingly at his legs. "Sullah showed me his tally stick. Not bad. How's his grasp of the memory work?"

"Better than reasonable on the Lore," said Granny Crooshah, "but he needs a little more work on the Annals. He sings very nicely, by the way."

"Hmph." Granny Dillah prodded Cadon's belly and the skin over his ribs through his soft leather shirt. She pinched the hard muscles of his upper arm. He managed not to flinch, but he wished with fervor that he could be facing a rabid hillcat or a charging boar, or almost anything other than a pair of grannies weighing him up before a loan negotiation. He breathed a charm to the Old Man: *not my breeches, forefather,* please *not my breeches.* But Granny Dillah was now peering critically up at his face.

"Good-looking boy, I must say. The dark curls and the eyelashes—that's the Wolf strain coming out. I wanted his father Codor for our Baskallah, you remember, but you Foxes got him for Nurrah instead."

"There had already been a Wolf loaned to the Roebucks in that generation, Dillah. It wouldn't have been right."

"Perhaps, Crooshah, but Codor Wolf's father was a Hare. We needed a bit of that strain. Still do."

"Well then, you'll get a small dose of the Hares through this one, if you take him," Crooshah said rather snippily. "See his mouth? Very shapely, and fine teeth. That's a nice straight nose, too. There's the Hare strain for you."

"The nose is Red Deer, I think, dear Crooshah. Wasn't Nurrah's father loaned from the Red Deer?"

"Indeed, my dear Dillah—but I think you'll find if you search your memory–"and they were well away. Since neither of them told him he could leave, Cadon stood in a hunter's freeze and tried to be inconspicuous, hoping they would forget him and drift off while still caught up in the minutiae of the People's tangled bloodloans. With luck, they never would get around to inspecting the contents of his breeches.

***

Just after sunset, Cadon fished a nice bit of haunch out of the firepit and shook the ashes off it, ignoring the wistful eyes of the dogpack. He did not feel well. The grannies, augmented at a late stage by Sullah Fox and Manah Hillcat, had dismissed him at last; but by then he barely had time to find his mother Nurrah and his sister Pilshah and display the woven wonder to their admiring eyes, before they had to go and prepare for a women's moot taking place that evening. Nurrah had taken time to weep over him a little, though, which he assumed had something to do with the dark plotting of the grannies.

He knew perfectly well he should have been expecting it, this being his seventeenth summer and the year of his man-making. Signs and whispers had been cropping out for months, speculative glances from Grannies Sullah and Crooshah and Minnah, special treats and sorrowing glances from his mother, the odd ribald remark from the uncles: *It's just as much fun with women, laddie, just a different bivouac.* Further, it was a rare man whose loan was not arranged at the time of his man-making, though Cadon suspected the grannies had their options organized years ahead. There was no doubt he'd be trothed off at this Caucus and spend the next few years of his life on loan, fathering two children for another lineage. The only question was, which lineage? Now it seemed clear it was going to be the Roebucks, in which case the match would have to be Luah.

After a few bites, he hoyed across the firepit to his cousin Lusil and tossed the rest of the chunk of meat to a surprised but grateful member of the dogpack. Cadon should have been hungry, but he was not. His belly had been mildly uncomfortable all day, and the close-range scent of cooking meat made it worse. Nerves, he supposed. There was nothing wrong with little Luah, nor with the Roebucks, aside from Granny Dillah, nor for that matter with the institution of marriage, as laid out at the beginning of the world by the Old Man and the Old Woman. There was not even a virgin he'd prefer in one of the other families. It was just that time was passing too quickly. The man-making, eagerly anticipated only a few days ago, was now lying square across his path like a river that could only be crossed in one direction. Cadon, like any good hunter, liked to have alternate routes and the option of retracing his path.

His cousin Lusil was still sidling around the firepit as their far-uncle Furin Fox came out of the shadows, shoved a few dogs out of the way, and sat down heavily beside Cadon. Furin hissed, "You did a stupid thing, boy, if you went where I think you went."

"I'm happy to see you too, uncle," Cadon grinned. He had no intention of talking about his prize yet, except to his mother and sister, who had promised to help him get rid of the death-stench that still clung to its fibres. Pilshah had already taken it to the creek for a first dipping, though she had promised to stay upstream and keep out of sight of the place where the others were splashing about in the shallow water.

"You went to one of the holes where the savages live, didn't you?" Furin insisted.

Lusil squatted down in front of them, his eyes round. "What was that about savages?"

"*Hush.*" Cadon pulled his cousin nearer to make the three of them a little closed circle. "You'll hear the whole tale of where I went, but you'll need to wait for the man-making. Believe me, Uncle, I'll have lots of stories to tell you, enough for more nights than you can think of."

"Stories!" said Furin scornfully. "Stories! You thickhead! I know very well you went to the savages. Did they try to kill you? Or did they try to keep you?"

"Neither one," said Cadon, without thinking. Then he shut his mouth again, aware he had already said too much, determined to say no more. Why should he mute his own thunder beforehand, even with these two? Not, he admitted to himself, that there would be much of a story to tell unless he thought up some good embroideries.

"So, Cadon, you're admitting that's where you went. You have no idea how lucky you are," Furin said bitterly. "I was kept in cold misery for eight long winters by those bleeders, and I was damned fortunate to escape in the end."

"Kept in misery?" Cadon hooted, disbelieving. "I thought you were welcomed as their honoured guest. You told us—"

"What I chose to make stories out of was all true, except for that one small detail. And there's a great deal more that I chose never to tell you. But the savages live just as I described, as you've seen now with your own eyes. What did they say to you, boy?"

Cadon shifted his feet. "Not much," he said.

"That doesn't sound much like the savages. They did nothing but talk when I was there, talk and work in their damned fields. Too tired for anything else most of the time, except now and then tottering off to fight their brother savages in the next village."

The next what?" Lusil broke in.

"Village. Settlement. Place where savages live," Furin explained impatiently. "It's like a Family of the People, only with many more of them, and they stay always in one place, all the year around, in berths that can't be taken apart for moving. And they don't hunt much, except each other now and then."

"Family against family?" Lusil persisted. "I don't believe you. The Old Woman would stop them."

"The savages are not like us, Lusil. And their Old Woman is not like our Old Woman. The savages have some very strange ideas." Furin scowled. Cadon nudged Lusil, hoping he would let the subject drop, but Lusil was unstoppable.

"What strange ideas, Uncle?"

"Nothing," said Furin, looking down his nose at the two boys, "that I could make you understand easily. For one thing, the savages' Old Woman is not a granny, and she does not care about bloodlines. And the savages' Old Man is cruel, and he's no hunter, and you would not believe me if I told you what he makes the savages do. And they fight with each other, and a few times they've tried to fight with us, though we mostly keep out of their way. And that's all I want to say."

"How can they—?" Lusil began, but Furin hushed him with a gesture so furious that even Lusil had to notice it. Cadon sighed, feeling ten instead of two years older than his bed companion and near age-mate. Lusil had a tendency to fall asleep during story-time, and had trouble with the Lore and the Annals. He was not stupid, and his tally stick was impressive for his age, but feats of memory did not come naturally to him. Somebody was going to have a hard winter in a couple of years, coaching Lusil's recall for the recitations that would accompany his man-making. That person was unlikely to be himself, though, Cadon thought, since he would almost certainly be loaned to the Roebuck lineage for those years. With that thought, he hunched himself on the ground with his arms wrapped around his shins, partly to ease the continuing dull queasiness in his belly, partly to deal with a foretaste of what nostalgia was going to feel like, all too soon. Furin watched him gloomily. Lusil, accustomed to following Cadon's lead, looked uncertainly from his cousin to his far-uncle.

"Well, Cadon?" said Furin at last. "At least tell me this about the savages, and set my mind at ease. Are you certain none of the buggers followed you here?"

"Very certain," Cadon answered, thinking of the scattered bones, the silent huts, the family of corpses under the woven coverlet. "And that's all I have to say, Far-uncle. Wait until the man-making for the rest."

Frowning, Furin rose and stalked away. Lusil bit into a chunk of meat speared out of the fire and chewed contemplatively. "Don't worry, I won't ask you any more about where you went," he said when he had swallowed. He inclined his head closer to Cadon's, and his voice became low and guarded. "There's something I have to tell you."

"What is it?" Cadon asked, without much interest. His stomach really was unsettled. A throbbing ache was starting behind his eyes.

"There's a women's moot tonight."

"I know, my mother told me. So?"

Lusil glanced around without moving his head. Nobody was paying them any attention. "Mairn Roebuck and I are going to watch it from cover and see what happens, and you can come too if you like."

"To the women's moot?"

"Keep your voice down! Yes, why not? I've always wondered what happens at their doings, and I bet you have too. We can't ask *them*, and the uncles who know anything about it won't tell us. Tonight is our chance to find out. And it's good timing for you."

"What do you mean?"

Lusil grinned. "I guess they'll be talking about you tonight."

Cadon moaned softly at that reminder of his fate, but he felt a stir of interest. What Lusil was proposing was a piece of pure mischief— possibly dangerous, certainly disrespectful, and liable to get the Old Woman upset enough to start chucking minor hazards around if she noticed. On the other hand, it was the sort of cheeky little revolt the Old Man would enjoy watching. Strictly speaking, it was not forbidden. It was officially assumed that no such act would ever occur to well-reared boys and men of the People. The fact that most of the men, even including the shamans, had spent at least one night of their lives spying on women's magic from the cover of a dark tree was tactfully ignored. And he, Cadon, might hear something about the terms of the next five years of his life.

"All right," he said, "I'll come too."

***

Much later in the evening, Cadon nudged his cousin. Granny Minnah Fox, the rearguard, had finally sidled out of the camplight in the direction of the hill. Crooshah and Sullah Fox and the Roebuck and Hillcat grannies had vanished discreetly some time past. The younger women and girls had been disappearing in ones and twos ever since. The men of the three bands, studiously unaware of their womenfolk's withdrawal, were diligently improving on old hunting tales around the fire, while getting good and sotted on a strong infusion of happygrass. This was correct behaviour on such a night, and the young men knew it well. One grain more of good sense, and Cadon would have been glad to stay by the fire; one grain less of youthful curiosity would have led the same way. He nudged Lusil's arm again.

"Not yet," Lusil whispered, "I want to hear Salm's Backwarder story."

Cadon grimaced. Devising tall tales about the Backwarders, who farted from the mouth, spoke from the arse and did all manner of other amusing oddities, was a popular fireside entertainment in the all-male hunting camps, especially a series of speculative tales about the Backwarders' women, but this was not the time. Moreover Salm Roebuck was an easy drunk—the gourd only had to pass him twice before his tongue became loose and his stories exceptionally dirty—and he had a way of making a story last a very long time, because he kept losing his own trail. Tonight he was drunk enough to have forgotten that this was, in practice if not in fact, a mixed camp. By a polite fiction, the men were not supposed to notice the women were gone. The sort of stories fitted for a hunting camp were therefore not suitable, and everybody was honour-bound not to start quarrelling or permit matters to turn even recreationally violent. Cadon listened for a moment before leaning towards Lusil's ear again.

"Might as well come now. Salm won't get far with this tale."

Indeed, even before Lusil could answer, Rithin Hillcat was coughing pointedly and calling in a bullmoose voice for the gourd to come back to him. On Cadon's right, Faras Roebuck made a forthright and rather controversial statement on the relative merits of thrusting versus throwing spears, bound to stir up heated technical debate. On Lusil's left, Pinne Fox called heartily for Mil Roebuck to tell his two-reindeer-with-one-arrow story *again*.

"But there was this woman, see," Salm began again, "this woman of the Backwarders, who met a man of the savages in the forest—listen, Faras."

Faras Roebuck raised his voice and kept going. Salm, subsiding, appeared to fall sleep where he sat. Cadon slid backward into the darkness behind the circle and waited for Lusil and the young Roebuck, Mairn, to join him. He knew Mairn fairly well, a stocky boy with a pleasant face and better-than-average tally stick, who was also destined to become a man at this Caucus. Not too steady on his feet at the moment, Cadon noticed. He and Lusil both looked as though they had imbibed a little too freely of the happygrass for those about to undertake an entertaining act of mischief. Cadon thought again of backing out, but when Lusil set off through the inner cluster of forest berths, he shrugged and followed. It was about time, he thought, that Lusil took his turn at walking in the lead.

***

From the dark edge of the circle on the far side of the pit, Furin watched the boys leave. He had expected them to go, had even considered letting them know that he knew what they were planning, but it was harmless enough mischief. He had done it himself once, at about their age. Now he knew not to bother.

He reached across Salm Roebuck for the gourd, took a good pull at it, and passed it on to Pinne Fox. Cadon was a fine lad, and the most beloved of his Fox nephews, though it would never do to let him know that. Furin had been Cadon's sponsor ten years ago, when the boy passed over to the men's side of the camp, and he took a mentor's pride in Cadon's strength and skills. It would never do to let Cadon know that, either. Most of all, the boy must never know how much Furin would miss him when Cadon travelled on with the Roebucks at the end of this Caucus.

But what a risk Cadon had taken, putting himself in the hands of the savages—and how lucky he was to come back at all. Furin pondered grimly on the eight years of his life he had lost to those unclean bastards, not to mention any chance of being loaned. No youth or maid would greet him as father at the Caucus; Stennah Aurochs, whose bloodline would have been tied to his, was already a matron by the time he returned from captivity. Yes, he had fathered three babies in the savages' village, but they had all ended up in burial pots under the hut floor—and a good thing it was, too, considering the miserable circumstances they were born into. Now he could hardly remember the faces of the women who had borne them.

The gourd came around again, but Furin took only a judicious sip before passing it on. It was a clear head that he wanted, and the chance to ask Cadon some hard questions when the lads returned from their bit of fun. The more Furin thought about it, the more curious it seemed to him that the savages had not instantly tethered Cadon to a stake in the middle of a field, and set him to slaving in the sun. There must be something his far-nephew was not telling him.

***

The mischief-makers moved on silent feet along a minor path, with the sort of stealth that came naturally after a lifetime spent learning to hunt. Outside the main bivouac, Lusil halted to get his bearings in the near-darkness under the trees. The only light was a glimmer from a forest berth visible a short stone's-throw away, an outlier that was of the camp but not in it—a single berth, rather crude, no more than a hasty lean-to with a small fire in front of it, by which a woman sat nursing a swaddled child. Cadon recognized the woman as Annah Roebuck, little Luah's near-cousin and some degree of far-cousin to himself; her grandfather had also been a loan from the Wolves. He almost stepped forward to greet her before he remembered the illicit nature of their expedition—and then it occurred to him to wonder why Annah was not with the rest of the women at the moot. The other surprise was how Lusil and Mairn looked straight through her without speaking, and how Annah herself, after a quick frown in their direction, shut her lips and looked away. Then Cadon saw the swollen curve of her belly, and he understood. Between five and six months gone, while the first baby was not even a two-yearling yet. When Annah looked up again, the skin around her eyes was red with more than the firelight. She said nothing as the young men filed past her.

So, Cadon thought sadly, the moot might be as much to do with Annah as with himself and the eternal granny game of matchmaking. The Roebuck grannies would want to minimize poor Annah's scandal as well as her sorrow; better, perhaps, if the decision could be made before the Caucus proper. Still, it was hard on Annah, and shameful for her husband—Djeen Eagle—and the worst part of it was yet to come. An unsanctioned second baby, when the first was still in arms! One of the babies was doomed. Times like this, the Old Woman could seem like a ruthless old bitch. He dared to turn and send a small wave of friendly acknowledgement in Annah's direction, but he was not surprised when she simply averted her eyes.

He did his best to put her out of his mind.

***

Finding the moot was a childishly easy exercise in tracking. Almost any trail that trended uphill could serve at the beginning, until they should come into earshot of the festivities. They were even lucky in their lighting—the trees, not very thickly set, began to turn silver on their eastern flanks as a quarter-moon rose above the lip of the valley. Cadon forged ahead in the end, aware the others were hanging back to let him take his usual leading position. Annah's sadness and the ache in his belly were forgotten in the pleasure of following a trail. Snapping twigs and rustling branches were not a problem; nervous giggles might be, if those two idiots could not control themselves. Cadon felt nothing like laughing, but Mairn and Lusil were having far too good a time.

"Shut up, Mairn, or you'll have your Granny Dillah down on us like a rockfall."

"Oh, she's not so bad," Mairn began, but he broke off, sniffing the air. "Do you smell that?"

Smoke, but not from the roasting pits back in the bivouac. The breeze was coming off the crest of the hill, and the camp was downwind anyway. Also, the smoke had none of the savour of burning meat, but rather a musky richness that reminded Cadon of herbal draughts the Fox grannies prepared when some family member had a cold or a flux. His ears caught a sharp crackling noise—probably lightning dust—and a moment later there was a voice on the wind, a distant but sufficiently familiar high-pitched voice. Granny Sullah Fox, without doubt. The moot was already in progress.

A step later, his stomach heaved and his knees almost gave out under him. Gulping, he swerved aside to let Mairn take the lead, not caring for the moment whether the others thought he was showing fear. He knew himself it was not fear, not even fear of the wrath of Granny Dillah Roebuck. It was a surge of honest nausea, and he was convinced for a moment he would lose the tiny amount of meat he had choked down earlier, along with the small draught of happygrass sitting unhappily on top of it. Cadon bent over with his head braced against the smooth chill of a tree trunk, and after a few seconds the sickness passed. Mairn and Lusil, not noticing he had stopped, proceeded noiselessly into the silver and black stripings of the forest ahead of them. Cadon willed some force into his knees and padded after them.

Chapter Four

The Lumps in the Oak

Within the next half-watch of the night, Cadon learned why none of the men who had ever spied on the women's moots had much to say about them. There was not much to say. As far as he could tell, very little of any interest happened throughout most of the proceedings, and even that little did not happen very fast.

Granny Sullah's voice, the sound-beacon that led them, was just finishing some sort of invocation when they came within sight of the women's fire. A loud *crack* froze them like deer, but it was just sprinkles of lightning dust being thrown on the fire, flaring prettily with starbursts of white sparks. By the time they finished a hunter's creep through the trees around the edge of the circle, and a lizard's climb into the forks of a well-placed great oak, no voice in particular was standing out from the others. A great many of the women took turns speaking, each change of turn marked with a pinch of lightning dust on the fire, but they all spoke in low tones that carried towards the ground or into each other's ears instead of up to the trees. As a group, the occasional ripple of quiet amusement was about as loud as they permitted themselves to become. Cadon did not dare compare his observations with those of Mairn and Lusil, since any whisper they made was almost certain to be heard.

Crouching bored and uncomfortable in the fork of the oak, Cadon thought with longing of the men's magical gatherings. Raucous, rousing, boastful of both the future and the past; much symbolic slapping of the Old Man's back, much dancing and pounding on things and posing with spears and bows. Normally quite drunken, which was part of the attraction. The happygrass might give you, on at least a temporary basis, the eagle's sharp sight, the bear's strength, the roebuck's speed, the hare's invisibility, the fox's strategic cunning, the stamina of the steppe horse, the potency of the bull-aurochs. If a shaman happened to be present, he might drop a few pinches of fungus into the happygrass, and then the visions would become truly wild—sometimes even a manifestation of the Old Man himself, wreathed and bearded with leaves, tongue sticking out between his grinning lips. And when most of the participants had dropped with exhaustion, there would always be a few to carry on singing and pattering in a slightly confused fashion on the ceremonial drums, until the next shift woke up again and staggered back to their feet. The women's moot could hardly be more different.

They sat quietly in neat concentric circles around a tidy, restrained fire, grannies near the centre, matrons and virgins mixed on the periphery, all the females of all ages of the Roebuck, Hillcat, and Fox families—except Annah. The only males who had a right to be there were the nurseling boys under four winters of age, including the yearling at Yarrah Roebuck's breast. Cadon noted the Roebuck yearling well, trying to remember whether Annah's authorized child was a boy or girl, and wondering whether the existence of Yarrah's boy in the Roebuck clan would affect the grannies' decision. Maybe Annah Roebuck's superfluous child would not have to be killed. The Old Woman sometimes broke her own rules. Uneasily, wondering if the Old Woman ever attended the moots personally, Cadon scanned the dark trees for any sign of her floating form, sharpened his ears for a hiss from the serpent she carried in each hand.

A poke from Mairn brought Cadon's wandering mind back to the great oak. He looked along Mairn's pointing finger. Little Luah Roebuck (not so little now, he noted) had risen from the outer circle and was picking her way towards the grannies in the centre. Definitely not so little; the year and some months since the Foxes last made fire with the Roebucks had seen her sprout in the most astonishing directions. Cadon found himself leaning a little further than was prudent over the oak's stout branch in order to watch her better: curves and grace, smooth dark hair, interesting tremors under her flexible leather shift when she walked. She stood lissomly beside the fire, between Grannies Sullah Fox and Dillah Roebuck, holding something at arm's length and revolving slowly to display it to the watching women. A knotted skirt, the twisted fibre strings dangling stiffly from the braided leather intricacies of the waistband—her marriage skirt. The women murmured approval, and more lightning dust crackled and flared in the fire.

Cadon swallowed dryly. He was suffering a revelation: his first inkling as to why Goran Horse might be so reluctant to leave Bintah behind, now his time on loan was finished. And was Luah blushing, or was it just the warm firelight on her face? Then, in Granny Minnah's muted utterance, Cadon caught what might be his own name. Mairn poked him again in confirmation, Lusil reached down from the next-highest fork to rap him very quietly on top of his head. To Cadon's distress, the women chose that moment to indulge in one of their choruses of laughter, not so soft this time, more like snickers with distinctly ribald overtones. Luah, looking pleased and swaying her hips, made her way back to the outer circle. It appeared to Cadon as if the loan negotiation had been ratified, and he felt surprisingly cheerful about it.

The next entertainment consisted of parading a few of the younger girls, the ones who were a year or two short of making their own marriage skirts, but old enough to have the grannies thinking ahead. These included his sister, Pilshah, which startled Cadon. More lightning dust, another bout of monotonous but rather pretty chanting. This was followed by a tedious interval during which Cadon's mother, Nurrah, recited that part of the Lore that dealt with ensuring the bloodlines and the ties of loyalty between family to family, and with the Old Woman's warning to keep the branches of the People well pruned. Cadon knew roughly what that word meant. Pruning was what women did to trees in the fruit forests in the autumn, for strange magical reasons known only to themselves and the trees. He thought sadly of Annah and her overburdened branch. What pruning would be undertaken there?

While Nurrah moved into a recitation of the bloodloans of the Fox lineage, the situation in which the young men had placed themselves became suddenly more precarious. Three dark figures detached themselves from the outer edge of the women's circle and headed straight for the foot of the great oak. Cadon smothered a gasp and tried to make himself look more like an innocent lump on a branch. Above him, Lusil had a quiet little convulsion and grew still. None of the women looked up. Stopping under the oak not quite below Mairn, they knelt on the ground. A glimmer of light spread between them and brightened when the smaller figure bent and blew on it. Embers, Cadon saw, spilled from an ember-basket into a nest of prepared kindling. The new fire flared with a pinch of lightning dust before settling into a steadier glow as the fuel caught beneath the kindling, and then most of it vanished from sight as one of the women placed a dark object hood-wise across the flames. In a stray flicker of light, Cadon recognized the grannies Crooshah Fox, Sarvah Hillcat, and Missah Roebuck, Annah's mother.

The only sound was the voice of Baskallah, Nurrah's age-mate in the Roebuck family, moving on to a recitation of the Roebuck loans and lines. Then it was Pasannah Hillcat's turn. When she finally finished working her way through the present generation, the silence was unbroken for a long uncomfortable time—particularly uncomfortable for Cadon, whose dull stomach ache was now enlivened by sharp shooting pains in the lower gut, raising the fear that a belch or fart might escape him at this inconvenient moment. He did not see how their situation could get worse, until it did.

At one moment, the women were sitting quietly around the larger fire; at the next, with no warning, the whole moot was in motion towards the oak. Grannies Sullah Fox and the dreaded Dillah Roebuck led the way, Sullah carrying a burning brand, Dillah with a small object cradled in front of her. They stopped at the muffled fire and waited for the others to gather around them again, in not such a tidy circle this time. Cadon had a fearful few seconds of certainty that the women had known all along they were there, and were gleefully proceeding to spring their trap—that is, to set fire to the oak tree and roast themselves a few interlopers as a sacrifice to the Old Woman.

Miraculously, nobody looked up. All heads were bent towards the little fire, crackling under its clay hood. Only the matrons were chanting, some obscure chorus about `pruning', which Cadon could not quite catch. The virgins were rapt and silent on the fringes, the grannies clustered in the middle. Granny Dillah Roebuck, in the unsteady light from Sullah's brand, was closest of all to the fire. The object she was chafing was no bigger than her hand, a little bulbous tube of a thing, pointed at one end. When Cadon recognized it, he hastily averted his eyes. Some unknown woman had laboured to mold it that day, with clay and lightning dust and her own spit, using her own body as a model. This was serious women's magic. Granny Dillah held it at last to the flat bosom of her shift, then tossed it under the fire's hood.

Nothing for a few moments. A gurgling in Cadon's lower gut sounded as loud as a bear's lovecall to Cadon's own ears, but no accusing faces pivoted to search him out. A few moments more, and all the grannies were crouched on the ground, with the glow of the small fire throwing their facial wrinkles into high relief as they peered into its heart. A sudden sharp *ping*—then another, and a scatter of small mysterious raps against the clay hood. A murmur swept around the circle as Granny Dillah poked into the hidden embers with a stick and raked something into the open. Cadon peered down at the top of her head, the thick greying coil of hair secured with ivory spindle-pins, the jutting triangle of her nose. Other tops of heads gathered near hers as she examined her recovered prize, but they did not get too close. Even Granny Sullah Fox kept a cautious minimum distance. Cadon suppressed another vehement protest from his gut. The night seemed unnaturally warm, and he prayed to the Old Man that no beads of the sweat starting to roll down his face would fall on anybody.

"We have an answer."

Granny Dillah's voice, reedy in the open glade, was followed by an expectant silence. She surveyed each of the faces around her in turn before her voice rose again, louder and sharper. "The Old Woman speaks for the child *inside* Annah's body."

So that was it, Cadon thought. The clay woman-thing dancing herself to fragments in the fire was Annah Roebuck; this decision was what Annah Roebuck was waiting for, down in her lonely forest berth. He heard a few indrawn breaths and one long exhaled sigh—he traced that to Granny Missah, Annah's mother, who perhaps had been unguarded enough to become too fond of the grandchild she already had. Of course, Annah's unsanctioned pregnancy also reflected badly on Missah, and her shame demanded she would be the one to go off with Granny Dillah before sunrise, to dig the grave. Cadon reflected, as he often had before, that men were lucky: they were generally required to kill only animals and a few overly aggressive savages.

"I am not finished!" Dillah snapped. Startled, Cadon nearly lost his grip on the branch. "The Old Woman says this is to be no quiet shame for the Roebucks to bury in the forest and then forget. She says we must unbirth the child Sashah in the presence of the Caucus. Afterwards, she must be left in the keeping of the Ones Before."

Seen from above, the heads made an agitated pattern: faces swinging to faces, lips coming close to ears, clusters of three or four forming and reforming. The only concensus was a general shift away from Granny Dillah's position, leaving a clearing around her. The messenger, Cadon thought, was being blamed for the message. Nobody liked having to kill an infant, but a quick snap of the neck and a quiet hole in the forest were kinder than slow starvation in the dark, in the silent company of the Ones Before.

***

That was effectively the end of the moot. Before the moon was a handspan higher in the sky, the big fire was given one last magnificent handful of lightning dust and then smothered and kicked to death, and a steady outflow of murmuring dark figures nearly emptied the glade. All that were left were

Granny Dillah Roebuck, still crouching over the smaller fire, and a young Roebuck virgin waiting quietly at the edge of the trees. There were also, still unseen, the three oversized branch-clumps on the great oak tree: two of them feeling cramped and bored and sorry they had come to such a colourless event; the third feeling all of those, plus having to concentrate fiercely on keeping his lower gut quiet. As the minutes dragged on, another physical necessity became urgent to Cadon. He peered down at Granny Dillah with impatience and a spark of genuine hatred.

"Granddaughter, I did not like what I heard in this fire."

The attendant—Roosah Roebuck, Cadon recognized her at last—bent over the old woman's hunched figure. "Nobody did, Granny, but it's all up to the Old Woman. It's late now, the moot's over and you must be tired. Come back to camp and get some rest."

"Don't talk down to me, my girl. The Old Woman may have left us, but this fire still has something to say. Listen carefully."

Their heads came together over the remains of the small fire. Abruptly, Granny Dillah reached out with a stick and knocked away the hood. As smoke and sparks drifted up towards the observers in the tree, the old woman rocked back and forth on her heels, her chin propped on her knees and one ear turned to the fire. "Yes," she said, "I hear you. Roosah, can you hear the words?"

Roosah dutifully held her ear so close to the little hearth that her hair was in danger. "No, Granny," she said.

"Then clean out those dirty ears and listen again. Listen for these words: *death and doom.* Do you hear them now?"

"Sorry, Granny."

Dillah Roebuck made a noise that sounded to Cadon like the growl of a she-wolf. "The fire is telling me more about what is coming. We're doomed, Roosah. These are the last days of the People."

"That's what you said last year, Granny."

"So what if I did?"

"And the year before that, at the last Caucus. Ma told me." Roosah sat back from the fire and tossed her tail of dark hair over her shoulder. "I'm sorry, Granny, but I just don't hear any words in the fire."

Cadon was glad he could not see Granny Dillah's face. The set of her greying head on her hunched shoulders was already enough to set his shame-and-fear reflex spinning into operation. Roosah might be allowed to talk pertly to a granny, since she would be one herself one day, given luck and a long enough life, but Cadon would sooner leap off a cliff. This was the dark side of the respect for the Old Woman and her fleshly counterparts that every son of the People was taught from his beginning breath. The last response he expected from Dillah Roebuck was a low, ungrudging laugh.

"The fire doesn't lie, Roo, but it's never very clear about timing. Are you really so eager to watch our doom arrive? I've seen it coming for many years, and I hope it delays for many years more—but I'm afraid it has come much closer since the last time I listened to a fire."

Sighing, the girl stood up. "If you say so, Granny. But I doubt it'll come before sunrise, so let's go back and get some sleep."

Granny Dillah said nothing as she permitted Roosah to help her to her feet. She spat into the bright embers, head cocked as she listened with polite attention to the sizzle. A quick and expert scattering of the fire, and the two women vanished into the trees, the younger trailing a little behind the elder. As soon as Cadon judged they were out of earshot, he slid down the tree and tore frenziedly at his breeches.

"That's disgusting," Mairn said a few moments later, having just completed a more leisurely descent. "What a stench, Cadon. What have you been eating? Don't you Foxes know how to find good shitting places?"

"Shut your face," Cadon said, fairly amiably now his immediate urgency was dealt with. The night was too hot for him to feel like taking proper offense, though he noticed vaguely he was the only one sweating.

Lusil joined them. His problem had been too much liquid at the happygrass session, coupled with a touchy bladder. The noise of a small waterfall seemed to go on forever. The grannies, if present, would have nodded knowingly about the bladder and pointed out that his father was a Bear. Cadon leaned against the trunk of the oak while he waited for the deluge to end. After the initial relief to his bowels, he was starting to feel bad again. Worse, in fact. Much worse. The closest he had ever come to feeling this bad was the memorable occasion of his first hangover.

On the way back to the bivouac, they made a wide detour to avoid Annah Roebuck's forest berth.

***

The main camp was peaceful. Cadon, trying not to stagger too obviously as he followed the others towards the firepit, had just one target in mind, to lie down before he fell down. There was plenty of room now. Most of the uncles had vanished inside the berths, leaving a thin strew of younger men curled up and snoring on the hard ground near the fire. The only uncle visible was Furin, wide awake and glaring at the flames. He looked up with no sign of pleasure as the boys approached.

"I know where you've been. First the savages, now the women's moot. I tell you, Cadon, you'll come to a bad end."

"We all will, according to that Roebuck granny," Lusil chuckled. Cadon said nothing. He let himself collapse towards the ground in a fairly controlled fashion.

"Which Roebuck granny? Dillah?" When Mairn nodded, Furin's face became watchful, the face of a picket listening to twigs crackle in the undergrowth. "What did she say?"

Cadon did not hear Lusil's answer. A fiery hand had just reached right inside his belly and grabbed his guts. He clamped his lips shut over a groan and shifted onto his right side with his knees drawn up to his chest. The relief was momentary; the hand took a firmer hold and twisted his innards in the opposite direction.

"Cadon, what's wrong?"

"Nothing, Uncle."

Why was it so hot? The campfire had become an inferno, sweating him into fine, dry ashes. He groaned and managed to pull himself a few inches into the darkness before his bowels gave way and reduced the agony by a tiny degree. The fire seemed hotter than ever, but he lacked the strength to crawl farther; and that hardly mattered, because even the darkness was burning. Furin's voice penetrated the fiery fog in his head: *Cadon, Cadon, what have you brought us?* He listened distantly, only just able to bear the pain as long as he kept himself doubled up.

Indeed, he seemed to split himself in two: one part to observe and hear the ministrations of Furin, the anxiety of Lusil, the rapid arrival of his mother Nurrah and a selection of grannies; the other part to drift towards a confused sleep attached to a different set of dreams. The man-making was only two days away. It was high time he thought through the details of his story and the flourishes that would accompany his narrative. He only realized he was rehearsing at full voice when somebody put a hand over his mouth.

Granny Dillah Roebuck was there, crying doom—no, that was a phantom from earlier in the evening. There were only Fox grannies around him, and one of them was pouring something sweetish into his mouth. He vomited it out and let himself detach and float away again. There was not-so-little Luah to ponder, and the thought of Annah Roebuck's doomed child to avoid; the man-making to prepare for, the huts of the savages to forget. With so much to think about and to keep him awake, he was asleep in no time.

***

He did not waken properly for days after that. It was true his eyes opened frequently, but the fever-ridden fits of raving and struggling that broke his coma now and then were not real consciousness. Much of what he later remembered involved violent colours whirling inside his head, hot as the heart of a volcano, tormenting his eyes whether his lids were open or shut; and always, always, there was the twiddling of that hot hand inside his belly. Early on, in rare lucid flashes, he was aware that ropes were binding him to a litter, and he watched treetops flow overhead like a green sunlit river. He wondered if it was time for the man-making yet, and fumbled for the right words to explain how he came by the woven wonder. There were voices now and then, but at first they were too distant to understand. Later, they shrieked into his ear with the power of a storm-surf. Towards the end, they only wept.

He remembered hearing a woman's voice at some point, damning Cadon's name and his seedings to all generations, and it seemed to him that this must be the voice of the Old Woman herself, hissing like one of her own twin snakes; then a man spoke, the Old Man using Furin's voice, rough and sad, bidding Cadon goodbye. Sometime later, somebody held Cadon's head to give him a drink of water. That was the last he remembered until he had slept his fill and sweated out the worst of the damnation, and then he wakened into the world of Granny Dillah Roebuck's direst prophecies.

Chapter Five

Some Pillow Talk and a Debut

Far to the east, on the night of the women's moot, a very different sort of rite was taking place in the palace of the Lord in Earth. The Dreeves were clumped on one side of the viewing stands and the Hithes on the other, buffered by a good scattering of Fruhs, Kilves, Sundes, Varns, and a few from the lesser great factions. Prefect Caviram Hithe thought this separation was just as well, since violence, which was officially banned in the god-king's conjugal bedchamber, was very much in his thoughts. The night's fiasco was clearly Grandis Dreeve's doing. It seemed almost unfair that Calviram could not climb straight across the Fruhs, Kilves, Sundes, Varns and all the rest, and stick something sharp into the Recorder's black and devious heart. On the other hand, Calviram knew his role in the Hithe order. He was the designated diplomat, the man of words and manners, the wielder of subtler weapons than knives. It was his elder brother, General Hoderil, who was the man of blood. Calviram glanced sideways at his brother's grim profile.

On the vast fleece-strewn bed in the centre of the chamber, their sister Chanithel, the Consort of the Lord in Earth, was sitting cross-legged and slump-shouldered in her fine bedgown, her face hidden in the ruins of an elaborate coiffeur. Filkamos, the Lord in Earth, was sprawled on his back with his mouth open, snoring sonorously. Chanithel was trying very hard, Calviram would give her that. With thoroughness and earnest application, she had run through the whole long list of the conjugal arts, some of them twice. The most active response from Filkamos had been a fit of giggles some time back, and mostly he did not even seem to notice she was there. In the presence of all these witnesses, the Consort was signally failing to put herself in the way of conceiving an heir, and this was surely the Recorder's fault as much as hers. Naturally, it could not be the fault of the Lord in Earth.

The general put his lips close to Calviram's ear. "He's drugged."

"Of course he's drugged. He's always drugged."

"More drugged than usual. Or a different drug. The consummation wasn't anything like this."

It most surely was not, Calviram thought. On the night their sister was conjoined with the god-king, Filkamos had been tireless, even manic, bouncing about on poor Chanithel for hours and hours. Not very pleasant for the girl, but Calviram's pity for her was blunted by the fact that, even after all that bouncing, she had failed to become pregnant. The few times the Lord in Earth had sent for her since then had been repetitions of the first. But how could Chanithel succeed in her duty to the Hithe faction when the Palace Master controlled the god-king's meat and drink, and the Palace Master was presently a Dreeve?

Calviram looked across the stands to where eight lordly Dreeves were watching Chanithel's humiliating performance, some of them with ill-hidden satisfaction. The Palace Master and the Recorder were sitting a little apart from the others, heads close together over a small stack of tablets in the Palace Master's lap. Calviram would have given the tip of his right forefinger to know what Villamar and wicked old Grandis were discussing with such perfectly blank faces.

***

"Prefect Calviram is looking at us again."

"Let him."

"Grandis, I think he suspects—"

"He'd be a fool not to, and the Prefect is no fool." The Recorder looked up from the tablet in his hand, met Calviram's eyes, and gave him a honeyed nod across the weaving heads of lesser witnesses. Calviram nodded just as affably and offered the Recorder a graceful wave before turning his attention back to the conjugal bed. The Recorder permitted himself a twitch of the lips that was not at all friendly.

"All the same, Villamar," he said, "I think we'll try a different tactic the next time the Consort is called to her husband's bed. We can afford to be obvious, but we can't afford to be predictable."

"But if she should become the Electa—"

The Recorder's fingers tightened on the tablet. Sometimes his cousin irritated him almost beyond bearing. "That will *not* happen. We cannot have the General lording it over us as the Shield of the Electa. I'd slit the little cow's throat with my own hands first. But it will not come to that—the Hithes were able to land her in the boy's bed, but the Consort does not necessarily become the Electa, and that's all that counts."

Down on the great bed, the young woman in question pushed her hair away from her face, visibly took a shuddering breath, and started again. Very pretty she was, like all the Hithe women, the Recorder generously admitted to himself, but about as seductive in her despair as a piece of mouldy old bread.

"Were you perhaps thinking," the Palace Master began delicately, seeing where the Recorder's eyes were fixed, "that the Consort Chanithel might, let us say, eat something that disagrees with her in the next little while?"

"Villamar, as always you are attacking the wrong end of the problem," the Recorder sighed. "If anything should happen to the Consort, the General will simply produce one of his other three sisters from the Hithe stronghold, each of them with as good a chance of becoming Electa as our darling Damissel. Would you murder them all? Even the lesser families would start to notice. Think again."

The Palace Master's hands were not moving, but he had the faraway look of someone counting slowly and painfully on his fingers. "So," he faltered at last, "we go after General Hoderil instead?"

The Recorder beamed. "Very good, Villamar. If there is no brother to stand as the Shield of the Electa, the girl cannot even enter the circle. So it is the General who must eat something disagreeable, not the girl. I leave it to you to work out the details."

The Palace Master looked a little happier. "It should not be too hard to arrange."

"Something slow, mind you. His passing should appear natural."

"We have ample time before the Day of the Electa," the Palace Master said. He looked thoughtfully across at General

Hoderil. His eyes narrowed, as if estimating height, girth, and dosage.

"Myself, I would not grieve," said the Recorder, "to see the General fade away, though I'd be disappointed if his illness were completely painless. A little suffering would not be out of place, Villamar, if your people can manage it. But not so much suffering as to raise a suspicion of foul play."

The Palace Master clicked his tongue softly in agreement. "Long illness, some pain, nothing suspicious. Anything else? What about Calviram?"

"I have given the Prefect some thought as well," the Recorder began. Then, like everyone else in the stands, he leaned forward, intent on the conjugal bed. The Lord in Earth was stirring.

***

Chanithel's shoulders ached, also her knees, her head, and the back of her neck. She paused for a moment and glanced up at the stands, at the ranks of bored and critical eyes, the busy styluses of the scribal observers as they recorded every frustrating, futile, shaming moment.

Then Filkamos stirred. Chanithel picked up the tempo, daring to hope. She heard the whisper of robes on the stands as the witnesses craned forward, apparently daring to hope as well. Everybody was tired. Duty on the stands in the divine bedchamber did not usually mean staying awake well into the night, and she was horribly certain they all blamed her. She stole a quick glance up at her brothers. Like the rest, they were watching with impassive faces, and not a scrap of sympathy for her pains. How she loathed them! Even more than she loathed her husband, who chose that moment to flop onto his belly, snort like a piglet, and fall back to sleep. Biting her tongue to keep from shrieking, Chanithel switched to the next of the conjugal arts.

***

General Hoderil Hithe covered his eyes and muttered to himself the sort of curses that one can only pick up in the army. Calviram, ever the diplomat, controlled himself better, though he was burning to stand up and tell the whole damned lot of them to go elsewhere and screw themselves silly if they liked, the witnesses, the observers, the bodyservants, the guardsmen, and especially the happy couple. It was clear this conjoining was wasted. He glanced towards the Dreeves, saw the Recorder and the Palace Master were again bent over the tablets in Villamar's lap, cursed himself for not likewise bringing something to read. Lucky buggers, he thought. Then it was eyes to the front again, boredom competing with fury competing with the imperative to keep a straight face; and over all, a conviction that Chanithel might have better luck if she would only stop sniveling.

***

"I'm glad that's over," said the Recorder some time later. They were back in the Palace Master's offices, hearing the footsteps of the night guard pacing the square outside the windows. Mercifully, the Lord in Earth had wakened up enough to demand to be taken back to his tower rooms; and so the vigil in the bedchamber had ended at last, and the Consort was sent shamefaced and unploughed back to the Great Household on the arm of her bodymaid. A good night for the Dreeves. A look to cherish on the faces of General Hoderil and Prefect Calviram Hithe. Which reminded the

Recorder: there was still an item of urgent business to discuss before he retired to his own chambers for an abbreviated sleep.

"Concerning the Prefect Calviram Hithe…" he said to the Palace Master, as he poured them each a measure of wine.

"Must we do this now, Grandis?" The Palace Master yawned hugely.

"Yes, we must." The Recorder picked up one of the tablets he had perused in the divine bedchamber and tossed it to his cousin. "I like the idea you put forward—a pleasant sea voyage to keep him out of the way until after the Day of the Electa. We don't want him taking Hoderil's place in the circle, after all. But not to Tshinn, Villamar. The mission must be a real one with a real purpose, nothing that looks trumped up, or the Hithes will be too much on their guard."

After another cavernous yawn, the Palace Master held the tablet close to the candle and scanned the hen-scratchings on the grey surface. "You want to send him to visit that fat vassal king in Lazoon?"

"It's a suitable mission, in my opinion. Lazoon is a year behind on the tribute. The Oversight could legitimately decide to send a prefect on a tour of inspection, even without us pushing for it. Prefect Calviram Hithe would be a logical choice."

A tired smile dawned on the Palace Master's face. "Lazoon is at the far backside of the empire. Ten or twelve days to sail there, ten or twelve days back, and considerable work in between to keep an inspector busy. He could be gone for months." He hesitated, and added delicately, "Do we—do we want him to come back at all?"

"We rather do, Villamar, and I thought you understood that. It is only General Hoderil who needs to have a tragic fatal decline. Let me see that tablet again." The Recorder read on a few lines, and tapped the tablet with a gold-tipped fingernail. "What pathetic excuses these petty kings make! The blood-plague we knew about—but does that fat idiot think Lazoon was the only place in the world to be bleeding from it? Mori and Liske and the Kreslin Vale have been hard hit too, but they're still managing to make their payments."

"Lazoon was worse hit than most, I believe," said the Palace Master thoughtfully. "The previous dispatch said survivors from upriver were gathering for refuge in the chief town. I suppose they want to be near that loathsome temple of theirs, but it could leave half the territory reverting to wilderness. How can they hope to feed themselves at that rate, much less meet their obligations to us? You're right, Grandis, a mission to Lazoon is most genuinely called for. I don't imagine the Hithes will question it."

Reading further, the Recorder grunted. "The fat fool's whining about how bad the harvest will be, since no one is out planting the fields. Listen to this, Villamar: *Your devoted subjects in Lazoon cry out for the merciful bounty of Great Balimhavar.* So not only is this King Cretin asking to be forgiven a year of tribute, he's asking us to send him food. Ah, well, let me think on this."

Pensively, Grandis blew on the surface of his wine and watched the pattern of ripples rebound off the sides of the chalice. The auspices were good. "Yes," he said, breaking the patterns with his finger, "the case of Lazoon is ideal, for the treasury's sake as well as ours. Maybe shipping a few galleys of grain to Lazoon before next winter would even be a worthwhile investment in the long term; but the Oversight would naturally want to send an inspector along first, to check how truthful Lazoon was being about its troubles. Also to collect what tribute he can make the fat vassal scrape together." He tossed the tablet back to the Palace Master.

"A substitutive payment—that alone could take quite a parcel of an inspector's time. If Lazoon cannot remit—" the Palace Master glanced at the tablet, "—fishmeal or textiles this year, the inspector could be authorized to accept partial payment in youths and maidens, don't you think?"

"Absolutely." The Recorder grinned, and raised his chalice to the Palace Master. "If I put it to the Oversight tomorrow, he could be gone within days, and away for six months or more. And, Villamar—"

"Yes?"

"The thought of Calviram Hithe spending months in a backwater pesthole like Lazoon makes me happy. *Very* happy."

***

On the same night, far to the northwest, a ritual of a yet another nature was being enacted on the portico of the great temple in Lazoon. About a thousand pairs of eyes watched from the muddy plaza below the portico, but the view of the Heavenly Fathers, likewise that of the five thousand eyes of the night sky, was blocked by a mist rolling in off the sea and fetching up against the ridge that arced northwards behind the town. The mist made golden spheres around the torches, dampened the rags of the spectators and crept into their bones, hung like a curtain spun by spiders across the mouth of the stage. It worried Valdur Il Jinoon, whose debut as Master Speaker this was.

"Do you think it's getting thicker?" he whispered.

Zayn hissed back, "Shut up. They'll hear you out there."

"But *do* you think it's getting thicker? What if they can't see me at the back?"

"Hush. This is a serious matter, Valdur, a message to the Heavenly Fathers. It's not about you."

Of course it's about me, Valdur wanted to say, but it hardly seemed tactful. He leaned around the side of the portico again, to peer at the crowd, until Zayn pulled him back among the cutter priests and the speakers' chorus, of which Valdur had so lately been a member.

"Calm down," muttered Zayn. "Stand still. Don't worry, it'll start soon enough."

Valdur took a deep breath to compose himself. Zayn was right, this was a serious matter. Out on the stage, the guest of honour was already strapped into the Doorway of Heaven, waiting to receive the urgent message he would bear to the skies. It seemed the Heavenly Fathers were outdoing themselves lately with punishments for Lazoon. As if the burdensome treaty with Balimhavar were not enough, they had sent the plague. As if the plague were not enough, they had sent the famine. And as if the famine were not enough, they had sent a cat-demon, a *lagosh,* to terrorize the countryside upriver from the town. Terrible tales were arriving of the cat-demon's bloody ferocity and long, sharp claws, the shredding and partial consumption of its tragic victims, tales which Valdur was already mentally organizing into the narratives and ritual enactments he would eventually be required to perform. Tonight, though, would just be the litanies, the tedious clunking litanies, to accompany the flaying of the messenger and to impress upon him (it was a man tonight) the message he would take to the Heavenly Fathers.

Still, Valdur told himself, even if he could not fiddle with the text of the litanies, he could certainly sharpen up the delivery. His voice was pure and flexible, strong in both the high and low registers, and he had practiced saying the words as if they actually meant something interesting. The standard gestures grabbed more attention if one exaggerated some and underplayed others, and he had worked out a few twists that should capture the crowd without getting him into trouble with the purists. If only he could get started!

Zayn poked Valdur in the side. Things were moving at last. The spearmen of the king's constabulary emerged from the passage and took their places around the edge of the stage. Next, the drummers and pipers. Following them, heavy feet shook the wooden floor as the king lumbered with infuriating deliberation towards his seat near the Doorway of Heaven. Valdur fought an impulse to get behind the great trundling ball of lard and *push*.

"Get ready," murmured Zayn.

"I know," Valdur hissed.

Then it was finally time to step out into the view of the crowd, and all was instantly well with Valdur, dirt-born orphan of the wormly peasant Jinoon. The plaza was a torch-ringed carpet of faces, all fixed on him. He felt the power of his great talent filling the air around him, like the golden mist-halo englobing the torches. His voice soared from the first word; the crowd, wearily accustomed to ignoring the litanies as background noise to the messengers' howls, perked up and began to take notice. With the first of his innovative gestures, appreciative murmurs broke out here and there. When the mist began to clear a few moments later, it was generally taken as a sign that the Heavenly Fathers themselves wished to enjoy the fine performance of Lazoon's new Master Speaker. Valdur Il Jinoon had arrived.

Chapter Six

Waking up in the New World

Cadon drifted, open-eyed and not unpleasantly, through the upper layers of a half-sleep. Above him was a sloped stone ceiling, which he recognized in a hazy way as one of the caves under the massif, though not the resting place of the Ones Before, nor its antechamber. He tried to raise his head, swallowed nastiness, closed his eyes, and gave up. When he kept himself still, he was comfortable. The voices in his ears had fallen silent.

Though his body still felt too hot wherever one patch of his skin touched another, he was eased by something cool butted up against him and half-circled by his arms. Cool like a rock, he thought, but not hard like a rock. He folded his body into a snake-curve around it, ending with his forehead pressed against its clammy surface. It smelled a little like meat on the turn, but there were stronger odours around that were far more repellent. Cadon slid his hand along the swell of coolness in a way that felt habitual, feeling hair pass under his fingers. He assumed for the moment it was a badly scraped hide. But when he opened his eyes, his field of vision was dominated by a nipple, human, male. Dark tattooed chevrons radiated from it like the petals of a meadowsharp.

"Lusil," he whispered. "Lusil, wake up."

Lusil lay quietly in his arms. Cadon lifted his head away from the cold breast and shook his near-cousin a little, then a little harder. Lusil's head lolled. His mouth and chin were crusted with something dry and black. Twin black tracks ran in parallel from his nostrils down his left cheek and into the hair around his ear.

"Stop it, Lusil. Wake up."

Lusil's skin was pale on the surface, almost translucent, mottled underneath, as if bruised by a fist battering outwards from the inside. In the dim light, his eyeballs glittered red between half-open lids.

"Lusil! I'm warning you." Cadon, disentangling himself in a sudden panic, gave his cousin's cold chest a shove and scrambled upright. Still no response. Cadon shoved him again, quite hard, with his foot. Lusil flopped sideways and came to rest with his body twisted at the waist, a position that looked almost impossible and certainly painful. Cadon bent down without thinking, to pull him straight—saw in the dimness that somebody else was acting as Lusil's partial pillow, a young man with the crescent tattoos of the Horse family on his bare chest—saw there was a woman of the Wolves lying next to him, with a small child draped across her body—

Cadon stumbled backwards and felt the ground yield under his feet. He fell heavily, one hand landing on somebody's cold face, his own cheek in some fecal-smelling material with the consistency of drying mud. They were all around him: Eagle, Aurochs, Horse, Brown Bear, Red Deer, Wolf, Roebuck, Fox. Surely that was Granny Crooshah a few bodies over—Cadon was judging by the familiar pattern of the waistband, because the face was black and distorted. Cadon retched: nothing there to bring up. He worked himself into a position where he was not standing on anybody, and saw there was some order to these bodies, that they lay in closely-spaced rows, and he scrambled towards the glimmer of the cavemouth along one of the narrow lanes between. He had to scramble over a small hill of something at the entrance, barely noticing it in his frenzy to be out, and then he burst into a golden midmorning light.

Water first. He became conscious of a terrible thirst and the heat of his head. He took his bearings automatically, remembering that the river wound along the eastern face of the massif, and set off with shaking legs and untrustworthy vision. The fresh air was a help after the noxious vapours inside the cave; even so, he was already on the bank, scooping water into his mouth, before he realized that no bivouac sounds were coming to him, though the wind was blowing down the valley from the right direction; no cooking smells, dog-smells, people-smells, were on the wind either. Nothing came to him but thin whiffs of the same stench he had wakened to inside the cave. Something slipped inside his head.

Clearly the Caucus was over, the People had moved on, and Cadon had somehow been left behind. He did an excellent job of forgetting about the cave and Lusil, Granny Crooshah's blackened face, the long rows of still, stinking forms. All that mattered was getting some supplies and setting off soon enough to catch up with the Foxes before they ranged hopelessly far ahead. His mother and Pilshah would be worried about him. The grannies would be annoyed that he had messed up their loan plans for him, but he could bear that. He stumbled into the cool water to wash himself and his befouled clothing—his mother, whom he very much wanted to please, was particular about his habits—and then he threw himself down on the bank to dry off in the warm rays of the sun.

***

Cadon awoke from a dream of his mother, stern-faced and dangling a dead serpent from each hand, leading him silently through the shadows of a strange, cold forest. The feel of the dream lingered after he opened his eyes. He half-expected to find Nurrah keeping watch beside him, but nothing moved on the bank or in the trees that fringed the river. Then he remembered that his mother was already far away, and he must follow. He sat up unsteadily, noting that the sun was already nosing down between the hills west of the massif, and that his raging thirst had been replaced by a raging hunger. He was in no shape to go chasing anyone through the days of quick-marches that followed a Caucus, when the People hurried to disperse themselves before the forest complained of their weight. So, food first, he told himself. But before he could arrange food, he had to make or find some hunting gear, because his pack was missing, as were the blades he normally wore on his upper arm and at his waist. There was a good source of flint on top of the massif, but it was reserved to the use of the Ones Before, and there was a taboo against any but the shamans gathering it. Even the easy-going Old Man would be annoyed if he broke that rule. Cadon hovered on the bank, fuzzily trying to work through the intricacies of the problem, treating it as a hunting puzzle, approaching the answer, losing his place, starting over, trying to shake off his stupidity and weakness and the desire to sleep again.

The very small part of him that was keeping a clear picture of the world said: *Why don't you go get Lusil's blade? It's still in his arm-sheath. You saw it there just now.* The larger part of him admitted that was a good idea, or would have been if Lusil were not already far away towards the mountains. Perhaps even now the Foxes were setting up their forest berths and watching for him to come, far-uncle Furin impatient for his help, Lusil skiving off without Cadon to keep him in order, Granny Crooshah storing up reproaches and small penalties, Nurrah making the honey-tongues he loved, Pilshah brushing the dust out of the fibres of the woven wonder…

He did a belly-flop into grim reality. The woven wonder—the Caucus—the man-making. The Caucus must have finished by now, and he had missed it, but that was rapidly becoming the least of his worries because he was starting to admit to himself that he remembered the cave. He stopped pushing the image away and brought it forward for close examination. It seemed Lusil could not be in a distant bivouac, doing his best to avoid being useful. He was here, in the cave under the massif, dead, and so were Granny Crooshah and Nurrah and Pilshah and the Roebucks and the Bears and the Wolves and everybody else.

Everybody but Cadon Fox.

***

He pelted through the forest, stumbling every few steps, often falling at full length, winded, bruised, and not caring. He spotted the cavemouth just above him and tore his way towards it through the brush rather than losing precious moments along the path. The stench rolling out from the interior was much more powerful than in the morning—the day had been hot. Now it was early dusk, and the cavemouth gaped black and menacing in front of him. Cadon could see nothing of the interior beyond a careless stack of twisted forms just inside the entrance, the stack that he now remembered climbing over in his daze of the morning. Dozens of forms were heaped high, many of them known by name to Cadon.

Arms were tangled with legs and heads in graceless disorder, the whole cemented with unspeakable black matter—just like the savages, Cadon thought irrelevantly, back in the silent huts, glued inside their badly cured coverlets by their own bloody fluxes.

"Well, bugger me silly. Here's one come back from the dead."

Cadon jumped almost high enough to brush the low ceiling with his head, but one thought kept him from fainting: the thought that if he did, he would collapse straight into that noisome heap of corpses. Still, his heart had never beaten half so fast, not in the most hazardous of hunts nor the most gruelling of chases. He whirled to face his attacker. Granny Dillah Roebuck peered up at him.

He fell to his knees, but not in fear. No one who looked as solid and sour as Granny Dillah Roebuck had any chance of being mistaken for One Before. Rather, he fell in weakness and shock, and in feverish relief that he was not completely alone, though the dissonant part of him was asking in dismay: *if everybody is dead except me and one other, why does that other have to be Granny Dillah Roebuck?*

"Well—it's you, Cadon-Fox-that-was. I should have expected that."

"What?" he said.

"Or perhaps I should say, Cadon-Fox-that-*never*-was."

"What?" he repeated.

"You're not even dead, you know. You've been unbirthed—almost the last words that were spoken before the Caucus fell to pieces, and the People broke apart. You were never even born." Scowling, she detoured around him to reach the pile of the dead. There was a burden on her shoulder, a bundle wrapped in a soft leather hide. It was the corpse of a female child of three or four, Cadon saw a moment later, after

Granny Dillah unwrapped it and laid it gently at the edge of the jumble of corpses. Unlike the others, the child had been properly washed and her face painted red.

"What's happening?" Cadon croaked.

Granny Dillah turned and glared at him through the gathering darkness. "The doom I've seen coming for years, that's what happening. Though it didn't happen quite as the voices in the fire told me it would, and apparently, Not-Cadon-Fox, it's you that we have to thank for it. That's according to the man who would have been your far-uncle Furin Fox, if you'd ever been born." She turned away from him to speak the forms for a child dead within the first handful of its years, and her voice was matter-of-fact and slightly hoarse in a way that told Cadon she had said those words more than once, even many times, in the previous few days. He was still standing there helplessly with his arms dangling when she finished the obsequies, took him firmly by the elbow, and led him out of the cave. He tottered along beside her.

"On the first day when people began to die," she said conversationally, "there were still enough strong arms left to wash the bodies as they should be washed, and mark the faces, and haul the dead up to the antechamber of the Ones Before. The second day, we left them dirty and laid them in rows in this lower cave. The antechamber was filling up, and there were precious few strong arms left to get the bodies up the massif. Yesterday we just piled them by the entrance. Today—"

Cadon's head was aching and he was beginning to feel insubstantial, a cloud blown along by the powerful wind that was Granny Dillah Roebuck. He looked down at her and saw that his eyes were doing strange things with her face, obscuring her edges with jagged pulses of light, and placing drops of iridescent rain on her cheeks, as if she were weeping beads of rainbow; whereas, of course, Granny Dillah Roebuck was generally famous for never weeping any substance at all. He smiled at the very idea of her weeping. It was such an amusing idea, indeed, that he laughed out loud. A hand glittering with jagged outlines, but solid enough for all that, flew up to clip him hard alongside his ear. It hurt, but it helped.

"*Today*," she continued, much louder, "there's only me to wash them and carry them up, but it doesn't matter any more. Only the little ones are left, and I'm strong enough to carry them, the poor mites."

He tried manfully to think that over. "Does that mean," he asked at last, in a very careful voice, "that everybody else is dead?"

"Dead or gone," she snapped back. "The Hares were late for the Caucus, they only arrived three days ago, and quick-marched right out again when they saw what was going on. If the Old Woman wills it, they may be safe. Of the rest—well, perhaps two in every ten."

"Dead?" Cadon asked in horror.

"No, boy. *Eight* in every ten are dead. The last four shamans died yesterday. The Eagles have been wiped out altogether. The Red Deer, very nearly. The Hillcats have not fared so badly. About half of them were still on their feet when they pulled out two nights ago. The Brown Bears, maybe ten survivors. The Foxes—"

"What about the Foxes?" Pure terror worked a miracle. His mind had never been so clear. He stopped and swung the old woman around. *"What about the Foxes?"*

Her face did not soften. "Your mother was Nurrah, your sister was Pilshah, correct? I can assure you they died early enough to find a place in the antechamber of the Ones Before. The Foxes had very bad luck. Many of them are dead—though a couple of your uncles are not, nor is your mid-cousin Manac and your far-aunt Minnah, and one or two of the children. Unless they've died since, which is all too possible these days. Anyway, they left just before sunset last night. Your father was Codor Wolf, correct? I did not see his body, but I know he's dead."

She had thrown most of those words at him from the end of a dark tunnel of increasing length, filled with the sound of drums. He found shortly thereafter that he was sitting on the ground with his head between his knees, and Granny Dillah was pinching his shoulder in sharp, painful nips, presumably intended to wake him up. "Stop that," he said.

One last extra-sharp pinch. "Then up you get, you not-born Cadon Fox, or I'll leave you here. I want to get back to the little ones." She pulled him to his feet—either she was stronger than she looked or he had lost some weight—and set off down the path as if not caring whether he followed or not. Two drunken steps later, he was falling again; and there was Granny Dillah to catch his arm and hold him upright until his head stopped spinning and the world was back in some kind of balance. They walked on in silence. Cadon kept his mind as blank as possible. There was no subject in the world that he dared to think about. Only once did a stray thought manage to get past his pickets and give rise to words.

"Granny Dillah, you didn't say what happened to the Roebucks."

She walked a little faster.

"Who of the Roebucks is still alive, Granny Dillah? Is Luah—"

"Luah is dead," she said harshly, "and the Roebucks—"

She shut her mouth, let his arm drop and quickened her pace until she was a step or two ahead of him and he could not see her face. Her back looked more hunched than usual.

"The Roebucks?" he prompted.

"Myself," she grated over her shoulder. "Also six others, who banded together with the Wolves and Foxes still living, and left in the night. Plus—"

"What? Who?"

"Plus," she said snippily, "one who, like you, cannot die because she has never been born. Now, shut up about the Roebucks. In fact, just shut up." She turned and took his hand again, the better to pull him along at a pace that took no account of his misery and weakness.

***

Granny Dillah Roebuck led Cadon to one of the smaller and cosier of the many caves under the massif. A fire was burning low in a hearth in one corner, with a firepot of broth nestled in the embers. At least a dozen forest pallets of ferns and pelts had been built along one wall, but only three people were in residence, all of them children, and two of them were dead. The third was a girl-child perhaps halfway through her second year, lying listlessly on her pallet of rabbit-skins and ferns. Her eyes were huge in the tiny face. All babies looked somewhat similar to Cadon, but this one did remind him of someone, or something, just outside the range of being properly remembered. He thought about it as he watched a stone-faced Granny Dillah move the dead children onto one pallet and cover them with a pelt. Then she picked up the living child, who seemed more and more familiar to Cadon. The memory involved firelight. It was just before he got sick. Lusil was there, and Mairn Roebuck, and somebody else, who was nursing a child and saying nothing.

"Granny Dillah," he said, sipping from the gourd of warm broth she had given him, "is that Annah Roebuck's child?"

"That's right, boy. Her name would have been Sashah, if she'd ever been born." She was holding the child and letting it suck broth off a twist of soft leather. She did not seem particularly tender towards it.

He sipped and watched. "Granny Dillah?" he repeated.

"What do you want now?"

"You keep saying this child and I were never born, but I don't think you can be right about that."

"Oh, really?" she said.

In other days, such a tone and such a look on a granny's face would have stopped Cadon cold, but he was past caring. "If I really had been unbirthed, Granny, you wouldn't be talking to me. You wouldn't be seeing me, or hearing me, or feeding me, or feeding that child—"

"I hate to disappoint you, boy," she cut in, "but I'm probably the only person in the world who will talk to you, with the possible exception of your far-uncle Furin, and he may have left last night with the other Foxes. I can assure you that you have indeed been unbirthed. Codor Wolf was never loaned to the Foxes, and he never sired a son out of Nurrah Fox. You never existed, boy. Your name does not appear in the bloodloans and generations in the Lore, though how much the Lore matters now, I really couldn't say."

She had shocked him. "How could the Lore *not matter*?" he said. "Without the Lore, the People would forget who they are, and the grannies wouldn't know what loans to arrange, and—"

"Without the People," Granny Dillah broke in, mocking his tone, "the Lore is of no use to anyone. We've spent all the years of the world, we grannies, ever since the time of the Old Woman and the Old Man, keeping the tree of the People strong and well-pruned—a hundred generations of careful birthings, of bloodloans weaving the families together, every one of them lovingly planned and worked out and negotiated, and every one of them remembered by name in the Lore, and now all of that is finished and gone. All wiped out in four days of dying! Do you really think the People can recover from this, Not-Cadon-Not-Fox? That's what you've gone and done, my boy, you have cut down the tree of the People, root, trunk, and branch."

The child Sashah began a weak, fearful wailing as Granny Dillah's voice rose. Cadon fought his impulse to cringe; she was a granny, but she was also an unpleasant old wolf-bitch whose bitter accusations were making him even more miserable than he already was, if that were possible. "I didn't do anything," he broke in.

"Did you go to the huts of the savages?" Granny Dillah asked mildly.

"Yes," he admitted.

"And did you bring something back with you?"

"Yes, but I didn't cheat thim. It was a fair trade."

"It was a curse, boy. Your uncle Furin Fox testified to the matter before the Caucus, and the Caucus agreed."

That hurt. "So far-uncle Furin was my accuser?"

"Not happily. He was fond of you." She dipped the twist of leather into the broth and offered it again to Sashah, who stopped crying and sucked at it hungrily. "Speaking honestly, the Caucus did not need an accuser. You were the first to come down with the illness, and you raved at the top of your lungs about going to the savages and finding them all dead, and bringing back a woven thing which your mother and sister were washing for you—by the way, they were the next after you to fall sick with this curse—"

Cadon buried his face in his hands.

"—and it was suspiciously similar to a curse Furin once saw chew up a settlement of the savages, so altogether it seemed safe to conclude that you were the right one to blame. Wouldn't you agree, Cadon-Never-Born?"

He could not answer. He was inside his head watching his mother and sister exclaim at the beauty of the woven wonder; watching his sister bury her face in its softness and then wrinkle her nose at the smell. He watched his mother take a few critical sniffs and theorize that a sprinkling of oak-ash, a good beating with a green branch, and then a rinse in the river would do miracles. They had been so proud of him, so eager for the man-making where his offering would shine, so sure he was destined to be a big man. Instead, he had brought a killing curse down upon them.

"What was strange," he heard Granny Dillah's voice go on, "was that, while most of the People were dying, a few of us never became ill at all. A few became ill and recovered, like you—by the way, they knew perfectly well you were still breathing when they left you in that cave—but some of us old people, who were ready for death, never got so much as an upset stomach. Well, the Old Woman never was fair, and I don't mind if she hears me saying it. Though, of course, it was perfectly fair that *you* should have survived, Cadon-the-Walking-Catastrophe. Since you brought the curse to the People, it's only fair you should suffer its afterburden."

Cadon wished she would shut up.

"Because, believe me, this curse is beyond any doubt the worst disaster ever to befall the People, but I'm old enough to have seen a few lesser disasters in my time, and I know that the afterburden is always, always the heaviest and most painful—that the survivors are not always the lucky ones—that grief can be worse than dying, many times worse—"

Cadon could no longer bear to listen. He stumbled out of the cave and into the forest, leaving Granny Dillah to talk out her own version of grief and madness with no one but Sashah to hear.

Chapter Seven

The Unborn and the Not-Alive

Cadon sat on a boulder at the edge of a large clearing, in a forest that would remain dark until the half-moon rose in an hour or so, and for the first time in his life he felt lost. Girdling the western portion of the massif was the rocky flatland where the families would camp during the Caucus, spreading themselves in an array of fire-circles that was the most magnificent manmade sight these children of the forest would ever see—under normal circumstances. Here he seemed to be on the correct flatland, yes, properly rocky in the way he remembered, with the great dark bulk of the massif blocking the eastern stars, just as it should; and he was surrounded by the black humps of festival berths, and by at least some of the correct smells, left as recently as two nights ago: wood fire, roast deer, wet dog.

But the flat vale was silent and dark. The comfortable smells were almost overwhelmed by the stench of loose bowels and rotten meat. Cadon wondered why no scavengers were padding around the rocky outcrops or quarrelling to get into the death-caves and the berths. Perhaps there was something about the stink of this curse that drove even the carrion-eaters away.

He fell asleep for a while. When he awoke, prodded by a hunger so intense that it was agony, the moon was well risen and a decent light lay across the valley. Looking around, he thought how displeased the Old Woman and the Old Man would be with this sight, before he remembered how unimportant all that business had become. The Old Couple dearly loved a tidy bivouac, and loathed wastage, and were horrified at any rubbish left lying around old campsites when a family moved on. The silent berths among the ashes of the fire-circles might look normal at first glance; at a second, one would see how shockingly the ground was strewn with packs and pelts, abandoned gourds, foodstuffs, minor bits of household equipment. Bodies. Not many of the latter, though, and after he dropped to his knees by the first one and turned it over, he knew not to bother with the rest. The few dead dogs appeared to have perished from wounds inflicted by other dogs, not by the same sickness. Cadon wondered nervously where the rest of the dogpacks were, and hoped they were eating well enough to keep them friendly. Food was very much on his own mind.

Keeping a good distance between himself and the dark berths, where the death-stench was mightiest, he searched for and found some unspoiled supplies—a basket of berries only slightly overripe, a string bag of crabapples, a packet of honey-tongues well-crusted with ants. He ate ravenously and returned some of it involuntarily to the earth; ate again and managed to keep most of it down this time, and felt much the stronger for it. He contemplated a packet of dried meat strings but decided he could not face chewing it quite yet. He put it in his pocket for later and then took it out again and threw it away, because he suddenly decided there was not going to be a *later*.

With this new thought in mind, he searched for and found a greasy torch and an ember-basket where the embers were still warm enough to be coaxed into use. He did not light the torch yet, since the moon was sufficient to get him up the massif. The cavern of the Ones Before was theoretically barred to him now, since he had never been born, but there was nobody around to stop him going in and explaining his situation and begging their intercession with the Old Man and Old Woman. It was not, he thought, as if he had deliberately set out to destroy the entire root-stock of the People; it was something that simply happened. All he wanted to do, if the Ones Before would let him, was curl up in one corner of their antechamber until he was really dead, as opposed to being just unborn. It seemed little enough to ask, until he remembered the magnitude of his misdoing.

Up the massif he went. It was not an easy hike for one who was still weakened by illness, but he struggled on up the trail in the moonlight and through the celebrated places, one by one. It was a sad parody of the pilgrimage he would have made with his entire kindred under happier circumstances. Here was the little rocky clearing where the Old Man and Old Woman first conjoined; the crescent-shaped plateau where the Old Man met with the Prey Spirits long ago and worked out the terms of the hunt; the beginning of the winding side-trail that led to the Old Woman's Place, the snake-haunted cavern where the Old Woman gave birth to the Nine Hunters and the Nine Virgins, the eldest of the People. From polite habit, Cadon kept his eyes on the ground as he passed that point.

He topped the western edge of the massif and then there was nothing above him but the moon and the five thousand eyes of the night sky. Below him, moonlight caught the upper canopy of the forest and left vast deeps of shadow underneath. The river was a winding strip of cold silver light. Otherwise, nothing. The great fire-circles of past Caucuses would never be seen here again. Sighing, Cadon turned to trudge across the wide plaza of the man-making place.

There was a stir of movement ahead; he was too unhappy to be afraid. He even thought he might welcome a predator, since he could use a fight. In the unlikely event that he won, he would have a fresh gift to take to the Ones Before, which might help his case. If he lost, he would be dead in the sense of no longer breathing, and that would be equally good. But it was not one of the great bears or great cats that waited for him near the platform of the man-making place. It was worse. It was Granny Dillah Roebuck, wrapped in a fine but overly large deerskin cloak, and holding in her lap a swaddled bundle that Cadon assumed was Annah Roebuck's never-born baby daughter.

"Here at last, Cadon Fox. I knew you'd come past here eventually, on your way to pester the Ones Before."

Since it was dark and his face was in shadow, Cadon felt free to grimace his despair at being tracked down by the last person in the world he wanted to see, even if she was the last other person in the world who would acknowledge his existence. "What do you want?" he asked. "You shouldn't be talking to me."

"I'll decide that. Let me guess—you *are* on your way to join the Ones Before, aren't you?"

"Yes," he admitted.

She hoisted the sleeping child to her shoulder. "Well, come along then. Sashah and I have been waiting for you."

He drew back in horror. "I want to go alone."

"Really?" she said. "And how do you imagine you'll talk to the Ones Before? Are you a shaman suddenly? Or maybe a granny?"

"I—"

"You have no idea how to approach them. I, however, know very well. Here, you take the child."

Before he could protest, he found himself carrying Sashah—a slight burden, which he would hardly have noticed a week ago, but now one that weighed in his arms like a boulder. Also before he could protest, he found the old woman's fine fur cloak being thrown around his shoulders, and her fingers knotting the drawstring at his neck.

"You're not well yet," she said, "and you should really be asleep by a fire with a good hot dose of some infusion inside you. Still, we may as well get this over with, and then we'll see about dosing you." She walked on, and he found himself catching her up. "Cadon Fox," she said as he came level with her, "do you hear echoes in this place? Do you see shadows? By rights, it should be well and truly haunted. Look at the platform."

Where she was pointing, the moon illuminated a richness that made Cadon gasp. A treasure was heaped on the man-making platform—gleaming pelts, iridescent shells, rare stone crystals and a chunk of shining ore—the gifts for the Ones Before, still unbroken and unburnt since the man-making had been permanently interrupted. Cadon caught himself looking for his own woven wonder.

"Yours isn't there," Granny Dillah said, as if she had been listening to his thoughts, "because it was burned-in-shame along with your tally stick, at the same time as you were unbirthed. Too late to break the curse, alas. There were those who wanted to burn you in shame too, but Furin Fox made himself difficult, and we settled for dumping you in with the dead. Very briefly," she said, looking up at him with a hard smile, "I was one of those in favour of burning you, but I understood almost at once that it would never have helped. Do you know why?"

"No, Granny Dillah," Cadon said uncomfortably.

"I don't suppose you do. Tell me something: in the hunt, is it the arrow that kills the buck, or is it the hunter?"

Cadon did not want to play this game. "The arrow?" he guessed.

"Wrong. The hunter kills the buck. The arrow is only the instrument, the extension of the hunter's hand. So there you are."

"What?"

"Gather your wits, boy. This great dying must be the doom I've seen coming our way, from long before you were born. As if some great hunter was stalking the People for many years, and finally caught us in a thicket and shot us in the heart with his arrow. You, boy, have the uncertain honour of being that arrow."

Cadon shook his head slowly in the darkness. He had only the vaguest idea what she meant, and no energy to work it out, and he dimly disapproved of the suggestion in the first place. There was nothing in the Lore about such a stalker on the track of the People. Nor, strictly speaking, was it proper for her to be talking about the hunt. She didn't catch him talking about women's things, did she? On the other hand, if the idea kept Granny Dillah off his back long enough for him to find a quiet end in the caverns of the Ones Before, then he had no real objection. He grunted something noncommittal and made to move on. She stopped him with a hand on his forearm.

"I haven't finished telling you what happened here, right here on this spot, on the day of the man-making. You were sick as a tree-rat, so you'd been left in the Fox circle down in the valley, being tended by your mother and sister, who were not feeling very well themselves; but there were other boys to be made into men, and their offerings were piled just as you see them now." She gestured at the glories on the platform.

"Your offering was still with them then. The Fox grannies decided they did not want you to wait until the next Caucus, and so your near-uncle Xirn stood proxy for you. That woven thing from the savages was getting a lot of attention from the shamans, and everybody else. It might have put you on the path to being a big man, who knows? Your far-uncle Furin objected, but nobody listened to him, just as nobody ever believed me about the doom I saw coming. Anyway, the man-making had started and we were about ten families into the General Recitation when things began to go bad."

Sashah was rapidly gaining weight in his arms, but Cadon ignored the strain. He could imagine the scene: a great crowd of the People covering the roof of the massif, all dressed in their best, shining with facepaint, feathers and shells, and dusted with gold; the candidates for man-making standing in perfect stillness in full view of the massed lineages, muscles oiled, hair shorn, young beards trimmed to the skin, eyes somewhat distant with last-minute mental review of their own Recitations. He should have been there himself.

"Don't tell me," he said. "I don't want to know."

"Part of your punishment, so shut up and listen. It started out as a very small slip, even amusing at first. We were well into the General Recitation, and the lads were all standing there as still as you please, and a handsome well-formed bunch they were, too, though you would have been the flower of the field, Cadon-Fox-that-never-was. Then Mairn Roebuck, the son of my own daughter's daughter, swayed a little and toppled slowly sideways onto Wayr Eagle, who wasn't expecting it, and Wayr toppled sideways onto Somer Hillcat, who stepped sideways into Chir Bison, who knocked against Dorn Red Deer, who shoved Chir back hard enough to push him sideways into Somer Hillcat, and so on back down the line. The faces on them all! Side-splitting, really, until our poor

Mairn began spewing like a geyser into the crowd, which was not at all funny. I remember my far-nephew Mil was beside me. He had been laughing, but he choked at the smell of Mairn's vomit, and sat down very hard on the ground. Somebody brushed past me; it was Furin Fox carrying that young cousin of yours over his shoulder—what was his name?"

"Lusil." Touch-memory of cold skin. Cadon shuddered, and the child stirred in his arms.

"Lusil Fox, yes. Vomiting all down Furin's back, with worse than vomit running down between his legs and onto the front of Furin's tunic. I caught Furin's eye—we were friends for a long time, Furin and I—and I could see he was thinking along the same lines as I was."

Cadon turned his face away. He really did not want to know. He knew she would tell him anyway.

"What we two were thinking was this: *this is only the beginning. It will get much worse.* The sun was shining, the shamans were undisturbed, some of our kindred were still laughing, and all of them were well-fed and strong and beautiful—but they were the walking dead. Furin knew that as well as I did. Mairn and your young cousin were taken away and the man-making carried on to its finish for the day; but by the time the General Recitation was done, nearly half the Foxes and Roebucks in the crowd were dizzy or puking and whispers were starting to spread. I did a fair amount of whispering myself: *first Cadon Fox—two days later, his family and fellow-travellers—two days hence, who will it be?* Meantime, your young sister fell ill after the rest of us went up the massif, and she was dead by the time we came down in the evening. Many died that quickly, once the dying began. Nurrah lasted until the next evening, but by then the sickness was everywhere. You know the rest."

"Why didn't I die?" This was a cry of anguish, not a question, and Dillah did not bother to answer. Cadon badly wanted to be not-breathing dead, and he had a good idea how to accomplish it. About forty paces away, the edge of the massif made a long sheer drop onto a plain of broken boulders, the site of the few executions carried out by the Caucus over the generations. It would be a shameful way for him to end, a guarantee that the Ones Before would have nothing to do with his spirit; but then he remembered he did not have a spirit anyway, being unborn and all, and at least his end would be quick, his grief and desolation would be over, his guilt would be punished. He took a step in that direction.

"Don't you dare," said Granny Dillah. She clambered awkwardly up onto the man-making platform and began rummaging through the glistening pelts of the offerings. Cadon realized where the exceptional deerskin cloak he was wearing had come from. "I know what you're thinking, Cadon Fox," she added, "and I'm telling you to stop thinking it."

"If you're worried about Annah's child," he said sulkily, "I would put her safely down before I—did anything."

"That child is your burden, and you can never set her down. You two are unborn, and I am not-alive, and we're going to go to the Ones Before to see what we can do about it." She pulled on a coat of rare golden marmot-skins—a sure winner, Cadon thought, once his woven wonder was out of the contest—and gingerly lowered herself off the platform. As she set off towards the eastern end of the massif, Cadon followed her pensively. One of her phrases echoed in his head. So the old sow was not-alive now, was she? There were generally three ways to become dead. The first was to stop breathing; the second was to consider yourself dead; the third was to be considered dead by the rest of the People, whether you liked it or not. But in which sense was Granny Dillah not-alive?

Dulled by his own misery, he had not stopped to wonder why the old woman was still at the massif. The sky was blue, grannies tended the sick. Nothing there to wonder at. But now he saw there might be something more to it. Perhaps she was just as much an outcast as he was himself, and the child Sashah. You could not unbirth a man who had been loaned or a woman who had herself birthed a child. The most—and worst—you could do was to regard them as not alive, and treat them as such until they obliged you by no longer breathing. Cadon, relieving the pain in one shoulder by shifting the child to the other, caught up with Granny Dillah and shortened his stride to fall into step with her.

"What did you do?" he asked.

"You'll need to be more specific," she said primly.

"You're not-alive, you said. Was that your own idea?"

"No."

"Then you must have done *something* to be cast out."

"Oh, that," she said. "I told the truth, that's all."

"The truth about what?"

She sighed. "Three days ago, I told a gathering of big men and grannies and the last two surviving shamans that the People were finished. That some Great Hunter had caught up with us, and it would save us all a lot of struggle and pain if we simply gave up and joined the Ones Before. Better, I said, that the few of us who were left should finish all together in our own sacred places, than drop dead in the forest with no one to do the obsequies and bring the headbones back and ensure us our welcome among the Ones Before."

"What was wrong about that?"

"They were out of their minds with fear," she said sullenly. "I was the one who had foreseen this catastrophe. In their terror, they confused *foreseeing* it with *making* it. There was some talk of burning me in shame, too. Sandah Horse remembered me predicting the very form of the curse—nonsense! I had no idea what form it would take. Calnah Red Deer remembered me foretelling the very day and hour it would break out. Nonsense again. Minnah Fox remembered me mumbling words of ill-wishing at the women's moot last week, and again at the man-making—all nonsense. But it was enough to make them blame me."

Cadon frowned. "I thought they blamed me."

"They did, but fear makes people stupid. They blamed me as well. They came to me the next day and told me I was no longer alive, and could bugger off now and let my body catch up with my spirit. At the time, I was too busy nursing the sick to pay them any heed, and many of them were dead by the same evening. Well, the others have gone now, as far as I know, and I've got nobody to tell me I'm not alive. That seems to make a difference."

"You're..." *dead*, he was going to say, but practical considerations stopped him. If he caused Granny Dillah to realize she was dead, what on earth was he going to do with the baby? "...fine," he finished lamely.

Chapter Eight

The Cave of Smiles

The stench was apparent long before they reached the edge of the massif and started down the well-trodden path that led to the antechamber of the Ones Before. It poisoned the air. It woke Sashah up, whimpering and wheezing into Cadon's shoulder. It crept into the pores of Cadon's skin and made him feel he would never be clean again. It sent Granny Dillah into a fit of coughing that ended in retching, which in turn set Cadon's fragile stomach off. And when he had recovered enough to see straight, he passed Sashah back to a pale but unsubdued Granny Dillah and worked grimly on reviving the embers in the basket and lighting the torch.

The eastern face of the massif was in moon-shadow now, and the cleft leading to the antechamber was dark as death. It was cold, as well, but the sweat rolled down Cadon's face and joined with the torch-smoke in stinging his eyes. He hesitated at the cleft, his gorge rising again, until Granny Dillah pushed past him and made a determined effort to trade the baby for the torch. He twisted away from her in a little act of rebellion. Holding the light high, he began to pick his way through the smothering corruption of the antechamber.

He liked caves, or thought he did. But this was a very different matter from, say, the Prey Spirits Cave on the south side of the massif, where the painted herds of bison and steppe horse and aurochs thundered promisingly across the walls, while the shamans danced in their animal skins and sweating drummers pounded on the drum-rocks at the back of the chamber and the People oohed with appreciation and wonder. That was magic—this was darkness, foulness, the hovering of things unseen.

It was also damned hard to pick his way. Cadon did not want to look at the festering dead, but he really did not want to step on them either. Nor was it comfortable to look up, or straight ahead at the walls. In the unsteady torchlight, the painted forms of this cave were in fitful motion. The Nine Hunters, firstfruits of the Old Woman, seemed to turn their antlered heads to follow his progress. The Nine Virgins glowered and stirred. The Prey Spirits tossed their horns in his direction, and their eyes shone red. It worked best, though still imperfectly, to focus on a point a few inches in front of him, and let his downward peripheral vision take care of his feet.

Another dilemma: these were his beloved dead, and as much as he feared them, he grieved for them as well. His mother and Pilshah were lying there somewhere, along with his cousins, aunts and uncles of all degrees, his friends and cousins in the other families. One of those silent forms might be Luah Roebuck, who would have borne his children. That might be the face of his father, Codor Wolf, on which he narrowly avoided treading. And was that lumpen figure to his right Annah Roebuck, swollen with her other unborn child? Or somebody else entirely, swollen with corruption? He tried to deaden himself and see nothing, feel nothing, but he could not block out the stink and the jerking shadows and the slide of dead flesh against his feet.

In the far wall was a ragged opening twice as high as a man, roughly arched at the top. Cadon had been through that archway twice in his life, once as a baby to be shown off to the

Ones Before, and once at the Caucus where he joined the hunters, along with the other boys of his age-grade. As a newmade man, he would have come down here to burn the woven wonder as a gift. Granny Dillah would have visited sometime during this Caucus, if only to leave Sashah with the Ones Before as per the Old Woman's instructions. Sashah would never have left at all. Cadon could hear her snuffling softly in Granny Dillah's arms.

They passed under the archway together. The air was close, but the space felt wide and high, and the torchlight did not reach as far as any wall. At least, Cadon thought, the floor here was clear of the recent dead, and he was getting used to the stench. He made no protest this time when Granny Dillah passed Sashah back into his arms and took the torch. This was her territory, not his. He followed her for a couple of paces before he abruptly became aware that the sound of laboured breathing in his ears was not coming from Sashah, but from somewhere in the darkness to his right.

"Who's there?" His voice echoed off the high unseen ceiling.

"Never mind them," Granny Dillah snapped, "just keep out of my way. Take the baby and go sit by the door."

Them? He dared not ask. He sat down on the cold stone floor by the archway with his back against the wall and watched Dillah as she moved confidently forward. A natural table of rock took shape in the torchlight. Someone—*not* Dillah—coughed in the darkness, and Cadon's heart drummed painfully, but the granny took no notice. The cough was not repeated, and a moment later Cadon noted that the stertorous breathing had stopped as well. Spirits or demons, he supposed, but Dillah Roebuck could deal with them if anyone could. For the first time, he found himself glad to be in her company.

Dillah hunched herself over the table of rock. "That's a relief," she said over her shoulder. "The Aurochs girls did their duty before they all fell ill—did I tell you how badly the Aurochs family fared? Anyway, it was their year to get the fuel stacked for the fire and fill up the firepit and the lamps." She fell into mutters as she bustled around the table, and the light began to grow. She was lighting caucus-lamps, Cadon realized, shallow stone bowls of oil with a twist of wick that would burn for several hours with a surprisingly steady and smokeless light. There must have been dozens. When the tablestone was ablaze with them, Granny Dillah fitted the torch into a crevice at one end of the slab and began spreading the lit caucus-lamps, two by two, around a widening perimeter on the floor. Gradually, as she worked, the Ones Before emerged from the darkness.

The People maintained that the fleshless faces of the Ones Before were perpetually smiling in welcome, but they did not look very welcoming to Cadon. They were there in their thousands, solidly packed against the walls to a height even he would have trouble reaching, empty dark eye-sockets and racks of excellent teeth somewhat dulled by the soot from centuries of gift-burnings. Yes, they were smiling; but it occurred to Cadon that *everybody* was smiling under the skin, whatever their intentions, and he had much to fear because he really was guilty, and because he had the gall to come before them without a spirit.

Sashah, in contrast, was delighted by the golden light of the caucus-lamps and the thousands on thousands of cheerful teeth. She sat happily enough in Cadon's lap, smiling back, chatting to herself, kicking her hard little heels against his thigh. After a while she put two fingers into her mouth and subsided thoughtfully against Cadon's chest. He gave her a drink from his gourd, and a moment later she was asleep again.

Feeling himself beginning to nod off as well, Cadon swatted his own cheek so hard the tears came to his eyes. Even so, minutes later he was again watching the chamber shift around him, as if it intended to spin as soon as his control slipped. He blinked, fighting sleep, floating despite himself on a little cushioned cloud as he looked around the glowing chamber—neat piles of logs and kindling for a gift-burning that would never be lit—solid walls of wide-stretched grins and fathomless empty eyes—the inscrutable stares of Furin Fox and Granny Aturah Wolf and Basik Red Deer with his prize-winning foliage of silver-grey hair and beard, framing his face like the Old Man's wreath of leaves—

"No more of that screeching," Granny Dillah said over her shoulder. "You don't want to wake the dead right now, believe me. And there are others in here who are dying, and should not be disturbed."

"We're not dying, we're *dead*," Furin Fox growled, "and so are you, Dillah."

"All in good time," said Dillah. She sited two more lamps on the right side of the chamber, bringing more flesh-covered faces out of the darkness, all of them near or over the great age of forty except for Chir Bison, who was Cadon's age-mate. But Chir was sprawled dead on the floor with his head cradled in his grandmother Soonnah Bison's lap, and Granny Soonnah's face was tearless and blank. Basik Red Deer was also looking quite blank, but Cadon thought he might actually be dead, as opposed to not-alive. The others, an old man of the Eagles and a Hillcat granny, looked on with mild interest.

"You should be sitting here with us," Furin went on to Granny Dillah. He glanced uncomfortably at Cadon, but did not acknowledge him.

"I would not sit with you, alive or dead," Dillah retorted, "and I have things to do that are not your concern, so just hurry up and stop breathing, will you?"

"Come now, Dillah," Granny Aturah Wolf said with reproof in her voice, "we're doing exactly what you recommended three days ago. What made you change your mind?"

"Three days ago," Granny Dillah said bitterly, "you were ready to set me on fire for recommending it. What made *you* change your mind?"

"We consulted with the Old Woman," said Granny Aturah, rather smugly. Furin sighed and said nothing.

Granny Dillah sniffed. "Very convenient for you, 'Turah. The Old Woman always had a way of telling you exactly what you wanted to hear. Don't think I didn't notice. As for me, I was too busy nursing the sick to indulge myself in idleness and despair. Maybe if you'd stayed and tended the children with me, we could have saved a few more."

"Yes, I see you've managed to keep Annah Roebuck's girl-child breathing. Why did you bother, Dillah? She's unborn. And as for that vile unborn who would have been called Cadon Fox—"

"I'm planning to have my own little chat with the Old Woman about them." Scowling, Dillah turned her back on the row of still-breathing corpses, and resumed her mysterious business near the great firepit where gifts to the Ones Before were customarily burned. Cadon shrank against the wall, keeping very quiet and trying to block out his awareness of his far-uncle's presence on the other side of the cavern. Unfortunately, though now he craved oblivion, he was no longer in danger of falling asleep. Furin Fox, one of the touchstones of his childhood, the acknowledged master of story-telling and a fine hand at teaching hunt-games to his nephews, no doubt blamed him for the curse and wished him worse than dead. Cadon raised his eyes, caught Furin staring at him, and dropped his head again when Furin looked hastily away.

Granny Dillah certainly was working very hard. Glancing around, Cadon saw she had shoved most of the piles of bonfire fuel hard against the repeating skull-pattern of the walls. Now she walked into the remaining darkness on the near-left side of the chamber, where she had placed no lamps. There was a scraping noise, and a moment later she reappeared in the light dragging a large basket behind her. The basket was piled high with what looked like deerskin bags about the size of Cadon's fist.

A movement from Furin caught Cadon's eye. His far-uncle was sitting very straight on his haunches, with a puzzled frown on his face. When Granny Dillah began distributing the little bags among the piles of fuel along the walls and stuffing many into crevices among the skulls, he started up as if to say something, and then sat back again. He began to look worried as he watched her make a large heap of the bags, several tens at least, in the right-hand corner of the chamber, not far from himself. Granny Aturah looked only faintly interested. The others watched incuriously. Cadon's view was blocked by the tablestone. He slid upright against the wall, with Sashah against his shoulder, in time to see Granny Dillah open one of the little skin bags and start pouring out a line of silvery powder between the firepit and the fuel against the wall.

"What do you think you're doing, Dillah?" Furin Fox rose again to a half-crouch.

"Ignore her," said Granny Aturah. "She'd never dare."

Granny Dillah barked. Cadon realized she was laughing, but the sound had no mirth in it, and froze the blood and spit and marrow in his body with a cold sense that something was about to happen, something that would make even the existing disaster seem trivial. Dillah returned to the basket and stuffed a large number of the skin bags into the pockets of her magnificent marmot-skin coat. She kept one in her hand as she drifted back towards the firepit.

"Dillah?" said Furin Fox. "Dillah, stop this."

She took a lamp from the table and dropped it into the firepit.

The kindling at the near end of the firepit exploded into flame. Cadon jerked with the shock and Sashah woke up squalling as he clutched her too tightly to his chest. He poised himself to take flight through the antechamber, but Granny Dillah's voice came irritably from the vicinity of the firepit: "Damn you, Cadon, can't you keep the tyke quiet?"

"What's the point of this, Dillah?" That was Granny Aturah's disapproving voice.

"You're dead, I can't hear you." Granny Dillah's hunched form was black against the flames dancing over the firepit. She waved her hand over the fire—bright white sparks rushed upwards, crackling among the yellow tongues of flame. Lightning dust, Cadon thought, but he had never seen it used so prodigally, scattered over the fire by the handful instead of in tiny pinches. In her still-powerful voice, Granny Dillah began to sing. Cadon did not know this song, and he listened to the words with growing dismay. They were not complimentary about the Old Woman.

"Dillah, no good can come of this." Furin Fox was standing now. Aturah Wolf reached up to tug at him—"Sit down, Furin, the Old Woman will see to it that nothing happens"—but he took a hesitant step towards the firepit. "Dillah," he said, "do you know what you're doing?"

She stopped to say, "Perfectly," then sang louder. Even in his terror, Cadon was shocked by the words. Furin made a sudden movement towards the head of the firepit, where Dillah had laid the line of lightning dust, but Dillah stopped singing again, leapt to intercept him, and pushed him back with ferocious strength.

"You're insane," Furin shouted into her face. "When the fire reaches those bags—"

"I do know what will happen," she hissed, "and as for being insane, who was it who recently allowed most of her children to drown in a lake of their own vomit and shit—me or the Old Woman?" Furin tried to twist away, but she melted into him and pulled him down.

"Aturah!" Furin gasped, "The lightning-dust! Break the line of dust from the firepit. Kick it! Hurry, woman!"

Granny Aturah slumped back against the wall.

"Aturah, *please*."

Aturah Wolf folded her hands and gazed into the distance. Soonnah Bison did not move, Nosor Eagle looked at the ceiling, Pasannah Hillcat examined the floor. Incredibly, Furin Fox was now flat on the ground and Granny Dillah was kneeling on his back and pounding at him with her small but unusually sharp-knuckled fists. Cadon saw his uncle's desperate eyes turn at last to him.

"Cadon!"

"You can't talk to him, remember? He was never born."

At this point, Cadon realized he was dreaming. Nothing so absurd could be real. He settled back with a sigh of relief, nestling Sashah more comfortably against his shoulder. He would have to remember the details of the dream later, so Granny Crooshah Fox could interpret it—whether it was the last dream of his boyhood, or the first of his manhood (somehow he could not quite fix when the dream began) it was bound to be significant. In this dream, Furin Fox wrestled himself half clear of Dillah and shouted again to Cadon.

"Wake up, boy! You must—"

The flames reached the line of dust, raced along it in a firestorm of sparks and sharp crackles, caught on the tangled brushwood fuel at the foot of the wall and began to spread towards the caches of little deerskin bags. One of the logs caught fire. Granny Dillah rolled off Furin's back and leapt upright, shaking her fists above her head. Furin struggled to his hands and knees but made no further attempt to reach the firepit. To Cadon, he looked like a well-trained hunting dog crouched to point, all fierce concentration.

"All right, Old Woman," Granny Dillah screeched over the roar of the flames, "*talk to me!*"

Furin, on his feet now, grabbed her arm and shouted something that Cadon could not catch, but it looked urgent. Granny Dillah shook him off, and Cadon had no difficulty understanding her screamed answer: "Make up your mind, Furin Fox! Are you alive or dead?" Then she turned away from him to face the slowly spreading heart of the flames: "I'm listening, curse you! So *talk*!"

Cadon checked the progress of the flames. On the left they had almost reached a pair of the skin bags; and since it was only a dream, he was eager to see what would happen when the lightning dust began to burn. A large noise, presumably, judging by what happened when a meagre pinch was sprinkled on a fire. Indeed, when the bags caught fire, the noise was so loud and the flash so bright that Cadon thought actual lightning had struck inside the cave. And that was only two bags. How interesting it would be when Dillah's larger piles caught fire.

He looked over to see what unusual thing Granny Dillah might be up to now. Oddly, she and Furin were just picking themselves up off the floor, shaking their heads in a stunned fashion. Then she began waving her fists and shouting, though in a peculiar ringing silence because something seemed to be wrong with Cadon's ears; while Furin, with many fearful glances at how the fire was proceeding, staggered along the row of the not-alives, shaking shoulders, shouting into ears, seeming to plead and urge. None of them moved except Granny Aturah Wolf, who first battered at him with her fists and then curled up into a ball on the floor.

Another lightning strike, but it was also on the left side of the chamber, and the flames were still creeping towards the great pile of bags on the right. Granny Dillah was standing in a listening posture now, though Cadon himself could hear nothing over the clangor in his ears. Suddenly Furin Fox was there beside him, jerking him to his feet and screaming words that looked like *Go! Run!* and shoving him towards the archway with Sashah shrieking soundlessly in his arms. Cadon took one tentative step and then another, and then he was pounding through the noisome craw of the antechamber, stumbling and retching, not caring now what wet horror his feet plunged through because he had decided that he was not, after all, dreaming, and the flames had been very, very close to a ten-year cache of lightning dust, and though he was bereaved and unborn, he still rather did want to keep on breathing.

He was out of the cleft into the cooler but still stinking night before he stopped and collapsed onto the ground. Sashah's wails were thin and distant-sounding, but at least he could hear her now, and he held her very close because Annah Roebuck's daughter appeared to be all he had left of the People—until the next moment, when two gasping figures flung out of the cleft and threw themselves towards him. Half a heartbeat later, the earth rumbled and shook and toppled the newcomers off their feet. A great flame gouted from the cleft, lighting up the moonless shadows as brightly as high noon, remaining as a vivid ghost-image in Cadon's closed eyes for many minutes. He coiled himself into a protective ball around Sashah and waited for the world to end; and when he could hear again and the ground had stopped moving, he sat up and soothed the weeping baby and looked around to see who else had escaped the holocaust. A fine red glow from the mouth of the cleft gave him more than enough light.

Furin Fox lurched to a sitting position, holding his head. Beside him, Granny Dillah Roebuck looked dead, but Furin seized her shoulder and shook her violently.

"Why, Dillah, why?"

She opened her eyes. "I had a very big question to ask," she whispered, "and a very big question needs a very big fire."

Furin opened and closed his mouth several times in rapid succession, like a gasping fish with something hugely important to say. "Ngh," he said. He collapsed onto his back and put his arm across his face.

Granny Dillah painfully sat up and squinted into the shadows at Cadon. "Is that you, Cadon Fox? And is Annah's child still breathing? Good. Come closer. I have a message for you."

Cadon came to crouch beside her. The red glow from the cleft was fading, and he could hardly see her face, but she smelled of singed hair and smoky marmot-fur. She put her hand on his cheek.

But before she could speak, Furin sat up convulsively. "Cadon, get away from that murderess!"

"Murderess? Whom did I murder, Furin Fox? That bunch of dead people?"

"You know what I mean, Dillah! *And* you destroyed the Ones Before!"

She frowned at him. "That was an act of kindness."

"*What?*"

Granny Dillah dropped her hand from Cadon's cheek. Bewildered, Cadon stayed where he was. "The People are dead, Furin Fox," the old woman said in the sort of voice used to reason with idiots. "Those pathetic few who fled into the forest are not the People. We were one body, held inside one skin by bloodlines and bloodloans, and now our body is dead. There are no shamans left. There will never be another Caucus. Would you have the Ones Before starve slowly for want of gifts and offerings and the shamans' songs? I would not. How could I leave them to that fate?"

"You're lying," Furin said bluntly. "You did it because you were angry."

"Well, yes, that too." Her face was in near darkness, but she sounded impatient. She put one hand on Cadon's cheek again, and the other hand on Sashah's. Sashah, the usual two fingers in her mouth, sat quietly in Cadon's lap. "Welcome, children," Dillah began. "Listen carefully. This place where you find yourself is the world of those who breathe. That which you see above you is the sky. That which you see below you is the earth."

"Please, I don't understand," Cadon interrupted. "Is that the message from the Old Woman?"

"No, nephew," Furin said in a strange, flat voice, "it's the midwife's greeting to the newly born. Congratulations."

"Let me get on with it," Granny Dillah snapped.

"Go ahead. It's not a bad idea. But if you think you can fool the Old Woman with a trick like that," Furin added drily, "you'd better think again."

"The Old Woman? Why would I bother to fool her? Old Bitch, more like."

Furin and Cadon uttered near-identical exclamations of horror. Cadon recoiled from Granny Dillah's hand, but she shifted her fingers into a quite painful grip on his hair, and pulled him back. Then she cupped his cheek again and drew breath to speak.

Cadon put his hand up to her mouth. He felt tired and ill and close to tears, and the child was heavy in his lap. "Please, you said you had a message for me from the Old Woman."

"I have, but not from the Old Woman. Though it is true that she spoke to me from the fire. What she said was, *burn them.*"

"Oh," said Cadon. Now his head was aching.

"That's right, that's exactly what she said. *Burn them, burn them, burn both of them.* I don't think we'll listen to the Old Woman any more."

"All right," he said stupidly. "So who is the message from?"

"From me, Cadon Fox."

"Oh," he said. He heard a grunt from Furin, and was surprised at how approving it sounded. Then he started to drift again. How wonderful it would be to sleep, he thought, to sleep forever on a soft pile of pelts in a cosy forest berth. The red glow brightened again in the cleft. The stench of decay was enriched by a gamy smell of something roasting. He dragged his mind back when Granny Dillah pinched his cheek, quite hard.

"Stay awake, boy! I'm birthing you into a very different world. You have no future in the places where the People used to walk. The Old Woman will be walking there, and she is a madwoman. You must take Sashah and go far away."

"Yes, Granny Dillah." Cadon found himself beyond protesting. A different world? It was a terrible thought, but the old world was as dead as his mother, as dead as Lusil, as dead as Annah Roebuck and Aturah Wolf.

Furin Fox grunted again. "It's not bad advice, Cadon. The Old Woman isn't all you need to worry about. There's not a survivor of the People who doesn't know you brought the curse. But Dillah, where should he go?"

"Somewhere that's as far as it can be from the world of the People."

Silence from Furin; then, "Do you mean a city?"

"A city would do nicely. "

"That's harsh, Dillah."

"What's a city?" Cadon asked.

"You'll find out," Furin growled, when Granny Dillah did not answer. "And what is he supposed to do there, hey? Find something, do something? See visions? What?"

"No point asking me, Furin Fox, because how would I know? Perhaps the savages will have some suggestions."

"You're sending him to the savages?" Furin sputtered. "On purpose?"

"That's generally who lives in cities. And as for me, since I am dead, I shall be an unquiet spirit, and walk the earth for a little—with these newborns, if there's nothing better to do."

Furin sucked in a loud, indignant breath, and Cadon braced himself for an explosion of rage. It did not come. Instead, Furin held his breath for a long few moments; and then he muttered something indistinct and struck the ground hard with his open palm, as if declaring surrender in a wrestling match. "Fine, Dillah, have it your way. And since I no longer have a comfortable cave to be dead in," he added pointedly, "I may as well come along too. And the sooner we go, the better, so get on with it, Dillah Roebuck."

"Fine by me. So shut up. Cadon, listen carefully." Dillah again cupped Cadon's cheek. "That which is wet is water, and it falls from the sky as rain. Are you getting this, boy?"

"Yes, Granny Dillah," said Cadon. He fell asleep sitting up a couple of minutes later, whereas Granny Dillah carried on stating the obvious for quite a long time before she too began to snore. And three days later, two newborns and two ghosts left the massif of the Caucus behind them forever, and turned their feet towards more savage places.

Chapter Nine

Travelling Unhopefully

The five thousand eyes of the night sky, looking down, might have noticed a few patterns changing during the next turn of the seasons. A brace of new volcanoes sparked in an arc of islands at the waist of the Earth. Halfway between there and the night glow of the icecap, fringing the shores of a large inland sea, some of the cities and towns glittered more brightly than before. Farther north, in contrast, many small lights were extinguished altogether. The fire-circles of the People no longer wove a shifting web across the high places, though a few points of flame continued to wander northwards, vanishing one by one over the months. The upper reaches of an entire river system had been swept clean since the previous autumn.

During the last week before the Longest Days, the eyes of the night may have observed the lights of a large vessel as it crept westward along the coast of an inland sea, towards the mouth of that same river system. Of the many men on deck or in the rigging, and therefore visible to the five thousand Watchers, only two stood idle by the railing, night after night. One was tall and well-made, with a rich cloak to protect him from the chilly sea air. The other was short, thin, and simply dressed, wearing the black sash of a Balim chattel-clerk under a plain black cloak. Night after night, the taller man watched with bored resignation and occasional resentment as the dark shore slid past on the starboard side. The smaller man, whose station in life did not entitle him to facial expressions, merely looked ready to serve at all times. Only once, towards the end of the journey, when the ship sailed past a clump of lights denoting a town of average size, did something like grief and longing cross his face, and he watched those lights hungrily until a headland eclipsed them.

Converging on the same rivermouth, but from the north, a lone campfire marked out a leisurely trail of light down the valley through the summer months, continuing its slow journey long after the ship dropped anchor outside a stinking estuary. Never did the campfire shift more than an easy day's walk from night to night, and sometimes it lingered in the same place for several sleeps in a row. The Watchers could reasonably conclude that the four people staring into its flames, night after uneventful night, were in no particular hurry to go anywhere in particular.

***

Indeed, the journey down from the massif would have been the best travelling of Cadon's life, if he had been fit to appreciate it. For two months or more, while the summer blossomed around them in golden days and silver nights, they worked their way unhurriedly down the river from empty settlement to empty settlement, keeping mostly to the ridges and high river terraces, on a quest for any breathing savages. Cadon expected at first that his elders would push on urgently, but Dillah and Furin seemed content to amble down the valley in a way that was most unlike the People's customary smart pace, and to stop frequently in well-favoured bivouacs, even for days at a time. In physical terms, life had never been easier.

Food was not a problem. Wherever they camped, Dillah barely had to leave the bivouac to gather a day's worth of comestible plants. Hunting was ridiculously easy, given an abundance of strangely obliging sheep and goats in the meadows around the abandoned settlements. Much of the time, Cadon found his eager prey seeking him out and stalking him through the high grass, bleating hopefully. Those he did not choose to slaughter, he often had to chase away. Well fed and well rested by the easy pace, he noticed one day that his strength was returning to him, and Sashah had lost her starveling look and become decently babyish and pretty. Furin was as robust as Cadon had ever seen him, and even Granny Dillah seemed to stand straighter, with some of her accustomed burdens off her back. They were recovering, and so was he.

That seemed wrong to Cadon. Grief and guilt were the air he breathed—they should also have been the food he ate and the water he drank. It felt wrong that his body was not continuing to be punished with weakness and pain; wrong that he should be strong and unscarred when so many others had joined the Ones Before; wrong that, now and then, he could forget the accusing ranks of the dead for even a moment and take pleasure in the warmth of the sun, or the taste of meat.

***

One lazy afternoon, Furin paused from gutting Cadon's latest goat and gazed thoughtfully down at the riverbank, where Cadon was skipping stones across the water for Sashah's entertainment. Furin remembered, with a sharp pang of loss, doing the same thing to entertain the infant Cadon, years ago on a far northern shore. "I'm worried about the lad," he said abruptly.

Dillah looked up from the lapful of green pods she had gathered around the bivouac, and frowned down the slope towards the river. "I can't imagine why. Look at him. He's stronger every day."

"Perhaps so. But he's changed, Dillah."

Dillah shrugged and went back to shelling the pods. "Changed in what way?"

"I'm not sure. He looks the same, sounds the same, hunts as well as ever. But—"

"Well, you know him better than I do. Pass me that cutter, would you?"

Furin passed her the flake, but his eyes returned immediately to Cadon. "We hunters had high hopes for him, from the moment Nurrah passed him over to us. Bright, fast to learn, lots of initiative—"

"Maybe too much, seeing what he did."

"—the kind of lad," Furin continued, ignoring the interruption, "who might very well have become a big man in due course. Faras and Crooshah certainly thought so."

"I know, it came up in the loan negotiations. So what's different about him now?"

Considering, Furin lifted out the goat's liver and cut away the gall. "He's like a child again. Like an seven-yearling spending his first winter with the hunters, content to follow along and do exactly what he's told. There's no fire in him now." Furin tossed the gallbladder to Dillah, who cut it open and poked around inside.

"Two lovely stones," she said, wiping her fingers on the ground, "and that's a good omen. I'll keep these to make some charms for the youngsters. But as for Cadon, Furin Fox, I am not at all surprised by what you tell me. Remember he was unbirthed, and then brought freshly into the world. Maybe his new spirit needs time to catch up to his body."

"So it's normal? He'll be himself again?" Furin sniffed the liver, and took a savouring bite.

"Normal?" Dillah laughed, a little sourly. "There is no *normal* in this. He had all the sorrows of the world hit him smartly over the head, all at once—and unlike you and me, he had no experience of sorrow to soften the blow. I'll take a share of that liver, thank you."

"Here you go." He tossed her the rest, suddenly not hungry. Down by the riverbank, Cadon was now waist-deep in water, giving Sashah either a bath or a swimming lesson. Both of them were laughing, a rare sight. Perhaps it was an omen, Furin thought; a sign that they should settle down right here, all of them, never move again, become like the savages who lived like trees with their roots deep in the soil. Then he remembered what that felt like, and shuddered.

"Dillah," he burst out, "what are we doing? Where are we going?"

She cocked her eye at him. "We're going to the city," she said around a mouthful of liver, "to meet the savages. I thought you knew."

"But why? Why?"

She swallowed. "You asked me that before. I didn't know then, and I still don't know. But it's starting to look like we'll live long enough to find out." She surprised him with what would have been an uncharacteristically sunny smile if not for the blood smeared around her mouth.

"There is a reason?"

"I expect so."

"But you don't know what it is?"

"Not a clue."

Furin sighed. "I'll have a little more of that liver after all," he said.

***

The search for savages settled early on into an undemanding routine: a watchful march along the ridgeback overlooking the river valley, keen-eyed survey from a distance whenever a settlement was spotted, a quick search for bodies to see whether the curse had also visited there. Invariably, it had. All they found was silence and darkness, in the huts and all around them: untended bodies on the way to becoming bones, wilderness overtaking fields and trackways, nets and coracles rotting on shingle banks. Cadon began to suspect the savages had been wiped out even more thoroughly than the People. He could see that Furin and Dillah were thinking along the same lines, but nobody wanted to be the first to say it; and so they travelled on, through one village-corpse after another.

They bypassed four settlements. One, because Cadon recognized it as the place where he had obtained the woven wonder, and there was no need to see again what he had already seen. A second, because Furin recognized it with loathing, cursed it comprehensively from the ridgetop, and refused to go any closer. A third, because the grove it was built in had been burnt to the ground, and all that remained amid the blurred pattern of fields were skeletal ash-trees rooted in one year's vigorous second-growth scrub. A fourth, because the visible skeletal remains were human, five of them, and they were nailed upside-down to tree trunks along the opposite riverbank, much damaged by scavenger-birds. Only Dillah splashed across the shallow water for a closer look, and she came back pale and angry.

***

They fared on down the valley, which day by day broadened and flattened and curved southward as it approached the sea, though the northern edge of the floodplain continued to be a range of high blackstone ridges. Day by day, their bodies grew stronger. Day by day, their hopes dwindled of finding any living savages. One night, as they sat around the fire, Furin finally came out with it.

"If we find nobody alive at the river's mouth," he said without any preamble, "it may be that we will *never* find anyone alive."

"Why do you say that?" Dillah asked.

"I keep catching salt on the wind," he said, "and that means we're getting close to the sea. As I recall, the savages used to talk a lot about the settlement at this river's sea-mouth. They said it had more huts than the sky has stars, and they also said it was the place where the *king* lived. That was the word they used for a big man, a *very big man*. They were required to send some of their grainstocks and animals to the king every year, or else."

"Or else what?" Cadon asked.

"I don't really know, but I imagine it was unpleasant. They always sent the goods. Anyway, the point is that the sea-mouth settlement was said to be much bigger than the others, and if there's anyone still alive, that's where we'll find them. It might even be where any survivors from upriver would go for refuge. If anyone survived."

"And if not," said Dillah, "and if we find this settlement as dead as the others—"She stopped to give her full attention to dealing with a cracked mutton bone for Sashah, who was in her lap. "This, dear baby, is how you get the marrow," she said, demonstrating.

The men watched impatiently. “Well?” Furin said. “What's your feeling, Dillah? What were you going to say? What if we find no savages alive?”

She only looked at him inscrutably over Sashah's head, and shrugged. The matter was not renewed. By this point, Cadon had seen enough of both his elders to make a general observation: since leaving the massif, Furin *never* pressed on with conversations that Granny Dillah wanted to drop.

***

It was the next day when they found their first trace of living savages. Oddly enough, it was in the form of a dead savage, or most of one, fresh enough to have been killed less than a week before.

“Hillcat, of course,” said Granny Dillah, peering up at the cadaver in the tree. At her feet, midges swarmed around the dried brown puddle far below the savage's dangling hand. The smell they had come to investigate was thick enough to taste.

“Poor old thing,” said Furin. “The cat, I mean. Haven't seen anything like this for years. Hillcats don't usually turn to man-meat unless they're old and their teeth hurt. We should try to get out of its territory before it gets any ideas about Sashah, else we might have to kill the poor beast.”

“So you're just worried about Sashah. What about me?” Dillah sniffed.

Furin grinned. “You and I are too old and tough to worry. See how the poor sod in the tree was young and tender. Check him, Cadon.”

Cadon, who had just ascertained to his own satisfaction that nothing was stalking them at that moment, hoisted himself up into the tree, the hillcat's stash, grimacing at the closer exposure to the stench. He could see the cat had done its best to jam the body into a deep crotch where the tree forked, but much of the savage's forepart was draped on its back along a large branch, with the head and remaining arm dangling in balance on either side. The savage was male and young, perhaps around Cadon's age. There was no face left to judge by—probably lost to one good swipe of the hillcat's paw, plus the depredations of the birds—but where the skin of the chest and arm was undamaged, it looked smooth and young-muscled. Cadon could see no tattoos. Around the neck was a tangle of knotted thongs, at least a dozen, each holding an object that looked like the sort of amulet grannies would make. Around the waist were a few bloody tatters of some unfamiliar fabric, and a leather waistband with leather pouch and empty knife-sheath still attached. Cadon nerved himself, closed his eyes and took a good sniff. He reckoned the savage had been ripening for at least three days, and was to the point where even the gums of a toothless beast could pull a substantial meal off the bones.

"I'd say three days, far-uncle, maybe four," he called down.

"Then the cat could come back at any time," Furin called back. "We'd better get out of its way. Come on down, Cadon."

Cadon hesitated. All summer long they had been viewing corpses, and this was just one more. On the other hand, those others were already months old. This one was so recent that the young savage's spirit might still be hovering close by, forlorn, frightened and unfreed, waiting powerlessly to watch the demolition of his own physical remains in the jaws of the hillcat. Cadon propped himself more securely in the tree-crotch and peered thoughtfully around the grove, through the branches of yellowing leaves. There were many sombre shadows. He thought of Lusil, unwashed and unshriven—but at least Lusil had a host of spirits for company, whereas this poor savage was helpless and alone. "Granny Dillah," he called down, "can't we do something for him?"

She turned her face upwards. "He's dead, boy. That's why he smells bad."

"I mean, can't we say the forms for his spirit?"

Dillah's face came as close as it ever did to softening. "It's decent of you to think of that, Cadon Fox, but remember he was a savage. We don't know if the savages have spirits like ours."

"*They* think they do. They're just not sure about us," Furin said.

Dillah turned to him with interest. "So the ones you stayed with did have obsequies for the dead?"

"Oh yes. They buried them in the ground close to the settlement; and then," he paused impressively, "they *left* them there."

"What, the whole body? And they never dug it up?" Dillah was fascinated but disapproving. "What about outcasts and unborns?"

"Oddly enough," Furin said, "they didn't seem to have unborns in the way we do, though stillborns and dead babies were buried *under the huts*."

Dillah made a sound of wonder and disgust. "Didn't they smell?"

"They did indeed," said Furin, "but not for long. Outcasts weren't buried at all. The few I saw were just spiked up like those ones in the settlement back there, and left for the birds."

"Strange," Dillah said thoughtfully.

Cadon began to regret his charitable impulse. The hillcat could return at any moment, and here they still were, standing around discussing the savages' funerary practices. "If we're going to do anything," he called down, "we should do it soon. That cat—"

"Quite right," Furin said. "I'll tell you. We'll just take the head along, and do some decencies when we've got more time."

Cadon nodded, satisfied. It was what they might have done for one of their own hunters under similar circumstances. Taking the head did not break the Old Man's bargain with the Predator Spirits, since there was not much meat on the headbones to begin with, and the cat would hardly miss it. Also, heads were light and easy to carry, especially after they were boiled. With his hafted blade, Cadon hacked through the savage's neck and dropped the head to Furin's waiting hands. He cut through the waistband and gathered up the pouch along with the tangle of amulets from around the savage's throat, leaving behind the waistband itself and the empty sheath. After a final sniff that attempted to detect beyond the stench of the hillcat's stash, he scrambled to the ground. Granny Dillah had already cut away the skin and matted scalp and was dropping the remainder into a hide bag. She held out the bag for Cadon to add the amulets and the savage's pouch.

"It smells pretty high," she said, pulling the string tight. "I wonder if it won't draw the cat after us."

"Only if the beast is greedy," said Furin. "We've left it all the best meat, after all. If it chooses to follow us for the head, we'll have no choice but to kill it."

"Hear that, lovey?" Dillah said to Sashah. "Doesn't that make you feel safer? Pick her up, Cadon, before she finds the scalp. She's putting everything in her mouth these days."

***

Through the rest of the day they saw abundant signs that the hillcat's territory lay along their chosen route to the sea, even encompassing a number of abandoned settlements. It was also clear the cat was not native to the valley, but was a wild interloper from the north, like themselves. This landscape was tame. The overgrown remains of fields were becoming continuous along the river, with ragged second growth marking where the forest had been burned or hacked away. As well, the dead villages were larger and linked by many narrow tracks. There were no signs of other predators, nor any of the fierce scavengers who could be just as dangerous, and the herds of wistful sheep and goats that flocked to them upriver were also lacking. The hunters' impression was that the hillcat, however old and enfeebled, had moved in and had everything its own way for a while, but had recently exhausted the supply of easy prey and moved on to the surviving savages. According to Furin's experience, that made the beast both more dangerous and easier to trap.

Therefore, they travelled warily that day in the expectation of being attacked before they were ready, keeping downwind of any shelter a stalker might use. Later in the afternoon, when Cadon's sensitive young nose caught a trace of cat on the breeze, they adapted Minic's Defense to fit a very small group. Cadon covered the rest of the party from one vantage point while they hurried to the next defensive position, and then he ran to catch up while Furin covered him. It made the day's journey slow, but strangely restful. Cadon realized with shock how much he relished the counter-stalking, and how deeply he hoped the cat would attack.

As evening fell, they sought out a place to arrange a confrontation with the stalker, a gully on the side of a well-treed ridge, with a single narrow approach to act as a trap. Granny Dillah grumbled a little at having to be the bait ("very nice for you, Furin Fox, sitting at your leisure up that tree, while I do my chores with a cat staring at me from the undergrowth") but Cadon guessed she was enjoying the excitement. Sashah, well-fed and mildly drugged, was half-buried under a bush for safety not long after nightfall, and Furin and Cadon took to their agreed positions in the trees.

The hillcat turned out to be greedy. When it broached the bivouac in the late evening, Dillah was just immersing the savage's headbones in a waterpit, brought to boiling with stones from the fire. She paused at the double thwack of Furin's spear and Cadon's arrow striking the cat's vitals, looked up at the animal's roar of outrage, and moved back a few prudent steps when the great spotted body hit the earth just beyond the circle of firelight. Furin, landing beside it almost at once with his blade out, hit the ground badly and staggered backwards into an unsuspected hollow. Dillah, muttering dark complaints as she avoided the cat's flailing claws, cut its throat herself to finish it off. When Cadon arrived out of the trees a moment later, she was wiping the blood off her sickle-blade and peering thoughtfully inside the great cat's mouth.

"I don't imagine the skull is worth taking. The teeth are bad."

Cadon grunted. Tactfully, he did not point out there was no longer much reason to collect trophies, since there was no longer a caveful of Ones Before to impress, nor a Caucus of other hunters to boast to. Neither was there much point in doing a forest offering to the Old Man. Anyway, the pelt was mangy on the back and scored with terrible scars on the flanks and one shoulder, and was thus useless for anything more than trimming or patching items made from better pelts. The steaks would be practically inedible, only worth eating for the traces of cat-spirit they would pass on to the consumers. Cadon's jaws ached at the thought, but he moved around to the haunches as he tested the sharpness of his blade.

"Hold on, Cadon." Furin, who had been sitting on the ground examining his injured ankle, got up and hobbled over.

"We're going to skin it and cure it properly, and we'll take the skull as well."

"Why, far-uncle? Look at it, it's a wreck."

"Never mind. Dillah, is the waterpit big enough to take the cat's headbones along with the savage's?"

"I suppose so," said Dillah, "but the boy's right. See those teeth?"

"Never mind the teeth," Furin repeated patiently. "Cadon, you start skinning, and I'll get the head. Dillah—"

"I'm busy," she said. "*Somebody* has to dig up the baby."

***

They did not travel further for several days. Cadon dug a second waterpit, sufficient for boiling up the pelt and various other body parts with one of the tanning cakes from Dillah's pack, while the headbones of cat and savage bubbled companionably away in the first. Dillah extracted a selection of organs and disappeared into the forest. Cadon had no idea what she planned to do with them, and he did not want to know. She did not, in any case, go far before she built a separate fire and set to work making some exceptional smells. From time to time, Cadon heard her voice raised in a chant or a song.

There was no time to hang the cat-steaks for the month or so that would render them digestible. Furin, restricted by his injured foot, spent much of the first day tenderizing them with a hammerstone, while Cadon fed the fire now and then. Otherwise there was little for either of the men to do except renew their supply of sharp blades from the cores in their packs, and play games or make mudpies with Sashah until she exhausted herself and climbed into Cadon's lap to fall asleep. Cadon, drowsing in the afternoon hush with the baby nestled against him, realized from time to time that he was dangerously close to being at peace, and pushed the thought away. By rights, he should never be at peace again. Anyway, the wind that blew in from the west bore a sharp tang of the sea, and he knew their journey, for better or worse, was almost over.

For several evenings after the hillcat was killed, they chewed their way dutifully through the steaks. On the fourth day, the catskin was pegged out to dry before Dillah went to her separate fire in the morning. She returned in the evening with many small bags of mysterious substances to add to the stock in her pack. On the fifth day, the headbones were taken from the waterpit and polished up beautifully. The savage's headbones were returned to the original bag, with his bloodstained amulets and belt-pouch. The cat's skull, Cadon admitted, looked impressive despite its broken and blackened teeth. The next day after that, they moved on again along the ridge overlooking the valley; by mid-morning of the following day, they saw the ocean spreading out before them, with the huts of the city on its shore. It was time, at last, to meet the savages.

Chapter Ten

Meeting Savages

Cadon, crouched in a crevice on the highest eminence of the blackstone ridge, looked out across the delta below. In a sheltered cranny about ten minutes' scramble below and behind him, his catch of the day was roasting on a spit, while Furin rested his sore ankle and prevented Sashah from investigating the fire too closely. Spread out before and below Cadon was the river's mouth, visible as a sheen of broken moonlight on the water. He estimated there were several hundred huts lighted from within on the flats across the river, some of them quite large, and he could make out at least as many dark humps with no lights showing, which he deduced were empty huts. Before sunset he had also seen a few score of huts on the near side of the river, linked to the main town by a narrow bridge, but no lights showed there at all.

Something hissed at him from just below his feet.

"Up here," he whispered back. He reached down to help Dillah haul herself into the crevice. "I can see lights. The savages are alive down there, for sure."

Dillah grunted, "At last," and craned past him to see over the edge of the crevice. She studied the spread of lights thoughtfully, a ragged circle around a bright centre, a little too far away for any noise to carry across the river. In an unnecessarily low voice, Cadon told her how many lighted huts he had counted, and his inference that this place was somewhat less than half dead, and must therefore be somewhat more than half alive. He paused at the expression on her face. He expected her to be pleased, because they had found what she said they must look for. Such a vast aggregation of huts must surely qualify as what she and Furin called a city. Instead, she looked rather like he felt himself, uncertain, unhappy, even frightened. It bothered him to see this odd combination on Granny Dillah's redoubtable face. He thought, as he watched the old woman look down on the city of the savages, that perhaps they would do very well to turn their steps northward at this point and head back to a more familiar unknown as fast as their feet could carry them. Finding the city as dead as the upriver settlements would have been a curious relief. It was one of those times, he decided, when travelling was so much better than arriving.

***

"So now that we've found them," Cadon said that night, after he and Dillah returned to the campfire, "what do we do about them?"

Short silence around the fire. "Well," Furin said hesitantly, "we go in and trade things with them. It's not that hard."

"But we'll come back to this bivouac, won't we?"

"Damned right," said Granny Dillah, shifting the sleeping child in her arms. "I'm not setting foot in one of those hut things, Furin Fox. I haven't forgotten your stories about body-bugs."

"I agree, we'll come back to this camp. In fact, Cadon and I will go in alone tomorrow, Dillah, and you and Sashah will stay here, at least until we see how they receive us. It's on account of Sashah, you see, in case we have to leave in a hurry. The savages are very slow runners, but even so…" He paused apprehensively, as if expecting Dillah to protest, but she only nodded and went on staring into the fire. Furin continued with relief. "There are some important things you should know, Cadon, so listen carefully. First of all, *you must not laugh* when you hear the savages talking."

"None of us," Dillah said primly, "would be so rude as to laugh at people in their own bivouac."

"Why would I want to laugh?" Cadon asked.

"Because they don't talk right, boy."

"How do they talk, then? Like the Backwarders?" Cadon grinned involuntarily at the image. Furin gave Cadon a warning frown and twitched his head towards Dillah.

"I don't know what you're talking about," he said. "As for how the savages speak—well, they don't know the real names for many things, and so they make up their own. And when they do use the proper names for things, they don't say them properly. But don't worry, I'll be able to understand them well enough."

Granny Dillah nodded. Cadon nodded too, though his mind was still grappling with the bizarre concept of *making up names for things*. How was that possible? Everything had its proper name, bestowed upon it by the Old Man and the Old Woman themselves at the time they molded the mountains and wept the seas. Grannies and shamans were there to make sure the words were correctly remembered from generation to generation. What was wrong with the savages?

"And another thing," Furin went on, "don't ogle the women. That means *you*, Cadon Fox. Or the men, for that matter. They're funny about buggery. And there will certainly be at least one large hut there of the sort they call a *temple*—we'll keep clear of it if we can. It's where their Old Man lives, and we want nothing to do with Him, trust me. But if we do have to get close to it, then we approach it in the same manner as we would the Cave of the Prey Spirits, say, or the Antechamber of the Ones Before. Do you understand?"

"It might be the proper place to take the young savage's headbones," Granny Dillah pointed out.

Furin shrugged. "Perhaps. We'll see. Now, try to be polite at all times. They're touchy, in my experience, but we'll give them no cause to take offense. They—"

"Did you offend them the first time, far-uncle?" Cadon asked. "Is that why they treated you so badly?"

Furin scowled. "I did not offend them. The truth is, I was caught by a flash flood near the Icehead and got carried downstream. I washed up near one of their villages, naked and half-drowned, and they seemed to think they owned me after that. This time will be different, because we're not naked and we're not half-dead, and most especially because we have things to trade. The savages love traders. So keep your mouth shut and your eyes open tomorrow, and let me do the talking. Any questions?"

Granny Dillah grinned at his tone, but said nothing. Cadon said, "What will we be trading?" He had wondered about this a few times as they trudged the crest of the high blackstone ridge. They were each carrying a few spare pelts, and Granny Dillah had her herbs and doses and a number of bags of lightning dust, but it seemed a pitifully small stock.

Furin reached for his pack and took out two leather bags, each double the size of a fist. He tossed one across to Cadon, who carefully loosened the drawstring and shook some of the contents into his palm. They glittered in the firelight.

"Gold, isn't it?" Cadon said, not impressed. He poked at the rough nuggets with one finger. Furin opened the other bag and spilled a clinking cascade of shells into his lap: shells from the northwestern littoral, though Cadon's critical eye could see they were not terribly fine ones. They were not the sort to be selected for a man-making gift to the Ones Before, for example, and certainly not as fine as the strings he had traded for the ill-bringing woven wonder.

"Those shells are not very good," he said.

"The savages won't know the difference."

"And why the gold? I thought you said the savages don't make themselves beautiful."

"But they seem to like it, and who cares why? I used to pick up a few nuggets every time we crossed that stream in the Bearpelts, in case I ever needed to trade with them."

Illumination dawned. "Is that what the hillcat's headbones are for?"

"Of course. Believe it or not, we can probably trade the cat's skull for several days of food."

"But why, far-uncle? Why would we want to trade for food? The forest is full of things to eat."

"We won't be in the forest, boy. We have to start thinking in a new way now we're going among the savages, else we'll end up sweating in their damned fields."

Cadon shook his head in wonder at the ways of the savages. Surely the effort spent finding things to trade for food would be better spent in simply finding food. The more he learned about these people, if people they were, the more mysterious they became.

"Now listen," Furin went on, "We'll just take these with us tomorrow, and maybe a couple of spare pelts. We'll leave the other pelts and the hillcat's headbones with you, Dillah. Apparently no trader shows all his goods at one time. And don't ask me why not, because I don't know."

In silence, deep in thought, Cadon poured the nuggets back into the bag and pulled the drawstring shut.

***

The next morning was spent in the first general titivation in three months, including a good bath and some artful self-decoration. Between the last blackstone ridge and the floodplain, a long, slightly brackish slough gave the travellers a place to strip off and bathe in the warmth of the early autumn sun, hidden from the premature notice of the savages. Dillah's pack yielded a magnificent shirt of woven leather strips, which she instructed Cadon to put on. Surprised and touched, he began to thank her. She turned away, and he realized the shirt had probably been woven for Mairn Roebuck's loaning ceremony.

Though she was not going into the city, Granny Dillah also took the opportunity for a change of clothes and some ornamentation. For Sashah, there was a tiny new tunic fringed to her knees; for Dillah herself, a supple leather shift that should have been worn by a somewhat larger and significantly younger woman. Cadon found the sight of her in it faintly embarrassing, though Furin grinned at her and clicked his tongue appreciatively. Cadon stared at him aghast—*clicking his tongue at a granny*. Dillah snorted.

"I mean it, Dillah," Furin said, "you look just like you did twenty years ago."

She gave him a sour look as she finished ornamenting her own hair and started on Sashah's. "Twenty years ago, let me think. That would be about the time you were trying to cram enough of the Lore into your head to pass your man-making, and I was midwifing my first grandchild. I was an old woman even then, Furin Fox, so don't you think you can flatter me that way."

"Did you know, boy," Furin said to Cadon, but with an eye on Dillah, "that twenty years ago she was a byword for beauty, though she was already a matron and about to become a granny? Zann Hillcat, who was loaned to the Roebucks for her, never wanted to go back to his own family. Maroc Wolf threw himself off a cliff and got himself made unborn as well as dead, because he couldn't have her. I myself was—"

"—a young fool then, and now you're an aging fool. And I haven't been a beauty for a very long time, as the boy can well see, and if I was a byword for anything at all in the last days of the People, it was for my extreme old age and bad temper. Don't think I didn't know."

"Just as you say, Dillah," Furin said, but Cadon perceived he was hiding another grin. No doubt, Cadon thought, he had been joking from the beginning about the old woman's past beauty. Cadon was relieved, because he did not want to believe that beauty could vanish so completely.

"Right," said Furin at last, slinging the small pack of wares on to Cadon's back, with the thrusting spear and mace secure in their loops. Over his own shoulder, he slung the bag containing the headbones and amulets belonging to the young savage from the forest. When they were arranged and balanced, he expanded his chest and thumped it once, twice, as if he were the huntmaster on the brink of a hunt. "Now," he said, "we will go into the city, find the trading place, set out our goods, and *be friendly.* Are we clear?"

Out of a hunter's habit, Cadon breathed, "Old Man, pray help us."

Dillah, who had been looking amused, turned bitter. She said, "Forget that, Cadon Fox. We left the Old Man and the Old Woman far behind, and there's no one to help us but us. Just be careful."

***

Nobody was working in the fields on the near side of the river, though some ground was under cultivation and should have been harvested already, according to the knowledgeable Furin. The few huts they passed were abandoned and in bad repair, but no dead savages lay untended inside their sagging walls. As the travellers neared the bridge, following mazy little paths through the patchwork of neglected fields, they heard nothing but silence ahead of them.

“I don't understand,” said Cadon. “I thought you said they had to work all the time. Where is everybody?”

As if to answer his question, a clatter of drums broke out on the other side of the river. Startled, Cadon reached for his mace.

“Looks like they're having a celebration,” Furin said dubiously. “It's about the right time for harvest-home, though they don't seem to have done much about the harvest. I'd forgotten how awful their music sounds.”

“Is that music?” Cadon asked, grimacing. “And is that their idea of singing?” he asked a moment later, as they approached the bridge, and a human voice joined the confusion of noises ahead of them.

“I suppose so,” said Furin, though he looked worried.

“It didn't sound like singing to me. It sounded more like somebody screaming.” It swelled out again over the thudding drums.

“No,” said Furin positively, “it's a song. I know the savages, remember? And it may mean we're in luck. If we arrive in the middle of a celebration, they'll be inclined to welcome us warmly. Don’t worry so much.” Furin spoke heartily. His confidence had returned.

They pushed through a line of densely planted bushes and found themselves on a broad sandy strip of beach, just short of the river's opening to the sea. The bridge, a solid structure of flat wood on logs like branchless trees growing out of the water, was unguarded. Still no savages were visible on the far bank.

Cadon paused in mid-bridge to turn and look back towards the high ridge and the distant mountains of the Bearspaw range. On the edge of the forest, he could see the small figures of Granny Dillah and Sashah, and saw Dillah raise her hand in a wave. He had a moment of wild hope that she had changed her mind, and was signalling them to come back—*whoops, lads, sorry, must have misheard that fire, don't have to go to the city after all*—but then he saw her turn and vanish into the forest. He ran to catch up with his uncle.

But when they reached the townside end of the bridge, Cadon began to feel better. The high bubbling shriek that Furin called a song had not been repeated for some time, and the drums were augmented instead by the wail of many breathy pipes, which Cadon found quite pleasing. A broad track, very dusty, led from the bridgehead into the huge tract of huts, most of which were larger and in better repair than any Cadon had seen before. And so many of them! They stood thick as forest trees along the track, in most cases set in a patch of dust-blown pod-plants and bare scratched earth. Smells of bird-dirt, goat, and human sweat hung about them, mixed with the cheerful traces of recent cooking plus a whole palette of less attractive odours. In fact, the city stank to the skies of waste and rot and chronic filth, stank with a rich and highly interesting tapestry of stinks. Cadon sniffed avidly, trying to unweave and identify the exotic strands of the pattern.

Still, it seemed to him that the city smelled much more exciting than it looked. The city of the savages was a plain and colourless place, a wasteland of grey dust, pale straw, and stunted things struggling to grow. He wondered if the people of the city would be similarly stunted, like the corpses he had seen in the settlements along the river, and all at once became uncomfortably conscious of his own height and breadth, the flowers and feathers he had woven into his hair, the brightly dyed neckband of his leather shirt. He was glad Furin had decided against face-paint and gold dust.

"We must be getting close to the centre," said Furin. "Time to make a little noise."

"What's the use?" Cadon said. "They'll never hear us over their own racket. There's that singing again—but far-uncle, I really can't believe that's a song."

"You know nothing about music," Furin said. They turned the corner and stopped dead. After a moment Furin added, "But in this case, I suppose you may be right."

There were the savages at last. To Cadon's eyes, they were not impressive, except in numbers. They were mostly short, thin, and not very healthy-looking, and they were boringly dressed all alike in greyish shifts that hung as far as their knees. At present it was mostly backs that were visible, hundreds and hundreds of backs, many more than the People could have mustered even at the height of a Caucus. They filled much of a dusty plaza outlined by large structures of a sort that was new to Cadon, tall and square, with walls that shone white in the midday sun. At the far end of the plaza, broad timber steps led up to a covered platform, which formed the forepart of the largest and whitest structure of all. On the platform, there was a solid wooden frame just higher and wider than the man strapped cruciform to its corners, and it was this frame that the savages were watching so intently. And no wonder.

The People were accustomed to blood and the many ways it could be made to leave the body. They also had an excellent knowledge of internal bodily structures, the various tubes and sacks and channels and spongy tissues, the flexing fist of the heart, the bones and sinews, the raw meat of muscles. They were just not accustomed to seeing so many of them on display all at once, especially in a still-living body, and apparently by intention rather than misadventure. Cadon shifted his eyes queasily towards the sky, bothered by a memory flash of flayed and dessicated remains nailed to the trees of a distant village. Furin whispered, "You know, they seem to be in a strange mood today. I think we should leave before they notice us."

Too late. When Cadon forced himself to look towards the portico again, he saw there were more figures on it than the man-shaped horror howling in its wrist-straps in the wooden frame. A daunting number of them were armed with spears, and all of them were scowling at Cadon and Furin with no sign of the hoped-for welcome. Worse, some of the closest savages, the ones at the very rump of the crowd, were turning around to see what those on the portico were regarding so balefully. They did not look friendly either. It seemed like a good time to test Furin's memory of how fast the savages could run.

Too late again. Footsteps behind them: a large party of savages, carrying staves, was approaching from the direction of the beach. At the sight of Cadon and Furin in their finery, most of them stood still with their mouths gaping, but some recovered and began fanning out purposefully to cover the side road and cut off any chance of retreat. At the same time, bolder members of the main crowd began to arc around to meet the others, placing the visitors at the centre of a shrinking circle of faces.

Eager to maintain the courtesies, Cadon and Furin smiled hugely and raised their hands in a greeting that was normally taken to mean, *I would not dream of drawing weapons in your bivouac, my fine new friends.* The savages did not seem to be familiar with the rules. Cadon surmised they were not going to be politely blind to the knives in Furin's belt and his, and the spears and maces in their pack-loops. On the contrary, a few of the savages brandished their staves rudely enough to make Cadon, vicariously embarrassed, blush on their behalf. Furin muttered, "They're even worse than I remember, these savages, just a pack of ignorant louts, not a clue how to behave. Well, we'll show them what good manners are. You, there! Most fond and friendly greetings!"

The savage addressed, an alarmed-looking twig in a filthy shift, skipped backwards a couple of paces, but was pushed forward again by the indrawing crowd. Furin sighed through a slightly forced smile. "Cadon, perhaps it's time to demonstrate our good intentions." He took the bag containing the savage's headbones off his shoulder and began to fumble with the drawstring.

Cadon let himself relax, relieved at his uncle's quick thinking. Chances were the unfortunate savage had come from this very city—Cadon did not believe there could be two such enormous gathering places in the entire world—and his peers and elders would surely welcome the headbones back, and be cheerfully disposed towards their kinsman's rescuers. The savages watched Furin with a gratifying eagerness as he let the bag fall away and held the skull high in one hand. In the other, he flourished the tangle of bloodstained amulets.

Proud of the pains they had taken with the headbones, Cadon was puzzled by what happened next. The savages did not appear grateful. They drew back in something like horror, looking from the handful of amulets to the skull to Furin with obvious fear and hostility. Furin, maintaining his broad smile, took a couple of steps towards the twig-thin savage and drew breath to speak further.

Cadon saw the blow coming, but did not believe it in time to stop it. That is, he saw a savage trot up behind Furin and aim a stave at the back of his far-uncle's head, connecting with a crack that sent Furin hurtling into the thin savage's unwelcoming arms. Still gripped by disbelief, Cadon felt his pack jerked backwards, taking him with it; when he twisted sideways to recover his balance, he found himself plunged into a foul-smelling embrace, hard against somebody's scratchy shirt and prominent ribs. It came to him that he should perhaps forget the courtesies for the moment and break a few savage bones. He butted with his head at the man grasping him, then slipped his arms out of the packstraps and retrieved his thrusting spear in one smooth motion. He was not conscious of drawing the mace, but somehow it was already in his other hand.

Clawed fingers clutched him from the rear. He shook off them off and jabbed backwards with an elbow, heard a crunch and a cry behind him. Swinging with the mace and thrusting with the spear, he cleared a space around himself, hoping to work his way towards Furin's crumpled body. But there was no sign of Furin, nothing but a lake of heads rippling around Cadon, screeching mouths, maddened eyes, clawing hands, kept at bay only by the length and speed of his spear. Then over the heads of the crowd he saw men with *very long* spears approaching from the direction of the portico, and the coldest and calmest of his instincts informed him that his only hope, and ultimately Furin's, was to retreat. Swinging, thrusting, he worked towards the edge of the square, the crowd giving way before him, and at last the ring of faces around him broke. He leapt forward then, through the gap, and in the course of the next few minutes proved that his far-uncle had told at least one important truth about the savages. They were very slow runners indeed.

***

Cadon spent a major part of the afternoon laying a number of probably unnecessary false trails for the benefit of the savages, all the while frantic with fear for his uncle. When he had heard no shouts behind him for some time, he doubled back across the blackstone ridge, and surveyed the site of the bivouac from the cover of the rocks. At first glance, it looked like bad news: no Granny, no Sashah, no packs. On the other hand, a second glance showed no hearthplace, either, no footprints, nothing to suggest the little hollow had ever been used as a campsite. His first impulse to panic died a sudden death. He abandoned cover and walked into the centre of the hollow.

"Granny?"

A small pack dropped from a nearby oak. Dillah followed with less speed and more dignity, Sashah slung on her chest. "About time you got back, boy," she said gruffly. "I was watching from that outlook of yours—saw you burst across the bridge and turn inland, with a pathetic swarm of savages puffing along behind you. What happened? Is Furin dead?"

"I don't know." Cadon told the story briefly and wearily, aware of how little there was to tell, sick in his belly at the thought of what might be happening to Furin. The only point Dillah made him repeat concerned the savages' reaction to the headbones from the forest, after which she nodded grimly.

"Do you see, Cadon?" she said. "They must think it was Furin who killed that young idiot whose headbones we so kindly rescued for them, fools that we were. Well, it's obvious what we have to do."

"I know, Granny Dillah, I have to go back and rescue him."

She patted his arm. “Not bad,” she said. “You’re partly right. Now listen to me.”

***

By the time they were ready to leave the bivouac, the shadows of the trees were long and dark down the slope of the blackstone ridge.

“Hold still.” Dillah was doing a hurried last-minute job of securing the hillcat’s pelt around Cadon’s shoulders, and arranging the empty skin of its head hood-like over the ruins of Cadon’s coif. “And carry the hillcat’s headbones right up in front of you, where the savages can’t miss them.”

“Granny, please listen. I still think you should stay here, and I should—”

“—sneak into the city under the eyes of huge numbers of hostile savages, and rescue him all by yourself, I know. Ha! Get yourself captured right alongside him, more like. And then I’d still have to use my wits to save both your skins, if the two of you still had skins to save, so I think we’ll just go straight to my plan, thank you very much, and spare me the bother later on.”

“But Granny—”

She grasped him by his elbows and stared fiercely up into his eyes. “Would you march straight into the lair of a hillcat and expect her to sit quietly while you poked at her with a stick?”

“No, of course not.”

“Exactly, because you know she’d take your face off. You’d lure her into the open, you’d play on your knowledge of how the big cats think. Well, it’s the same here. They seem to think Furin killed their hero—we take them the real killer—they let

Furin go. Nice and simple." She released his elbows and moved around to inspect the back of the pelt.

"But why do I have to wear the catskin? I'm not a shaman, I'm not even a Hillcat. I'm a Fox. It isn't right, Granny Dillah, it isn't proper."

"There is no right and proper any more, Cadon Fox. We left all that behind us with our dead. And as far as we know, there are no Hillcats left, either, except for those with real tails and spotted skins. Hold still! As for the pelt, you'll wear it because it needs to be the first thing the savages notice. You think they'll wait for us to dig the skin and bones out of our packs? No, son, you've got to go in there with the pelt draped over you and the headbones held high for everybody to see. It's what the shamans and we grannies used to call a dramatic effect. Can you get at your weapons easily?"

He reached under the pelt to check for the mace, the sheathed knives, the two thrusting spears. "Yes."

"Good. Let's hope you won't need them." She made some fine adjustments. "There, Sashah, doesn't he look nice?"

Sashah, drowsing on a forest pallet with two fingers in her mouth, looked up at the sound of her name, so trustingly that Cadon felt his heart break for her.

"We're taking her into danger."

"I can't let you go alone and that's final. You're a bright boy and a good boy, but you don't know your arse from your headbones yet. Somebody has to do the thinking. And we can't leave the child here, can we? What would happen to her if we never came back? So let's get going."

She picked up her pack, easily enough now that she had lightened it. Most of its original contents were in a shallow pit with the men's packs, while the little bags of herbs and remedies and lightning dust that she thought fit to bring along, plus a flint core in case new blades were needed, and several days supply of emergency jerky, added up to less than half the burden she was accustomed to carrying. Sashah, slung on Granny Dillah's front, neatly counterbalanced the weight behind. Dillah's sickle and butcher blades were not visible, but Cadon was certain they were there somewhere.

And so they ventured off to the huts of the savages for the second time that day, armed with truth and justice, a mangy catskin, and a large assortment of concealed weapons.

Chapter Eleven

Night Life in Lazoon

Savages, thought Calviram Hithe. *Savages.* Bloody-minded bloody-handed mannerless savages, uneducated, badly dressed, cursed with greasy hair, rotting teeth, and charnelhouse breath—and that was just the aristocracy. The peasantry, an unwashed half-naked herd of hollow-eyed foul-smelling flea-ridden starvelings, hardly seemed human at all. And Lazoon itself was a fit setting for them, a cluster of noisome hovels perched on the edge of a fish-stinking shit-stinking beach, centered on the pathetic plaza with its graceless box of a so-called temple and the filthy roach-infested stye they seemed to think constituted a palace. He'd been right, Calviram told himself, to see this inspection tour as a petty payback to the Hithe faction for levering his sister Chanithel into the god-king's bed as Consort, much good it had done them. That smug Dreeve diumvirate, the Recorder and the Palace Master, were surely still celebrating Chanithel's most recent failures, but Calviram amused himself by contemplating what machinations his brother Hoderil would even now be setting into motion against them. Truly, the woes of the Dreeves were only just beginning. But as for here and now, if he had to sit on that platform just one more time, breathing in the stench of these yokels while watching the pig-king's hard-eyed priests de-flesh another shrieking sacrifice—

The interpreter sought his attention with a discreet cough. "Honoured Prefect, sir? The king desires me to tell you the time has come."

Calviram nodded graciously and took his place beside the king in the procession towards the portico, now lit with numerous torches against the gathering darkness. In the plaza below, it appeared that most of the surviving population of the Lazoon valley was assembled to watch justice being done, a multitude of reasonable size for such a minor provincial kingdom. Several thousand eyes followed the progress of king and imperial inspector towards the two seats of honour placed side by side under the canopy, conveniently close to the skinning frame where the Wild Man captured in the morning had been secured all afternoon. A little too close, in fact. A fine backspray of blood from the morning's messenger had spotted Calviram's third-best gown of expensive Balim linen and possibly ruined it altogether—his valets had clucked in despair when they stripped it from him for his afternoon rest. He supposed it was good policy for Balimhavar to tolerate local religious customs as long as the tribute continued to flow; still, the flaying rituals of these Lazooners were a little too protracted for his taste. Why not a clean, simple knife across the throat or the belly, or a quick and tidy plucking-out of the heart, like any civilized sacrificial rite? He was allowing this one to proceed because it was a punitive sacrifice, where torture could have a beneficial effect on the watching populace, but he swore it would be the last he would sanction before he left this piss-hole kingdom in a few days time.

Anyway, the tribute was *not* flowing. His report would be harshly worded on that score. The problem of the man-eater was real enough, and the blood-plague had undoubtedly hit

Lazoon a crushing blow, and the town was indeed crowded with famished refugees from upriver, and it was quite true the fields had been left to parch or run riot with weeds; but the plump pig's response to these crises had been most unsatisfactory. Begging food from Balimhavar, indeed! There was plenty of food in Lazoon—that is, the nobles, the priests and the constabulary were all eating well enough. Why would these provincial rulers never understand the most basic principle of economics? As a pump had to be primed to give water, so the peasantry had to be fed if they were to produce a taxable surplus. There might be temporary benefits from increasing the tempo of sacrifices and the brutality of the constabulary, but too many dead peasants could mean no food at all in a year or two.

No, things had to change in Lazoon. Instead of grain galleys, Calviram would recommend dispatching a strike force to commandeer and distribute the existing foodstocks, and a party of trained hunters to go after the man-eater—the *lagosh*, they called it—so the peasants could safely be driven back upriver in the spring, back to their suffering fields. Then, naturally, a garrison of reasonable size should be installed, headed by a competent governor sent out from Balimhavar, though that honour would not, he vowed, go to Calviram himself. At any rate, he saw no reason to doubt that Lazoon would be back on a tribute-paying basis in a year, two at most, given proper management. And if the fat king objected, he could easily be deposed. In fact the pig-man would himself make an impressive sacrifice, possibly even a popular one, though with his acreage of skin, the cutter priests might have to flay him in shifts. Calviram grinned at the image, and the king nodded back at him with vigour and incomprehension, smiling vastly as they lowered themselves into the seats of honour.

Before them was a pedestal on which the evidence of the Wild Man's guilt was displayed before the sorrowing eyes of the population: the shining clean skull presumed to be that of the hunter-hero Kazfon il Mar, and the tangle of protective amulets which Calviram had watched the king put around the young man's throat barely two weeks before. It was a pity about that boy. An offspring of the constabulary class, he was much less scrawny than most Lazooners, indeed quite well-muscled, and handsome in a way that would have gone down quite well in the court of Balimhavar. Calviram's orders included collecting a levy of young Lazooners for part-payment of the client kingdom's arrears, but what a sad joke that was. There was a bare handful left that would not disgrace Balimhavar's meanest stable, much less its court. The fat pig had been sending the man-eater a regular diet of hunter-heroes ever since the beast began its depredations in the spring, far up the river valley. And week after week the cutter priests had made the plaza echo to the howls of formal sacrifices, whose essences were sent screaming off to the forest to augment the powers of the heroes, or else up to the sky with anguished messages for the Lazooners' obviously deranged deities. Calviram arrived too late to preserve most of them, but he might have requisitioned Kazfon il Mar if he hadn't thought the young man had a good chance of actually killing the man-eater, which would have increased his value considerably as a prize for Balimhavar. Poor lad.

Once more, Calviram considered pointing out to the Lazooners that the Wild Man in the skinning frame was almost certainly innocent. Those two neat holes in the top of Kazfon's skull looked to Calviram like the marks of teeth, large curving fangs such as might be found in the jaw of a great cat; but if this discrepancy did not bother the Lazooner judges, he saw no reason to make trouble for himself by bringing the matter up. His brief was to collect tribute and information, not to interfere unnecessarily.

Of course the Wild Man was interesting in his own right. Calviram had vaguely heard of the Wild People before, but they generally ranged too far to the north and west to be of much interest to Balimhavar. His interpreter, Hari, knew very little about them, but he was a city boy from Liske, the next river valley to the east, whose language was close enough to Lazoon's to be workable. As for the Lazooners, they reported that the Wild People were not much better than animals. No gods, no temples, no priests, no kings, nothing in the way of lore or history or arcane wisdom. Neither did they tend fields, raise herds, mine for copper or gold, or weave cloth. Mind you, thought Calviram, the Lazooners also said the Wild Men spoke only in hog-grunts and bird-calls, and had no real language, but he had heard this one cussing his captors in what sounded like perfectly fluent Lazoon-speech, a few words of which he himself could understand. So perhaps the Lazooners were not such a reliable source of information after all.

Furthermore, in matters of physique, this specimen of the Wild Men put the Lazooners to shame. Half a head taller, for one thing. Calviram looked him over with grudging admiration. The captive was not young, perhaps even in his late thirties, but his body was lean and strong and muscled like a professional court athlete back in Balimhavar. Even though the mob had beaten him bloody before the constabulary managed to take possession, four strong men had been required to secure the ankle- and wrist-straps of the skinning frame, and he was still able to stand upright and defiant after a waterless afternoon in the sun.

And there was something else of interest—the contents of the ingeniously constructed bag the other Wild Man had left behind, the one who escaped the mob. A leather pouch of exotic shells that would be much admired in Balimhavar was intriguing enough, but even more exciting was a pouch of very fine gold nuggets of great purity, as good as the best that ever came out of Mori or the famed goldbeds of Perall. Naturally Calviram had appropriated both pouches at once, in his role as representative of the Lord in Earth—at which the fat pig's face had fallen as far as it could, considering the large number of chins holding it up. Calviram had briefly contemplated appropriating the Wild Man as well, to find out on the god-king's behalf whence this interesting golden treasure had come, but he held back after a few seconds of thought. The people of Lazoon *needed* to see an execution—innocent or not, this Wild Man had to be flayed alive for the murder of Kazfon, the ill-fated son of Mar—but there should be plenty more where he came from. Calviram would recommend, therefore, that troops should be sent as soon as possible to locate and pacify the Wild Tribes and annex their territory. Meantime, he would take steps to ensure that credit for discovering this source of gold and excellent slaves remained firmly where that credit was due. That is to say, with himself; and thus, indirectly, with the Hithe Faction.

What a pity it was, he thought, that the other Wild Man had not been captured. He would have liked one to take home as a sample.

***

In most of the previous sacrifices Calviram had witnessed in Lazoon, the central figure had been considerate enough to keep quiet until the cutter priests' knives were actually under his or her skin. This one was not so obliging. The moment the speaker priest opened his mouth to begin the litanies, the Wild Man burst into song in a deep, tuneful and notably powerful voice. Calviram assumed at first it was some kind of death lament, but it sounded too cheerful for that. He crooked a finger at the interpreter.

"What is he singing, Hari? Is it his death song?"

The interpreter's cheeks were slightly pinker than could be accounted for by the glow from the torchlight. "No, honoured sir, he is singing about—about the nobles of this place."

Calviram saw changes sweeping across the faces in the plaza below: from their usual state of sullen stupidity to disbelief, from disbelief to—here and there—dawning enjoyment. "What are the words, fool? What is he saying about them?"

"He is saying," Hari began hastily, "that the nobles of this place are fat when others are thin, and…er…break wind with their mouths and eat with their arses and…um…copulate by blowing their noses because they have no—I am sorry, honoured sir, some of the words are not familiar to me. And he is singing now about the…uh…the man beside you, sir."

"The king, yes, go on."

The interpreter bit his lip, as if not quite trusting himself to speak. But the Wild Man stopped singing then anyway and sagged unconscious in the frame, because one of the Lazooner spearmen had knocked him quite hard on the head in response to a furious gesture from the pig-king. After a minor stumble the speaker priest picked up the invocation where he had left off, but it was clear to Calviram that the mood in the plaza had lightened. The speaker priest was not quite managing to recapture his audience, many of whom were gazing speculatively at the king and the dignitaries on the platform. Snorts that suggested imperfectly suppressed laughter were breaking out in odd corners of the plaza. Then somewhere in the crowd, somebody managed to produce a farting noise of incredible volume, and outright laughter began to spread. The king took action at last. He cast a significant glance at the Lazooner spear-captain, hauled himself to his feet, and waddled with ponderous menace to the edge of the portico platform, swinging his gaze back and forth across the multitude. Calviram could not see his expression, but the corporate face of the crowd turned blank and sullen once again. Kingly force of character? Perhaps, but Calviram suspected it had more to do with spearmen of the constabulary taking up strategic positions around the margins of the plaza. This incident, too, would go into his report.

***

One valuable skill frequently exercised in court training and diplomatic service was the ability to let one's mind wander while not losing track of anything significant that was being said or done. Calviram's expression did not change as his thoughts roved from his sister Chanithel, frail buttress of the Hithe hopes, to his several expensive wives back in the capital, and to the upcoming triumph on the Day of the Electa; and then to the foulness of Lazooner cuisine, the feast he would indulge in on the happy occasion of his return, the acquaintances he would like to see strapped into the Doorway of Heaven in the Wild Man's place, starting with the Recorder and the Palace Master—but when the speaker priest's voice changed to mark a new stage in the proceedings, he came to attention immediately. Hari had explained there would be a trial by shade, where the spirit of the murdered hero himself would testify through the body of the Master Speaker, describing the circumstances of the crime and pointing out his murderer. The process sounded, if not exactly interesting, at least less horribly soporific than the other customs of Lazoon. Indeed, Calviram leaned forward after a minute or two, beginning to take a closer interest in the Master Speaker himself, a weedy little youth whose robes looked too large around the body and showed signs of being inexpertly turned up at the hem. Calviram had not taken much notice of him before. His delivery of the standard litanies had been better than adequate in previous sacrifices, and his voice was strong and surprisingly appealing, but there was not much anybody could do to make a standard litany interesting

But now the little Master Speaker's voice deepened to a menacing growl as he prowled the rim of the portico, glaring down at the people in the plaza through a thicket made of his own fingers. A shiver seemed to ripple across the crowd. They were transfixed.

"He is starting with the story of the lagosh," Hari whispered.

"I can see that."

"Lagosh means a large spotted wildcat from the mountains."

Calviram interrupted in a fierce whisper, "I know, I know! Now shut up." He was transfixed, too. Over the next short while, the little priest became by turns a farmer dying a hideous death in his own field, in the slavering jaws of the lagosh…a maiden cowering hopelessly in her hut as the beast broke through the walls of straw…an innocent trader torn to pieces on a forest trail…a brave mother saving her child at the cost of her own life. He did a reasonable impression of the child, too, mourning his shredded mother. Then his voice turned mournful, and all over the plaza tears began to flow and wails tore the air.

Calviram watched thoughtfully. He knew he was seeing a born storyteller, a natural mover of the hearts of crowds to horror, pity, and rage. Very interesting. A little crude in technique, perhaps, but histrionic talent on that level was wasted in Lazoon. He had an arresting face as well, clean-featured and astonishingly young in repose, but malleable as wet clay. And his ears did not stick out, unlike some of them. Sixteen years old, maybe seventeen? Young enough to be retrained, anyway. Calviram leaned his head back to catch the attention of the interpreter, who was watching open-mouthed, as rapt as all the rest. Hari started guiltily and bent close to Calviram's ear. "I beg you pardon me, honoured sir. He says—"

"Never mind what he says. What's his name?"

"The Master Speaker, honoured sir? His name is Valdur. Valdur the son of Jinoon. And now he is saying—"

"Never mind, damn you! I'll tell you when I want to know something." Irritated, Calviram turned his attention back to the unfolding drama. Valdur il Jinoon somehow gave the illusion of being taller than when Calviram last looked. His voice resonated with courage and resolution. He was the hero now, Calviram inferred, poor Kazfon himself, bidding his people a stalwart farewell; and then he was hunting the lagosh through the dense forest, armed with his strength and beauty and the amulets of the Heavenly Fathers' favour. The lagosh (Valdur switched roles momentarily) fled before him. But alas! The lagosh had the low cunning of a fox, and the treachery of a serpent. Valdur moved now as a snake might move if it took to walking upright. His voice became an evil thunder, rumbling in rhythm with the drums. But when had the drums started to beat? Calviram had been too absorbed to notice, but he heard them now, even felt them vibrating inside his own bones. By Filkamos, he thought, perhaps he should requisition a few of those drummers as well. Reluctantly, he was finding himself impressed.

So now there were two Wild Men on the platform: one of them shaking his head groggily as he started to wake up in the

Doorway of Heaven, the other stalking an invisible hero through an imaginary forest. The drummers beat faster...the pipes joined in...the murderer struck...the multitude howled. And suddenly little Valdur was the hero again, gracefully dying, and as he died he pointed a steady accusatory finger at the Wild Man in the skinning frame. The crowd exploded with fury and applause.

There it was, the proof was in. And now that the guilt of the accused had been established and the mob was properly primed with bloodlust and rage, it was time for the Master Speaker to efface himself, and the cutter priests to take over. Three of them, one more than was needed for a normal workaday message, were already advancing from the rear of the portico with their copper blades flashing like gold. In the frame, the Wild Man shook a bloody lock of hair out of his eyes and warily watched them approach, over his shoulder. He bared his teeth in a growl— excellent teeth, Calviram noted wistfully—and strained against the leather straps at his wrists and ankles. They held. Then the first blade lightly touched the Wild Man's chest and began to trace the initial cut off-centre from the collarbone to the groin, leaving a thin red track behind it.

Barbaric. Boring. *Slow.* The cutters would spend ages marking parallel verticals down the upper body before sliding the knives crossways to remove the skin in neat strips, meantime weakening the sacrifice before the more delicate detail-work around the joints and genitals. How could the Lazooners watch the process over and over again without getting tired of it? Calviram sighed and looked away from the Doorway of Heaven, where everybody else's attention was so bloodthirstily fixed. He drummed his fingers on the armrest of his chair. He composed a sentence for his report on the subject of religious reform in Lazoon. He gave some thought to the

Hithes' next moves in the game of Balim power. He wondered whether Chanithel had yet pulled off the politically astute move of getting pregnant. He wondered what his brother the General was doing towards the Day of the Electa. He stifled a yawn. Then he frowned and sat up straight.

A strangely shaped skull was sitting all alone on one corner of the portico, on the relatively deserted side where the temple faced the palace across a narrow courtyard.

Calviram squinted. He was sure the skull had not been there before. He leaned forward to get a better view, and yes, it was definitely solid and real, not a trick of his eyes. Likewise the disembodied hands that suddenly appeared palm-down on either side of it. Perhaps this was a movement in the punitive-sacrifice ritual? If so, the interpreter should have briefed him more fully. "Hari?" he said.

"Honoured sir?"

Before Calviram could begin the question, he saw the hands tense as if bearing a heavy weight, and a bizarre head rose out of the shadows and into the torchlight—a human face peering out with an anxious expression from the open mouth of a large cat-beast. Shoulders followed, broad shoulders, then a long body and longer legs, and suddenly a tall figure swathed in a spotted skin was straightening itself on the edge of the platform, holding the skull in front of it with an air of polite uncertainty. That is when the screaming started, both on the portico and down among the crowd.

"Lagosh! Lagosh!"

No, Calviram decided, this was not part of the ritual. He deduced this from the fact that he was suddenly almost alone on the portico, except for his own bodyguards, who had their spears raised and ready and were looking to him for instructions; the Wild Man in the skinning frame, who was unable to leave; and Hari, who would have left if Calviram had not been clutching his wrist. In the plaza, a wide emptiness took shape close to the portico, though large portions of the crowd were making angry noises from a safe distance. The long-legged lagosh-man looked around in confusion, a confusion so perfectly evident that Calviram found it difficult to be afraid of him.

"Don't kill him yet," he said over his shoulder to his spear-captain. To Hari he said calmly, "If you try to leave, I'll order them to cut your arm off at the elbow. I mean it. That's better." Then he rose to his feet and faced the lagosh-man across the portico, spreading his hands in a dignified welcome.

The face in the beast's throat brightened. The lagosh-man held the skull high—Calviram recognized it as the skull of a large cat with rotten but impressive teeth—and took a few eager paces forward before stopping again. His eyes shifted cautiously to the poised spears and then back to Calviram's face with something of innocent enquiry in them. He called out a few words that sounded rather like Lazoon-speech to Calviram's ears.

"Down your weapons—for now," Calviram told the spear-captain. "Hari, do you understand him?"

"Mostly, honoured sir. He says…he says he brings you most fond and friendly greetings. And *she* says—"

"She?"

The interpreter pointed down at the plaza, where a lone old woman, curiously lumpy front and back and with her hands planted on her hips, occupied the large clearing recently vacated by the crowd. She shouted again. Calviram noted with disquiet that the crowd had already begun to draw in again, and their mood was ugly.

"She says to give the headbones of the… the something… to…well, to you, I suppose, honoured sir. And *he* says—"

"He?"

"The Wild Man in the Doorway of Heaven, honoured sir. He says to get him out of the…uh, something to do with copulation, honoured sir…the *something* straps before he bleeds to death, sir."

Calviram looked from the old woman to the Wild Man, then to the lagosh-man, who was now advancing with careful steps as if worried he would trip over his own feet. He was holding the cat-skull awkwardly in front of him like a gift whose appropriateness he rather doubted. Comprehension dawned. Also visions of costly shells, much gold and many slaves with breathtaking bodies and beautiful teeth, like the one before him now. *Thank you, thank you, Lord Filkamos and all your fathers in Heaven,* he prayed under his breath.

Over his shoulder, he said, "Cut the Wild Man down, and get the old woman up here, fast as you can, before that damned crowd of barbarians decides it's a lynch mob. These people are now valued guests of Balimhavar." Then he arranged his mouth in a smile of genuine and heartfelt welcome and stepped forward to meet his guest, his prisoner, his prize.

Chapter Twelve

Saving Skins

There were three small square openings high in one of the walls, through which Cadon could count about fifty of the five thousand eyes of the night sky. There was a door as well, but the kind man who had greeted them on the platform had asked them very politely not to go through it until he sent someone to fetch them, and a reasonable request made with such courtesy by a fine new friend could not be denied. Staying put felt like a good idea anyway, because the savages in the great square had divided almost immediately into a large number who apparently wanted to kill them, and a smaller but fortunately more efficient number who wanted to stop them being killed, and Cadon reckoned it was the latter who were now guarding the door from the outside. Up until a short while ago there had also been an old man in a ridiculous headdress trying to fuss around Furin's injuries with an ointment pot, but Granny Dillah got rid of him with one good blow from her eyes. Now they were alone.

The chamber held three broad benches softened with cushions and woven blankets, and another bearing a tray of small roasted birds and some suspicious-looking edibles that Cadon had no intention of risking. He sat abstractedly on one of the benches with Sashah in his lap, feeding her with shreds of birdmeat, which he partly chewed for her first. He was still shaken.

"What happened out there?" he asked after a while.

"I was—easy, Dillah, for pity's sake—wondering about that myself," said Furin.

"Keep still, then, for pity's sake." Dillah had already cleaned and stitched the five hair-fine scorings down Furin's bare front and painted them all with an intensely green paste from the pack. Now she was slapping poultices of an equally intense yellow onto the most purple of his bruises. In the lamplight, he looked like he was wearing a bright and badly executed version of the woven wonder. "There," said Dillah, "you'll live. At least, if you die in the next few days, it won't be those cuts that kill you. But it's a good thing we stopped them before they stripped off any skin, or you'd be in some real pain now. And as for what happened back there, it's obvious."

"This pain is perfectly real," said Furin. "And what's obvious?"

"It's obvious the savages are insane. They don't talk right, they have no manners, and they behave like a rabid dogpack. They're insane."

Furin snorted skeptically. "I don't think it's as simple as that."

But Cadon, trying with only partial success to review the evening's events, felt he could well believe it. Everything had seemed to go sensibly enough at first, from their unremarked arrival in the centre of the city, to the happy discovery that Furin's skin was still largely intact, and the mannerly welcome from the savage in the shining robe—and then the night fell into nightmare. All he retained was a string of crowded pictures involving many people shouting and waving fists or spears at each other, two or three throats being cut, a glimpse of a very angry savage who was far too massive to be true, and near the end of it all, a circle of snarling faces held back by a picket of spearpoints. After a hideous few minutes of this, shocked and breathless, they were hustled off the portico inside a flying wedge of spearmen, down what appeared to be a long torch-lit tunnel, to this room. The only sane picture that Cadon could conjure up was that of the kind savage with his arms spread in welcome. He held on to the picture gratefully. At least there was one person in this new world they could trust.

***

On the other side of the palace, in what the Lazooners had the presumption to call the Great Hall, Calviram reclined at his ease on an eating platform with Hari hovering behind him, anxiously fiddling with the ends of his black sash. Also present were the pig-king, a gaggle of priests, a small army, and a large number of resentful nobles. The catskin and skull lay in the middle of the Hall surrounded by a protective circle of ashes. Outside in the plaza, a large mob growled its displeasure at being cheated of the blood and skin of the Wild Men.

Calviram's ease was a fraud. There was real danger in the air, to himself as well as to the Wild Men. He was vividly aware that his complement numbered only twenty troopers, plus his personal staff, Hari, and the galley crew quartered outside Lazoon. Any sign of uncertainty on his part, and the king might remember this awkward statistic as well, while temporarily forgetting in his fury that these twenty were only the tip of Balimhavar's mighty spear. Even reminding him of what Balimhavar would do to Lazoon should any harm come to its inspector might be taken as a sign of weakness. Calviram did not want to be avenged, he wanted to get home safely. But he also wanted the Wild People.

Therefore he reclined and ate honeyed grapes with an unconcerned air, while the pig-king thundered and brayed up and down the room. When he finally ran out of breath, Calviram said without looking up, "Hari, send someone for poor Kazfon il Mar's holy relics, and tell this royal nothing to be patient until they come. I want to show him something."

He smiled at the fuming king while they waited. He could smell somebody's stench of fear and hoped it was coming from Hari and not himself. When a cutter priest came in carrying the skull and amulets of Kazfon il Mar, he stretched lazily and got to his feet. "Tell the king," he said, "that in Balimhavar, the guilty are always punished. Murderers are always made to suffer. The Lord in Earth will be happy to find that Lazoon shares our passion for justice."

The king responded with a blast of speech that set all his cheeks and chins in wild motion. "He says," Hari faltered, "that he is happy to hear that the Lord in Earth will be happy."

"Then ask him why he is so eager to execute the Wild Men, when it was clearly a great cat who murdered his villagers."

"Honoured sir, he says they must be lagosh-demons who can also take the forms of men. He says they must be flayed first with hot knives, then burnt in a great fire while they are still breathing. He says, if this is not done, the Heavenly Fathers will punish Lazoon for shirking their duty of justice. He says—"

Calviram interrupted, "He's repeating himself. Ask him if the Heavenly Fathers would punish Lazoon if an innocent were executed by mistake."

"He says most assuredly, honoured sir, which is why they first conduct the trial by shade. He says the lagosh—"

"Enough." He took the skull of Kazfon il Mar from the cutter priest and held it up so everyone could see, tapping with his gold-tipped fingers at the two neat holes punched through the crown. "You will all agree, I think, that these are the marks made by the lagosh's teeth when it dragged the body of your poor hero to its lair?" He waited while Hari translated this, waited a little longer until it was clear that everyone did agree, even the sullen king, and then waited a little longer still because one learned in the court of Balimhavar that timing was everything.

At last, moving deliberately, Calviram stepped inside the circle of ashes and picked up the great catskull. "This is the skull of a dead lagosh, is it not? Yes? Note the teeth? Now watch closely."

This was the risky part. What if he was wrong? What if there was more than one cat involved? But when he brought the two skulls together, the long curved fangs of one slid neatly into the holes on the crown of the other. "See?" Calviram said triumphantly, "here is your murderer. Tell them, Hari."

But even when Hari told them, the cream of Lazoon looked blank. Calviram sighed. "Tell these clods to listen carefully. This is the skull of their killer-lagosh, the great cat who terrorized the villages and slew Kazfon il Mar. And if the skull is here, it cannot also be inside the head of the Wild Man who was wearing the catskin. Neither can it be inside the head of the other Wild Man, nor the crone. The lagosh is dead, and Lazoon has narrowly escaped executing innocent men. They should be thankful to me for stopping them from incurring the wrath of the—Hari, put in whatever it is their gods are called. And they should also be grateful to the Wild Men, because it is clear to me that the Wild Men have destroyed the lagosh-demon for them."

This seemed to be sinking in at last. The fat king became glassy-eyed with concentration as he tried to follow the logic through to its end, while other heads were already nodding with surprised comprehension. Finally the king, frowning with mental effort, stepped into the circle of ashes to take a closer look at the conjoined skulls. To Hari, he addressed a few wondering words.

"He says he does not see how this can be so, honoured sir, because Kazfon's shade pointed out the murderer through the hand of the Master Speaker."

"Then the Master Speaker must have been wrong." Pleased with progress, Calviram spoke without thinking. The shocked silence that followed Hari's translation told him he had made a mistake. He turned at the sound of rustling behind him and saw that, where a moment ago the priests and nobles had been evenly distributed along the wall, there was now a wide and growing stretch of masonry visible, with a single lonely figure framed in the centre. A moment later, it was lonely no longer, if the troop of Lazooner spearmen who encircled it could be called company. The young man looked familiar.

Hari breathed into his master's ear, "Bearing false witness is also a crime."

Calviram groaned inwardly. It seemed that being surrounded by idiots was making him slow. The young man was the Master Speaker who had conducted the trial by shade, Valdur Son of Something—now Valdur the Doomed, if Calviram knew the Lazooners.

"They will mete out to him the penalty intended for those he falsely accused," Hari added helpfully.

Of course they would. That even seemed reasonable to Calviram. Flayed with hot knives and burned alive, wasn't it? But, he mourned, what a waste of talent! He had fully intended to take this one back with him. With a little training in Balim-speech and a few refinements of technique, the poor sod could have been an adornment to the sacral dramas of Balimhavar, not to mention a credit to the Hithe faction. Oh well, he thought, if it came down to a choice between saving the Wild

People or saving the skin of this miserable provincial priest, no matter how talented, he would take the Wild People without a second thought.

He kept his eyes on the little speaker priest's face as the spearmen conducted him, not without deference, to the ash circle. The priest did not look especially frightened. Rather, he looked tolerant but mildly impatient, as if he had better places to be. So perhaps Hari was exaggerating the danger—after all, this Valdur was the man who barely two hours before had blown the hearts of the Lazooners around like a pile of dead leaves. But as the interrogation proceeded, Calviram shook his head sadly and looked away. He did not need to know the speech, the priest's tone was enough. Too much honesty, too little humility. The flippant overtone was a terrible idea. What was the fool priest thinking of?

Hari maintained a low-voiced commentary. Yes, Valdur stated with admirable calm, he certainly had pointed the guilt-finger at the Wild Man in the Doorway of Heaven. Why? Well, whom else was he going to point it at? The honoured visitor from Balimhavar, perhaps? One of the nobles? The king himself? Some poor random peasant from the plaza? As for the shade of Kazfon il Mar, well, Valdur certainly thought he saw the poor confused thing pointing its spectral finger at the Wild Man. But shades were far less reliable than was generally believed. Alas, the shade of Kazfon must have been mistaken. Valdur did, of course, offer his sincere regrets to the Wild Men and to anyone else who might have been inconvenienced by his unfortunate error.

There was a long, gravid silence after he finished speaking. Then the king spoke, very coldly, his chins wobbling with solemnity. Even before Hari translated, Calviram knew the little priest had touched the torch to his own pyre.

"The king says, the priest Valdur il Jinoon has tried to fling excrement onto the memory of the hero Kazfon il Mar. How could a hero possibly make a false accusation, even after death? It is unthinkable. So for trying to shift his blame, the priest will now stand in the Doorway of Heaven for three days and three nights without food or water while his skin is taken from him in *very* small pieces with *very* hot knives—did I mention, honoured sir, the Doorway of Heaven is what they call that skinning frame?"

"I knew that," Calviram murmured. He watched the king tear a ring from Valdur's hand and slip it onto the finger of another speaker priest. This abomination was at least partly his fault, he thought. Ten years of diplomatic experience, and he could still come out with a spontaneous unguarded statement. Well, he would learn from his mistake. A shame the little priest would die from it. He looked up as Valdur the Doomed was escorted past him, and their eyes met.

If there had been one dust-mote of pleading in the little priest's face, nothing would have happened. With mild regret, Calvimar would have watched Valdur marched off to the Doorway of Heaven, and then he would have thought up a variety of diplomatic excuses to avoid the temple portico until his galley departed these grimy shores. But Valdur's expression was distinctly wry. His face said he was a man in the power of baboons, a songbird smothered in the birdlime of carrion crows. As he passed Calviram, he gave him a rueful half-smile and lifted one shoulder as if to say, *oh well, what would you expect of this pig-pack of barbarian clods?*

After the briefest of all possible hesitations, Calviram's hand shot out and grabbed the priest's shoulder. "Hari! Tell the king that I propose to grant Lazoon a signal mark of esteem, bestowed on very few of our client states."

"Yes, honoured sir?"

Calviram let his fingers turn into claws, which dug deep into the little speaker priest's flesh. "Tell him I am so impressed by the justice he keeps in Lazoon that I wish to do him a great honour. Tell him I will take this piece of filth, this blood-streaked accuser of innocence, this slanderer of the heroic slain, back to the capital with me, to be punished there."

Hari consulted with the king.

"He wants to know—in what way, exactly, is this a mark of esteem, honoured sir?"

With an icy smile and a little shake, Calviram released Valdur's shoulder. "Tell the king that men from all the nations under the sky gather in Balimhavar. Tell him all these men will see the priest's terrible fate, and will learn to use the name of Lazoon as a byword for justice and piety, and Lazoon's king as the very type of the wise ruler. Tell him that Lazoon's fame will spread like a…like a something or other. I leave the details to you, Hari."

There was another consultation, briefer this time. The king looked pleased.

"He wants to know, honoured sir: do you swear the priest will be punished?"

"Tell him," said Calviram in a deadly voice, "that I am offended he would even ask such a question. Tell him I guarantee, as a servant of Filkamos the God-King of Balimhavar and Lord in Earth, that the priest Valdur will get exactly what he deserves."

"Then he says, so be it, honoured sir, and thank you very much."

***

Some hours later, but long after its usual bedtime, Lazoon was dark and quiet. Unsettled after the excitements in the portico, the mob had lingered on in the plaza for some time, hoping to see the lagosh-demon in his magic second skin strapped into the Doorway of Heaven. Rocks were collected, in case of a stoning—rotten vegetables were far too precious to waste. But eventually a rather nervous speaker priest appeared on the portico and told the populace to go to their beds for now, that a formal proclamation would be made in the morning. The sharper-eyed noted the ring of the Master Speaker on this priest's hand, though he was not the wildly popular Valdur il Jinoon. Talking this over, and starting a seedbed of wild rumours, kept the crowd lingering a while longer, but at last the plaza was empty and the torches died. For the most part, Lazoon slept, from the king snoring among his six fat wives on a specially reinforced platform, to the peasants scratching fleabites in their dreams.

But not everybody was able to sleep. In the priests' quarters, the new Master Speaker lay shaking with the worst attack of nerves he had ever experienced in his young life. Outside the palace, in the huts of the town, several newly made widows and orphans, bereaved during the violence in the plaza, sobbed into their straw pallets. Inside the palace, four Balim guards remained very wide-awake outside the door of a small chamber; while inside the chamber, Cadon lay curled protectively around Sashah's warm little body, alive to every sound. Two doors away, Calviram and his scribe worked diligently with stylus and tablet by the light of candles brought from Balimhavar. And in the anchorage just east of town, on board the massive Balim galley, the ex-Master Speaker of Lazoon was engaged in making a poem.

Personally, Valdur was surprised to find himself in any shape to do that. He suspected that making poetry might have been difficult while standing in the Doorway of Heaven, especially if the mob were allowed to stone him. He did not doubt they would have stoned him, too, given permission, no matter how much they had enjoyed him as a Master Speaker. Earthbound people, he reflected, were just as fickle and cruel as the Heavenly Fathers.

He had not meant to bear false witness. How was he to know the Wild Man was innocent? His job was not to get at the truth. His job was to stand up and tell the multitude what it already knew, but in a memorable and exciting fashion. He was good at it, too, perhaps the best Master Speaker who ever held a multitude in the hollow of his hand. And yet, if that prissy-faced sod from Balimhavar had not stepped in, he would be losing bits of himself painfully over the next few days with the full approval of the crowd who had applauded him only last night, and then he'd die. Life was full of surprises.

His current situation was also surprising. The Balim spearsmen had dragged him ungently out of the Great Hall and through the familiar alleys of Lazoon, bumping him along like a side of mutton on a meathook whenever he lost his footing—but as soon as they were out of the town, they straightened him up and dusted him down, slapped him jovially on the back and led him the rest of the way, just a bunch of jolly boon companions who happened to be carrying large spears. His expectations of being thrown chained into a stinking rat-infested hold, ankle-deep in slimy green bilgewater, also went unfulfilled. The cabin where he found himself was a strange shape, but clean and comfortably furnished with cushions and carpets. The spearsmen handed him a skin of decent wine and a plate of cheese, pointed out the cupboard holding the chamberpot, and left him alone. He was unbeaten, unstoned, unsliced, and thoroughly confused.

Never before, he thought happily as he settled down with the wineskin, had he seen better conditions for the making of a poem.

Chapter Thirteen

The Hero's Farewell

A good round belly was a beautiful thing among the People, but only in the company of other good round bellies. In the company of sunken bellies and fishspine ribs, like those of the savages milling about in the torch-lit plaza outside, it was both an accusation and sufficient evidence of guilt. Surely, Cadon thought, the matrons and grannies of this place would advance on the fat man at any moment with harsh words and some local variant on the fasting penalty. But there was nobody in the chamber who looked remotely like a granny or a matron except Granny Dillah herself, though some possible virgins were circulating among the eating platforms with trays of roasted meat.

"Fat-arsed warthog weasel," Granny Dillah whispered into Cadon's right ear. "Ought to be ashamed." She glared at the fat savage until Furin reached across from his own eating couch and gave her a gentle nudge. "We're guests in his bivouac," he said. "Stop *staring*." So she glared at the steaming hunks of meat on the platters instead, muttering darkly to Sashah.

Sweating under the heavy catskin, which he had been required to drape over himself again, Cadon looked curiously around the great chamber. It was as large as the cave of the Ones Before, an enormous construction of stones and mud mortar, the walls as solid-looking as cave walls but somewhat smoother, the thatched roof supported by two ranks of tree shafts carved crudely in the shapes of men. The air smoked with torches. Several score of savages reclined on the eating couches or stood in clusters against the walls, and some of them were fat, but not one of them could approach the girth and weight of the man Furin called the *king*. Cadon watched surreptitiously as this *king* turned his head to speak to the kind man called Calviram, affording Cadon an astonishing side view of his rolling profile and several chins, and, under the bearskin, a glimpse of a robe shining with many colours.

Cadon was more and more inclined to take Granny Dillah's view of things. The savages must be insane. Yesterday, they were gleefully shredding Furin's chest and falling about themselves in a murderous rage, killing each other in the process of trying to kill their visitors. Today, they were heaping their visitors with gifts and far more food than was good for anyone. There had been a baffling ceremony as well, out on the platform in front of a plaza teeming with thin-faced savages—savages who screamed just as loudly when Cadon appeared in the catskin as they had the night before, but this time, he gathered, with approval. Then somebody told a long story involving a mighty hunter, and did a reasonable imitation of both a hillcat and somebody stalking a hillcat, though he was not as convincing as the young savage who had prowled the platform the night before. But something was wrong. Cadon could understand quite a bit of what the story-teller said, enough to make him anxious to set the record straight. He tried to interrupt at one point, to tell the young man it was technically Granny Dillah who killed the hillcat, but Furin hissed at him to shut up. When the story was done, the watching savages cheered with a noise like a cloudburst falling on a bare stone mountain, and the fat king himself advanced rather alarmingly on Cadon to hang a wreath of flowers around his neck. And all the while, the kind man with the strange name of Prefect Calviram Hithe sat watchfully on a grand seat near the rear of the platform.

Then came the feast. Cadon's eating couch was next to the king's, in a place of honour second only to Prefect Calviram's. The king turned to him now and again with a huge smile and a few words—*"Good meat? Good meat?"*—but mostly addressed himself to his own brimming platter. The food was fine, Cadon thought, though he felt guilty at its abundance. But the earthenware jugs held a sweetish golden liquid, quite pleasant, of which he drank a fair amount before realizing it had the same effect as a happygrass infusion. He was still thinking this through when music began to happen, some pipes and drums that he enjoyed, some largely incomprehensible but tuneful singing, a number of dancing virgins who did much of their most interesting writhing in his immediate vicinity. Everybody was being most kind.

Gradually, Cadon began to realize how wonderful he felt. He looked around in a mist of good feeling. The chamber was beautiful. The virgins were beautiful. The fat king was beautiful. Even Granny Dillah was beautiful—yes, even she. And everybody was smiling at him. Everybody liked him. Everybody *loved* him. That realization was as dazzling as the torches. By the Nine Hunters, he was a Big Man among these people, a hero, a hillcat-slayer, a stalker of demons and a fine personage altogether. If the Ones Before could see him now, they would surely smile on him with approval.

He allowed another cup of the golden liquid to be poured for him, and had started to raise it to his lips when Granny Dillah caught his eye. He knew that look on a granny's face, and his cup faltered for a second, but he was no boy now, he was a man, a Big Man, and nobody had ever appreciated him as much as these wonderful, wonderful, wonderful people. He drained the cup and looked around at their faces, appreciating all of them right back, and their sheer beauty and kindness moved him to the point of weeping.

"What are you sniffling about, boy?"

He beamed at her through his tears. "Which one of you is Granny Dillah?" he said. "Never mind, you're both beautiful and I love you."

"You what?"

"I love you. I love everybody!"

"Furin," said Dillah, "I think we should get your drunken nephew out of here. Furin? Furin, for pity's sake! Wake up!"

Cadon's attention wandered. Smiling faces surrounded him, blurred by happy tears. Then the torchflame flickered in a draft and the unsteady light worked a strange shift on the faces, deepening the darkness around eyes, hollowing cheeks with shadows, highlighting teeth. Awed, Cadon sat up. Now it was the Ones Before who surrounded him, magically restored, and clearly forgiving him, approving his rebirth as a man of the city. A Big Man. And that man-shaped pillar—was that Lusil, hero-worshipping him from across the chamber? Was that his mother forming in the smoke of the torches beyond the king, his sister taking shape in the shadows of the far corner? He turned his head to tell these grand omens to the others, but at the sudden movement the great chamber blurred again, this time into the semblance of a meadow of face-flowers nodding in a hot wind. Then even the face-flowers dimmed and dissolved, and the meadow fell away into a charmed golden darkness.

***

Calviram was carefully keeping himself sober through the dreary hours of the feast, in anticipation of the next day's rigours, but the Lazooners' ghastly excuse for wine was hardly tempting anyway. In fact Calviram was reasonably content. Only one more day to suffer, and his labours in Lazoon would be finished, and he would be back in Balimhavar in ample time for the Day of the Electa. Even now, his captain was loading water and supplies for the return journey, aided by the interpreter Hari—no Lazooner in the room was sober enough to say anything worth translating anyway, up to and including the fat king. Calviram sincerely hoped the king would be too hung over to haggle much on the final day of diplomatic settlements. By this time tomorrow, he thought, the Balim mission would be safely on its way home.

In fact, the sooner they were at sea, the better. The king had been unhappy about yielding up the gold and shells from the Wild One's pack, even though Calviram generously agreed to count them as a small part of Lazoon's tribute payment. And the greedy ball of blubber had still not come to terms over the Wild People, having deferred any discussion of them until after tonight's feast of thanksgiving. Perhaps, Calviram thought, he should just requisition the two males for Balimhavar, and let Lazoon keep the crone and the child. He yawned and looked across the fat king at the younger male, who was snoring on his eating platform with a beatific smile on his face. The older male was asleep now too, after first attempting to pull the least repulsive dancer down onto his couch beside him, and then rolling off it himself, to sprawl giggling on the hard floor until hauled back up by a couple of serving girls. Calviram pondered this interesting fact, that both Wild Men became stupid-drunk and passed out so early in the festivities. However tall and strong they were, he mused, they obviously had no great tolerance for wine—a piece of intelligence he would be sure to include in his report, since it might be useful to eventual slave-taking expeditions.

The old woman, on the other hand, was still awake and looking disgusted, as well she might. Calviram shared her disgust at the clod-footed dancing girls, inedible food, undrinkable wine, unspeakable manners. On impulse, he decided he rather liked her; and on further impulse he decided to include her in the shipment to Balimhavar as well, and damn the fat king if he protested. And if the old woman were taken, then why not the girl-child too? Yes, he thought, he would take them all. The youth was a beauty, the man was a fine specimen, the others had at least some novelty value. Calviram was composing the terms in which he would introduce his prizes to the critical eyes of the Balimhavar courtiers when he became aware that somebody was panting unpleasantly close to his ear.

"What is it, Hari?" he snapped. "I thought you were helping the captain with the deliveries."

"Honoured sir, I most humbly beg your indulgence; but I heard something of terrible import, and hastened here to tell you." The interpreter glanced over his shoulder at the pig-king, and the Wild Men snoring on their couches.

"Well?"

"I have been talking with Valdur il Jinoon, honoured sir, the little speaker priest you sent to the ship. He said there will certainly be a messenger dispatched tonight."

The prefect sighed. "Another damned skinning?"

"Yes, honoured sir."

"By Filkamos, what's it for this time? The lagosh is dead. What more do these idiots want from their unspeakable gods?"

Hari leaned close to whisper directly into Calviram's ear. "Honoured sir, Valdur said the Heavenly Fathers will need to be thanked now, and with a thank-offering of blood. He said the people of Lazoon must send a message of gratitude to the Heavenly Fathers, or their sufferings will be renewed and redoubled. And as I came through the plaza, I could see the Doorway of Heaven is even now being set up again."

Calviram sighed. "Savages. They'll take any excuse for a bloody sacrifice. Well, too bad. I'm not going to get involved this time. We're sailing tomorrow, by the grace of Filkamos and the Lords in Heaven, and what happens in this benighted place no longer concerns me. Let the poor sod who comes out as governor take care of crushing these barbaric practices." He waved at Hari to vanish, but the interpreter nervously cleared his throat.

"Valdur said this message must be special, honoured sir. A thank-offering, he told me, must be the very best Lazoon can offer."

"I suppose that makes sense. What of it?"

"He reckons it will be the lagosh-killer himself who is sacrificed, honoured sir. In fact, he is sure of it."

The prefect stared across at the sleeping youth, sprawled in his catskin, decked with flowers. "What nonsense is this, Hari? What are you talking about? They're piling the lad with honours."

"Being sent as a thank-offering to the Fathers through the Doorway of Heaven," Hari said gravely, "is the greatest honour of all."

Calviram digested the information in silence. So this was why the lardball king had not wanted to talk about the Wild People until after the feast. By the time the final talks started, the younger Wild Man would be, if not already dead, then at least missing so much of his skin that he would hardly be worth requisitioning. An unsubtle tactic on the pig-king's part, but it would have worked if not for Hari's loyalty and initiative. Which meant Calviram was in the unfortunate position of owing Hari a debt of gratitude. Either the little chattel-clerk would have to vanish over the side of the ship some dark night between Lazoon and Balimhavar, or he would need to be taken deeper into Calviram's circle of trust—something to think over. But meantime, the debt would have to be enlarged a little.

"How many of my troopers are in the town?"

Hari whispered back, "Eighteen, honoured sir. The four who were escorting you, and the others I brought with me from the ship."

"Good, good. Now listen carefully." Calviram put his lips close to the interpreter's ear and murmured his directions. "And quickly," he added, "before these animals finish setting up their accursed Doorway to Heaven." He watched Hari thread his way through the eating platforms towards the great double door, unnoticed by the feasters.

A few minutes passed, even more slowly for Calviram now that he was anxious instead of bored. He felt a touch running up his thigh, and was revolted to see it was one of the scrawny dancing girls, dressed only in a few strings of beads and a drunken leer. He swatted her hand away and kicked out with one foot to discourage her further, praying to Filkamos that Hari would damned well hurry up and get back before he, Calviram, was forced to murder somebody out of sheer distaste.

Trouble. Four identical shaven Lazooner priests, a matched set, had arrived at the doorway. One of them was conferring with the guards there, while casting businesslike looks in the direction of the Wild People. Damn Hari's dragging feet and drooling stupidity! Why was he taking so long? Calviram sat up straight, stretching and yawning, and casually lifted himself off his platform. A couple of armlengths away, the pig-king snorted in his sleep. Calviram strolled around the end of the royal platform, paused to make a lordly goodnight wave in the unconscious pig-king's direction, and walked past the sleeping youth to the platform where the crone was reclining with the child. She glowered at him as he approached, but gave him a nod that was courteous enough.

He bent over her, scrabbling for the few words of this abominable language that had somehow managed to elude his defenses and become lodged in his mind. "Old woman," he said, fumbling, "come knifes…come bads." Shielding the gesture with his body, he pointed towards the doorway, and saw her eyes widen as she looked past him. "Priests…knife…boy…lagosh…bads," he added, plucking words from the air.

She gazed up at him soberly. "I'll give *them* knife-boy-lagosh-bads," she muttered, and he had no trouble constructing her meaning. She sat up and secured the child in the sling on her bosom, and somehow a wicked-looking sickle-shaped antler inset with sharp stone flakes was already in her hand when she stood up. "Furin! Cadon!" That was in a vicious whisper, followed by a string of words that Calviram inferred was insulting as well as vehement, and he glanced nervously over his shoulder to see if the priests were taking notice. His heart lifted—Hari was just visible in the dimness beyond the doorway, a pale anxious face peering past the phalanx of guards. The spear-captain of the Balim troopers was right beside him.

"Good mans helps come," he remarked to the crone. She responded with a snort, and punched the older Wild Man's shoulder with a sharp-looking little fist. And again. The third time, the Wild Man shook his eyes open and groaned softly. The old woman hissed into his ear, which only caused him to try burrowing deeper into the soft cushions of the eating couch. Casting an eloquent look at Calviram, the crone moved on to the younger of her associates, but by then Calviram could see his Balim troopers moving across the littered floor towards them. Hari was still by the door, engaged in amiable conversation with one of the shaven priests, whose littermates appeared to have left already. Calviram addressed a further prayer to Filkamos, a prayer of gratitude that Hari had the good sense and initiative to adapt his orders.

"Good mans these," he whisper-hissed to the crone as the Balim troopers arrived at his side. She cast them a look of deep suspicion, but mercifully kept her sickle to herself as they linked arms around the shoulders of each of the snoring Wild Men and began the laborious process of walking them to the door. The Lazooner guards parted at the doors to let them pass, with Hari and the remaining priest strolling ahead a few paces, still in conversation. Too easy, Calviram thought, then took it back as he glanced behind and saw the Lazooner guards following them into the corridor.

Hari said over his shoulder, "I told the priests you offered the strongest arms of Balimhavar to escort the Wild Man to the Doorway of Heaven, and take the others back to their quarters. They were honoured, honoured sir. But your troopers know what to do."

And they did it very smoothly. Even Calviram barely caught it happening. One hard knock on the priest's shaven head, masked from the Lazooner guardsmen by the crush in the corridor—and before Calviram could take a breath, the catskin was on the priest, a Balim helmet and cloak were on the younger Wild Man, and two troopers were bearing the swathed priest towards the portico, followed by the Balim and Lazooner honour guards. Hari stepped back to let them all pass, beckoning to Calviram and the remaining troopers, with their burden of Wild Men, to do the same. "Now we go this way, honoured sir," he said, pointing to a side-branching corridor. "We should hasten to the ship, if it pleases you."

Calviram tamped down any visible reaction—it would not do to let Hari know how relieved he was, nor how impressed. Instead, he nodded brusquely and motioned the rest of the party onward, the crone with the girl-child, the Wild Men now tottering half-conscious between their guards. With luck, the ploy with the catskin would win them enough time to reach the ship and get under way; assuming, of course, that the decoy priest stayed unconscious for long enough, and none of the other priests approached him for a while after the Balim troopers fastened him into the Doorway of Heaven, and the catskin didn't slip off his face, and....

"Faster," he hissed, "*faster...*"

Chapter Fourteen

Better Things Happen at Sea

So it was that these survivors of the People, in happy ignorance of their new status as imperial chattels, were carried eastward along the coast of the great inland sea. In the town they left behind them, a cutter-priest with ears like a jug woke up sore-headed in the Doorway of Heaven, a Messenger by default. In the city they were sailing to, far to the east of them, the chief scion of the eminent Hithe Faction lay in state for the seventh and last night appropriate to his station, all the better preserved by the poison that had killed him. And in the same city, in the heart of the Great Household, that nobleman's sister wept under an embroidered coverlet, and prayed her other brother would return from the western dominions before all was lost.

Far to the north and west, meantime, other splinters of the People were having adventures of their own. The Hares, who had arrived at the fatal Caucus after the main spearthrust of the sickness and fled the valley within an hour of their arrival, had still lingered too long. The sickness broke out among them within a few days, and about a week after that, seven shocked survivors linked arms and stepped all together off a high cliff. So the Hares were extinct, along with the Eagles, the Red Deer, and the Aurochs; also the Hillcats, who had a grave misunderstanding with a river—a consequence of having no surviving grannies or shamans around to keep them straight with the river spirits—and were wiped out by a flash flood. The remaining Wolves, Foxes and Roebucks, who had banded together, were mostly in good health but were gravely confused, and the big men of the three families were starting to quarrel among themselves. Of the other survivors, some were slowly starving to death in remote mountain passes as a vicious early winter fastened on to the north, some were already safely back through the mountains, and a few (largely Horses and Black Bears) had been forcibly added to the workforce of a farming chiefdom on the high inland plain. It was normal for the People to be so scattered, but this time there would be no Caucus to bring them together again. There would never be another Caucus. The People were a people no longer.

***

Cadon was not seen on *Balimheit*'s deck until the evening of the first day at sea, and his far-uncle Furin was not seen at all until the morning after that. This was due to the Lazooners' wine, which was somewhat toxic even to those who were used to it. Dillah, however, with Sashah strapped to her front, was on deck before the first sunrise, and neither of the females seemed bothered by the slight roll of the ship. The Prefect was sequestered in the aftercabin, but Dillah had a long and reasonably comprehensible talk with the interpreter Hari in the morning and another with Valdur il Jinoon in the afternoon, and was there again at sunset when Valdur helped a giddy Cadon up the stepway from the forecabin.

"About time you stuck your head out of that hole, boy," she said to Cadon.

Cadon glanced around wildly, then grabbed the rail and hung on. His knuckles were as white as his face. "This isn't Lazoon," he said.

"You worked that out, did you?" said Dillah. "Hadn't you noticed the floor was moving?"

"I thought it was just me. I'm not well."

"No more than you deserve, Cadon Fox."

"But—" He gawked upwards at the bellied sail, down at the oars plying the water from the covered oardeck, across the broad strip of glittering waves to a low silhouette of hills. "Where are we? What is this?"

"This is a boat, Cadon. You know what a boat is."

"Yes, but—but why did we leave Lazoon? I was a big man in Lazoon. They liked us there."

"I suppose they did, in their way," Dillah said grimly. She watched Cadon fold himself double, and lower himself onto the deck with his back against a railpost. "Valdur," she sighed, "be a good lad and amuse Sashah for me. I need to talk to this unworthy young person for a little."

She waited until Valdur had carried off a charmed Sashah before hunkering down on the deck beside Cadon. "My boy," she said, "let me tell you why we left Lazoon. Do you remember that wooden frame the other night, where those louts with no hair were about to peel your far-uncle's miserable hide off his unworthy bones?"

"Of course."

"Well, lad, *you* were going to be next.

"Next?"

"The next to lose his skin. After that obscene feast, they planned to lash you into the frame and skin you alive. And that is why we left Lazoon in such a hurry. Do you understand?"

"I suppose," Cadon mumbled. He slumped a little lower against the railpost.

"Keep listening, Cadon. That Valdur boy, he told me *why* the Lazooners kill people in such a horrible way. Put your head up and listen! The people of Lazoon do not know the Old Woman, only the Old Man. Old Men, I should say, because they call them the Fathers—as if there could be Fathers, and no Mothers—and they give them gifts, just as we used to give gifts to the Ones Before. Which is why you and your fool uncle nearly lost your skins."

"They wanted to give our skins to their Old Men?"

"Apparently. Though I'm not sure why the Old Men would want them."

"Unh."

"Breathe deeply and put your head between your knees. But don't stop listening, because there's more. It appears we're being taken to a city. A *real* city, Cadon, just the kind of place where I said we should go."

"Lazoon seemed real."

"Lazoon was real enough, but not much of a city, according to young Hari. That's the lad who knows the Prefect's words. Valdur's a Lazooner, Lazoon is the best he knows; but Hari told me about a city that could hold ten Lazoons in its bounds, and more savages than the sands of the sea."

Cadon fumbled with this concept through the mists of his hangover. "There can't be that many savages in the whole world."

"We'll find out soon enough. That city—Hari told me the name, but the sound of it is too strange to hold on my tongue—that city is where we're going. He says the huts of this city are like high hills, and the hut of the king is like a mountain that touches the sky."

Cadon mustered a weak grin, to show he appreciated Hari's wild imagination and strong narrative skills, but he ended with a moan, and worse. Dillah waited impatiently for his full attention.

"I've left the best for last, Cadon. Hari swears on his own thigh that the Old Man and the Old Woman—our Old Ones—*dwell in that great city, in bodies of flesh.*"

"Oh?" said Cadon.

"And we'll see them with our own eyes."

"Oh," said Cadon.

"Hear them with our own ears."

"Well," said Cadon.

"You're such a joy to talk to, my lad. Of course Hari didn't call them by those names—these savages have stupid ways of saying even the simplest things. But Hari said they're the great man-spirit and woman-spirit of the world; and who could that be, if not our Old Man and Old Woman?"

"Hmm," said Cadon.

"Do you understand me, boy? When we get to the city, the Old Man and Old Woman will be there already."

"I understand." Cadon swivelled his head on his neck to gauge the effect, and decided to rest a while before trying again. The deck tilted back and forth, slightly but distressingly. He swallowed and asked, from the heart, "Will we get there soon?"

"Not for days. But is that all you can say?"

Cadon leaned his head back against the railing and turned his hollow gaze on Granny Dillah. "Do you believe what that little man says about the Old Ones?"

"Why not? We know the Old Ones have walked in the forest and the mountains, have walked everywhere in the world from the tundra to the southern sea. I see no reason why they shouldn't walk in the cities as well."

"Fair enough. But—do we want to see them?" Cadon gingerly turned his head and spat over the side. "The Old Woman told you to burn me alive—she told you to leave Sashah to starve to death in the dark. You didn't, and she might be angry about that. And you—er—destroyed the Ones Before. She might be angry about that, too."

"No angrier than I am at her," said Granny Dillah, with a harder edge to her voice. "And yes, we do want to see the old wolf-bitch, we want to see her very much. I want to tell her exactly what I think of her. In fact, I can hardly wait."

Cadon closed his eyes. Behind his eyelids, he could see the scene playing out: Granny Dillah shaking her fist under the nose of the great progenitress, dressing her down like some shamed miscreant at the Caucus hearings. In his mind's eye, the granny and the old crone-spirit had the same face, wore the same minatory expression, and confronted each other across a space that crackled with lightning and sizzled with the hissing of the Old Woman's snakes. That would be something to see.

"Is this why I have to go to the city?" he asked. "To meet with the Old Ones? Is that what the fire told you?"

She was silent for so long that he half-considered opening his eyes again. At last she said in a weary voice, "I don't know, my son. I suppose we'll find out when we get there."

***

The next morning, an order issuing from the Prefect Calviram in the aftercabin began a new phase in the Wild Ones' experience. They sat with Valdur il Jinoon in a cluster on *Balimheit*'s afterdeck, with Sashah napping in Cadon's lap, while Hari, nervous but resolute, faced them from the relative authority of a low stool.

"The Honoured Prefect," Hari began in the speech of Lazoon, "has told me to begin instructing you in the speech of great Balimhavar."

"*That's* the name I was trying to remember." Granny Dillah nudged Cadon. "Didn't I tell you it had an outlandish sound? How do these savages make such funny noises?"

"Let Hari talk, Dillah," Furin mumbled. Somewhat restored by one of Dillah's concoctions, but still shaky, he had propped himself up against the foot of the aftermast.

"Ah, so the dead speak," Dillah said acidly.

"Shut it, Dillah. Anyway, you're dead too."

"Balim, the speech of the great city of Balimhavar," Hari said, raising his voice, "is the language—"

"I may be dead, Furin Fox, but it pleases me to continue breathing."

"The speech of the—"

"Well, it also pleases *me* that you're still breathing, Dillah. But I wish you'd stop talking so much."

"And I wish you'd stop drinking so much. How will those wounds on your chest heal, if you go on filling your body with poisons? And as for your disgraceful behaviour that night—"

"The speech of the great city of Balimhavar," Hari began again, almost in a shout, "is the language of the Lords in Heaven, spoken in the world from the time of its foundation."

This managed to snag Granny Dillah's attention. "That's simply not true, young Hari," she said. "It was the Old Man and the Old Woman who first named all the things in the world. We of the People remember those first words, and what's more, we use them correctly, and they're nothing like those bird-squawks your men from the City make."

"I hate to agree with her, boy," Furin put in, "but she's right."

"Of course I'm right. Hari, we can't understand a word those men from the City say, not a word," Dillah went on. "Why, even the Lazooners speak better than they do. At least we can understand most of of what you and Valdur say, though you could both use a great deal of improvement. I suppose I could teach you to speak better, but you'd need to listen very hard, and learn to say all the real names for things, and to say them properly."

Hari groped for an answer. Valdur grinned. Furin moaned softly. Cadon waited with interest to see who would end up on the low stool. And in the cabin below, Calviram Hithe, who was keeping an ear on the proceedings through the vent in the ceiling, was pleased at the liveliness of the lesson. If Hari could have the Lazooner and the Wild Men speaking even a few courtesies in Balim speech by the time they reached the city, it could add significantly to their value.

He was sprawled on a pile of cushions, sipping a good wine that was almost the last of the stock brought with him from Balimhavar. This was more or less where he meant to spend the rest of the journey. He had no intention of going on deck. The landscapes slipping by on one side of *Balimheit* were boring and dotted with inexpressibly ugly shanty villages, while the empty sea on the other side was vaguely unsettling. The sea might be a fine thing to view from a flower-hung balcony on the Hithe estate, set on its proud promontory on the east side of the city, with the Balim fleets jagged on the horizon and making Balimhavar's mastery of the earth easy to see for oneself—but the useless, undisciplined expanse of the open sea made even Balimhavar seem insignificant. He did not like to think that way.

He listened absently to the voices above him. The little Lazooner seemed to be talking at least as much as Hari—perhaps he was helping Hari explain things to the Wild Ones. Indeed, Calviram found it interesting that the speech of the Wild Ones was so close to that of Lazoon and Liske. Could it be, he wondered, that they were brother races? Or that one was the father of the others? And how would that affect the policy of Balimhavar when the question of pacifying and annexing the wild tribes was brought before the Council? On the subject of which, he had a number of ideas he was eager to pass by his brother—the Hithes *must* grab the initiative in mining this stunning new resource Calviram had discovered, and Hoderil was the man of action, the great General, the brother whose sure-footed violence meshed so well with Calviram's silkier diplomatic talents.

In fact, Calviram was starting to think that presenting the Wild Men simply as part of the Lazooner tribute, or even revealing their existence too soon, could be a tactical error. At the moment, they were effectively a Hithe secret—but once he presented them to the Council, it would be harder to stop the Dreeves, sly sods that they were, from somehow creaming off part of the benefit. Could he delay exhibiting them? Or—even better—could he cut them out of the Lazooner tribute altogether?

As the lesson grew more spirited overhead, Calviram cast an appraising eye on three small crates lashed down in a corner of the cabin. They contained the more valuable nonhuman items of tribute he had extracted from the pig-king, including the Wild Men's gold and shells and a fair collection of jade, jet, gold and carnelian beads from the necks of the pig-king's wives. Would all that, plus the little priest, plus the bales of Lazooner woollens in the hold, be a respectable enough harvest to satisfy the Council? He rather thought so.

But if he reserved the Wild Men as Hithe property, what about the crew and troopers on this ship? What about Hari? What about his own valets? They all knew about the Wild Men, and Calviram had no doubt there were spies on board for both the Dreeves and the Council in general. Buying their corporate silence was really not practical. A spy would happily take the bribe, then spill the secret anyway to his masters. Stopping in Liske to change crews would take too long, even assuming the Balim garrison could supply enough warm bodies. Calviram sighed at the possibility that the whole of *Balimheit*'s complement would need to die before any of them touched foot on Balimhavar, though he was sure Hoderil and their invaluable cousin Sallik could arrange it easily enough. The matter of Hari, however, required more consideration. The Liskan was clever and so far loyal, and was becoming uncomfortably indispensable. Would it be better to buy him outright from the Council—or to dispose of him?

Another thought, guilty but insistent, rose once again in a dark corner of Calviram's head. Did everything *have* to be for the greater glory of the Hithe Faction? The Day of the Electa would take place not more than a month after his return to Balimhavar. If Chanithel became the Electa, then it was Hoderil, as the elder brother, who would have the honour of becoming the mighty Shield, whereas Calviram would remain where he had always been, in Hoderil's shadow. Of course he would never dream of betraying his beloved brother, nor the Hithe clan, nor mighty Balimhavar—perish the thought—but who would it hurt if he, Calviram, kept a quiet monopoly on the Wild Ones for the time being? Hoderil would have his powerful new position. Surely Calviram could save something for himself.

He frowned at a burst of new noise from above—not the language lesson, though certainly the new scholars had been noisy enough until a moment ago. No, these were the sounds of the captain issuing orders, a hubbub from the oardeck, a high rising call from the bow lookout. Calviram listened, swore to himself, then surged to his feet and snapped at the valets to bring his mantle. *Ship ahead!*

***

Up on deck, Valdur il Jinoon had been amusing himself by wondering how long it would take the crone from the forest to bring poor Hari to tears. Valdur had not himself helped matters by reciting one of his middle-length poems, and innocently inviting Granny Dillah to help him bring it into line with the words of the Old Ones. And then, since Hari seemed to be gathering strength to assert himself, Valdur followed up with a second and longer poem, which Granny Dillah happily parsed for him at great length. The fact was that Valdur liked Hari, and was eager to learn the speech of the great city, if only because he would not shine in his recitations if nobody could understand him; but for now it was entertaining to watch the crone slice through the interpreter's earnest intentions like a ploughshare through soft loam.

Then he looked up and was interested to see a mid-sized galley rounding the next headland, not more than a half-hour's sail from *Balimheit.* The bow lookout shouted something back to the captain, words that became Valdur's first real lesson in the Balim speech: *ship ahead.* A few seconds later, Valdur heard soft-soled boots hissing up the aft stepway, and turned to see the Prefect himself emerge, pulling a mantle over his linen tunic. The Prefect's face was grim.

By this time the entire language class was on its feet and drifting towards the forward railing, peering with interest and much commentary at the oncoming ship. Valdur moved up beside Hari and touched his shoulder. "What do you make of it?"

Hari appeared to have put the disaster of the language lesson behind him for the moment. He shook his head thoughtfully. "I don't know. Not a pirate—can you remember the last time a pirate was fool enough to hunt on this coast? Not a fishing vessel either, the lines are too sleek."

"It's not ugly enough to be a Lazooner boat, that much I can tell you," said Valdur. "And it would surprise me if it were even headed for Lazoon. The only outlander ship we'd had in months was this one that we're standing on. Unless it's from Liske—Liske isn't far ahead of us, is it?"

"It's not far, but I'd know a Liske galley if I saw one, and that's no Lisker. And anyway—" Hari paused, squinting at the approaching ship, where wind-whipped banners were becoming visible on the mast. "Anyway, it's another Balim ship."

They both turned at voices behind them. The Prefect himself was politely but firmly herding the Wild People towards the forward stepway, and the Wild People were making a mild fuss, but going peaceably enough. Valdur tried to make himself inconspicuous, in case he too would be shuttled below; but the Prefect looked straight at him, and said nothing, and so Valdur relaxed. He noted that the Prefect's grim look had already been replaced with the same diplomatic blankness with which he had watched a large number of Messages being sent through the Doorway of Heaven.

Hari nudged Valdur, suddenly excited. "It's not just a Balim ship—it's carrying the banners of the Hithe Faction."

"All right. And that means…?"

"I think it means they've come all this way to meet the Honoured Prefect, who is a Hithe—the Hithes are a great clan, very powerful in Balimhavar. So these are friends and family of the Prefect, and I'm sure there will be rejoicing when the two ships meet."

Valdur grunted. The Prefect did not look to be brimming over with joyful anticipation, and he noticed the troopers' spear-captain was distributing a supply of blades and spears to his command. On the other hand, the weapons were being broken out with a distinctly perfunctory air, and the troopers were chatting casually among themselves, in no way like men girding themselves up for a serious battle at sea; so maybe Hari was right after all.

"Look there, Valdur!" Hari was pointing at the prow of the other ship, the angle of which was now occupied by an imposing figure whose mantle flashed in the sun as if threaded with silver. And then Valdur saw another banner being shaken out and attached to the bowsprit at the tall figure's feet, a shining scarlet square, gold-edged, looking large enough to make a four-man tent.

"Oh," said Hari. And he added, "Oh, dear."

***

Calviram resisted the urge to reach behind and claw at the line of fleabites so annoyingly situated just above his left buttock. This was something else to blame the filthy Lazooners for, and another grudge to hold against the Recorder and the Palace Master and the Dreeves they represented. As for this ship approaching, he was not pleased. For one thing, it was a damned nuisance to have another set of witnesses to the existence of his prize chattels. Yes, he had been able to get the Wild People below, out of sight, but he was not sure how long he could keep them there without actually drugging them. One crew could be silenced about their existence—but two? And if this ship carried an inspector from the Council, coming to check on the progress of his mission to Lazoon, then it was a grave insult as well as a damned nuisance.

He squinted past Hari and the Lazooner priest, trying to make out the flags on the newcomers' mast. The flags of Balimhavar were there, for sure, and—his heart began to beat more easily—the Hithe banners as well. The figure standing in the other ship's prow was starting to look familiar, and Calviram suspected at first that it was his brother Hoderil in the flesh. But no, he could see now that this was an older man, with white hair flying in the wind, and he was kitted out in the garb appropriate to a Balim court diviner. Calviram moved up to the bow railing beside Hari and the Lazooner just as the great gold-edged scarlet banner was unfurled.

"Oh. Oh dear," Hari said beside him.

"Gods in Heaven," Calviram breathed.

Hari glanced at the Prefect before returning his excellent eyes to the oncoming galley. "I believe, honoured sir," he said, "that it is your eminent cousin Hillisam Hithe standing in the bow. And have you observed the mourning banner?"

"I'm not blind," Calviram said through clenched teeth, "and it's hardly the size of a loincloth, is it? Of course I've observed it."

"I am sorry for your loss, honoured sir."

"Don't be sorry," Calviram said, keeping his eyes on the distant figure of his cousin, "until we find out who's dead."

***

"No! It can't be!"

"Alas." Hillisam Hithe bowed his head in a dignified posture of sorrow.

"But how? How?" Calviram angrily motioned to the valets to refill both wine beakers, and then get out. Hillisam Hithe waited until they had vanished up the stepway of the rear cabin before answering.

"As I said, Calviram, there are clear signs your brother was poisoned—"

"Yes, I heard you. We'll talk about Hoderil later. But the Day of the Electa! They're plotting to have it over with before I return, aren't they? But how can even the Recorder get away with moving the day forward? The priests and diviners would never stand for it!"

Hillisam Hithe abandoned his posture of sorrow and sipped his wine. "Of course they would—they already have—because the order came from the one mouth whose lightest word must always be obeyed."

Calviram gaped at him, and then emptied his beaker in a gulp, and filled it again. "Filkamos gave the order," he stated in a flat voice.

"Indeed he did. Apparently it has been ordained from the beginning of the world that the Day of the Electa should henceforward fall on the first new moon after the equinox, not the last before the solstice. This comes directly from the lips of the Lords in Heaven, through the lips of the Lord in Earth."

"It comes directly from the Recorder, through the lips of his empty-headed drunkard of a puppet king." Calviram spat the blasphemy in a vicious whisper.

"Cousin, be careful what you say! What if the valets hear you?"

"It doesn't matter," Calviram said, "because they're all going to die soon anyway." And then he realized his old plans were now in ruins, because the damned Dreeves had made themselves an earthquake in the political landscape of

Balimhavar, and the need to silence *Balimheit's* crew was almost certainly past. Everything must be rethought.

His cousin was looking at him curiously. "Why are the valets going to die soon?"

"Perhaps they won't," said Calviram shortly. "Tell me, when did the Lords of Heaven decide to change the Day of the Electa? Was it before or after my brother was murdered?"

"Conveniently enough—for the Dreeves—Filkamos made his pronouncement the day *after* your brother succumbed to his, er, fever."

"I see. The first day of mourning, when the clan was islanded and could do nothing."

"Calviram, we did not even hear about the proclamation for two days afterward. But what could we have done anyway? Filkamos had spoken."

"So what did you do? And if everything is already lost, why did you come all this way? Just to torment me with the bad news?"

Hillisam abruptly looked his age, and mortally tired as well. He laid his white head back against the heap of cushions. "I was sent to fetch you back. All is *not* lost—not yet. Chanithel can still be the Electa, and the Hithes can still gain the power we need. But Chanithel cannot be chosen unless there is a brother present to be her Shield."

"You mean me."

"She has no other full brothers left, has she? By murdering Hoderil, and sending you to Lazoon, and deviously messing with the Day of the Electa, the Dreeves hoped to cut out Chanithel and elevate their own snippet—and what would happen to the Lady Consort then, eh? Chanithel's life would not last out the year, though that would be the smallest of our problems. But if we get you back to Balimhavar before the new moon, we can still confound these damned Dreeves."

"And I would act as the Shield in Hoderil's place."

"Well, yes. Who else is there? As to why I was sent to fetch you, this chunky ox of a Council ship could not possibly reach the city in time, but our *Hithe Pride* out there can have you in Balimhavar with days to spare."

It took Calviram something under the length of a breath to absorb this, readjust his plans, and begin organizing his thoughts on vengeance. He strode to the stepway and called for the valets to return and start packing. "I shall have quite a bit of baggage," he said, turning back to Hillisam, "including several extra passengers and three crates. And when we've got it all stowed on the *Pride*, you will tell me everything you can about my brother's death."

Chapter Fifteen

Other Things Happen at Sea

Liske was a glowing sprawl of lamps in the night, bright enough to dim the stars above it, and twice the spread of the Lazooner lamps that Cadon had first viewed from the ridge across the river, only days before. There was little time for him to be awed by the sight, though, because the *Hithe Pride* skimmed past the harbour mouth with sails set and a full galley shift still rowing, despite the hour. At the beginning of that swift passage, Cadon, Furin and Valdur were sitting amidships under a lantern with Hari, learning strings of nonsense syllables that Hari assured them made perfect sense in the Balim speech; but when the lights of Liske came into view, Hari left them and moved to stand silently at the railing, gazing shoreward.

"Hari's a Liskan," Valdur explained in an undertone. When the others looked at him blankly, he added, "From Liske."

"What's Liske?" asked Cadon.

"That is," said Valdur, pointing towards the shore, where the outlines of tidy streets and squares could be picked out in the pattern of lights, not at all like Lazoon's messy straggle of huts. "He says it's been ten years since he was requisitioned there as a boy, and he's not set foot in it nor had news of his family since then. He'll be unhappy we're not stopping."

Catching all that, Cadon nodded. He was interested in the way the savages had feelings about the little patches of dirt where they had been born, often strong enough to keep them grubbing in one miserable place all their lives when there was a whole world to hunt in. True, Hari had long ago left his natal patch of dirt, but at this moment he did not seem happy about it, judging by the sad set of his shoulders as he watched Liske dwindle into the blackness beyond the stern of the *Pride*. It was all very strange. Cadon glanced curiously at the ex-speaker-priest beside him.

"Valdur," he asked, "were you unhappy at leaving Lazoon?"

The ex-speaker-priest shrugged. "Not at all. If I'd stayed, I'd be without my skin by now, and shrieking my throat out to the Heavenly Fathers. No, I was delighted to leave Lazoon, and especially delighted to leave our Heavenly Fathers."

Cadon nodded again. From what he had seen of the Heavenly Fathers' handiwork, Cadon could well understand. He rather wished he could say the same about his own Old Ones, that he had left them far behind and would never have to think about them again. Even rebirthed, with a fresh and reasonably unsullied spirit, he was in no hurry to see them, or to revisit his guilt and sorrow. Unfortunately, the Old Ones were as ambulatory as the People, and made a habit of popping up everywhere the People went.

But he was less sure than Granny Dillah about one thing—that the Old Man and Old Woman would already be waiting for them in the city of Balimhavar. When Cadon questioned him, Hari confirmed the part about the great man-spirit and woman-spirit; but he confused Cadon by talking about something called the Day of the Electa, when the flesh for the woman-spirit would be chosen—just the woman-spirit, though, because apparently the Old Man already had the flesh he required, otherwise known as the Lord in Earth. And the one most likely to become the Old Woman's flesh was in fact a *young* woman, about fifteen years old, very beautiful, definitely not a crone, and actually the Prefect's own sister. But, Cadon reasoned, if the Old Woman had been walking the world from its very beginning, how could she be young and beautiful? Or somebody's sister?

Certainly Cadon had seen the shamans become flesh for various spirits—the prey spirits, the Nine Hunters, the occasional Ones Before—however, the possession was strictly temporary, a borrowing of the shaman's flesh that would leave the shaman ill and weak for days. And yet Hari said this young female would be the woman-spirit for as long as she lived, and her Shield would be the most powerful force in Balimhavar, after the Lord in Earth. And then she would die. How could the Old Woman die? Cadon, mulling over the unlikely details, watched the interpreter crane over the rail for a parting view of the lights of Liske. As soon as Hari rejoined them, he thought, he would ask all the questions all over again and see if he got the same answers, because none of this was making any sense.

***

Everything made sense now. From the beginning, the mission to Lazoon had been a trap, a move in the Dreeves' game. *We celebrated too soon*, Calviram told himself bitterly, *when Chanithel became the consort—we lowered our guard, and now Hoderil is dead, Chanithel's usefulness (which was never great) may be finished, and I am on a ship beyond nowhere, watching the execrable outposts of empire crawl by.*

He was on deck because the open air, however chilly, was preferable to the *Hithe Pride*'s cramped and smelly aftercabin, which he was sharing not only with his cousin Hillisam Hithe, but also with the captain, the Wild Men, the crone, the small child, the ex-speaker-priest of Lazoon, Hari, the three chests of valuables, and the pitiful fraction of his luggage that had been transferred onto the *Pride*. Speed was being purchased at a ghastly cost. Even his valets had been left behind.

Hillisam Hithe drifted up the stepway and joined Calviram on his pile of cushions and fleeces. "She's still singing to the brat," he said tersely. Calviram muttered a curse. He wondered if the crone were doing it on purpose, so as to have the aftercabin to herself. "We could simply clear the cabin—tell the lower orders they must sleep on deck," Hillisam went on.

"*You* be the one to tell her that," Calviram grunted. "Anyway, we want them to reach Balimhavar in good health and good looks, and the captain tells me there's a storm coming by morning. Even the galley shifts will be sleeping under cover tonight."

"When they sleep at all," Hillisam answered absently. He was watching the little group near the railing, Calviram's prizes and the Liskan chattel-clerk, engaged in what sounded like a lesson in simple High Balim. "They're magnificent, those Wild Men of yours," he continued. "Pity the only woman you could get was that harridan below."

"I took what the Lords in Heaven provided."

"Surely. Well, it can't be helped."

They sat in silence for a few minutes, watching as a few lamps showed briefly on the distant shore and vanished astern. At last, to break the silence, Calviram asked, "Who is the girl the Dreeves will be putting into the ring? Is it Damissel again?"

"I think so. You remember her from the consortship affair?"

"Yes, I remember her. Vicious little virgin who just happens to be Grandis Dreeve's niece and some degree of cousin to the Palace Master. I know her brother Darrasat somewhat better. We suffered under the same tutors in the Temple College."

"And did your childhood sufferings forge a bond between you?"

Calviram snorted. "There is strong mutual feeling, of a sort—we have loathed each other from the beginning. On the day Darrasat becomes the Shield, we may as well bury the Hithe treasure and fortify the estate. Hillisam, we must arrive in time."

"Of course we shall, cousin. But if Darrasat Dreeve still manages to become the Shield..."

"Well?"

"Nothing. Because it won't happen. Don't worry about Sallik and the others sitting on their hands while they wait for us. Things are happening in Balimhavar. Moves are being made. All we need to do is get you back in time." Hillisam Hithe looked appraisingly at the four figures by the railing, two short and two very tall, and he pulled a fleece from the pile up around his shoulders against the chilling night. "And what you've brought with you could be helpful to our cause, as well. If properly used, that is..."

Calviram cleared his throat, wondering if his cousin's suggestion was what it sounded like. "I agree," he said carefully, "they're an unusual resource. It has even occurred to me that—er—including them in the Lazoon tribute might be a waste of their potential. But if you're hinting we should—"

"I'm hinting nothing. Though I would point out, this is a delicate time for the Hithe Faction. Anything that might swing the balance on the Day of the Electa is a *good* thing."

"You're saying we should present them among the Hithe gifts on the Day of the Electa." Calviram's voice was low and flat.

Hillisam winced. "So blunt, cousin."

"No one can hear us. But as for this idea, Hillisam, I—I don't know. It would seem…"

"Also a waste?" suggested Hillisam impatiently, when Calviram had hesitated too long. "Never mind that. If there's a whole forest, we can afford to burn a few sticks."

Calviram did not reply. Of course he had already thought of appropriating the Wild Men—who wouldn't?—but he found himself dealing with a strange repugnance to the idea of using them in *that* way. Obviously, he had been away from the court of Balimhavar a little too long.

A gust of wind shook the sails and sent dark figures swarming up the masts. Out of a suddenly starless sky, the first drops of a cold rain spattered on the deck. Calviram held his face up to the rain, grateful to the Lords in Heaven for interrupting his uncomfortable thoughts. "Here comes the storm," he said. "We'd better get below." As he bent to the unaccustomed labour of gathering up his own cushions, he prayed fervently that none of his new cabinmates was given to snoring.

***

The storm turned furious by morning and carried on for three full days and nights, a period of unrelieved wretchedness for most of the residents of the aftercabin. Calviram was one of the afflicted, though Valdur was worse hit, and the life of Hillisam Hithe was several times despaired of, at least by Hillisam Hithe. Furin and Cadon avoided much of the unpleasantness by sleeping most of the time, often with

Sashah snuffling between them; but Granny Dillah and Hari, both of whom were offensively unaffected, whiled away many hours conversing with each other. Hari even talked Dillah into learning a few words of Balim speech, as a personal favour to him.

When at last the storm blew itself out, and the *Pride* stopped behaving like a leaf in a torrent, the invalids clawed their way out of their unspeakable bedding and stumbled up the stepway to the deck. The news from the haggard captain was not good. The *Pride* was a messenger ship, designed for great speed on short journeys between Balimhavar and the nearer possessions. What the ship was not designed for, besides comfort, was long battles with high wind and water, especially in inshore waters, and the captain had wisely decided to run for the open sea early in the storm. The ship and most of the oarsmen had survived, but (as the captain estimated to a Calviram quivering with rage and residual seasickness) they might get into Balimhavar as many as three days later than planned.

"That will be cutting it quite fine," Hillisam murmured as the captain finished speaking. "Our margin was only about five days as it was."

"We'll be in time." Calviram spoke grimly, to his cousin but for the captain's benefit. He did not need to elaborate. The captain's sun-leathered face turned a shade paler, and he bowed himself away and down to the oardeck to pass the fear on to the rowing master. When he was gone, the Hithes turned idly to watch a fleet of small fishing vessels approaching them from the horizon that hid the distant shore. Otherwise the sea was leaden and empty, and the post-storm sky was a wash of dead blue holding a watery sun. The air was cold and stank of salt. The *Pride*, normally trim and pretty, looked grubby and discouraged after three days of storm-batter, and her deck was infested with dazed-looking deckhands starting to clean up the mess. Ugliness, Calviram thought, was all around. He sighed.

"Whether or not I become the Shield of the Electa," he said, "I shall never leave Balimhavar again." His tone was conversational, but his cousin looked at him sharply. "*Never,*" Calviram added.

"That sounds like a solemn vow."

"More like a promise," said Calviram, "a promise to myself."

***

Cadon had liked the previous ship better—more room, and more people to watch climbing those branchless tree trunks the sails were attached to. But this one had the advantage of speed, cutting like an otter through the smooth silver billows, and creating a wind equal to that of running full-tilt down a steep hill. Furthermore they were all alive and still together, including their new friends Valdur and Hari, and they were still under the protection of their kind friend the Prefect. Therefore, it seemed they had not lost by the change of vessels.

And now, with the thoroughly unpleasant storm over, the days were filled with interesting sights both on and off the ship, spiced by the varied smells of the sea. He could have watched the shore forever. Amazing clusters of huts, large and small and in all colours, passed in procession along the coast, all given strange names by Hari—Seluss, Cornmart, Loosiun, the Principate of Hoshe. Day by day, the stretches of wild coastline dividing these places of the savages grew narrower, and gradually turned into expanses of bare autumn fields, and meadows cropped by moving dots that Cadon assumed were large goats or strangely shaped deer. Hari called them "cattle".

There were more ships around, as well, which Cadon thought would please the Prefect and his white-haired kinsman. Instead, the few troopers on board and a number of the off-shift oarsmen were kept constantly armed and watchful, and the face of the ship's big man—the captain, Hari called him—was permanently creased with worry. When questioned, Hari was noncommittal. Yes, they were approaching Balimhavar; yes, the ships thereabouts were friendly ships. No, they were in no danger of attack. The Prefect, he mumbled, was just being careful. Then he adroitly shifted the conversation to Cadon's commendable mastery of some basic courtesy phrases, and the fact that Sashah had started to include a few words of High Balim in her babbles. Lulled, Cadon dismissed the extra tension among the savages as just another mystery of their behaviour, and forgot all about it. Furin and Granny Dillah, however, who were sitting close by, continued to watch the other ships with deep suspicion. Furin kept a knife discreetly tucked into his boot-top, while Dillah kept her sickle close to hand.

***

"We must be extra vigilant, Hillisam—they'll have worked out long ago the *Pride* was sent to fetch you, and they'll be watching for us."

"Watching for us? If I know the Recorder, he knows exactly where we are. We've been seen from at least a dozen ports since we entered the strait, which means a dozen possible messages to Balimhavar already. The *Pride*'s speedy, all right, but she's no match for the mirror-towers, or even the post-horses."

"So if they ambush us, it'll be—where do you think? Near Fils Isle, where the strait is so narrow?"

"That would be the obvious place. So obvious, I'm sure we can discount it. Anyway, Sallik will be keeping an eye on the shipping, and if a battle galley so much as casts off its mooring ropes, he'll know."

"Assuming it casts off in Balimhavar. There are other ports, you know." Hillisam surveyed the smooth waters of the strait, dotted with ships, edged on both sides by strings of hamlets and fields that rolled down to the shore. He shook his head thoughtfully. "Anyway, I don't think it's a battle galley we need to worry about. The Dreeves wouldn't dare attack us openly in the strait—they'd be more likely to use an innocent-looking fishing scow, and try to board us by night. So I say it again: we must be vigilant."

"Rest easy, cousin. We'll be in Balimhavar by tomorrow midday, with two full days in hand before the Recorder's show. And when we get there, we can stop worrying about the Dreeves for the moment and start worrying about the Lord in Earth."

Hillisam heaved a deep sigh. "That boy is difficult, it's true; though I'm sure the Lords in Heaven and Earth always have been difficult, the whole mad string of them. If they weren't, you wouldn't need diviners like me to interpret the Heavenly Will. But as for Filkamos—you know, it's not entirely Chanithel's fault that her consortship hasn't worked out as well as we hoped."

"It's not a matter of fault, but of failure," Calviram growled. "We moved earth and sky to put her there, and all she had to do was captivate him. Heaven knows, she's pretty enough. But you saw the last conjoining before I left—rather, you didn't see it, because nothing happened. I'd give a finger or two to know what the Dreeves used on him."

"I imagine the man to ask about that would be Grandis Dreeve," Hillisam Hithe said thoughtfully.

"Oh, I'd like to ask him. I'd like to put him in the truth chair, and see what he'd say with a great iron spike up his backside."

"That was crudely expressed, Calviram, but an attractive picture. Though you know you'd never get a man of the Recorder's rank into the truth chair, even if the Dreeves would stand for it. Unless, of course, you..."

"...become the Shield of the Electa," Calviram finished for him. He had a hungry look in his eyes.

***

At about the same time as Hillisam was defending Chanithel's efforts to her brother, the girl herself—Blessed High Consort of the Lord in Earth, and until recently the favoured contender for the title of Electa—was in the early stages of dressing for the great event. Chanithel wept a little as the hairdressers began the long process of combing, curling, oiling and scenting her very long brown hair—not because they were hurting her, though they were, but because she was starting to realize the pain was all going to be for nothing. However much she suffered to be beautiful, the next day was virtually guaranteed to be a disaster.

Where was Calviram? He should have been back days ago, but there was still no word of the *Hithe Pride*; and now the Lords in Heaven had decreed the Day should be moved forward yet again, two full days earlier. She wished the Lords in Heaven would make up their all-powerful minds. So it seemed that tomorrow she would stand unchampioned outside the Circle, with no brother to stand beside her, and therefore no chance the Electa would choose to be manifested in her. Instead, that unprincipled, simpering slut of a Dreeve would catch the spirit: Damissel, whom she had hated since they were small girls together, learning the mysteries of the Temple in the care of a stern Sisterhood; Damissel, whom she narrowly beat out for the consortship, and who responded by making Chanithel's life in the Great Household a misery; Damissel, darling of her poisonous relatives, the Palace Master and the Recorder, who did everything they could to scuttle Chanithel's consortship of the Lord in Earth.

That was her worst failure, but she did not see how she could possibly have succeeded, not with all of *them* ranged against her. Yes, the consortship had been consummated in front of witnesses, but in a fumbling, drunken fashion that was most painful and unpleasant, and she had cried on her bodymaid's shoulder for many nights after. And then, though he maintained a constant stream of bedmates and lesser wives through his chambers, including Damissel, he had sent for his consort only once since they were conjoined, and spent the whole of that occasion in a snoring, dribbling sleep. Humiliating, that was, especially with the half the officialdom of Balimhavar watching her performance with critical eyes. And what message did it seem to carry from the Lords in Heaven? On the whole, she thought, if she had to be a kind of human sacrifice for the good of the Hithes, she would have preferred a nice clean cut across the throat.

She hated Filkamos. She hated the Hithes for giving her to him, and her brother Hoderil for dying, and her brother Calviram for being on the other side of the empire. She hated the Dreeves as a matter of course. She hated the hairdressers for torturing her hair, and the masseuses for rubbing icy ointments into her skin with almost enough force to leave bruises. It might be a blessing and a relief, she thought bitterly, if Damissel did take the title of Electa—because then Chanithel would be doomed, and at the moment death seemed like quite a fine idea. She just wished she did not have to have her hair done first.

***

Also at about this time, a naval engagement was taking place several days' sail to the west, the culmination of a series of events beginning about a week before. The departure of the *Hithe Pride* with Hillisam Hithe, though discreet, had not gone unnoticed by the Recorder's spies, and the Recorder had correctly interpreted the intelligence in a heartbeat. The result was that a second messenger ship, the Dreeves' *Glider,* hastily refitted with a battering prow and filled with a larger than usual complement of Dreeve troopers, had set off quietly from a shipyard on the edge of Balimhavar the following evening. Since this in turn did not go unnoticed by Sallik Hithe's spies, a third messenger ship, the *Hithe Pelf*, had set off the following afternoon from the port of Fils Isle, with a minor Hithe cousin on board. The race was on.

The *Hithe Pelf*, unhampered by the extra weight of a battering prow, came within sight of *Glider* just off the point of Cornmart, and dropped back to stay unnoticed. Then came the storm that sent the *Hithe Pride* far out into open water. Both the pursuing ships were close enough to Kiruz to refuge in its safe harbour amid a mass of other shipping, and spent three days battened down in the shelter of the mole. When the storm weakened, the *Hithe Pelf* managed to steal a tide, and crept out of Kiruz before the Dreeves' ship even learned of its presence. Thus, the *Pelf* was the first to encounter the Council ship *Balimheit* the next day, as the latter lumbered innocently along the coastline with a hold full of Lazooner tribute and the bulk of the Prefect's baggage.

But the Prefect himself? Transferred to the *Pride*, *Balimheit*'s captain told the minor Hithe on the *Pelf*; left several days back, just before the big storm began to settle in. *Balimheit*, he went on, had beaten its way into the shelter of Liske just in time, and heard the *Pride* had been seen in passing—it was ominous the *Pelf* had not encountered it, since the galley route hugged the coastline all the way to the strait. Perhaps the *Pride* had sunk in the storm? Or perhaps its captain had run for the open sea to ride out the worst of the weather?

The Hithe messenger wasted no more time on *Balimheit*. He turned his ship around and flew before a westerly wind; shortly afterwards, he encountered *Glider* off a deserted stretch of coastline. The latter, mistaking the *Pelf* for the *Pride,* took advantage of the lack of witnesses to ram and sink the Hithe vessel, and to make sure there were no survivors. By the time *Balimheit* rounded around the headland, the Hithe *Pelf* was a scatter of wreckage and bodies on the water, and *Glider* was already over the horizon, halfway to Kiruz.

None of this affected the prospects for the Day of the Electa. The Recorder, who had not risen to his high position by planning for only one contingency at a time, had regarded dispatching a fast galley to intercept the Prefect to be no more than a good first-level plan. The second-level plan was to engineer a further pronouncement from the Lords in Heaven through their representative on earth, an edict that would make one more tiny adjustment to the Day of the Electa.

***

"What do you mean, it's *today*?"

"Today, Prefect. That's the message. The Honourable Sallik will have your cortege waiting at the harbor. But he said to tell you to *hurry*."

Calviram stared at the messenger. He, Calviram Hithe, had not slept properly for many nights. For the same length of time, he had been forced to dress himself, wash himself, wrap himself in coarse and unclean bedding, breathe the same foul air as a passel of lowborn underlings, and survive on food he had no wish to identify or ever remember. Through all these sufferings, beneath his anxiety regarding the Day of the Electa and mild regret at his brother's death, he had held on to one shining prospect: a proper bath in hot scented water, followed by a proper meal, followed by sleep under a soft cover in a room that did not smell of unwashed bodies and a still-incontinent small child. One such day, he assured himself, would set him up for the rigours of battle with the Recorder and the Palace Master, and with the Lords in Heaven themselves, if it came to that. Now he was to be denied even a hot bath.

He looked east across the water, to the sky just beginning to lighten in the hour before dawn. The messenger ship's approach had happened just the way Hillisam predicted it might, a small galley creeping up to the flank of the *Pride* in the darkest hour of the night, top-heavy with troopers. However, instead of boarding the *Pride*, the little galley hailed it, insistently and annoyingly enough to shake Calviram out of his uncomfortable doze even before the captain sent a sailor down to rouse him.

Hillisam appeared up the stepway, wrapped in a fleece. He was followed by Hari and the younger of the Wild Men—Cadon, his name was—who looked enragingly bright-eyed and wide awake. Hillisam gazed warily at the messenger. "Well, well. Sallik's man, aren't you? What's the news from your master?"

It was Calviram who answered. "The news is that the damned Recorder has played us another nasty trick. Today is the day, Hillisam."

"What day? I don't understand."

"Grandis Dreeve has named today as the Day of the Electa," Calviram snapped, "and don't look at me like that, I'm not blaspheming. I know very well the order came from the Lords in Heaven, but I strongly suspect they were taking up a suggestion from the Recorder." Calviram paused as a large chest was heaved up onto the deck of the *Pride* from the boat below. He looked questioningly at Sallik's messenger.

"Regalia, silks, ceremonial weapons," the messenger said, "and also the hairdressing supplies. He sent hairdressers, too."

"Very good of him," Calviram said sourly. "Well, if we're to be there by noon, we'd better get moving." He growled an order to the captain, a single order that set many others in train within moments. With unnecessary vehemence, he told Sallik Hithe's messenger to get the damned hairdressers on board forthwith, then disengage his toy boat and get out of the *Pride*'s way. Hari, he shoved towards the stepway with snarled instructions to rouse the aftercabin and get everybody on deck. Hillisam, with clear distress on his face, followed Hari down the stepway. That left only Cadon.

Calviram watched him thoughtfully. The younger Wild Man seemed unaware of the turmoil breaking out around and under them—sailors swarming up masts to change the set of the sails, the rowing master bellowing on the oardeck as he added an extra oar to each bench, a sleepy howl from the dratted child in the aftercabin. Cadon, however, was leaning gracefully by the railing, apparently sniffing the dawn air with interest and appreciation. Calviram sniffed it himself, and thought he detected a faint, vanishingly faint, taint of the city under the smell of the sea. In fact, Balimhavar was not far now.

They would be in time. They *must* be in time. And Hillisam's hinted suggestion, so repugnant to Calviram a few nights before, was now inescapably the thing to do.

The young Wild Man may have felt Calviram's eyes on him. He turned and gave Calviram an enchanting smile, and in halting Balim wished the Thrice-Honoured Master a good morning and a flower-strewn day from his humble and most unworthy servitor. A set phrase, obviously learned by rote, but (Calviram thought) delivered in a way that was a credit to Hari's teaching skills. What a sad, sad waste. The Prefect responded after a moment with a gracious nod, and Cadon smiled again and turned back to the sunrise.

Calviram continued to watch Cadon with resignation and a degree of regret. If ever there was a time to gamble everything on one cast of the bones, this was it. All doubt was gone, the decision was made. He would, after all, shamelessly appropriate the Wild People, plus the boxes of gold and shells and the jewellery extorted from the consorts of Lazoon, though he would spare the little ex-speaker-priest. When he stepped into the Circle of the Heavens by Chanithel's side that very afternoon, he would have a dizzying array of gifts to offer the Lords in Heaven and tempt the woman-spirit of the Electa. Nobody would know about the Council's claim to any of this stolen property until *Balimheit* trudged across the harbour bar in a few days' time, and by then the truth would not matter; because either he would be the Shield of the Electa, and above the truth, or Darrasat Dreeve would be the Shield, and Calviram would in fatal difficulties anyway. There was nothing to lose.

Such a pity, he thought with genuine sadness, watching Cadon watch the sunrise, that the Wild People would have to be sacrificed. He wondered if being burned alive was a kinder fate than being skinned alive, and decided it was, if only because it was quicker—so he had, after all, done them a favour in saving them from Lazoon. That made him feel a little better.

***

The first shout from the little ship had wakened Cadon. His dreams had been of the city, a city like an enormously swollen cave of the Ones Before, its towering huts built of bony grins and empty eye sockets piled in improbable profusion, its streets paved with headbones, its trees draped with unshriven dead. Footfalls taunted him, just out of sight. The breeze brought a whisper of voices, a scent of wood fire, roast deer, wet dog—salt sea. He turned over, instantly wide awake, and saw dark figures moving in the cabin, heard real whispers, saw the form of the Prefect briefly silhouetted against the grey square of the hatch as he ascended. Outside, the shouting ceased. Cadon rolled eagerly off his pallet and wrapped the coverlet around his shoulders against the pre-dawn chill. Then he moved cautiously across the dark cabin, bumping into one shadowy figure who turned out to be Hari, and then another, who was the Prefect's white-haired cousin. He trailed them up the stepway to the deck, where the Prefect was conversing with a young dark-coated man whom Cadon did not recognize.

Cadon bypassed them and went directly to the railing, where he first examined with interest the smaller craft bumping gently against the side of the *Pride*. Impassive faces stared back up at him from its deck, and he shyly decided not to try out his small stock of Balim phrases on them. Instead, he turned towards the part of the sky that was already lightening with the dawn, the direction in which he knew the city lay.

There was no visible sign of a city ahead, but Cadon discovered the trace of a new smell on the wind—more than just the salt air from the sea and the earthy scent from the cultivated shore a few spear-throws from the right side of the ship. There was an underscent that reminded him of Lazoon and the towns they had sailed past on the journey, but it was both ranker and spicier. He lost it as the wind dropped, then found it again, a little stronger than before. Perhaps it was the smell of Balimhavar, he thought, his excitement growing. He turned to find someone to share the moment, and found that Hari and the old man had gone below, but Prefect Calviram was still standing in the same place, staring oddly at him. There was a large box beside him that had certainly not been there before.

"Respectful greetings on this fine morning," Cadon said, to the best of his knowledge, somewhat limited by the tactful looseness of Hari's translations. He wondered if he had said it too badly for the Prefect to understand, because the latter just stared at him for a few seconds; then the Prefect nodded with a faint, courteous smile, and Cadon decided he had spoken correctly after all. Pleased with himself, he returned to watching the east for the first sight of the great city where the Old Ones waited, noting that the intriguing scent was already easier to catch on the air.

Chapter Sixteen

The Morning of the Electa

A few hours later, both the *Pride* and the aftercabin passengers were in a transformed state. All were very clean—the ship, from the ministrations of every available deckhand and many of the offshift oarsmen; the passengers, from a good scrubbing with water drawn up from the sea, followed by a rinse with the last of the fresh water in the deck butts. Cadon and Furin also marked the occasion by striking some fresh blades off the core in Granny Dillah's pack and shaving their several-days' growth of beard. They offered Valdur a blade to shave off the blonde fuzz that was gradually replacing his priestly baldness, but he declined politely and wandered away.

"To think," said Dillah, in a rare reflective mood some time later, "that it's no more than ten days since we washed ourselves in that cold river by Lazoon. Did you notice how much warmer these seas are? Who would believe we're in mid-autumn already? Right, Furin Fox, that's you done. I'll fix your face later. Take Sashah away, would you, and keep her clean, while I untangle this one's hair. Sit, Cadon."

"It's too bad about our packs," said Furin as he received a resplendent Sashah from Cadon's arms. "I don't feel right in these fancies from the Prefect."

"You look good, though, far-uncle," Cadon said sincerely. "You're healing up nicely, too." Cadon still retained the fine woven-leather shirt Dillah had given him before the approach to Lazoon, now neatly brushed and oiled. Furin's best clothes had suffered rather more than Cadon's, but the Prefect had issued him a tunic of some rich blue fabric to wear under the remains of his leather weskit, to hide the long vertical scabs from the cutter-priests' knives. Dillah scorned accepting anything from the Prefect's box—still thinking about those body-bugs, she explained darkly to Furin—but the profusion of beads and pendants and torques the Prefect showered on them from the chests of Lazooner tribute seemed to spark off in her a burst of wild decorative energy.

She wound many strings of tiny golden beads into Sashah's clean dark curls. She loosened and combed out Furin's long mane, and cunningly attached ribbons of gold and amber at the crown, so they swung and glinted among his barely grizzled black locks as he moved. A copper torque and a set of tortoiseshell hair ornaments, she set aside for her own head, but first there was Cadon's thick and unruly mane to tame and embellish.

"Ouch," said Cadon.

"I can't be any gentler, boy, there's a tangle here the size of an eyeball."

Cadon gritted his teeth and tried to distract himself by watching the passing shore, but Hari and Valdur caught his attention. He noticed with envy that, although enforcedly cleaner than before, the two of them were not being subjected to this intensive beautification, and were free to sit in idleness and comfort at the foot of the foremast.

"Hold still," said Granny Dillah.

"Ouch," Cadon repeated. He squinted at the interpreter and the ex-speaker-priest, noting how earnestly they were talking, heads close together. It struck him they were glancing frequently and rather furtively towards himself and Dillah. Then Hari looked up and met Cadon's eyes across half the length of the ship, and he abruptly turned his face away. Cadon pondered this. "Do you think there's something the matter with Hari?" he asked Dillah.

"What sort of something?" she asked around the bone hairpins in her mouth.

"I don't know. He looks—well, not very happy. Though yesterday he seemed excited about getting back to Balimhavar."

"It's true he wouldn't stop talking about it," Dillah said wryly. Cadon felt her hands pause in his hair, and reckoned she was peering sharply towards the two sitting near the foremast. He reckoned this because Hari, with what looked like a guilty glance their way, abruptly scrambled to his feet and vanished in the direction of the bow. Valdur il Jinoon in turn caught Cadon's eye, shrugged elaborately, and rose in a more leisurely fashion to follow Hari out of sight.

Granny's fingers commenced pulling at Cadon's hair again as she wove something metallic into it. "I see what you mean," she said. "He didn't want to look at us, and even his back looked unhappy when he scarpered. But he's a good boy, that Hari, and I swear there's something he wants to tell us. Maybe you should go talk to him in a minute, when I've finished with you."

"*Ouch!* Careful, Granny!"

She swatted his head. "Such a fuss. But that was the last, you're done now except for a touch of facepaint, and I won't do that until closer to the time. But I don't mind telling you, boy, you'll be a credit to the People when you meet the Old Man and the Old Woman, at least as far as looks are concerned. Off you go now—and *keep clean.* I mean that."

Released from bondage, Cadon wandered forward to find Hari and Valdur.

***

"Are you sure, Hari? Absolutely sure?"

"Yes. There's no room for doubt."

"But did the Prefect actually tell you that?"

"Of course not, but he didn't need to. I've lived ten years in the court of Balimhavar, I was there when the previous Electa was chosen, and I know their bloody customs. If the Wild Ones were part of the Lazooner tribute, the Prefect would send them straight to quarters in the Treasury, and present them for the first time at a full council caucus. Which is probably what he'll do with you. But there's only one possible reason for him to present the Wild People *to the court* on the Day of the Electa, and that's to send them as gifts to the Lords in Heaven…"

Hari's voice broke. He glanced aft again, to where the old woman was absorbed in putting the finishing touches to Furin's coif. Hari watched as Furin stood up and stretched to his full impressive height, magnificent in the tunic of blue Vaspan silk, with gold and amber glinting in his hair. He looked more like a god than the actual god-king did, Hari thought, and then pinched himself hard as penance for the blasphemy. He saw Furin take the child in his arms and swing her away towards the aft railing, to show her the clouds of seabirds trailing the *Pride.*

"Are you going to tell them?"

"Think about it, Valdur. What could I possibly tell them? Not to waste time on their hair, since they'll all be burned alive tonight anyway?" Hari watched Cadon sit down with obvious reluctance on the barrelhead, and saw him flinch when Dillah plunged the wooden comb into his hair. When Cadon shot a wistful glance along the deck, Hari looked away.

Beside him, Valdur il Jinoon heaved a sigh. "You're right, my friend, it's probably kinder to say nothing. It's not as if they could escape—well, the men might make it to shore, though I doubt Dillah could, nor the girl-child. Why don't you tell Furin and Cadon at least, and let them take their chances?"

"They wouldn't leave the womenfolk behind. Anyway, they'd be snatched out of the water before they were halfway to shore. Have you not noticed the vessels that keep coming down the channel, and turning to sail with us? They're the escorts sent by the Hithe Faction." Hari waved his hand overside, where six small, sleek and dangerous-looking galleys were keeping pace with the *Pride*.

"Ah well," said Valdur, "that's the end of it, then. So if you say anything to the Wild Ones, you won't be warning them so much as making them miserable before they really need to be."

"Exactly. And I'm also trying to imagine what the Prefect and all the other Hithes would do to me if I said anything and they found out about it, which they certainly would. Though I'll wager I'm doomed anyway."

"Why is that?"

"Because I was in Lazoon. I know about the tribute. So do you, but you're safe because you can't speak Balim, and can't tell anyone about it. Indeed, friend, you may be the only one of us who will live to see the sun rise tomorrow. But at least my death, if the Prefect has me killed tonight, will be swift and private, whereas the Wild People…" His voice died away, and he stiffened. "Valdur, she's looking right at us. I can't bear it."

By the time Valdur opened his mouth, Hari had jumped to his feet and fled. Valdur, catching Cadon's eye, raised his shoulders as if to express a mystification that he did not feel. Hari's distress was no mystery at all. Valdur found that he even shared it to some extent, since the Wild People were both endearing and entertaining. Furthermore, the poet in him was struck by the thematic richness of the situation as it developed—such grace and beauty destined for hideous destruction, such strength turned to helplessness, such freedom of spirit entrapped and immolated. What was about to happen to the Wild People was so damnably poignant. Already, Valdur had the first stanza of a poem roughed out.

***

Down in the aftercabin, Prefect Calviram was going through sufferings precisely parallel to those of Furin and Cadon. He was technically clean, though his sponge-bath had taken place in the grubby privacy below decks, and had not involved anything remotely resembling hot, scented water. The hairdressers were doing their best, but it was a job they would otherwise have started the day before, and their haste made them less gentle than Calviram might have wished. One of them was also seasick off and on, so an odour of vomit now mingled with the lingering hint of infant bowels, and warred valiantly with the fragrant unguents and oils produced from Sallik's chest.

Still, Calviram felt better. All the news was good. Hillisam's report from the main deck was glowing about the Wild Ones' state of good looks and cleanliness, so important in gifts destined for the Lords in Heaven. Sallik had come through with a large enough escort of fighting galleys to ensure no last-minute ambush before the *Pride* turned into the roadstead, and the latest bulletin from the captain was definite about reaching the Balimhavar docks well before the noon deadline.

***

Chanithel was in the second day of having her hair done, in common with most of the high court of Balimhavar. Unlike most, she was being hairdressed in the presence of representatives of all seven of the high factions, who were keeping official watch on the candidate for Electa, and a less official watch on each other. The forecourt of Chanithel's suite also held six undermaids, three hairdressers and their assistants, five troopers, a spear-captain, a divination priest, and Liddy, the consort's bodymaid. When the messenger from Sallik Hithe arrived, he had some difficulty pushing through the crowd to reach Chanithel's ear.

All was well, the message said, and the consort's brother would be at the Circle of the Heavens in good time. Chanithel inclined her heavily freighted head to acknowledge and dismiss the messenger, careful not to let it tip too far. Part of her court training was in balancing a court-dressed head on her neck, like an overblown flower on the slenderest of stems. If you did it just right, her tutors had told her, your neck and shoulders would not ache so *terribly* much by the end of the day. Chanithel had mastered the trick of it at last, out of self-defense.

Keeping her face blank, she watched the messenger pick his way out of the packed forecourt. "Liddy," she said.

"Yes, Blessed Consort?"

"Tell the spear-captain I need to be alone for a little while, for my—for my *private* functions. I am going to retire to my boudoir, and I do not expect any of the observers to follow me. Tell him that."

"Yes, Blessed Consort."

Chanithel bent forward as far as her coiffure would allow, and whispered, "If he protests, tell him I insist on privacy. If he still protests, go fetch the chamberpot."

"Yes, Blessed Consort."

Liddy did not have to resort to the chamberpot. The spear-captain escorted the consort and bodymaid to the boudoir, and stationed a couple of troopers at the door. Liddy closed the door-curtains and started for the cupboard where the chamberpot was kept.

"Never mind, I don't need it really," Chanithel said, giving herself the luxury of sounding weary. She set herself carefully down on a pile of cushions, taking care not to disturb the delicate balance of her hair. "I just wanted to take a few breaths without that nest of poisonous snakes flicking their tongues at me."

"Poor Chani, this is worse than the day you were conjoined. Shall I rub your neck?"

"Oh, please."

Liddy moved around behind her mistress and prodded the place where Chanithel usually got a knot in her shoulder in unhappy times. She tutted and turned away to oil her hands. "It feels like you have a pebble under your skin. But I don't know why you should be unhappy. It's good news about your brother."

"I suppose so. By now, I hardly care." Chanithel leaned her shoulder into the bodymaid's probing fingers. "Calviram will get all the power he could ever want if I'm chosen, and I imagine that will make him happy. The Hithes will get an advantage over the Dreeves, which has got to be a good thing—but do you know what's in it for me?"

"What?"

"More hairdressing," said Chanithel gloomily, "and more cold-oil massages."

Liddy smiled. "More corsetry," she suggested.

"More listening politely to the dowager consort."

"More nights of passion with the Lord in Earth."

Chanithel did not respond to that one right away. "You mean," she said brightly after a pause, "more nights with the Lord of Drunken Groping, or the Lord of Snoring and Dribbling. I'll tell you a secret, Liddy. Being summoned to my husband's bed is the only thing worse than *not* being summoned to his bed."

Liddy patted Chanithel's shoulder. Then she grunted as she dug her strong fingers deeper into the knot in the muscle. A rising chorus of voices on the other side of the curtain signified that the crowd in the forecourt was getting restive.

***

In another part of the palace, outside the Great Household, the Recorder Grandis Dreeve was pacing the floor in his public finery and raging to himself in mutters. When the curtain that covered the door was pulled aside, he looked up with a face of thunder.

The Palace Master entered with heavy steps and an air of despondency. "It's all true," he said, "the *Pride*'s been spotted passing Karno Head. At this rate, that Hithe sod will land well before noon. And there's more—in case you were thinking of arranging a surprise for the *Pride*, Calviram has now got half the Hithe galleys with him, and two hundred retainers waiting for him at the docks. We have to face it, Grandis, there's a chance we're going to lose this."

"We'll face nothing of the sort," the Recorder growled. "What's the word from upstairs?"

"Well, he's being difficult."

"That's nothing new. But is he dressed and ready?"

"I believe so, though the hairdressers had a great deal of trouble with him. He tried to throw one of them out the window. It's a good thing we had those bars put up."

"When are they bringing him down?"

"Just before midday. What are you thinking, Grandis?"

"I'm thinking," said the Recorder, "that Filkamos may be thirstier than usual on this important occasion. No doubt he would appreciate an extra supply of his favourite tipple. And I'm also thinking it will boost his spirits if I pay him a visit before he leaves his chamber, and we have a pleasant talk."

The Palace Master looked worried. "You've increased the dose twice already in the last month. As it is, the boy can barely speak without slurring."

"He doesn't need to speak." The Recorder opened a small jewel-chest on the table and, after deliberation, took out a single tiny vial. "One should be enough," he said.

"The observers will be watching."

"I'll manage," Grandis growled, as the curtain closed behind him.

***

Hari was definitely moody, and would not tell Cadon why, but Cadon felt he went some distance towards cheering him up, with Valdur's ready help. He noticed, though, that Valdur himself seemed a little distracted much of the time, gazing into the distance in the wrong direction, with his lips moving. But when Cadon asked Hari if the lessons in Balim speech would continue the next day, Valdur sat up and took notice; and the Lazooner and the Liskan exchanged a look that was pained on Hari's side, and wry on Valdur's, and somehow the question never did get answered.

For some time, the shores sliding past them had been lined with cultivated fields, interrupted by great stands of huts that fringed the beaches and spread far inland. Some of these towns seemed as large as Lazoon, to Cadon's eyes at least, and he expected as each came into sight that Hari would announce it was Balimhavar at last. Each time, Hari shook his head and kept his unaccountably gloomy face trained on the east. The scent Cadon had first faintly caught in the early morning was now strong enough for even Valdur to comment on.

Furin joined the watch, beautiful with facepaint; and then Granny Dillah came to the bow with Sashah in her arms. Even Cadon had to admit that Dillah looked not bad for such an old woman, with a sash of bright red silk tied around her leather shift, and the copper torque fixed like a wreath on her iron-streaked hair. Only her backpack, from which she refused to be parted, ruined the effect. Furin clicked his tongue at her admiringly.

She ignored him. "Cadon, I'll do your face now," she said.

"Fine, Granny Dillah," he sighed; but as he turned away, Valdur caught his arm.

"Wait. *Look!*" His finger jabbed towards the east. "That *must* be it, Hari."

"That is Balimhavar," Hari confirmed in a flat voice.

So there it was at last, the greatest city in the world. Cadon caught his breath: dismay, not wonder. He seemed to recognize it at first—tall crags and taller spires of rock rising above badland canyons; white facets and planes of limestone shining in the midday sun, banded with gold and blood-red. Not Cadon's favourite kind of scenery, since it was associated in his memory with dry watercourses and hot dust devils, the breeding grounds of scorpions and venomous snakes, places of menacing wind-sculptings that seemed to move while one's eyes were elsewhere. He could even put a name to it, and locate it on the map he carried in his head: it was the Valley of Death at the southwestern fringe of the mountains, a place to be crossed with haste and the protection of a shaman, to get to the rich wintering grounds beyond. He thought of his dream of a city of skulls, and his fingers fumbled for the amulet at his belt.

"It reminds me…" Furin began.

"Me too," Dillah said, "and I'm not happy. Cadon, does it remind you of any place?"

Cadon hesitated. The first impression was fading as he watched the city approach: not crags of rock, he saw now, nor piles of skulls, but massed huts of impossible height, riddled with openings, crowned with a spire whose summit seemed to scrape the underbelly of the sky. The fact that it was a manmade landscape did nothing to dispel his instinct of dread. He said, "It reminds me of the Valley of Death."

"Then it's not just you and me, Furin Fox." Dillah made a warding-evil motion with her fingers. "May the Ones Before be a shield to us on our journey through this place," she muttered. Cadon and Furin murmured the appropriate response—but beside Dillah, Hari jerked as if someone had stuck a pin into him, and he turned sharply to stare at her. She did not notice. He repeated her words in a mutter, and his eyes narrowed in thought.

***

Balimhavar was in sight at last, and in excellent time. Calviram and Hillisam Hithe followed the captain's messenger up the stepway into the brightness of the mild autumn morning, both of them splendid in court dress. Calviram carried over his arm one of the spare silks from Sallik's chest, for the adornment of Valdur il Jinoon—after intricate calculations and some debate, they had decided that all possible fuel should be thrown on the fire of the Hithe ambitions, specifically including the poet after all. Again, Calviram grieved at the necessity.

The gifts for the Lords in Heaven were all conveniently standing with Hari in the bow, goggling at the matchless vision of Balimhavar, its shining white-plastered walls, its towers that shamed the mountains. But, though he had hungered for the sight of Balimhavar since the very day he set sail for Lazoon, Calviram wasted no time in looking at it now. He stopped a little way from the group in the bow, and sharply summoned Hari.

"I'm coming, honoured sir."

The little interpreter was taking his own sweet time about it, Calviram thought irritably a moment later, and he was looking even more anxious and hangdog than ever. And it was not just Hari—even the Wild People, magnificent as they were in their finery, seemed to lack their usual vibrancy as they stared across the water towards the spires of Balimhavar. Calviram felt a stab of worry that they had somehow discovered how brief and painful their sojourn in the city would be. Only Sashah and Valdur seemed to be in reasonably good spirits.

"Hari, what's the matter with you?" Calviram hissed when Hari was close enough. "And what's the matter with the Wild People? Why the long faces?"

"I do not know, honoured sir," Hari said, his eyes downcast. "I think it's possible they don't like the look of the city."

"Well, that's too bad. Listen, Hari, you must take the crone's pack away. She's supposed to look like an object of value, not a damned beast of burden."

"She won't be parted from it, honoured sir. She refuses to leave it behind."

"Then *you* carry it for her. No one will be looking at you. And what's wrong with the older one's face?"

"His name is Furin Fox, honoured sir, and there's nothing wrong. His face has been decorated according to the custom of his people, that's all. Would you like him cleaned off?"

Calviram glanced at the nearness of the quays. "Never mind, there's no time, we'll be landing soon. Anyway, it looks quite otherworldly, and that's not a bad idea. Another thing, Hari, I've decided you'll need to accompany the cortege to the square, to keep the Wild People on their best behaviour. They trust you, don't they?"

"Yes, honoured sir." After a pause, Hari added, "They trust you too."

He glanced up as he spoke, and looked into Calviram's eyes. Calviram did not like his expression. He liked it so little that he was able to make another difficult decision on the spot, one that would see Hari quietly bought from the Council, and strangled when his duties as interpreter were finished. Say, by the end of the day. Too bad, because the little Liskan was very bright, and had been invaluable all through the journey to Lazoon. Calviram smiled gently and did Hari the honour of patting him on the shoulder.

"You'll give them their instructions, and tell them where to stand; most important of all, you will keep them calm and quiet throughout the entire proceedings. Do you understand?"

"Yes, honoured sir. And where is it that you want them to stand?"

Calviram's face hardened. "You know where. And Hari? One more thing."

"Yes, honoured sir?"

"Valdur il Jinoon will be joining the Wild People. This robe is for him. Get him dressed and hang a few of the gew-gaws from the Lazooner tribute around his neck, quick as you can. Understand?"

"I understand, honoured sir. I understand very well."

Of course he understood, Calviram thought. Hari understood everything, which explained the slightly cross-eyed look of reproach he'd been wearing since Calviram first told him to get the Wild People cleaned up for public display. No matter. In an affair of such importance, sacrifices had to be made. He knew in his heart of hearts he was doing the right thing for the Hithe Faction; and anything that was good for the Hithes was good for Balimhavar; and anything that was good for Balimhavar was good for the world. It puzzled him, therefore, that his own eyes dropped before Hari's steady gaze, and he could not bring himself to look at or wait with the Wild Ones and Valdur. Instead he slunk—yes, *slunk*—back to the aftercabin with Hillisam in tow.

***

"Hari, lad," said Granny Dillah, "what's wrong with the Prefect's hair?"

"Nothing's wrong," Hari said, "it's been decorated according to the customs of his people. Valdur, I need to talk with you." He drew Valdur midships, to where one of the chests of Lazooner tribute lay open, and he unceremoniously stuffed the silken robe into the priest's arms. "This is for you, Valdur. A gift from the Prefect."

"Ah." Valdur held it up and shook it out, the better to admire the deep duck-green of its shimmering folds, and the gold-wire embroideries at the neckband.

"Take some of the jewels from the box, as well," Hari added. "Take all you want."

Valdur lowered the robe and looked into Hari's face. "I assume," he said lightly, "that these fancies are for me to wear when I take up my temporary quarters in the treasury. Yes?"

"No."

"I see." Valdur paused and gave Hari a shrewd look. "Does that mean—"

"I'm afraid it does."

"Ah." Valdur turned and strolled to the railing. As he gazed thoughtfully towards the city, Hari followed him.

"I'm sorry, Valdur. I wish now I hadn't told you about—you know."

"About getting burned to death tonight?" The ex-speaker-priest shrugged. "Remember I was already a dead man in Lazoon—the Prefect gave me an extra week or so of breathing, that's all. And a very interesting week I've had, too."

"That's—a good way to look at it. But Valdur, listen—"

"Wait, that's not all. I'm delighted to be dying so far away from the miserable dungheap I was born into. And I'm happy," he said, focussing again on the shining silk, "to be dying dressed like a king. Though *not* the king of Lazoon."

With both hands, he seized the neckband of his shabby priestly robe, tore the garment open, and ripped it halfway to the hem. Then he stepped out of its ruins and threw the rag overboard. His loincloth followed. He stood naked for a moment, his face raised to the sun, then pulled the silk robe on over his head. The fit was better than reasonable, and he looked down at himself with evident approval. To finish, he drew fistfuls of beads from the chest and proceeded to hang a sufficient weight of them around his neck to drown him if he happened to fall overboard. There were spots of high colour in his cheeks, and his eyes were bright.

"How do I look?" he asked Hari.

"Very nice. Really. But listen, Valdur, I've been thinking—"

"Shall we go and show the Wild People how nice I look?"

"Yes, but Valdur, there is one thing—"

Valdur grinned hectically at the interpreter. "What? Are you going to ruin my last morning by being serious?"

Hari hesitated. "I suppose not. Never mind, then."

They walked towards the bow, side by side, Hari silent and Valdur strutting his new magnificence and declaiming one of his own poems in his most melodious voice. They found Dillah, Furin and Cadon watching the approach of the city with grim faces, apparently still in the grip of some dark suspicion about the place—not unjustified, Hari thought. Sashah, on the other hand, was hanging over Cadon's shoulder and crowing with delight at the bright Hithe banners flowing from the mast tops. Hari took a deep breath and gathered the gifts to the Lords in Heaven around him in a tight circle.

"Prefect Calviram has ordered me to give you your instructions," he said. "Now listen to me carefully."

***

It was a few minutes later when the *Hithe Pride* skimmed across the bar into the harbour. Four dead men, one dead woman, and one dead child stood in the bow, watching with various degrees of gloom and wonder as the towers of Balimhavar rose around them.

Chapter Seventeen

The Noon of the Electa

In his heart, Cadon had never quite believed Hari's account of the vast numbers of savages who dwelt in the city of Balimhavar. Now he did, because there they were. And as the *Pride* slid to rest alongside the dock, and a great herd of spectators pressed forward against the wooden parapets, he found himself wishing to be back in some place that was relatively familiar, for example the Valley of Death.

And there was the Prefect again, up from the depths of the ship in his uncomfortable-looking hair, a lacquered folly involving hardware entwined with braids and billows that could *not* be all his own. His gown, however, was a marvel of brilliant folds and deep, unnatural colours, down which an artificial beard spilled in perfumed and ribboned plaits. Cadon thought he looked very nice, except possibly for the hair, which looked frankly painful. Unfortunately, he no longer looked like the Prefect, in the sense of the kindly man who had greeted Cadon reassuringly on the platform in Lazoon, and treated them all with such courtesy ever since. It was also a little odd that he did not greet them now.

"Come along," Hari whispered into his ear, "and try to ignore the crowds. You'll be fine. And don't forget the—the other matter I told you about."

"Of course I won't forget," said Cadon, "but are you sure that's what I'm supposed to do?"

"Absolutely."

"But what should I say?"

"You won't need to say a word. In fact, it's much better if you say nothing at all."

"All right, then. So when do I…?"

"I'll tell you when."

***

Sallik Hithe was to be congratulated—but later, when the game was won and there was time for family talk. Even before the *Pride* was moored, he had the escort neatly lined up on the quayside, rank on rank, boxing in the open litter that would carry Calviram to the temple, the closed litter to whisk Hillisam Hithe ahead of them to join the other diviners, the ox-drawn wagon to carry inanimate gifts for the gods, and the small clump of animate gifts, both human and four-legged, who would have to walk to the burning field on their own feet. Sallik had assembled a decent collection of those living gifts, though the human specimens were obviously not long off the slave platforms of Balimhavar, and still somewhat undernourished. Not really Sallik's fault—no one outside the Dreeves could have predicted the festival would happen so early—but it was a good thing, Calviram thought, that he had the Wild People and the Lazooner to add interest and glamour to the Hithe gifts. He let Sallik supervise the transfer of the remaining Lazooner treasure to the already substantial pile on the wagon, while he took his place in the litter, and then they were ready to go. The sun was not yet at the zenith.

Cheering banks of faces lined the broad avenue and packed the open marketplaces that it bisected. Calviram, an expert in reading the moods of crowds, decided they were genuinely happy to see him arrive in time, which could be construed as a backhanded insult to the behind-the-curtain rule of the Dreeves. Or possibly they were just reacting to their first sight of the Wild People, who did (Calviram gladly admitted) look magnificent, even the crone. He had told Sallik to place them at the forefront of the other live gifts, walking slightly ahead as befitted their prize status and superior beauty. Judging by the way all eyes turned quickly from his litter to the procession of gifts behind it, the crowds liked what they saw and keenly anticipated the evening's holocaust. Calviram longed to look back at the Wild People as well, but it behooved him as a candidate, and as a lordly Hithe, to keep his overburdened neck as stiff as granite, and his gaze firmly forward and a little above the heads of the humble.

Now the litter was passing into the square that formed the temple's public forecourt. The colonnades at its margins were jammed solid with onlookers, and the windows and arched galleries overlooking the square were loaded to a point that was probably dangerous. In the centre of the square was the Hearthfield of the Lords in Heaven, the firepit of the gods, primed with enough fuel to keep a small town warm for a winter month. The stakes were already in place, too, perhaps sixty or seventy of them, a good-sized forest of stout poles planted among the tar-soaked logs and dried brushwood. Calviram felt a novel reluctance to look at them.

And now the platform was in view, raised a tall man's height above the level of the square, nested on three sides in its broad staircases of creamy stone. The entrance to the temple, a dark oblong at the platform's rear edge, was flanked by the ranks of courtiers who would witness the selection from close quarters, and then offer their grace to the newly chosen Shield. Hillisam would already have taken his place there, among the other diviners. Chanithel would also be there somewhere, but Calviram could not pick her out among the glittering bevies of court-dressed women, the termite-hills of hair. There *was* someone he recognized, though. The other processions were already drawn up at the foot of the grand staircase, and the back of Darrasat Dreeve's odious head was visible above one of the litters. In the other was a no-hoper from the Kilves—why, Calviram wondered, did the Kilves even bother? They were desperately outclassed. This was a game with only two serious players.

***

Here was the audience that Valdur had always dreamed of, the setting that was his natural home. The iridescent silk robe, with the colour and shine of a waterbird's plumage, was what he had been born to wear. The towering buildings did not awe him, since they were precisely what he had always known, deep in his gut, that buildings should be. At last, the stars which had carelessly despatched him to the womb of a backwater slattern with dirt under her nails were rectifying their mistake—too late to be of much good to him, he thought wryly, but better he should live one glorious day in Balimhavar than another drab decade telling stories to clots in Lazoon.

He was striding along beside the Wild People, with Hari a few steps behind. Now he leapt forward a couple of paces and, in a mood of abandon, commenced favouring the crowd with graceful and elaborate salutes, the kind he had tried a few times in Lazoon, and been roundly chastised for by the late Master

Speaker. This time, nobody told him off or ordered him to stop, except perhaps Hari, whose hissing for attention Valdur cheerfully ignored. He wove back and forth across the path of the Wild People, playing first to one side of the street and then the other. Around him, the cheers soared. He wondered what they might be shouting at him, but he did not much care.

A young woman, rather a pretty one, leaned out of an upper archway to throw him a flower, and he leapt high to catch it in midair. The mob roared its approval. *This is what my life should always have been,* he told himself, as he answered the girl with a broad grin and an especially florid salute.

***

"You know, the boy's not bad at that jumping and arm-flapping business," Dillah commented to Furin and Cadon. They were her first words since leaving the *Pride*—in fact, the first words uttered by any of the People on the streets of Balimhavar. Furin grunted back. Cadon barely heard her. Like Furin, he was fully engaged in trying to look in all directions at once, partly out of a hunter's caution on unfamiliar ground, and partly out of a simple desire not to miss a single thing. Nothing Hari had told them came anywhere close to the truth. Nothing of Lazoon's dust-blown squalor, or the towns glimpsed from the sea, had prepared them for these marvels. Nothing in his dreams looked anything like the solid, stone-fashioned reality. And, again unlike the rude and violent Lazooners, their thousands of new best friends in Balimhavar were greeting them with huge smiles and heartening enthusiasm. When a flower landed on the smooth pave in front of him, he bent to pick it up.

"They seem to like us here," he said to the others.

"They seemed to like us in Lazoon, too," Furin said drily, "between the times they tried to kill us."

Cadon thought that over. Was this a serious reminder to keep alert? All their surviving weapons were in Granny's pack, which Hari was obligingly toting. Close enough to retrieve, if the worst happened and the savages suddenly turned hostile, but about as much use as a thrusting spear against a tide of stampeding reindeer. Two men against a multitude? Plus Granny Dillah and her estimable sickle, of course, though she was also encumbered with a wriggling, wide-eyed Sashah. He caught himself muttering a prayer to the Old Man, and snapped his mouth shut—the next terror of the day might be a meeting with the Old Man himself, if Hari's word could be trusted. Would talking to him face to face have the same effect as a prayer? What should Cadon say to him, anyway? Hari had instructed him to say nothing, but that would be rude. Was there a protocol for such a situation? The prayers and protocols Cadon knew so well had nothing to say on that matter. And yet, long ago when the world was young, the People must have met the Old Couple regularly in the flesh. How were the great progenitors approached then?

"Granny," he said, leaning sideways so she could hear him over the crowd, "what does one say when meeting the Old Man and the Old Woman?"

"You personally will say nothing, Cadon Fox. You will leave it to me. And you, Furin Fox," she added, tugging on the arm of Furin's dazzling blue garment, "the same goes for you. I have a number of serious points to make to the Old Woman when we meet her, and I don't want either of you getting in the way."

"But Hari said…"

"Are you sure you'll get the chance, Dillah?" Furin had to raise his voice to be heard. They were coming into a larger clearing now in this forest of giant huts, and the noise of the people-herd was swelling.

Cadon did not catch Dillah's answer, and anyway forgot the question. He was too busy catching his breath as the view of the square opened up before them. Directly ahead was a hill of a building, a small mountain of dazzling stone, fronted with pillars like the trunks of giant oaks in the eastern forests. Towers thrust above the gleaming white escarpment, one of them tall enough so that Cadon had to tilt his head back before he could see its peak. The looming spires of the Valley of Death came into his mind again, and the voices of the people of Balimhavar became the howls of the searing winds that haunted that hostile place. A hole opened in the pit of his stomach, his steps faltered—and then he shook his head at his own stupidity, and strode on. They were here as the guests of the Prefect, weren't they? The Prefect would let no evil come to them in Balimhavar.

"Well, well." Furin sounded interested. "They're going to have a bonfire, it looks like. A big one, too. I hope we get to watch."

Opening his mouth to answer, Cadon walked straight into Valdur, who had halted abruptly in Cadon's path. Cadon caught him before he could be knocked over, and, though the late autumn morning was touched with a chill, Cadon felt dampness soaking through Valdur's shiny robe, and Valdur himself shaking under it. "You're sweating a river," Cadon said. The Lazooner did not answer. He remained rooted, gazing ahead at the vast firepit in the centre of the square.

"Perhaps, young Valdur," Dillah suggested, "you should just walk normally for a while?"

Hari's voice came from behind, touched with panic. "Valdur! Keep moving!"

Valdur started, shook himself free of Cadon's support, and walked on—soberly and in a straight line, disappointing the crowd. After a moment, Cadon followed. It occurred to him that Valdur might be sweating from more than his exertions, from nerves, perhaps, a fear of the vast number of eyes watching every move he made. Cadon thought it over, and dismissed it after a moment's reflection. Valdur would *like* having thousands of people looking at him.

***

"You're right, Furin, that must be a firepit," Dillah said judiciously as the party drew level with the Hearthfield's nearer end. "What are all the poles for, Hari?"

"I'll tell you later." Hari's voice was unusually hard. Dillah glanced back at him, surprised. This was probably the first time since leaving Lazoon that he had answered a question with anything less than far too much information. She looked past him, to the woeful faces of the scrawny lot bunched up behind their party, between the ranks of the troopers who had flanked them all the way from the harbour. Her eyes turned to the people of Balimhavar beyond the troopers, an animated frieze of grinning, spittle-spewing mouths and excited eyes, wild hands waving, fists shaking. It was flowers they were throwing, but she was suddenly not so sure about the quality of the cheering. A skyful of shrieking carrion birds, that's what it brought to her mind. She tightened her arms around Sashah.

"What are they saying, Hari? What are they shouting at us?"

Hari hesitated. "They're welcoming you most kindly to Balimhavar," he answered smoothly, but a little too late. Dillah favoured him with the kind of scrutiny that had become proverbial among the People, known in general as 'one of

Granny Dillah Roebuck's *looks*.' Hari stumbled. Dillah sighed and turned her face away.

"Never mind," she said over her shoulder.

***

Hari, under his breath, was busy saying goodbye—to Balimhavar, to the world, to any dim hope of seeing Liske or his long-lost kinfolk again. This was a precaution, based on the strong probability that his one desperate inspiration would come to nothing. Valdur's antics were a distraction at first, and a worry, until Hari reflected they did not make a spit's worth of difference. Why shouldn't the little Lazooner have his moment? Why shouldn't the mob enjoy a good bit of theatre from the doomed? As long as his charges could not understand what the mob was shouting at them, both sides could be happy for the moment. The only thing that mattered would happen soon enough, when the candidates reached the Circle of the Heavens.

Dillah suspected the truth about the stakes, Hari was fairly sure of that. And if she weren't already suspicious, the wails that were breaking out among the better-informed gifts in the rearguard as they caught sight of the Hearthfield would certainly set her instincts twitching. He prayed to all the gods and ancestors of Liske and Balimhavar, and for good measure to the older ones of the Wild People's forests, that she would say nothing to the others.

Especially not to Cadon. Cadon was not stupid, but he was straight as an arrowshaft, and had no gift for dissembling. Only in innocence could he play his proper role. Hari concentrated his gaze on the back of Granny Dillah's head and shut his ears to the misery behind him, knowing that, whatever happened to his immediate charges, those unfortunates in the rearguard were guaranteed to burn.

"Now, Hari?" Cadon asked as the procession halted behind the Prefect's litter.

"Not yet. But soon." Hari hefted Granny's packstraps higher on his shoulders—how, he wondered, did that bent little scrap of a woman manage to heave such a load around as if it weighed nothing? One short stroll from the harbour, and his shoulders already felt as if they were on fire. Then he glanced over at the stakes in the Hearthfield, and shuddered.

"What's happening now?' asked Furin.

"It's the invocation. You see the priests on the platform, in the black and scarlet robes? They're calling down the attention of the Lords in Heaven."

Valdur snorted, and Hari surveyed him anxiously. That dangerous glitter was back in the ex-priest's eyes, and the feverish colour was in his cheeks, and it was clear, between the sweatmarks and the strained seams at the armpits, that the silk robe would never be the same again. Yet Valdur seemed calm enough for the moment, until he threw back his head and let out a great bellow of laughter. "Is that what they call an invocation in Balimhavar? It's about as interesting as watching blood dry."

"Please, Valdur, hush."

"But this was my profession, Hari, I know what I'm talking about. Those old fools are meant to be getting the gods' attention, not putting them to sleep. The Heavenly Fathers of Lazoon wouldn't bother turning up to a show as dismal as this one, I can tell you. And they haven't even been able to capture the crowd! How will the gods hear anything over that racket?" Briefly, brightly, the sun flashed off his hair. Between that and the fire in his cheeks, Hari thought Valdur looked like a man about to burst spontaneously, and a little prematurely, into flame.

Hari wished he could stop thinking about fire.

"Calm yourself, boy, for pity's sake." Granny Dillah bent over to set Sashah down on her own tiny feet, then confronted Valdur with her hands on her hips. More gently, she added, "Don't upset the others." To Hari's surprise, Valdur stared at her and gulped a couple of times. Then he shrugged his shoulders and squatted on the ground to divert Sashah with a few fingertricks. Dillah turned to gaze hard towards the Fox men, who had their backs to her, and were busy estimating the size of the crowd. Furin was counting the heads in each section of the colonnade, while Cadon counted the sections, a variant of a hunting-party trick to estimate the size of a prey herd. They seemed quite cheerful again; but Hari, watching Dillah uneasily as she watched the others, thought he saw a look of sorrow cross her face, swift as a bird-shadow. She turned again to Hari. "The *moment* the Old Woman is chosen," she said in a fierce whisper, "you tell me. Do you understand? I *must* have words with her."

"I expect," Hari whispered back, "you'll know the moment without being told."

***

The Hithe procession drew up beside the others. Chanithel, standing a little to the left of the entrance, tried to feel good about that, as a way to distract her own attention from the hideous ache in her neck. Somewhere at the top of her head, something was unbalanced; she suspected sabotage. Perhaps a treacherous hairdresser, in the pay of the Dreeves. Behind her, she heard Chorath Fruh discreetly settling his bet with a minor noble of the Kilve clan. Apparently the odds on Calviram arriving in time for the Day of the Electa had shortened considerably over the last few days, which had a knock-on effect on the odds of her becoming the Electa. According to Liddy's sources of information in the palace baths, Chanithel was now the slightly favoured candidate, just a nose ahead of Damissel Dreeve, with Eliva Kilve coming in a very distant third. Chanithel did not much care. She noticed her surviving full brother was looking well, which she did not care much about either.

Three processions. Three arrays of gifts for the Lords in Heaven, to which they were entitled no matter whose hand the Lord in Earth chose to grasp in a few minutes' time. Three wagons of pretty things. Three unhappy clumps of sacrifices, on whom the honour of being sent to Heaven later in the day appeared to be lost. Bored and aching, Chanithel did not let her eyes linger on their faces—until she came to one small knot, standing just beyond her brother's litter, in attitudes that were unusual under the circumstances, attitudes of interest and high alert.

Two very tall men, two shorter ones, and an old woman with a small child. One of the shorter men, plainly dressed in the black tunic and sash of a Council-owned chattel-clerk, she discounted immediately. The crone and child were of no interest. The other three were curiously attractive. The tall men, outlandishly garbed, stunningly formed, were the finest gifts she had ever seen, in a lifetime of watching the Hearthfield, the noose, and the priests' thrice-blessed little knives in frequent use. But it was the other shortish man in particular who caught her eye, perhaps because he chose that moment to throw his head back in a great shout of laughter, which was lost in the bloodthirsty howling of the Balim plebs. She caught her breath—his head seemed suddenly to be wrapped in a dazzle of light. He was an angel, or even a god, or at least a good solid vision of unearthly beauty—but no, she corrected herself when the light shifted, it was only that the poor sod had very short fair hair, which had caught the sun for a moment. Anyway, there was no use mooning at him, because she was the consort, and he was as good as dead. She forced herself to look away.

***

The crowd fell silent at last, from which Cadon deduced the gods of Balimhavar had been invoked, and the Old Man was about to make His appearance. Cadon gazed up with some trepidation at the stone platform, and saw a glittering marvel emerge from the dark rectangle of the temple door: a golden hillock, it seemed to him, about the size of a forest hut, gliding across the platform as smoothly as a great legless beast sliding on slick ice. Its forward slope was cut in a series of shallow tiers, and on its summit was a construction that reminded Cadon of the fat man's seat of honour in Lazoon, but far, far richer, glittering in the sun from a thousand carven and polished facets. Two men rode the hillock, flanking the bottom of the staircase of tiers, and they were no more strangely dressed and coifed than any of the other notables of Balimhavar standing about on the platform; but the creature enthroned on the summit was something else again. A cloudbank of gilded hair hovered above his head, swirling around a tall, round-topped golden cylinder. A lustrous robe of many colours, belted and festooned with fine ropes of gleaming metal, swathed his slight body. A golden mask covered the upper half of his face, leaving visible only a young-looking mouth and chin.

"Why is he wearing a cock on his head?" Furin muttered to Hari.

"It's not a cock," Hari hissed, "it's a crown. Hush!"

"It does look like a cock, though," Cadon said, squinting to see it better through its own glare. "Don't you think so, Granny?" When she did not reply, he turned to look at her. There was shock on her face. "Granny Dillah?"

She reacted at last in an explosive whisper. "Of course it's a cock. But *that* can't be the Old Man, can it?" she demanded of Hari.

"*Shh.* Yes, it can. That's the god-king, the Lord in Earth, and that thing on his head is a *crown.* Not a co—"

"Wait, Hari. You seriously mean to tell me *that's* the embodiment of the Great Man Spirit of the world?"

"Yes. Shut up." Hari glanced at Dillah and caught her expression. "Please," he added.

"Is it time yet?" asked Cadon.

"No."

"Their pacing is terrible," Valdur remarked.

"Please, Valdur."

"But Hari, the merest novice in Lazoon could do better than this. Why, I myself…."

"So if *he's* wearing a cock," Furin broke in, "what will the Old Woman be wearing on *her* head?"

"…could give lessons to those dullards…"

"Please, all of you…"

Any further commentary was drowned by a blast of noise from a bank of ramshorn trumpets beyond the grand stairway. The great moment was coming to Balimhavar, along with the Lords in Heaven. Hari knotted his hands together to keep them from shaking.

***

The pain in Chanithel's neck and right shoulder could rightly be called agony by now, and none of the little tricks she had learned were of any use at all. Her stays were also cutting into her ribs, and her feet hurt from standing so long in the torturously tight gilded sandals. Let the Lords in Heaven choose whom they liked! Less and less did she care what the outcome might be, or what would happen eventually to her and the Hithes, just so long as she could get off the platform, kick off the damned sandals, and set Liddy's practiced fingers loose on the knots in her neck.

She was, therefore, too distracted to feel more than a flash of dislike when the dais of the Lord in Earth was rolled through the great temple door, freighted with the Recorder, the Highest Priest, and her husband Filkamos, and she was a few seconds late in noticing her brother had left his litter and was advancing up the stairway towards the Circle, scowling meaningfully at her. She moved to meet him, aware of Damissel and Eliva similarly crossing the platform towards their brothers, and the Lord in Earth descending from his dais, while the crowds watched breathlessly. Calviram took her hand when she was close enough—spitting, *Balim's sake, girl, pull yourself together*—and hand-in-hand they stepped over the outer line of demarcation, and into the Circle of the Heavens.

***

"Now, Cadon!"

"What?"

"Go! Quickly!"

"Oh. Right you are." Obediently, Cadon scooped Sashah up into his arms, strode past the litter and the Hithe troopers, and started up the stairs.

***

All over Balimhavar, for days afterward, the debate would rage. There were those who swore they had seen the stranger descend from the heavens on a ray of golden light; which, as the story developed, became variously a staircase of light, a wheel of white fire, and a burning cloud with lightning at its heart. Others would claim with equal certainty that he rose up through the solid stone paves at the foot of the temple stairway, which then healed themselves under his feet. Those who were standing close to the west edge of the temple staircase had a simpler and somehow less credible tale to tell—that the glorious stranger with the lovely child in his arms had walked up from the harbour as part of the Hithe procession—but the time came when even these observers doubted the evidence of their eyes.

However he arrived at the temple, there was general agreement about what happened next. He reached the platform unhindered by any of the troopers, and ducked his head politely to the invocation priests standing off to one side. Blankly, they regarded him back. After a glance over his shoulder, apparently directed towards someone in the Hithe procession, the stranger stepped forward and over the raised stones that marked the edge of the Circle of the Heavens, to halt beside Calviram Hithe and his sister Chanithel.

***

Calviram frowned, hearing the beginnings of a stir behind him—most unseemly. With the Lords in Heaven watching Balimhavar through nit-picking eyes, the people should know to keep silent, as should the troopers and most particularly the priests. Several thousand people whispering among themselves added up to a respectable tide of sound. A damfool spear-captain hissing orders at the bottom of the staircase was earning himself a long-term posting in the oarwell of a penal galley. And as for the nobles facing him on the platform—what were they all staring at with their eyes bugging out? The Recorder and the Highest Priest, keeping pace with the Lord in Earth as he drifted down the steps of the dais and across the far edge of the Circle, also looked fit to be stuffed and mounted. Calviram discreetly turned his head just far enough to catch what everyone else was gawking at.

The younger of the Wild Men smiled nervously at him from a distance of a few feet. He was *inside the Circle*; worse, he induced the dratted girl-child in his arms to pull her thumb out of her mouth and wave her chubby hand in Calviram's direction. Choked with horror, Calviram turned his eyes to the Lord in Earth, now drifting in their direction with a chilling grin on his lips.

***

Filkamos could hardly feel the weight of the crown on his head. Indeed, his head felt unnaturally light, buoyed up by its own contents, as frothy as the stones brought for his amusement from the volcanoes of Zerit. He knew there was some reason he was out there under the open sky, some *will* he should express on behalf of his brother-lords in the heavens, and he dearly wanted to get it over with and return to his tower and his friendly chalice. So why was he here? The reason kept spinning away from him. Through the eye-holes of the mask, he saw the broad charred square of the Hearthfield in a state of fuelled readiness, and deduced that a large-scale burning was involved, which could also explain the presence of great hordes of nasty plebs. Was he obliged to look at the gifts? Not really, because the Lord in Earth was not *obliged* to do anything, and anyway the Lords in Heaven would already have made a good, stiff appraisal of what was on offer. They would guide him when the time came.

He took a few deep breaths, and found this thinned the mists just enough to let him remember. Today was the Day of the Electa. His feet were already inside the Circle of the Heavens, and the candidates were before him. He swung his head around to catch them serially in the eye-holes of the mask. Damissel Dreeve on the left. Eliva Kilve in the centre. Chanithel Hithe on the right. Wasn't that one his consort? The consort would be the usual choice, but sometimes the Lords in Heaven had other ideas. Grandis was making his counsel clear by subtly nudging Filkamos onto a leftward course, away from the consort. What right had he? Irritated, Filkamos responded by deviating by degrees towards the right.

Then came an apparition—an astonishing figure that rose magically into view and stepped forward into the Circle, all golden skin and white teeth and dark, amber-bedizened curls. Taller than Darrasat Dreeve, even taking Darassat's high-piled hair into account. Handsomer than Calviram Hithe. Hardly the same kind of animal as Gavor Kilve. In this radiant apparition's arms was a very small, very pretty female.

Grandis's gasp of outrage was the only sign Filkamos needed. He stepped away from the Recorder and floated towards the apparition on a cloud of mischief, chuckling to himself. The apparition smiled brightly, against all tradition, and raised his free hand in a graceful greeting. Filkamos, grinning back, reached out to grasp the new Electa's tiny hand.

Chapter Eighteen

The Afternoon of the Shield

"What's happening now? Why is everybody...?"

"Move! Now!" Hari grabbed Dillah's arm and beckoned wildly to the others to follow, past the wagon and the litter and the staring litter-bearers, skidding to a halt at the foot of the great stairway. "No, Valdur, don't go up yet. It's a holy place, they'll slice us to ribbons if we go up now." But the troopers, like all the rest of this great concourse, were too busy gawping at events on the platform to notice them.

Regretfully, Hari glanced back at the other living gifts to the gods, still trapped behind the Hithe litter. Why should he feel as if he had abandoned them? He could not save them. He hardly knew yet whether Valdur and the Wild People would be safe from the fire. Nothing like this had ever happened before. All he had hoped for was to muddy the waters. Sending Sashah and Cadon into the Circle of the Heavens would at least confuse everybody, and perhaps buy the Wild People a few days while the court diviners thought things over. At worst, he'd thought, it might bring them all a death that was quicker and easier than being burnt alive on the Hearthfield of

Balimhavar. A no-nonsense bludgeoning, say, from unimpressed troopers. It had never seriously occurred to him that Sashah might turn out to be the Electa.

On the platform, a brave attempt was being made to carry on as if everyone were not in shock. The Recorder was visibly and literally prodding the Highest Priest to continue with the next stage of the Day, which was to shower blessings and scented oil on the chosen one and her supposed brother. Hari saw Cadon recoil, and prayed he would have the good sense to accept the blessing gracefully. Then realization hit him. Cadon was now, at least in theory, the most powerful man in all the Balim Empire barring the Lord in Earth himself. This was either much worse or much better than Hari could ever have imagined. It was certainly much stranger.

But he would think about that later. Who knew if the notables on the platform would abruptly decide the sacred day had been blasphemed, and turn on Cadon? And the others were not safe yet, not while they could still be seen as part of the Hithe procession, flammable fodder for the gods. He calculated their best chance of safety lay in ascending the stairs as if by right, as the near relations of the shining new Shield, wafting past the gauntlet of guards and priests and the daunting Recorder and the Lord in Earth himself, and brazenly joining the ranks of the nobles. They would not be entirely safe there, either, but nowhere was entirely safe. Hari kept a careful eye on the platform, praying he would recognize the right moment when it arrived.

***

Up on the platform, Cadon was in danger of succumbing to an acute attack of stage fright. It had not been so bad when he had his back to the square, and could not see the multitude of eyes behind him. As well, Cadon had taken courage from the fact that he was standing near their good friend and patron, the Prefect Calviram. Cadon had even judged it proper to address fond and friendly greetings to the youth with the large male organ on his head, especially since the youth himself had smiled in such a welcoming manner as he approached. And he clearly liked children too, since he had taken Sashah's hand and chucked her under the chin, giggling so infectiously that Sashah crowed with delight. But as for him being the Old Man, Cadon had serious doubts after seeing him at close range. He looked no older than Cadon himself. Neither did anybody on the platform look anything like a plausible candidate for the Old Woman.

And then the young man had stepped back, rather unsteadily, to totter back up the tiers of the golden hillock and collapse not very gracefully into the tall-backed seat at its summit. In the next moment, one of his companions rudely threw much of a jar of strong-smelling oil over both Cadon and Sashah, which would leave stubborn stains on their gala clothes. Cadon was annoyed, but good manners kept him silent. And then the young man's other companion, the nasty glowering one, snapped what sounded like an order at Cadon; and when Cadon did not move, he took him ungently by the arm and swung him around to face the multitude in the square.

More eyes than the night. A swelling floodtide of voices, yammering and ululating, a wind of whispers from the priests on the platform. That was bad enough, but worse was what he could not see: Granny Dillah and the others were not where he had left them. Sashah hid her face on Cadon's shoulder, but Cadon, with no such recourse, felt panic rising in his belly. Then a saving thing happened, the first of two.

Prefect Calviram was suddenly on his knees at Cadon's feet. He grabbed Cadon's right hand and pressed it first to his own forehead, and then to the brow of the pretty girl kneeling beside him. The glowering gentleman said something to him in a low, vicious whisper, but Calviram did not reply. Instead, he addressed to Cadon a torrent of incomprehensible words in a loud, public voice, then added softly and hesitantly in the Lazooner speech, "Not move. Not talk. Do happy." He demonstrated the last by stretching his lips in a wide, bright smile.

Cadon, though mystified, smiled back and obediently said nothing. And all at once Calviram and the pretty girl were gone, and another couple had taken their place, a large-nosed man and a girl who was clearly his close relative, and they repeated the hand-to-forehead manoeuvre; then there was another pair, and then a procession of invocation priests and troop officers and gaudily dressed personages of both sexes from the body of the platform, until Cadon's hand ached from the pressure of this stream of hard, sweaty foreheads.

Sometime during this ordeal, the second heartening event took place. Anxiously scanning the square for his own party between foreheads, Cadon happened to glance down; and there they were, clustered safely at the foot of the stairway, Granny Dillah with her arms akimbo and a puzzled frown on her face, Furin and Valdur grinning up at him, Hari poised like a bird on a branch, ready to fly. Relieved, Cadon pulled his hand away from the current forehead to wave at them, and at once—as if his wave had been a signal—Hari began to urge the others up the stairs.

***

Calviram managed to put aside his shock for the moment, as something to be indulged in later. He recovered quickly enough to be the first to offer his grace to the new Shield of the Electa, dragging Chanithel beside him, beating out Darassat Dreeve and his big-nosed sister by a very short head. Score one to the Hithes. It was a small but warming comfort to see the impotent fury in the Recorder's eyes. Indeed, Calviram could almost read the Recorder's thoughts. The interloper and his brat baby sister were still breathing only because Filkamos had touched the brat's hand in full view of the assembled multitudes of Balimhavar—but once the Recorder could get them out of the public eye, anything could happen. And probably would.

Unless he, Calviram, took a hand. He had offered his grace by instinct, without thinking; but by the time the tardy Kilves came forward to offer theirs, he had already realized there was a sizeable bright side for himself and the Hithe Faction. The consortship was already in their hands, in the person of Chanithel; and now the Hithes could claim kinship with, or at least take credit for presenting, the new Electa and her Shield. Cadon trusted him, Hari said so. And as the Recorder had his puppet in the Lord in Earth, so Calviram would have his, in the Shield of the Electa. It was almost better than being the Shield himself.

Hari, he thought. Hari was the key, the secret weapon, the only voice through which the new Shield could speak—and Hari must be kept that way. As he took his place among the nobles on the platform, Calviram discreetly crooked a finger to summon his cousin Sallik Hithe to his side, and whispered some instructions into his ear. Sallik slid away. When Calviram looked towards the square again, Hari himself was just cresting the stairway, in the wake of Calviram's other new best friends.

***

"See what they're doing? That forehead business? Do the same, just as soon as we reach Cadon."

For once, Hari's charges did not question him, debate among themselves, nor stop to observe the scenery. In fact, puffing under Granny's pack, Hari had trouble keeping up with them as they bounded up the stairway. The crowds in the square, having apparently decided this was the most entertaining Day of the Electa in recent decades, were thunderous in their cheers as Furin and Dillah muscled into the queue of nobles and knelt before the Shield, and noisier yet for Valdur's spectacularly dramatic genuflection. Hari had a bad moment when Dillah made to take Sashah from Cadon's arms, and another when she stepped towards the dais of the Lord in Earth with a purposeful look in her eye, but he was able to head her off before she did anything fatal. He was starting to shoo his charges towards the array of nobles behind the dais when he became aware that Cadon was holding the back of his hand under Hari's nose, and looking expectant.

"Not me," he whispered frantically, "I'm a chattel..." And then, on second thought, he dropped to his knees and pressed the proffered hand against his forehead. Who could fault him for obeying a direct expression of will from the Shield of the Electa? "Keep on doing what you're doing," he whispered to Cadon, before herding the others away.

A long file of nobles was waiting to offer grace to the new Shield of the Electa. Hari led his band straight past the queue to a prime spot a little apart from those who had already felt Cadon's hand on their foreheads, about halfway between the Hithes and the Fruh Faction. This caused a slight agitation among those notables, audible as a rustling of robes and confused whispers. Hari caught a glimpse of the Prefect Calviram and Hillisam Hithe, and swiftly turned his back on them, to stare determinedly out over the square. He was aware of a growing number of troop officers watching them uncertainly from the edges of the platform, as if waiting for orders.

"Look, there's the Prefect," Furin said happily, turning and waving towards the Hithe Faction.

"Stop that, Furin! Keep your eyes to the front. I'll explain later."

"You'll explain now, my son," Dillah said firmly. "What's happening? Why shouldn't we greet the Prefect? And when will we see the Old Woman?"

Hari sighed. "You've seen her already. The Old Woman—that is to say, the great woman-spirit of the world—the fact is, Granny Dillah…"

"Spit it out, boy."

"Well—it's Sashah."

"Sashah."

"That's right."

"Our Sashah?" Furin put in. At the end of the row, Valdur imperfectly turned a snicker into a cough. Hari nodded apprehensively.

"Our little Sashah," Dillah took over, "whom I midwifed myself? Little Sashah, who is just about to see her third winter? That particular Sashah is the Old Woman?"

"That's right, Granny Dillah."

There was a long silence, so long that Hari at last threw a desperate glance at Dillah's face. He feared she would be in a fury, getting herself ready to stomp over to the Lord in Earth and set him straight with a few well-chosen words, any one of which might break the protective spell that appeared to be woven around them for the moment. He was unprepared to see Dillah red-faced and shaking with mirth.

"If Sashah's an Old Woman," she snorted, "then what am I?"

Hari gulped.

"Never mind, Hari, that question was not meant to be answered. But what will happen to her now? And what about Cadon? Why is it *his* hand that's getting forehead-grease and heaven knows what else all over it?"

Hesitantly, still staring straight ahead, Hari summarized Cadon's exalted new status as baldly as he could. Dillah and Furin chuckled, but said nothing until he ran out of words.

"Fancy that, Furin," Dillah said, with a grin in her voice, "your young far-nephew, being such a big man."

"This is serious," Hari said.

"Maybe so, young Hari, but it's also very funny." Furin leaned across Dillah to poke Hari in the shoulder. "Imagine, grown people believing such things. By the way, did you know that Cadon is not actually Sashah's brother?"

"We'll keep quiet about that, if you don't mind," said Hari.

***

Sallik Hithe was lean and fast on his feet, a natural athlete and a good, quick thinker. These traits served him well on this Day of the Electa, with so many crowds to struggle through on behalf of the Hithe Faction. The first errand was relatively straightforward, once he had fought his way to the east side of the temple stairway: a low-voiced warning to the Domo of the Shield Guard, that a threat had already been made against the new Electa, that he should be extra vigilant, and that he should waste no time in offering his grace to his new master and taking up a permanent position by his side. That done, Sallik slipped out of the teeming concourse with six of his own toughs, to the deserted side streets that would take them to the back entrance of the Council offices on the west edge of the square. The skeleton guard, recognizing him, waved him through.

The man he sought was on the balcony of the second floor, with its frontage on the square and its fine view of the temple platform and the Hearthfield. The Council's Master of Clerks was not happy to be dragged away from the spectacle of the miraculous new Electa and her impressive brother, who had apparently dropped from the heavens—but a Hithe visitor was not one to be denied, not even on such a day. He took Sallik Hithe by the hand and led him towards his own records chamber, calling for wine.

Sallik Hithe had no time to waste on wine. How many speakers of the Liskan or Lazooner speech were among the Council's chattel-clerks? Four, the Chief of Clerks answered promptly, including the one now on loan to the visitor's esteemed cousin for the Lazoon mission. How much for all four? The price, the bribe, and the impression of a bill of sale were cumulatively the work of five minutes. Retrieving the three Liskan clerks from the happy crowd on the balcony took ten minutes more. Five minutes after that, in a cul-de-sac down the deserted street, all three were efficiently stripped, strangled with their own black sashes, and buried under a handy slop-heap.

***

Calviram was waiting until Sallik returned with the glad news that both errands had been successfully carried out, before making his next move. He knew that one of Sallik's missions had already borne fruit, because the Domo of the Shield Guard had discreetly moved a sizeable force onto the stairway, and remained on the platform after touching his forehead to Cadon's hand. Cadon and the brat were as safe now as could be arranged, barring a well-deserved lightning strike from the clear sky. Calviram eased his physical discomfort by imagining the Recorder's vexation. He noted with relief that the queue was mercifully diminished, and also that the glorious Electa had fallen asleep on the Shield's shoulder with two fingers in her mouth.

Sallik appeared at his side, and whispered in his ear. The news was satisfactory. Now he needed to put the fear into Hari, and *now* was as good a time as any, out in the open for all eyes to see, but no ears to hear. Nudging Chanithel to follow, Calviram sidled his way through his Hithe relations towards the exalted family of the new Electa, drifting to a position just behind Hari's shoulder. "You have some explaining to do," he said softly into Hari's ear.

Hari, staring straight ahead, showed no sign of being startled. "Explaining, honoured sir?"

"Yes, Hari. For a start, you can explain to me how one of the gifts I put into your care slipped his leash and ended up in the Circle of the Heavens. Well?"

"It seems," Hari said calmly and truthfully, "that a voice spoke to him and told him what to do."

"A voice? From where, Hari? From the heavens, I suppose."

"He did not say, honoured sir. But that would make sense, wouldn't it? Surely what happened must be the will of the Lords in Heaven."

"Oh, surely," said Calviram, with heavy irony. "But tell me, Hari, how is it that you and these other gifts are standing up here on the temple platform, where no common feet should tread? Did you hear a voice as well?"

"Why, no, honoured Prefect," Hari said, turning his head at last to look up at the Prefect with wide, honest eyes. "The Shield of the Electa called us to him with a wave of his hand.

There are ten thousand witnesses who saw him summon us. How could we refuse?"

"You've had time to think this out, haven't you?"

"I have no idea what you mean, honoured Prefect."

"Careful, chattel-clerk. I own you now—bought and paid for, not half an hour ago."

Hari only smiled. Then Granny Dillah craned around him to address what sounded like a question to Calviram.

"She gives you kind greetings, honoured sir, on this happy occasion," Hari said smoothly. And to Granny Dillah, he added in the Lazooner speech, "Yes, Dillah, he's heard the joke. He thinks it's hilarious about Cadon."

"He's not laughing," Dillah said, peering up at Calviram.

"His people are not great laughers," Hari said.

"What did she say?"

"She says she's sure the new Shield will use his power wisely."

"His what? By the Lords in Heaven, Hari, you don't take this seriously, do you?"

"What's he saying?"

"He says, he's happy that Cadon has received such a warm welcome from the people of Balimhavar."

Dillah surveyed them both inscrutably, and returned with a slight frown to watching Cadon accept the grace of the last few nobles in the queue. Calviram, biting his lip, wondered if he had been too hasty in trying to secure the monopoly on Liskan interpreters. Perhaps he'd had the wrong ones killed. Hari realized, with wonder and fear, how much he had enjoyed the last few minutes. The ramifications were beginning to sink in.

Chanithel, unnoticed by her brother, had meantime edged a little away from his side. Now she was directly behind the taller of the ex-gifts, with a good view of the profile and beautiful left ear of the young man beside him, the one whose hair was a dusting of sunshine over his shapely head. He may have felt her watching him, because he looked over his shoulder a few moments later, and returned her gaze with a usurer's rate of interest. Then he smiled at her. Breathless, Chanithel smiled back.

***

Cadon's right hand was numb and greasy. Sashah was a drooling dead weight on his left shoulder. Sometime in the hour or so he had been standing in the Circle of the Heavens, he had given up worrying about the thousands of watching savages, or indeed worrying about anything. Forehead followed forehead from an apparently endless supply—until at last he looked down and saw that nobody else was waiting to offer him this very strange greeting. His muscles creaked as he shifted Sashah to his other shoulder. She chose that moment to wake up and begin struggling to get down.

A touch on Cadon's arm. The glowering gentleman spoke to him, in words that Cadon could not understand. Cadon nodded politely and responded with a phrase that, as far as he remembered, would convey his respectful incomprehension. The gentleman looked puzzled, and even slightly angrier, while the young man who had touched Sashah's hand laughed out loud on his golden hillock. Perhaps, Cadon thought, embarrassed, he had not been absolutely accurate in reproducing that string of syllables. And then, happily, Hari arrived at his elbow, and whatever he said to the notables around Cadon had the pleasant effect of making them fall back a pace or two. Hari turned to Cadon.

"This is going very well, Cadon, very well indeed," he said. "Now go up and do that forehead business to the Lord in—

to the young man with the cock on his head—no, Cadon, *your* forehead, *his* hand—that's better—and now come down—turn around again and hold your hand out to the crowd—don't put Sashah down, they have to see her too—that's good—and smile, Cadon, smile as if you're giving every single one of the Balim clods in the mob his own personal greeting—excellent—and now, repeat after me, loud as you can…"

It was a longish speech, and although Cadon did not catch more than a few words of its import himself, he inferred it was an effective one. He heard his own voice echoing off the façades across the square, as he had formerly heard it echo off the rock walls of canyons in the mountains. In pauses between utterances, thousands of the massed people of Balimhavar cheered mightily. At one point, Hari hastily waved Dillah, Furin and Valdur forward, again to the delight of the audience, and the words he put into Cadon's mouth were evidently some sort of introduction. The greatest boon was that Granny Dillah was at last able to relieve him of Sashah.

***

Free! That was the refrain in Hari's head, counterpointed with "and still breathing," at least for the moment. He would worry about the breathing part later. Guiding the Shield of the Electa through the obligatory address to Balimhavar was the first priority, and that was going quite well. Survival was another matter. Still, a small portion of his soul was engaged in marvelling at his new personal status. Having one's grace accepted by an appointee of the Lords in Heaven and Earth was a token that one was of noble status, and a noble could not, by definition, be a chattel. He looked forward keenly to telling the honoured Prefect about his, Hari's, elevation. He also wondered, grinning to himself, whether the honoured

Prefect would be out the cost of one chattel-clerk, or whether the Council would give him a refund.

At an auspicious moment, Hari waved forward the rest of his charges, now officially redefined as Cadon's father, cousin, and grandmother. Eloquent words of introduction, of affirmation, and of promises for the future rolled off his tongue and straight onto Cadon's. The Shield of the Electa would be the Shield of mighty Balimhavar as well—the Electa would ensure that no pious woman went barren, that the fields would burst with grain—the Lords in Heaven and Earth, provided with such an avatar as Cadon, would make their faces shine upon the Empire in ways that were both general and specific and in all cases satisfactory. And then it was time for the feast.

"We'll go into the temple in a minute," Hari explained, while the people of Balimhavar were still giving Cadon's speech a resounding ovation, "and eat—but please, please, please, do not drink too much wine."

"And then what?" Cadon asked.

Hari did not answer at once. After the feast, they were to come out to the square again, and witness the despatch of gifts to the Lords in Heaven. He looked down towards the Hearthpit, and saw that troopers were already beginning to empty the wagons and strew the treasures from the three processions among the mounds of fuel. They were making a start with the live gifts, too, dragging the first group from the Kilve procession towards the stakes.

"What are they doing?" Furin's eyes had followed Hari's. "That's not what it looks like, surely?"

"I'll bet you it is," Dillah cut in. "I did wonder about those stakes. Hari?"

"It's—there's nothing we can do," Hari said. He was uncomfortably aware that the Recorder and the Highest were already in their places on the rolling dais, waiting for the Electa and the Shield to join them. "We have to go now."

"They're going to burn those people!" Cadon had worked it out as well. "That's not right!"

"They're gifts for the Lords in Heaven. We really do have to go now."

"Are they murderers?" Granny Dillah demanded. "Thieves? Rapists?"

"I don't know. Probably not. They're just chattels, that's all. But—"

"Have they been unbirthed?"

"Have they what?"

"Because if they aren't deserving of this, and haven't even been unbirthed," Granny went on, in a voice dark with disapproval, "then the Old Ones will certainly never accept them as gifts. Those shiny gew-gaws, yes, it's right and proper to burn those, and the animals as well. But burning people—I never heard of such a thing."

"As bad as those Lazooners," Furin said, adding, "No offense, Valdur." Valdur grinned.

"We really, really must go now." Hari was doing his best to block out the threats being uttered behind him in a vicious whisper: the Recorder, in a murderous mood. "I've told you, there's nothing we can do."

"Cadon could do something," Valdur suggested innocently.

"What?"

"Me? What could I do?"

Valdur turned to Cadon, still grinning. "You're the Shield of the Electa. As I understand it, you can do anything you want."

Cadon stared at him blankly. "I'm the what of the what?"

"Nobody's told him yet," said Granny Dillah. "But it's not a bad idea, young Valdur. Cadon can tell them not to do such a stupid thing. Hari, give him the words."

"I can't—we can't—" Hari began. Then he shut his mouth, and stared at her for a moment. Next he turned his eyes to the Hearthpit, to the stakes with two-legged gifts already drooping from them, and the forest of stakes still waiting; and then to a weeping woman being frogmarched across the fuel with a child in her arms, and past her to the hopeless queues behind the empty wagons.

"Cadon," he said slowly, "repeat after me." He rendered the words into the most formal register of Balim he knew. "*There shall be no burning*. . .shout it, Cadon!"

Cadon shouted it. His voice thundered the words.

Madness struck Hari. "And this, Cadon. *All the gifts are now the dower of the Electa*."

Cadon obliged, resoundingly. The crowd went silent, and Hari held his breath. Perhaps he had gone too far? The Recorder hissed a curse at the foot of the dais, the nobles stirred, the Domo shifted closer to his sacred charges. But then, from a hesitant beginning, the voice of the crowd grew—higher, deeper, louder, happier—until the plebs of Balimhavar were cheering with the full power of their lungs.

"See, Hari?" said Granny Dillah. "I told you it was the right thing to do, and the people of this place agree. Now what happens?"

"Who knows?" Hari breathed. But he had a number of ideas.

***

What a loud noise those plebs were making. Like the rain beating down on the roof of his tower chamber, which was where he wished to be. Was this farce not over yet? He had chosen the Electa, and drowsed through the new Shield's speech—who was he, anyway, and why hadn't the fires been lit for the great burning? Smiling vaguely, Filkamos coaxed his eyes to focus through the eyeholes of the mask. Curious. From the look of things, there was not going to be a burning after all. He wondered why not, and then he forgot to wonder at all. A wriggling little fish of a thought was playing just under the surface of his mind. A plan, a grand new mischief, and so simple to do. He longed to begin.

Chapter Nineteen

The Lords in Heaven Clarify Their Thinking

Dillah was right, and she was wrong. It was not the cancellation of an unblessed burning that so delighted the multitude on the Day of the Electa. On the contrary, a good burning was a much anticipated element of public rites, which could otherwise be quite dull. But on this occasion the people did not feel cheated of their entertainment. Neither were they upset that the Lords in Heaven had altered the terms of their lordship. Some sort of alteration was happening all the time: new taxes, new servitudes, new and deadlier penalties, new *wills*, spilling in profusion from the mouth of the Lord in Earth. Those were the changes one expected, and however difficult they might make the lives of the earthbound, one was at least assured that Heaven was operating normally. But this alteration had interesting implications, which were not lost on a bitterly experienced people.

First, there was the element of novelty in the previously immutable Day of the Electa. Then there was the dramatic appearance of the new Electa and her Shield, too beautiful and golden to be children of Earth. Clearly they were the offspring of the very Lords in Heaven, which meant their cousin, father and grandmother must have dropped from Heaven too, and possibly even the little familiar in clerk's clothing. If such a direct flesh-and-blood blessing had ever been granted before, it was far, far back in the legendary age of creation, when the first Lord in Earth had made his home among the primeval hills.

But it was the fate of the gifts from the great families that most astonished Balimhavar. Heaven had not exactly rejected the gifts—*that* would have been a sign that Heaven was turning its back on the city. But as the echoes of the Shield's words faded, claiming the gifts as his sister's property, all eyes in the great square of Balimhavar had turned fearfully to the Lord in Earth. From the ineffable smile suffusing the visible portion of his face, the great Lord appeared to be content with the Shield's decree. And it seemed he had nothing to add. Heaven's message was complete.

So, while troopers fanned out across the Hearthpit to gather up the reprieved treasures and cut the living gifts loose from the stakes, a tide of speculation swelled along the streets and across the squares of Balimhavar. The Lords in Heaven had *not* turned their faces from the gifts—they had simply decided to keep those assets in the world below, to dower the new Electa. But were they thus withdrawing their favour from the great old families? Was the Electa to mother a *new* great family, greater than all the rest, with a bloodline fresh from Heaven? And was the Shield to father lordly new children on the noble daughters of Balimhavar? That intriguing thought came at about the same moment to several noble daughters and their parents. Something even more intriguing occurred to Calviram Hithe.

Balimhavar's masses did not need the diviners to work out the signs for them. The Hithes, Dreeves and Kilves had received a moderate slap in the face, which grieved nobody outside the great families themselves, but the city as a whole was still in Heaven's good graces. Even better, this aborted burning was a stunning affirmation of Heaven's fresh covenant with Balimhavar. With hope fermenting in their hearts, the people of Balimhavar directed mighty shouts of gratitude towards the sky.

***

For the next five days, Hari's back itched continuously between his shoulder blades, at just the point where a knife would slide in with least effort from the user. His head throbbed from the strain of smoothing over the Wild Ones for Balimhavar, and Balimhavar for the Wild Ones. His instincts yammered that they were not safe yet, would never be truly safe, that their peril grew with every day the Electa and her Shield resided in their quarters in the Great Household. And, as if possible conspirators, assassins, spies, the Recorder, the Palace Master, and the entire Dreeve clan were not enough to give him nightmares, the dread prospect of court hairdressers loomed over the afternoon. But first, an old friend had craved the boon of an interview.

Hari waited for his visitor on a pile of cushions in the garden of the Electa's preserve, a cloistered square of fragrant trees and flowering thickets in the heart of the Great Household. For the moment, all his charges were accounted for and out of mischief. The personification of the woman-spirit was on the far side of the garden, playing under the watchful eyes of her Shield and the Shield's uncle. Granny Dillah, ignoring the anguish of a brace of gardeners, was squatting beside a fire she had built in a bed of rare royal velves, mumbling over some objects taken from her pack. Valdur, also sprawled on cushions near Hari's pile, appeared to be asleep, but Hari had every reason to believe he was working on a poem. From the shadows of the cloister, five of the Domo's troopers kept silent watch. Yes, Hari thought, all was well. For the moment.

Firm footsteps crunched along the gravelled path: the Domo of the Shield Guard, coming to announce the arrival of Hari's visitor. Wearily, Hari hauled himself up and trailed the Domo into the smaller reception hall, where a familiar figure was already installed on cushions and sipping from a chalice of wine from the Electa's excellent cellar. Hari caught himself before sheer force of habit led him to genuflect.

"Prefect Calviram, welcome," he said, in the dignified tone appropriate to addressing an equal. Hari had thought this through carefully, and practiced on Valdur, who had given him a few useful pointers on posture and delivery. Since Hari was no longer a chattel, he needed to avoid larding his speech with servile honorifics—but what *was* his status now? On one hand, a baseborn foreign chattel-clerk. On the other, a man whose grace had been accepted by Heaven, a nobleman of Balimhavar in the close confidence of the Shield of the Electa. Straightening his back, he looked across the wine tray and locked eyes with Calviram.

***

So the rabbit had a few hairs of the lion in his pelt. Calviram might have been amused, if his mission had not been so weighty. He noted with interest how rapidly Hari was adjusting to his new role in the Palace, how nearly the little clerk had perfected his air of peer-to-peer courtesy after only five days. "My felicitations, Hari," he said formally, "on your elevation to the ranks of the nobles."

"Your felicitations honour me, Prefect. As to my elevation, it was clearly the will..."

"I know whose will it was." The Prefect sipped again from the chalice, and set it down on the tray. "And I tell you, Friend of the Electa, I am happy for your good fortune, and content with this will. *Honestly* I am," he added, when Hari's eyebrows, freed from the constraints of chattelhood, rose skeptically. "Forget the formalities," Calviram went on, smiling the warmest of his diplomatic smiles. "Of course I'm happy for you. You're a clever little bugger, and you served me well from the moment we first set sail for Lazoon. If Heaven had not turned you onto a nobler path, you'd have had a fine future as a Hithe chattel."

"Is that why you tried to buy me on the Day of the Electa?"

"What other reason could there be?" Calviram spread his hands in a gesture of openness, but he was unpleasantly surprised. "Come now," he went on affably, "that's all behind us, and so is your old life. How are your charges?"

"They hardly know what's happened yet," Hari admitted, "except for Valdur, the Lazooner. He's been helping me get Cadon ready for tomorrow's reception, but I'm afraid the Shield's talents lie in other directions."

"Tomorrow? The feast?"

"His first state feast, plus his formal introduction to emissaries from the vassal kings. The Electa's whole family is expected to attend."

"That should be interesting for everyone." Calviram permitted himself a grin, then wiped it away. "*If* the Shield lives that long. Hari, we need to talk frankly."

"I'm listening, honoured…I'm listening."

Calviram covered his satisfaction at the slip. "Good. But my dear friend, why is your voice so cold? We are on the same side in this battle, after all."

"What battle is that, Prefect?" Hari's flat tone matched the blankness of his face. Calviram kept the smile, but his hand suddenly itched to clout the little Liskan's ear, as in the good old days, when his hold over Hari had included the power to have him cut into small pieces.

"Hari," he sighed, "you are, as I said, a clever young man. No doubt you have long observed how the court of Balimhavar is so unfortunately divided. There are some among the nobles, like myself, whose most fervent wish is to serve the Lords in Heaven and this great empire in piety and humility, with no thought of reward—and there are others who serve only themselves and their kin. You know of whom I speak."

Hari sipped his wine soberly. "I suppose you mean the Dreeves and their allies. But from the outside," he remarked, "one Great Family looks very much like another."

"You're not on the outside now."

Hari acknowledged this with a nod. "So you've come to warn me?"

"Nothing so meagre as a warning. I've come to talk about how we can help each other. The Wild People—"

"—have been chosen by Heaven," Hari said quickly. "No one can change that, Prefect, not even you."

"Nor would I want to. Believe me, Hari, I have nothing but their best interests in my heart."

"You were going to burn them alive."

"Well, yes. But I never wished them ill." Surprised again, the Prefect picked up his chalice and took a decent swallow rather than a ritual sip. "Hari," he went on, "where did you find this sharp tongue? The Wild People—"

"—are my sacred responsibility," Hari interrupted again, in a harder voice. "I will do nothing to harm them. I will have no dealings with their ill-wishers, nor take part in any plots against them."

"Quite right. Heaven and I chose you well." Calviram selected his best diplomatic mask for the occasion, a benign and reasonable face. "In that case," he went on, "you will be interested in what I have to show you."

He reached into his trailing white sleeve and brought out a clay tablet, covered on both sides with hen-scratchings, dried to the texture of a biscuit. Not baked to a state of permanence, though—this was a message that could revert to mud in moments, leaving no incriminating traces behind. The script, a kind of scribal shorthand, was a little beyond Calviram's own reading skills, but Hari was a trained scribbler. Calviram watched his face while he scanned the tablet, and saw the dawning of dread. And that was *good.*

***

"Pretty—I wish I could keep the box, Liddy, and throw away what's inside." Chanithel ran her fingers over the carvings on the lid of the little ivory chest. Her brother rarely sent her presents, and when he did, it was always with a purpose. It seemed to her that this was the worst present ever. "Did the messenger say how they're to be taken?"

"Only," said the bodymaid, "that each of you must eat one. Tonight, when your husband receives you in his bed."

Chanithel raised the lid again. Two crystalline sweetmeats, crimson, glistening with honey. The sight of them turned her stomach. She shut the lid.

"The messenger said the potion never fails," Liddy went on. "Imagine—it will bind your lover to you forever, make him helplessly your chattel, never to look at another woman. Oh, yes, and potency, stamina, and many children are guaranteed."

"Stamina," Chanithel repeated gloomily.

"All night long, the messenger said."

"Oh," said Chanithel.

"Apparently it was vastly expensive, and your brother sent all the way to Ris for it. You know, the vassal city with—"

"—the largest broods in the Balim empire, and the most faithful husbands. All night long. What a prospect. Maybe I should switch it for a sleeping potion. Or," Chanithel added mischievously, "for a poison." She laughed alone, but stopped when she saw Liddy glance at the doorway, which was covered only with a sheer cloth inadequate to block the sound of unwise jokes. "Liddy," she said, holding out the little ivory chest, "put this away for now. And then I suppose we should finish getting me ready. It's not every night my husband invites me to his bed."

Liddy slipped the little chest under a cushion and resumed rubbing warmed rose oil into her mistress's smooth shoulders. Chanithel closed her eyes and tried not to think about the night ahead—*stamina*—and found herself drifting towards sleep. An image floated before her eyes again, the image she had been trying to banish all week: a golden head catching the sunlight, laughing eyes glancing back at her over a well-formed shoulder…

"You're thinking of *him* again, aren't you," Liddy said crossly. "I despair of you, lady. We'll do your legs now."

Sighing, Chanithel stuck her legs out, settled back on the cushions, and picked up her beadwork. "I wish the box was for *him*, though. I wish I could give it to *him*, and not to Filkamos. *He'd* be bound to me forever then. And then maybe I could…" Her voice faded thoughtfully. *Escape* was not a word she had ever associated with herself. *Escape* was a word for chattels, prisoners, caged birds. She looked slowly around her boudoir, pausing to hate in detail each one of the numerous cushions, carpets, and bejewelled wall hangings.

Liddy slapped her gently on the ankle. "Tsk. Put him out of your head, Chani. You know it's useless, even if he is the Shield's brother. You're the consort of the Lord in Earth, and there's no undoing that, not even in death. What would your brother say if he knew what you've been thinking?"

Chanithel picked up a tiny golden bead with her needle, and jabbed the point through the linen as if the fine cloth were her brother's skin. "Liddy," she said slowly, "there's something I want you to help me with."

***

High in the highest tower of Balimhavar, the Lord in Earth gazed through the golden bars that newly ornamented his window. How many thousands of times he had seen that view! City, sea, hills, insect-people. Yet now, day by day, it seemed to him that the colours were brightening, the edges sharpening, the haze thinning between him and the world. Absently, he reached for the ever-present chalice at his elbow—but as he brought it to his lips, he remembered the new game, and discreetly poured the equivalent of a good mouthful over the edge of the sill, shielding the move from the observers in the walls. The dark liquid dribbled down the surface of the stone, already mottled with five days' worth of wine stains.

This was a wonderful game, the rules of which had come to him while he was bored at some feast not long ago, surrounded as always by watchful diviners taking notes on everything he did, from breathing to blinking. It was on the Day of the Electa, of that he was reasonably sure, though he could not remember much else. What he could recall most vividly was discovering the strange delight of moving in one direction while the Recorder tried to prod him in another; and later, at the feast, the related pleasure of *pretending* to partake, knowing the diviners were assigning a potential significance to every bite and sip. What a joke, to make them wrangle for days over the meaning of a meal he had only feigned eating! And how entertaining it would be if he should go on misleading those prying clots with their omens and auguries and ever-vigilant eyes, even after the feast was over.

That was how he had come to invent *the game*.

The rules were simple. Appear to eat and drink, but in fact let nothing pass the lips. Find clever ways to dispose of uneaten food and wine. Invent dreams. Conceal or lie about the small events of the day. Make things up. Hide a smile when some heavy affair of state is decided on the basis of an idle jest.

Of course, the game had to remain secret. If the diviners discovered he was starving himself, they would go ahead and debate about *why*, about what message Heaven was sending, and the joke would be lost. The first couple of days had been difficult, but self-denial and hunger pangs were novel in themselves. Now the hunger pangs were not as sharp, and the longing to reach for his chalice was fading. He smiled at his world through the golden bars. This was the best joke ever.

***

Ten years of being a chattel-clerk with a captive stylus in hand. Ten years of recording words uttered in silken aristocratic accents, knowing that what he impressed into the wet clay was at best artful half-truths, and often outright lies. Ten years of keeping his eyes from rolling in contempt and disbelief, ten years of faithful, unprotesting service to highborn ingrates, of being a useful piece of furniture with a skilled hand. Any small pleasure Hari had taken so far in his terrifying new life had nothing to do with wool robes, soft beds and good food, and everything to do with saying what he had always wanted to say to the likes of Prefect Calviram Hithe.

A pleasure, he realized as he scanned the tablet, that he could not continue to afford. For five days, his fear had been of a general variety, a knowledge that nameless enemies were all around. Now the enemies had names. The recto of the tablet listed five distinct plots against the Electa and her family, two involving kidnap, and the others murder. All the Great Families except the Hithes, Fruhs and Sundes were party to various of the plots, with the Dreeves naturally taking the lead. One comprehensive massacre had been planned for the previous day—a day when the most perilous situation Hari actually saw involved Granny Dillah's stern disapproval of the after-dinner entertainment.

"There are more on the back," said Calviram.

"I've seen enough." But Hari turned the tablet over and made himself read through to the end. Two more, one of which was scheduled to be in progress at just about that moment. He strained his ears towards the sounds of the garden—Granny Dillah's chanting, the Electa's babble, an unrestrained shout of laughter from one of the Wild Men. Still safe. Thoughtfully, he handed the tablet back. "So?"

"So you need friends, Hari." The Prefect idly studied the dainty chasings on his chalice. "The good will of Heaven is not quite enough."

"The Shield Guard—"

"—can be trusted, of course. But alone, they cannot protect you. Without the Hithes, you would already be dead, seven times over."

"You've shown me a tablet. Even if it's the truth, it proves nothing."

Calviram sighed. "Then try another tablet. Here." Hari hesitated before reaching out for it.

This one was larger and tidier, and had been baked into permanence. Hari recognized the style of the hen-scratchings: Kovolis, the head clerk from the records hall, whose primary task was to record the deliberations of the diviners.

"Note," said Calviram, "the date and the seal. Seven days ago, two full days before the Day of the Electa. And sealed by the Recorder himself."

Hari raised his eyes from the tablet to give Calviram a long and—he hoped—inscrutable look before he began to read aloud. "*Trust not the seawind. Look to the eastern hills. A stain is washed away. A new promise is made. The stranger's blessings multiply. A woman arises.* Is this supposed to mean something?"

"I hope you are not questioning the wisdom of the diviners. Look at the fourth line."

"*A new promise is made.* But it doesn't say by whom, or to whom."

"Prophecies never do. Now the fifth."

"*The stranger's blessings multiply.*"

"The Lord in Earth shattered a piece of imported crockery in one of his tantrums. Quite a positive omen, if you happen to be a stranger. Now put them together, Hari. *A new promise is made. The stranger's blessings multiply.* Do you see?"

Hari scanned the backside of the tablet again. A headache started to throb behind his right eye, and the vulnerable patch on his back itched furiously. He said, "I suppose you think this nonsense has something to do with the Wild People. Otherwise, why would you show it to me? But not all of it fits, Prefect. *Look to the eastern hills.* The Wild Ones come from the west."

"Not all the messages from the Lords in Heaven are connected. They're not storytellers at a feast, they're pointing the faithful in certain paths. And this path is marked as clearly as the lines on your hand."

Sighing, Hari handed the tablet back. "You're proposing an alliance, I imagine. A Hithe bride to bring the Wild Ones into the family. Poor Cadon."

Calviram looked offended. "Now you're insulting the flower of Balim womanhood. But no, that is not what I had in mind."

"You not thinking of marrying him into one of the *other* Great Families?"

"Of course not."

Pondering, Hari moved his fingertip around the smooth rim of the chalice. "I heard one of the Domo's men talking," he said in a low voice, "about Heaven having sent Cadon to found a new Great Family. There's a rumour in the city—"

"It's one of many," said Calviram briskly, "but again, no. The divination tablet suggests nothing of the sort."

"Then what?"

Calviram raised his head as if testing the air. Outside, Hari heard Valdur's voice start up, rhythmic and melodic, and he inferred another poem had been born into the world. Then the Prefect put his hand on Hari's shoulder to pull him a little closer.

"Think about the titles of the god-king. Run through them in your mind."

Hari, a veteran of the scribal pool, had written the full set of titles perhaps a thousand times in ten years. He shrugged the Prefect's hand away. "As you like. Lord in Earth, obviously. Lion of the Western Horizon, Bull of the Eastern Horizon, Troth of Eternity, Promise of the Fixed Star—"

"Stop."

"The Fixed Star?"

"Further back."

"The Promise?" Hari's headache, pulsing softly, spread to the other eye. Damning his new dignity, he reached over his shoulder to scratch between his shoulder blades. "So?"

"*A new promise is made. The stranger's blessings multiply.* Think."

Scratching felt wonderful, and gave Hari an excuse not to answer for a moment, while he tried to decide which of them was howling mad: himself, for thinking Calviram was suggesting what he thought Calviram was suggesting; or Calviram, for suggesting it. "You're mad," he said finally.

Calviram sighed, and his mouth drooped as if he had abruptly been plunged into sorrow; but to Hari, the Prefect's eyes seemed just as bright as before. "Not at all," he said. "It grieves me, naturally, but the diviners have spoken, and we are no more than their humble chattels. The Lords in Heaven do not want a new Great Family. They want a new *Lord in Earth.*"

***

In the Electa's garden, among the bloated flowers and sculpted shrubs, Valdur was holding forth to an attentive audience consisting of Sashah and a couple of songbirds. Cadon, sprawled on a soft carpet laid out on the grass nearby, listened idly and fought sleep. He could understand most of the poem, and supposed it was very good, but he had Furin's soporific snores on the carpet beside him, and a gutful of rich, unfamiliar foods to digest. In fact, there was not much for him to do in the daytime except fight sleep.

They had already explored every corner of their new quarters and found them stuffy and overfilled with cushions and carpets, and far less comfortable than the open air of the garden, though the weak autumn sun gave little warmth.

Vigilance did not seem called for. They did not have to hunt, not with those vast heaps of provender arriving regularly, far more than the six of them could eat; five of them, rather, since Granny Dillah would not touch what she called "that muck". It was still too light for him and Furin to set off on their nocturnal reconnoiterings of the neighbourhood, which they kept secret since they thought both Hari and the Domo would disapprove. Surely this was not what the Old Ones had in mind for him when they sent him to the city. Cadon sighed and turned over, to see what point Granny Dillah had reached at her fire.

She had stopped chanting some time back, and knocked the cover off her firepit. Now she was rooting about in the fading embers with her hazelwood wand, head cocked, dragging what he guessed were figurine fragments from the ashes: rough little heads and torsos molded from lightning dust and rich garden earth, moistened with spittle collected from each of them and sun-dried for the past three days. It was not the first time he had seen this women's magic. If he shut his eyes for too long, he found himself floating back to the branch of an oak tree in a dark forest, Lusil on the branch above him, his mother and sister and little Luah, the dead mother of his neverborn children, below in a crowd of hushed women, back at the brink of the world's end. So he kept his eyes open, and turned his head to look anywhere but at Granny Dillah.

***

"Sit still, Villamar, for Heaven's sake."

But the Palace Master continued to prowl the Recorder's chamber, tripping over cushions and his own feet in his nervousness, pausing to stare unseeing at the crowded square below the window. "What if it doesn't work, Grandis? What if—"

The Recorder gritted his teeth. There were times he found it hard to credit that Villamar was truly a Dreeve. "Of course it will work. Do I really need to explain it again? The poison will soak in through the scalp; the Shield will be dead by morning, without a mark on him. The Lords in Heaven will condemn the crone as a sorceress—we'll make sure of that—and the rest of that pathetic crew will be easy meat. Villamar, old man, this plan is proof against failure."

"You said that yesterday. And the day before, and the day before that. It's almost…" the Palace Master's voice dropped fearfully, "…almost as if the Lords in Heaven really have sent us this Electa."

The Recorder drained his chalice and threw it with some force at the Palace Master. It bounced off the old man's chest and fell unharmed onto the cushions at his feet. The Recorder found himself wishing he could throw something sharper than a chalice. "Do *not* let me hear such nonsense from you again," he said levelly. "This debacle is the Hithe Faction's doing, not Heaven's."

"But—"

"No buts. This will work, because there is no plot for the Prefect's spies to uncover. Nobody knows about it except myself, and now you, and the little mage who poisoned the pomade for me, and he has already been silenced. By tomorrow the upstart will be dead. The Hithes will be in confusion, and our troubles will be over. How can this fail? Who can do without the attentions of the court hairdressers? In fact, they should be arriving there just about now, and then the deed will be done."

***

Dillah was worried at first that this alien dirt might not be suitable, but she was reassured by the crackle of tiny explosions, the click and patter of shards against the thicker clay of the firehood. The fire, as well, had spoken with a clear voice and an unusual degree of sarcasm. The Old Woman—who was clearly not dear little Sashah, whatever these rabid idiots believed—was back on speaking terms with her. Dillah raked through the ashes once more, to be sure she had retrieved the last identifiable splinter of shattered terracotta, however minute. Then she gathered all the fragments in one hand and cast them to the ground between her feet. The pattern was clear and confirmatory. The fire had not misspoken.

She glanced around. Hari was still in the reception room with his visitor. She could tell him later. It would be better to get on with plans and preparations first, and *then* tell him, in case he turned awkward. They could not leave him behind, not even if it meant tying him up and carrying him flung over Cadon's back. The fire was pointedly clear on the subject of Hari, if a little hazy on some other matters.

"Valdur," Dillah called out, "waken the others. I need to talk to you all."

Valdur obligingly picked up the Electa and strolled over to the firepit, pausing to administer gentle kicks to Furin and the Shield of the Electa on the way. Cadon was on his feet at once, so presumably had been dozing rather than sleeping. Furin mumbled and tried to turn over, but Cadon hauled him upright. Dillah waited until they were all seated on the grass beside the bed of royal velves. She sniffed disdainfully when Furin yawned and lay back again with his arms crossed over his face.

"I'm amazed at you, Furin Fox," she snapped, "lazing around day after day with a full belly and an empty head. You'll be soft as a grub in no time. And you, Cadon, you're almost as bad."

"If you'd just *try* the food," Furin said from under his arm, "maybe your temper would improve. What will you eat when you run out of jerky?"

"The same as you, Furin Fox, honest food from the forest, gathered with our own hands, the way the Old Man and the Old Woman taught us."

Furin uncovered his face and stared up at the watery sky. "What are you talking about?"

"We need to leave this place. That's what the fire said. We have to go back to the forest."

"Leave? Forest?" Valdur sounded dismayed. Furin only sighed. Cadon made no sound at all, and Dillah was, for once, unable to read his face. Was he unhappy at the thought of leaving this unnaturally easy berth? Was he going to rise in revolt at last? Since the death of the People, he had followed her and Furin as a child might, as if his rebirthing had actually remade him as a babe in arms. This would be an inconvenient time for him to decide he was a man after all. The fire had spoken, and she knew in her marrow that it had spoken wisely. They *must* leave. She continued watching Cadon's face, and after a moment he met her eyes.

"Why did we come here?" he asked.

"What?"

"Why did we come here?" he repeated. "Why did the Old Ones tell us to come to the city?"

"Oh. That. Well…" Dillah hesitated. She made an honest effort to cast her thoughts back to that night at the massif, to the words in the fire and the words afterwards. Had she been the first to mention the city, or had it been Furin? And why, indeed? It had seemed like a good idea at the time, sitting outside the shattered corpse-cave of the Ones Before with the stench of roasting loved ones in their nostrils, but that was as far as her planning had gone. It had been like telling Cadon to fly to the moon, or swim to the bottom of the deepest sea. Neither she nor, apparently, the Old Ones, had any idea of what Cadon was supposed to do once he got here. If anything.

"I don't know why we're here," she said finally. "Maybe there is no reason. Sometimes there just isn't."

"Let's leave tonight," Cadon said.

***

"A new Lord in Earth? You *are* mad. Also, that's blasphemy." Hari edged away from the Prefect.

"It's not blasphemy if Heaven wills it."

Hari gulped his wine. "We know very well where Cadon came from, and it wasn't Heaven. It was Lazoon."

"But remember the circumstances of his coming. Remember how he appeared magically out of the empty air at the Door of Heaven, having taken the form of a divine lagosh-beast—"

"He climbed up the side of the platform," Hari interrupted, "wearing a catskin. I was there."

"So was I. I seem to recall his theophany somewhat differently. My memory of it will shortly become the canonical version."

"But—the others? *They* certainly didn't come through the Door of Heaven."

"Truly, Hari? Do you know all the ways of the Lords Above? Do I? Who are we to question the Lords in Heaven?"

Hari stared at the intricate pattern of glazed tesserae that made up the floor. "But Cadon doesn't speak the Balim tongue. He knows nothing of the courtesies. He talks about an old man with a beard of leaves and his tongue sticking out, and an old woman who walks around in the forest carrying a snake in each hand. He just looks confused when I try to explain about the Lords in Heaven."

"He can learn the language, if he needs to. Not that he will need to. How often do we hear the voice of the Lord in Earth? The divine Filkamos spends most of his time in his chambers, in a drugged haze. Surely the divine Cadon could manage that much."

"*He's not divine.*" Hari slammed his fine chalice down onto the tiles. "What will the Lords in Heaven do if you dare to put an ordinary mortal on the throne of Balimhavar?"

"Filkamos was born a mortal, Hari. He was born in the usual way, and eats his daily meat and opens his bowels like any child of Earth. And when he dies, the divine breath that inhabits his flesh will pass on to a new vessel."

"You're plotting to assassinate the god-king," Hari said flatly.

"No," Calviram said in a silken, reasonable tone. "I'm planning to carry out the will of the Lords in Heaven. And by the way, I'm coming round to thinking that Heaven has not necessarily chosen Cadon to be its new instrument. Heaven has been whispering to me that the Shield's uncle—Furin?—might be a better choice. Then Cadon could remain the Shield of the Electa, and the Lazooner could be drafted into the diviners' college. Yes, come to think of it, it was the divine Furin who appeared in the Door of—"

"No! I won't allow it!"

"I'm not asking your permission. I'm telling you what's already in progress."

"What?" Wildly, Hari threw himself off the cushions to the archway looking onto the garden—which, it now occurred to him, had been far too quiet for the last few minutes. But they were all there, sober-faced around Dillah's little fire, talking intently with their heads close together. The Domo's guards watched impassively from the shadows. Calviram joined him at the door.

"Rest easy for now, Hari. Nothing is happening here yet. But when it does, you must play your part."

"What part?" Hari asked bitterly.

"The same as before, to keep the Wild Ones in order. Try to do a better job of it this time. No more clever ideas."

"I refuse."

"That would be unwise. This is for the best, Hari. As the Great Household stands, the Wild Ones are doomed. Grandis Dreeve will not stop trying to kill them until they're dead—and you will die with them, along with many innocents. There will be war among the great families if we do not move swiftly. This is for the sake of Balimhavar, Hari. Think it over. And until I return, go nowhere."

Hari was saved from answering by a stir at the gate. The Domo was ushering in a crew of seven court hairdressers, accompanied by powerful wafts from the pomades, perfumes, hair-oils and aromatic face-paints they carried in their kitbags. Out in the velve bed, Granny Dillah shot to her feet and, hands on hips, advanced on them with a ferocious expression.

"What's she saying?"

"She's making her feelings known," Hari said, "on the subject of court hairdressers."

"Perhaps we should find a role for her in the new order," Calviram said thoughtfully, as the Domo swept the hairdressers out of the gate with more speed and less ceremony than when they arrived.

***

After his visitor left, Hari stumped out to Granny's fire to join the others. Mournfully, he sat down beside Dillah, took Sashah into his lap and looked around the circle of faces. They looked back at him inscrutably. How could he tell them? They had no idea of the many dangers they were in, he thought sadly, perils far beyond the simple prospect of sudden death. Ruthless gamesmen surrounded them, plotting to scoop them up and throw them down in dire patterns on a gameboard they did not even know existed. Calviram offered temporary safety, assuming his plan went well, but its success would only set off a new round of plots and counter-plots among a new set of enemies. Its failure, on the other hand, would certainly spark off both a civil war and a massacre of Calviram's candidates. He may as well, Hari thought, pin targets to the backs of the Wild Ones, to ease the job for the poor overworked assassins.

Valdur broke the silence at last. "What did the Prefect want?"

"Nothing much," Hari lied. "He brought us his personal felicitations." He hesitated, looking from blank face to blank face around the fire. Suspiciously blank. If he did not know better, he would almost think they had been adding another to the midden of conspiracies accumulating in the centre of the Great House. "What were you talking about before I joined you?"

Cadon opened his mouth to answer, but shut it again with a sidewise glance at Granny Dillah. Valdur coughed pointedly, Furin stirred. Granny glared at them all, then reverted to being inscrutable, and began to gather up the mysterious litter of burnt clay around her feet. "We weren't talking about much of anything," she said blandly. She tossed the fragments into the remains of her fire. "Something else, Hari?"

"Yes," he said, "one thing." He cleared his throat, the better to speak with firmness and resolution. "We have to leave."

"Leave?" Her voice was guarded.

"Yes, we have to leave—as soon as we can—tonight." He clenched his fists, expecting pained references to plentiful food and soft carpets.

"Fine," said Granny calmly. "As soon as it's dark."

Chapter Twenty

The Lord in Earth Goes Forth

In Balimhavar, the sky was never completely dark. The five thousand eyes of the night were dimmed to a few hundred, the others blinded by torches lining the wall of the Great Household, and the cumulative glow of myriad lamps, candles and courtyard hearths. The brightest star of all shone from the tower where the Lord in Earth looked down upon his kingdom, knowing all and seeing all, even through thatch and timber, plaster and stone. But not this night.

In the temple, the great water clock finished filling, and wheeled over to start its ceaseless task of filling again. Its attendant priest shouted to another, who hurried to the temple tower to call curfew. In the Great Household, a horn answered the curfew call, heralding the change of watch. Thus was each diurnal division in the reign of the Lord in Earth measured, signaled, and recorded, as had been done from the beginning of the world, and would be done until its end, untold ages hence. But on this strangest of nights, many notable things were taking place in a few drips of the water clock, hidden from the sky and the god-king's tower.

***

In the darkest passages of the Great Household, five separate bands of assassins moved with the quiet assurance of snakes in a rathole. Three of the bands served one master, two of them another. Those in one party were already wiping their blades clean from the first strike. They had taken the Domo, that incorruptible worthy, in the moments before the watch-horn was due to sound—coming upon him as he rose from his supper, half a room away from his knives and pikestaff, and leaving him bleeding to death in his own wardroom along with eight of the Shield Guard. The Domo stopped breathing as the last echoes of the watch-horn faded, but by then the assassins were on the way to their next appointment.

***

Chanithel was in new territory: a state of being unattended and having to find her own path. She had never felt coarse linen next to her skin, nor walked in a body so free from metal trappings, horsehair stiffenings, hair ornaments and tormenting shoes. So this was how it felt to be a common chattel, unblessed by heaven's special favour. So this was how Liddy *always* felt. Not for the first time, Chanithel found herself envying her servant.

Liddy's directions were detailed and precise. Fourth arch to the left, third to the right, then along the edge of the Dowager's garden, making sure to tread softly in the margin of shadows. Chanithel could hear mouth-harps playing in the Dowager's cloister, but the garden was empty. Then she was through the gardener's little gate and into the stone-floored corridor to the laundry annexe, and beyond that a dank passage through the servants' precinct. She heard the watch-horn sounding the change of watch, but it held no fears for her. This route would take her clear across the Great Household without passing a wardpost. She sent the Lords in Heaven a prayerful blessing on Liddy's head—and just as quickly stifled her prayer, not wanting to call herself to the Lords' attention.

She passed no one, though she heard the laundresses chattering in the courtyard where steam billowed from the wide-mouthed laundry vats. More people for her to envy, though not after tonight's work was done. After tonight, she would be happy—as happy even as Liddy and the laundresses. She hurried on, clutching the little chest more tightly in her hand, and letting the image of a sun-dusted golden head light her way through the darkest reaches of the passage.

***

Liddy had seen Chanithel to the first turning, handed her the little chest of sweetmeats, and sent her on her path. It was not easy watching her mistress walk away to certain disgrace and painful death, but Liddy had spent much of the afternoon hardening her heart. Walking back to Chanithel's rooms in Chanithel's clothing, she began to feel power for the first time: the wonderful weight of gold on her head, the beautiful tight shoes encasing her feet, the billows of stiffened silk around her body. This was how she would live from now on. Let the Hithes fall—let Chanithel pile the fagots around the foot of her own stake—let the Lord of Drunken Groping have at her *all night long*. After tonight she would be more powerful than that wet kitten of a Chanithel was worthy or capable of being.

What a wastrel of her birthright that girl was. Sweet, yes. Liddy, who had become genuinely fond of her, was sad they would probably burn her in the end. In the normal way of things, of course, Liddy and the other chattels would have gone into the fire with her, which was another good reason to betray her. As it was, Liddy might be able to save the rest, if she felt like it at the time.

She reached Chanithel's preserve just as the watch-horn sounded. Not much time was left before the god-king's attendants would come to fetch his consort. Hurrying, she refreshed the tracing of kohl around her eyes and rubbed rose oil into her throat and bosom. Next the veil, covering her from crown to shoulders. *A woman rises up.* That prophecy had been all over the Great Household even before the diviners' tablet was dry, and all the gossip pointed to Damissel Dreeve replacing Chanithel Hithe as consort. But Liddy knew better.

***

Calviram knew to a nicety how he should be feeling. A touch of anxiety, since the Lords in Heaven could be so captious; a twinge of regret for his sister, a measure of fear at his own temerity. Nothing very serious. His own wives and children were safe in the Hithe stronghold, and all reasonable precautions had been taken. Therefore, he was surprised at the sharpness of his discomfort as he trudged up the great staircase at the appointed time, just as the watch-horn sounded.

He could not, he told himself, be feeling guilty. Chanithel was a daughter of the Hithes. She should feel herself privileged to die for the benefit of Balimhavar. Also, the tincture in the sweetmeats was said to work very quickly and almost painlessly. Since she had not had the good sense to become pregnant with an uncontested heir, she would otherwise have been buried alive in the god-king's airless tomb on the death of that fuzzwit Filkamos. He was doing his sister a favour. She should be grateful to him if she knew.

That thought sustained him as he took his place among the other court observers in the conjugal bedchamber of the Lord in Earth, behind the divination priests in the stands that rose along one wall. Some witnesses actually enjoyed this duty, though Calviram was bored by it. The Lord in Earth would be brought down from his tower and decanted onto the broad bed, where he would be joined by some potential receptacle for an heir presumptive. The mating would be carefully recorded, for purposes of both divination and authentication of the issue. And when the receptacle was the consort herself, potential mother of an uncontested heir, the number of witnesses would roughly double. Tonight, the stands were filling up.

There was the Palace Master in the row ahead, paler and more fidgety than ever; and there, among the priests, was Calviram's uncle Hillisam Hithe, who was not party to the conspiracy—*his* shock and grief had to be seen to be genuine. Sallik Hithe, however, hovering near the southern archway, nodded casually and looked away. From this, Calviram inferred that Sallik's bands of cutthroats and kidnappers—also known as concerned citizens and loyal subjects—were in their appointed places. Just beyond Sallik, Darrasat Dreeve caught Calviram's eye and gave him an ironic wave. There was another head Calviram would be happy to see off its shoulders. He smiled tightly and waved back.

Chanithel should soon be on her way up from the Great Household, Filkamos on his way down from the tower. Now Calviram was committed beyond any hope of pulling back. He had tossed a stone towards a still pool. There was no power now that could stop the stone breaking the waters, nor the ripples spreading outwards in dread patterns. Calviram felt a terrible itch to pray, but there was nowhere safe to direct his prayers.

Tomorrow, though: tomorrow he would be able to pray again. The Hithes would not be blamed for Filkamos, because Chanithel would die with him, and who would believe the Hithes would assassinate one of their own? In the panic, Sallik's cutthroats would go straight for the Recorder and the handful of heirs presumptive. Hithe forces strategically disposed around the Great Household would seize the temple and the divination college. Others would go to safeguard the Electa's preserve. He and Sallik would have the honour of conducting the Palace Master and the Highest Priest to a place of safety in a Hithe stronghold, whether they wanted to go or not. Paid newsmongers were standing ready to whip the mobs up against the Dreeves for the crime of deicide, and to remind the people of Balimhavar about the Electa's male relatives, fresh from heaven. By tomorrow, if all went well, the elder Wild Man would be legitimized as the Lord in Earth, and Balimhavar would be saved from a civil war.

Altogether, he thought, things were working out rather well.

***

The Recorder stopped pacing his chamber for a moment when the watch-horn sounded. "Farewell, Domo," he whispered. And farewell, he added under his breath, to the Hithes and their Fruh allies, to the false Electa and Shield, to the damned inconvenient consort Chanithel. The plot was laid out like a series of stones balanced on end, each one set to topple the next in turn. First the Domo, to leave the Electa defenseless; then every living thing in the Electa's preserve, to engender popular shock and outrage; and then, with paid newsmongers loudly accusing the Hithes of the massacre, the vengeance killings of high-ranking Hithes and Fruhs could begin. *A new woman shall rise.* Damissel would become the consort, of course, and produce an uncontested heir, and Balimhavar would be saved.

A lake of blood would be spilled on the way, but that was the fault of the Hithes. It was they who had forced these actions upon him. If they had left him to do the sensible thing on the farcical Day of the Electa—throwing the interlopers straight back into the great hearthpit, and personally plunging a lit torch into the matchwood—none of this would have been necessary. Or if they had even let him murder the Wild Ones quietly in the days since then…but again and again Calviram Hithe had foiled him. And now nothing less than a killing blow to the Hithe Faction would serve, which would draw in others of the Great Families, and Balimhavar would inevitably be forced into a civil war; one which the Recorder fully expected to win.

Altogether, he thought, things were working out rather well.

***

Granny Dillah had been pleasantly surprised to find Hari in full and eager support of the Old Woman's orders, almost as though he had been thinking along the same lines. There would be no need to carry him, bound and gagged, like an extra pack over Cadon's broad shoulder. On the contrary, he was most helpful with suggestions, and even sent one of the Shield Guards to the market to buy parcels of cheap cloaks, ropes, and good copper knives, on the pretext they were gifts for his family in Liske. The only protest came from Valdur, who collared Hari while he was minding Sashah in the chamber where equipment was being discreetly gathered.

"Hari, this is madness. We're prisoners here. There's no way we'll make it past the first guardpost."

"Cadon is the Shield of the Electa. He can order them to let us pass."

"And then what? How do we get out of the city?"

"I don't know! We'll take it as it goes. But once we're past the wall and into the fields, we'll make for the hills to the north, and then for the mountains."

"Do you call that a plan? And why does it *have* to be tonight? How can we leave everything behind like this?"

"We'll take our lives with us," Hari answered abstractedly, "and that should be enough." He was trying to remember Cadon's patient instructions on lacing up a spare pair of forest boots from Granny's pack, through Sashah's interested interference.

"But think what we'll be losing! A hundred chattels, herds of good beasts, all the treasures saved from the burning place. They're ours, we can't just leave them behind."

"They're Sashah's," Granny retorted as she came in and scooped up the child, "and she doesn't want them. Here, Sashah, something to make you nice and sleepy."

"Hari, you have to make them understand. How can we survive on nothing if we just up and leave?"

Hari stood up and gingerly scuffed along the floor in the forest boots. "We'll be with *them*, Valdur. I think we'll be fine."

"Well, what about the Electa's regalia? And the gifts sent to her yesterday by the Fruhs?"

"The regalia belong to the office of Electa, not the child. The gifts—too heavy. We'll be on foot, moving fast."

Valdur, in despair, surveyed the twenty-piece gold-and-onyx dinner service—the seven alabastra as long as his arm, glimmering like fresh snow in moonlight—the quilted mantles iridescent with feathers—the heavy collars of lapis lazuli, gold and carnelian from across the mountains of Meruh. Never had he seen such treasures in Lazoon. The gew-gaws of the king's wives were like pebbles in a box of pearls by comparison; speaking of which, he gazed with longing at Cadon's festal garment, delivered that morning and hung out on a rack ready for the next day's feast: silver-shot brocade densely sewn with the finest grade of pearls. Discreetly, he edged closer to the garment and began unpicking a few of the largest from their settings.

"Are you ready?" Furin came in carrying a pile of light blankets from his sleeping chamber, with Cadon on his heels. "We should go before the other guards come back."

Hari frowned towards the door. "The Domo isn't back? But I heard the watch-horn a few minutes ago. Who's on guard?"

"The round head and the broken nose."

"Just the two of them?"

"Just the two."

"No sign of the Domo?"

"Not a hair." Furin tossed some blankets over to Cadon, and began rolling the rest tightly for attachment to one of Granny's newly cobbled packs.

"I don't like the feel of this," Hari said slowly. The Domo was never late. They needed his protection at least long enough to survive to slip past him; but where was he? Hari's vague unease slid towards dread. Perhaps they were already struggling unaware in the sticky interweavings of several spiders' webs. He swallowed hard and took a deep, calming breath.

"Did you hear that?" said Cadon. "Somebody's pounding on the gate." He started towards the door.

"No! Let the guards answer." Yet Hari went to the doorway with Cadon and peered with him through the shadowed cloister, to the gate on the far side of the garden. "It's a girl," he said, "a servant."

"It's the Prefect's sister," Cadon said happily. He started forward. Hari pulled him back.

"She can't be the consort, dressed like that."

"But she is."

"Cadon's in the right." Granny, her old pack already bulging on her back and Sashah's sling empty on her front, joined them at the door.

"She looks very pretty," said Cadon, "without those things in her hair."

Granny sniffed. Hari squinted at the visitor. He had seen the consort Chanithel from a distance several times, and closer up on the Day of the Electa, and he was compelled to admit the resemblance was striking. "Let her in," he called to the guard.

***

Birdsong, garden scent, moonlight: the two of them sinking together onto smooth grass, with the honeyed taste of the potion still on their lips; and then…*all night long*. That was the idea. But as Chanithel crossed the garden, she realized she had put too much of her planning into reaching the Electa's preserve, and not enough into what would happen next. How could she have forgotten the rest of the Electa's family?

"Why are you here, Madame Consort?" the familiar asked in a hard but respectful voice. She remembered his face—Hari was his name, a Liskan ex-chattel according to rumours rampant in the Great Household. Ex-chattel or not, he was blocking her way, and he was reinforced by the crone and a tall, very handsome youth whom Chanithel belatedly recognized as the Shield of the Electa. From the door behind them, the older Wild One emerged with the Electa herself drowsing in his arms, but there was no sign of the one she had come to find. No, this was not going at all as she had imagined.

"Madame, I ask again. Why are you here, and why are you dressed as a servant?" The familiar's voice dropped. "Do you have a message from your brother?"

Chanithel caught her breath, blessing him. "Yes! A message."

The ex-chattel's face paled in the torchlight. He hushed an incomprehensible commentary from the Shield of the Electa. "What is it?"

"It's—it's a message for the one known as Valdur. For his ears only," she added in a rush.

"Valdur? Why Valdur?"

"Never mind. I have to speak to him, now. Alone."

The little man stared at her suspiciously. "Without an interpreter, Madame Consort? He's got a few words of Balim, but you won't get very far." He muttered over his shoulder to the others, and then, to her surprise, motioned to her to follow him through the door.

And there at last was the golden one, as breathtaking as in her dreams; he was, it appeared, intimately fondling a figure in a shimmering robe in the shadows. He turned hastily as they entered, and she saw with relief that the figure was not a woman, just a festal robe on a rack. After a moment, the golden one smiled at her and spoke a few words to Hari in his musical voice, and Hari answered with a long stream of nonsense speech. In Balim, Hari added, "Quickly, Madame, say whatever it is you have to say."

"Well," she said. Nothing came to mind. She could see Hari's impatience and sense the scrutiny of the others behind her. So much for birdsong and moonlight. Valdur was dizzyingly close, close enough that at last she could feel his warm breath on her face. She fumbled the ivory chest out of her sleeve with shaking hands. "Here," she whispered, holding it open between them where the Liskan could not see. "*Please.*"

"What's that? What are you trying to give him?"

Please, please, please. Valdur grinned at her and picked one of the sweetmeats out of the chest.

Hari shouted, "Stop!"—half a heartbeat too late.

***

From the moment the Lord in Earth entered the bedchamber, Calviram knew something was not quite right with him. His gait; the way he swung his eyes around the chamber as if he had never seen it before; the secretive little smile at the corners of his lips. Calviram sat up straight, and noticed a few others doing the same, including the Palace Master and several of the diviners. The god-king hesitated at the edge of the bed before sliding across to its centre. That, too, was abnormal. Usually he just collapsed onto it, giggling. The observers scratched frantically on their tablets. Then the Consort was conducted in through the opposite door, and Calviram forgot the subtle oddness of the god-king's manner in the knowledge that Balimhavar's very foundations were about to be shaken.

That idiot girl Chanithel did not remove her veil. Calviram cursed her under his breath. This was not only a breach of protocol, but damned inconvenient for the grand plan. The witnesses needed to see her face, so there would be no question later that a highborn Hithe lady had been murdered along with the Lord in Earth. But already she was reclining on the great silken bed beside the god-king, and then she was reaching into the sleeve of her outer bedgown and drawing out a little chest. Calviram clenched his hands in his lap to stop them shaking. And then the Consort was taking two glistening red sweetmeats from the chest and offering one to the god-king, who accepted it with a peculiar smile and lifted it to his mouth.

***

"Not very polite of her," Granny Dillah muttered. "Not that I want any part of that foreign muck, but it's the principle. Share the least and share the feast, that's what I always…"

"Hush!" Hari broke in. He strode to Chanithel and caught her by her wrists. "What was that? What did you give him?"

Chanithel gazed at him wide-eyed over a mouth fully engaged with the sticky sweetmeat. Valdur swallowed his and said slurrily, "Cherry in honey. Very nice."

"But why did she—how do you feel? Do you feel sick?"

"Should I?"

"Maybe you should! How do you know that wasn't poisoned?"

"Why would anyone want to poison me? Least of all—" and here Valdur gleamed a smile at Chanithel and broke into heavily but charmingly accented Balim, "—this beautiful jewel on the brow of the night."

"Save it," Hari snapped. "We're leaving. *This minute.*"

"That might be hard," Furin said from his position at the courtyard door, "on account of there's a crowd of men at the gate, and they've just killed the guards. And now," he added, more brightly, "they're fighting each other." His report was confirmed by the clashing of pikes, hoarse shouts, and one short *glug* of a scream.

***

A scream—a choke of agony, surprisingly loud--burst from deep in the girl's rib cage. Even Calviram, who was waiting for it, was startled. The girl's body, flat on the fleece of the royal bed, strained to arch and writhe against the boned silk of her bodice. So much for the tincture being almost painless. Then she went limp, and a bright scarlet splotch appeared on the veil over her mouth. The Lord in Earth rolled away from her—Calviram watched for a scarlet gout from the kingly lips to match the one rapidly spreading across Chanithel's veil, but heads got in his way. They were all standing now, the witnesses and divination priests, tablets clattering to the floor, gasps and whispers spreading along the rows. Calviram stood with them. The girl's back arched again, violently enough to burst her trappings. Her heels drummed on the bed, then slowed and stopped altogether. Beside her, the god-king lay unmoving on his belly.

From the archway, Sallik's voice: "Murder! Murder! The Lord in Earth has been poisoned!"

The witnesses and divination priests wrenched themselves out of their first shock. Suddenly this was not a good place to be—who could forget the scenes of horror the last time a god-king was assassinated, though it was thirty years in the past? Tablets and styluses crunched underfoot as the stand emptied towards the great stairway. Calviram vaulted over the back of the stand, out of the crush, and ran along the wall to where the ever-efficient Sallik had the Palace Master in a grip of stone. Hillisam was slumped against the wall beside them, clutching at his heart.

"This is *your* doing," Calviram snarled at the Palace Master for the benefit of the witnesses still in hearing, "and the Dreeves will pay dearly for these murders."

"No! We did not do this!"

"A murderer *and* a liar. My dear sister died with the Lord in Earth—who but the Dreeves would dare to murder them both?"

"No!" wailed the Palace Master, but he stopped abruptly and put his hand to his mouth. Reading his expression, Calviram almost grinned. So even the Palace Master could not be sure of the full extent of the Recorder's tangled plans. All the better.

"Villamar," he said, more gently, "I can half believe you are innocent in this, but your house is not. We know who to blame, don't we? You will come with us, and I will guarantee your safety—for the time being. One moment, Sallik."

A loose end to be snipped. Chanithel's veil had to be removed. Her face had to be clearly seen by the few witnesses who had not yet fled the bedchamber. Feeling an odd distaste for the task, Calviram climbed on to the bed and clambered across the yielding surface to where the two corpses lay side by side, two waxen dolls half-melted on a hot griddle. The girl's veil was dyed a solid scarlet, shockingly bright in the light of the many lamps. The god-king was sprawled face-down, with one arm flung over his head.

Calviram knelt by the girl's side, feeling far worse than he had anticipated. Was this sorrow for Chanithel? Guilt at sacrificing her? Or was it irritation at how even in death she could disappoint him? Down the great stairway and through the windows, he could hear newsmongers already rousing the sleeping city with the shocking news. The Lord in Earth was murdered! The Dreeves had brought the curse of the Lords in Heaven down upon Balimhavar! Calviram closed his ears to the growing clamour and, nerving himself, pulled away Chanithel's veil.

And reflexively twitched it back, and sat frozen for a second with a thunder of blood filling his ears. Then he carefully remodelled his face and looked over his shoulder. Sallik and the Palace Master. Arhal Fruh, an ally. A pale and shaken Hillisam Hithe. A trio of inconsequential divination priests from minor factions. An elderly Kilve who didn't matter, because he had fainted. Several terrified chattels who didn't matter either, because even if they had seen something they shouldn't, they would not be able to talk about it after Sallik had their throats cut. And a good sprinkling of Sallik's trusted toughs, sufficient for the job.

"Are you coming, cousin?"

"Presently, Sallik. You go on to the temple—leave me here for a few moments with my grief."

"Your—grief?"

"My grief, yes," snapped Calviram, cursing Sallik for his slowness on the uptake. "My beloved sister has been foully murdered. Of course I'm grieving."

"Of course," Sallik said smoothly, recovering, "as are we all. I'll leave an escort for you."

"No! Just go—we need to be sure the priests are safe. Take everyone with you. And when the temple is secure, come back and find me in my poor dead sister's quarters."

"Are you sure, cousin?"

"Go!" Calviram covered his face with his hands and sobbed aloud until the scuffle of feet down the stairs died away. Then he dropped his hands and yanked the veil away. He stared down furiously at the blackened face of his sister's bodymaid.

"Damn Chanithel. *Damn her.* How could she do this to me?"

Calviram tumbled off the bed and yanked Liddy's body to the edge by her ankles. Nobody must see her. Everybody must think a high Hithe lady had died tonight. The consequences otherwise were too dreadful to contemplate. But there was still time to make things right—it was unlikely anyone would dare to approach the corpse of the Lord in Earth until well towards dawn, and most would be busy until then anyway, either killing or trying not to be killed. With a groan of effort, he hoisted Liddy onto his shoulder and staggered forward for a few feet, with no clear idea of where he was going. Nobody was on the stairway—but he heard screaming below in the middle foyer, and above in the concubines' dormitory in the tower. He cast around, panting under Liddy's dead weight.

The corbelled doorway on the far wall gave onto an open gallery overlooking one of the Household gardens. On a desperate inspiration, Calviram lugged Liddy over to it and threw the door open. The gallery was deserted, the garden below lost in shadows. Quickly, he stripped Liddy's body of the Hithe jewels and the consort's veil, and cut away the telltale bodice and stiff silken skirt. As an afterthought he slit her throat open to suggest a different cause of death, and then hoisted her to the top of the balustrade and tumbled her over. In the morning she would be just one corpse among many murdered on that bloody night, with nothing to connect her to the god-king's bed.

Especially if the *correct* body was in that bed by daybreak.

A variety of ceremonial daggers and swords had been dropped by the witnesses and diviners in their precipitate departure. Calviram bundled Chanithel's things into her skirt, and slung the bundle over his shoulder. Then he picked up a couple of extra daggers, and grimly set off to find his sister.

***

"Shouldn't we help them?" asked Cadon.

"Which ones, boy?" said Dillah. "They're all dressed the same." Lips pursed in distaste, she observed the struggling combatants through a screen of ornamental shrubbery. "Valdur," she added, "can't you stop that girl whimpering? Pat her arm, or something. She seems to like you."

"What shall we do?" breathed Hari. Clearly they could not hide for long in that narrow cloister between the shrubbery and the wall, because whoever won the war at the gate would certainly come looking for them. For his part, he was half-ready to march out into the battle and do his best to get in the way of one of the swords, on the theory that a quick end would be better than the agonizing one he saw ahead for them all. But how could he abandon his charges?

"I've had enough of these damned stupid savages. Let's go the other way." Furin was also watching through the bushes with disgust, and he spat on the grass as he turned away.

"There is no other way," Hari whispered dully. "We're trapped."

They ignored him. "What about the Prefect's sister?" asked Cadon, looking over Hari's shoulder at the dim oval of Chanithel's face as she clung to Valdur's arm.

"We're trapped," Hari repeated, a little louder.

"Well, we can't leave her here," said Furin, "not with those madmen hacking at each other in the garden. It's not safe."

"So we'll take her somewhere safer, and leave her there," Dillah said firmly, hitching her pack higher on her back.

"You're not listening to me. I said, we're *trapped*."

"Don't be silly, Hari. Cadon, it's time to leave." Dillah took the sleeping Sashah from Furin's arms, and worked her into the carrier sling. Hari turned to remonstrate with Furin, but Furin had vanished—and Cadon as well, Hari suddenly realized. He peered around wildly.

“How did you do that? Where have they gone? Have you—” Hari gulped, “have you made them invisible?”

“Don’t be a fool, Hari. They’re up there.”

Hari followed her gesture in the darkness. The walls of the garden courtyard were well-fitted stone blocks, rising sheer to almost three times Hari’s height and swelling inwards in a gentle curve to form a parapet at the top. Dimly, he could make out one tall silhouette already swarming up over the edge of the parapet, while another shadow, spiderlike and only slightly darker than the wall, was halfway up and climbing fast.

Hari brushed his fingers unbelievingly across the surface of the stonework. “How can they—?”

“Any child of the People could climb that wall,” Dillah whispered. “I could do it myself, ten years younger and without a tyke strapped to my chest. How do you think they’ve been getting out every night?”

“I didn’t know they had.” The end of a rope dropped past Hari’s nose. Granny Dillah pushed past him to tie the other packs to it, then gave it a tug. Smoothly, the packs dwindled up into the darkness.

“I’ll take Sashah up next, Hari, then the three of you come up, one by one. Unless you can climb up on your own.”

“I don’t understand.” Then the rope hit the ground at Hari’s feet again, and Dillah deftly caught it up and looped it around herself. A quick jerk on the line, and abruptly her feet were higher than Hari’s head, and all he could see of her was a dim and diminishing bulk above him. The battle-sounds thickened on the other side of the shrubbery—he twisted to peer fearfully through the leaves. It seemed more combatants had arrived since the last time he looked, and the fighting had spread farther across the garden to within a perilous few armlengths of their cover. More distant noises—shouts and shrieks—suggested the sleeping city was wakening into bloody chaos. Hari glanced up urgently, in time to receive a gentle slap in the face from the rope as it fell. He peered upwards, and dimly perceived Granny Dillah waving briskly at him from the darkness at the top of the wall. He took a deep breath.

"Valdur, this may be madness," he hissed, "but it's our only chance. Valdur?"

No reply. Except for himself, the shadows of the cloister were deserted.

***

Alone, truly alone. No concubines, no diviners, no observers in the walls. Filkamos rolled over and sat up. He dropped the bright red sweet onto the bed and wiped his hand on the fleecy counterpane. The girl had eaten one, and died. He had not eaten one, and lived. Therefore, the sweetmeats were poisoned, and it followed from *that* that somebody had tried to assassinate him. That surprised him, though it amazed him even more that he could pursue the logic through to its endpoint. It seemed a long time since he had even thought about thinking. He crawled to the edge of the bed, shedding the outer two layers of his bedclothes on the way.

The room was drearily familiar in one way, utterly strange in another. He sat on the edge of the bed for a few moments, trying to decide whether or not he was enjoying himself. On the whole, he concluded he was not. Solitude was a disappointment. The game of artful self-denial no longer entertained him. The novel clarity of the world was no longer pleasant, or even interesting. On the contrary, he was beginning to feel sick with hunger and thirst, and his whole body was crying out for a chalice of the soothing tincture. Small sounds began leaking out of his throat, sounds he could not remember himself making before, though he had heard them often enough when he hurt the concubines.

But was he not the Lord in Earth? Was he not brother to the Lords in Heaven? According to the orthodox wisdom, nothing and no one could harm him. Therefore, he told himself, it could not be fear that brought him to a startled crouch beside the bed when he heard many heavy boots thudding down the stairway from the tower; neither could it be fear that propelled him through the corbelled doorway, in the last heartbeat before the boots hit the bottom stair.

Chapter Twenty-One

The Night of the Savages

Strong hands reached out to pull Hari over the edge of the parapet. He lay panting for a moment on the broad stone ledge, not from exertion, but from the vertiginous discomfort of spinning up through the darkness on the end of a spindly rope. Welcome, he thought dizzily, to the world of the Wild Ones. Opening his eyes, he risked peering over the edge at the battle in the garden, which was clearly winding down. Eight assailants against three, then against two, and then against one desperately sword-swinging figure amid a litter of corpses. As Hari watched, that one fell as well. The victors consulted for a moment before fanning out across the garden and into the chambers of the Electa's preserve.

A smaller but also strong hand pulled him away from the edge. Granny Dillah, crouching beside him, put her mouth close to his ear. "We saw Valdur and the girl slip around the end of the shrubbery. Why did they do that? Did they say anything to you?"

"Not a word. They were right there—and then they weren't. So I came up."

Dillah grunted softly and shifted Sashah's sling a little on her front. "There's something wrong. This is not what the fire led me to expect."

Furin's voice hissed from further along the parapet, a quiet sibilance that only just reached Hari's ear: "Dillah, we're leaving. We can worry later about what the dratted fire said."

"Aren't we going to wait for them?" But even as he spoke, Hari heard a shout from below, and a furious agitation of the shrubbery. The searching figures converged on the end of the cloister where Valdur and the Prefect's sister had vanished.

"No point," whispered Furin out of the darkness, "because they've just been found." Hari heard him sigh as if in regret, and then whisper, "Move on, Cadon."

Disbelieving, Hari caught at Dillah's sleeve. "Are we just going to leave them?"

"Yes, boy, of course we are."

"But—"

She pulled his head close to her mouth again and hissed into his ear. "Hari, they chose a different path. We watched them choose it. And now we go on without them."

"But—"

"*Hush.* It would make no sense to go back for them, and we of the People prefer things to make sense. Now *come.*"

Hari raised his head high enough to see the pack-swollen figures of Cadon and Furin ahead on the parapet, crouched low and already moving towards the unknown with silent, fluid speed. Dillah followed on, not much inconvenienced by the sleeping child in the sling. Hari indulged in a last glance into the garden before crawling after them. In his heart, he was grieving for Valdur, of whom he had become fond, while also wanting to throttle the lost Lazooner for leaving them without a parting word. Indeed, it was unlikely they would ever know Valdur's fate, though Hari doubted it would be a long or a rosy one. He had time to distinguish two small prisoners within a circle of very large captors before Granny kicked back at him to remind him to move.

***

As the troopers converged, Valdur glanced once over his shoulder towards the top of the wall. Shadows flowed along the parapet against the darker sky, barely visible unless one was looking for them—and then they were gone. Without regret, Valdur wished the Wild Ones and the Liskan a safe journey to whatever horrendous wilderness they were so determined to reach, and put them out of his mind.

One of the troopers growled a question, of which Valdur could understand about half, but it was the prefect's pretty sister who answered. As far as he could tell, she was stoutly denying any knowledge of the whereabouts of the Electa, and demanding to be taken to the Prefect Calviram Hithe. No longer clinging to his arm, she stood imperiously by his side in an attitude that was at odds with her humble garb and former timidity.

Eight swords already dripping blood were raised around them. Valdur had a momentary qualm—perhaps parting company with the Wild Ones was not such a good idea after all. On the one hand the girl did seem remarkably well-disposed towards him, and she was the prefect's sister, and Valdur had grasped at her as his best means of not being dragged out of the lovely city and into some ghastly forest. On the other hand—*eight swords dripping blood.*

***

Something was wrong, outrageously wrong, and not just in the Great Household. Chanithel did not need the shrieks of distant murder to tell her that—bloodshed in the sacrosanct Electa's preserve was already a powerful sign of the overall wrongness of things in general. She had been terrified earlier, crouching behind the shrubbery with her beloved and his mysteriously vanished family. Now, however, menaced by the swords of thugs whose allegiances she did not know, she fell back on her early training in how to deal with the lower orders.

"You will take us to the Prefect Calviram Hithe. *Now.*"

The leading thug lowered his sword infinitesimally. "Who are you, woman? Where is the Electa?"

"I have no idea where the Electa is," she said frostily. "Now take us to the Prefect Calviram Hithe."

"Why," the strongarm asked in a mocking voice, "would the Prefect stoop to receive a bodymaid? Unless of course, you're a chattel of the Hithes, in which case you're in for a very bad time tonight, my girl. Are you a Hithe chattel?"

Chanithel's heart contracted, but she kept her nose in the air and her voice cool. "That is not your business, trooper. You will take us—"

"We will take not take you anywhere." The strongarm motioned for a torch, and held it first close to her face, and then to Valdur's. He whistled softly in surprise. "Lords in heaven! It's one of *them*—the Electa's kinsman. So where are the others, woman? I'll give you one chance to answer, and I'll cut your heart out if you don't. *Where are they?*"

"Up," Valdur broke in unexpectedly. He moved his arms in an eloquent gesture towards the stars. "They go up, up, up, as smoke when rising. Gone back to heavens." With a superb show of teeth, he smiled at the strongarm commander. Almost as one, the eyes of the troopers lifted to survey the dark, star-spattered sky, before falling again to the Lazooner's confident face.

"Sir?" faltered the second in command after a few seconds of wondering silence. "Are we still going to kill them?"

"What else are we here for?" the commander replied, but he too sounded uncertain to Chanithel's ears.

"But sir—no living thing has left the Electa's preserve, yet there's nobody here."

"What are you saying?"

"That maybe…maybe it's true the Electa and the others have gone back to the heavens. So maybe it would be blasphemous to kill these two, because maybe—"

"I'm not going to argue with you. We have our orders."

"Hold off on those orders for the moment." A sharp voice from the gate. The troopers started and turned, raising their swords and then lowering them again. Chanithel gulped back the taste of fear. She knew that voice, and therefore she knew who had just won this small corner of the struggle among the great houses.

Darrasat Dreeve moved out of the shadow of the gate and into the circle of torchlight, followed by a fair number of hulking men, also armed. He gazed long at Chanithel's face, clucked his tongue, glanced at Valdur, and returned his eyes thoughtfully to Chanithel. Staring back, Chanithel was unpleasantly struck by his resemblance to his repellent sister Damissel Dreeve, especially to Damissel gloating over the success of some nasty-minded chicanery in their school days, or in the petty rivalries in the Great Household. Somehow, the habit of loathing one Dreeve gave her a measure of strength when faced with another. She lifted her chin in defiance, but Damissel's brother laughed softly and made a gesture of respect so exaggerated that it was an insult.

"Uncle?" he said. "You must come see this miracle."

From the shadowed ranks behind him, an old man flanked by two wary guards moved forward into the light. Chanithel managed not to whimper, but it took *all* her early training. And here she had thought things could not get worse.

"A miracle indeed," said the Recorder, reaching out to pat Chanithel's cheek. "In fact, of all the many wonders taking place tonight, this may be the greatest. I believe you told me, Darrasat, that not half an hour ago you watched with your own eyes as the Consort of the Lord in Earth was assassinated in the very bed of her husband."

"Indeed I did, Uncle—yet here she is."

"I see that. The newsmongers in the city are crying out against us for her murder, and yet—here she is."

"Chanithel Hithe," Darrasat agreed with relish, "living and breathing."

The commander shifted uneasily and raised his sword. "So—do you want us to kill her, revered sirs?"

"Oh no," the Recorder purred, "we want you to keep her safe. In fact, we're anxious that not so much as a thread of her garment be harmed, not until this miracle is better understood."

"And the Electa's kinsman?"

Darrasat favoured Valdur with a longer look this time, and the Recorder's eyes narrowed thoughtfully. Chanithel risked a glance sideways, and saw with horror and admiration that Valdur was smiling back at the Dreeve lords with serene assurance, though he was showing the good sense to keep quiet. At last the Recorder asked the commander, "Are you certain the Electa and the others are not here?"

"No sign of them, revered sir. This one said—"

"We heard what he said. Up into the heavens. Fancy that. No, don't kill him, either. In fact, bring the two of them along."

"Revered sir?"

"We are going," said the Recorder, "from the site of one miracle to the site of another. Lively, now."

***

Calviram had stalked forth from the divine bedchamber with no thought but to scour the Great Household for his wayward sister. Chaos was spreading, and all Balimhavar was becoming the watershed for a river of blood—what a pity if it flowed to no good purpose because that stupid little trull, his sister, could not follow simple instructions. He should be a presence in the temple now, ostentatiously protecting the priests; he should be establishing the Hithes immovably on the highest moral ground; he should be ensuring the Recorder's head and body had parted company. At that thought, his teeth ground together.

It was not hard to dodge trouble, when trouble was making so much noise—shrieks, shouts, dying bellows, the clashing of bronze blades. Calviram gave a wide berth to the Electa's preserve, where a pitched battle was in progress. Ten men he had sent there to safeguard his protégées, ten of the best, though he was no longer sure he needed the Wild Ones to survive.

There were other skirmishes to avoid, and a few manned watchposts where he had to bully his way through, and he arrived at the entrance to the Great Household sweating under his heavy robe and breathless with impatience. The entrance guards were thankful to see him and full of questions—what was going on? Was it a coup? Why had they not been relieved at the sounding of the watch-horn? Calviram brushed off their questions and, as a Prefect of the Great Household, ordered them to let no one but Sallik Hithe pass the gate.

The forecourt, normally twittering like a birdhouse with the voices of women and children, was empty and eerily quiet. Not that Calviram cared: dead or fled or barricaded in their boudoirs, the fate of the god-king's other women made no difference to him. Finding Chanithel was all that mattered. Stealthily, he slipped along the corridor to her antechamber. Best not to frighten her, he thought; he preferred to have her walk to the god-king's bedchamber on her own feet. So he hid his little daggers in the bundle of fine clothing he carried, and pushed open the door to the antechamber.

"Chanithel," he called, "little sister, it's your brother Calviram. You can come out, child, I'm not angry with you. I've come to take you to safety." He put on a forgiving smile and parted the door-curtain to Chanithel's boudoir. The chamber, scattered with cushions and bright weavings and fragrant with Chanithel's perfumed oils, was empty.

Cursing, he ransacked the boudoir, then the rest of Chanithel's suite, finding nothing alive but a cage of birds and a couple of terrified undermaids hiding under a pile of cushions. He slit the throat of one to encourage the other to tell the truth; and when it was clear she knew nothing of where Chanithel had gone, he cut her throat too, for the sake of her silence, and raged to the forecourt of the Great Household. Sallik was just arriving at the entrance.

Calviram greeted him without ceremony. "Listen to me, Sallik. No time for questions. Chanithel is not dead. We need to find her and shut the mouth of anyone who might have seen her alive. We'll start here in the Great—"

"That will not be necessary, cousin," Sallik interrupted. "I know where Chanithel is. And I warn you, you're not going to like this."

***

Parapet became rooftop; rooftop gave way to raised terrace, terrace to ledge, ledge to rooftop, all set high above stone-paved courtyards and dim gardens of the Great Household. Their nightly excursions had given Cadon and Furin a reasonable grasp of routes through this difficult manmade terrain, and even though the backpacks encumbered them and Hari turned out to have a fear of heights, they crossed the Great Household and the outer palace at the equivalent of a good stiff walking pace. With a joyful heart, Cadon climbed and leapt and helped Furin haul the others up and across awkward places. Soon, this would all be left behind: the white manbuilt canyons cut by reeking streets, trodden by too many feet; the many-layered stench of the city, once so exciting; the crushing pressure of too many strange faces and strange voices, the cloying food and too-soft cushions. All that lay ahead of them now was clean forest and clear air.

They stopped to rest on a gently sloping rooftop not far from the tower that dominated Balimhavar, which they knew marked the location of the main temple square. Not the best place to stop, Cadon thought, as they were perched just above a raised gallery on which he had seen people walking a couple of nights before, and below that was a large square of trees where tonight screams came periodically out of the shadows. But even Furin and Dillah were puffing after the last scramble, and Hari looked like he had died on the spot where they dumped him, though he moaned when Cadon poked him.

"Which way now, far-uncle?"

Furin wiped his streaming forehead with the tail of his weskit. "Straight on, and bear left at the end. That'll put us just a leap from the outer wall."

"Hush." Dillah put her hand on Furin's arm. "*Listen.*"

Cadon heard it too. Something between and a grunt and a sob. Then a thud. Then the sound of a man weeping. After a long moment, Furin crawled to the edge of the roof and peered over.

"There's a man down there," he whispered, "weeping."

"Obviously," said Dillah.

A hand groped over the rim of the rooftop, then a second hand, scrabbling for purchase. Furin reared back. The hands vanished. There was another thud.

"Help him up," Dillah snapped.

"What?"

"Help him up. *Now.*"

Furin grumbled to himself, too far under his breath for Cadon to hear the words. But a moment later when the hand reappeared, he grabbed it. "I hope you know what you're doing," he remarked to Dillah. Cadon reached over the side as well and caught a handful of somebody's robe, and together they hauled the newcomer up like a drowned swimmer out of a river and laid him out on the tiles. Immediately he sat up and drew his knees to his chest. His robe flashed silver in the meager light. He wiped his dripping nose on the sleeve and gulped back a sob.

"Fine," said Furin, "we helped him up. Now what?"

Granny slid her arms back into the straps of her pack. "Now we take him with us."

"We do *what?*"

"You heard me. Here, he can carry Valdur's pack. That will lessen Cadon's burden a little."

Furin started to answer, but somewhere below them a door banged open and many booted feet stamped along the gallery which the newcomer had so recently occupied. Cadon held his breath until the tramping died away towards the centre of the Great Household. Then Furin exploded in a ferocious whisper, "Good for you, Dillah. You've just won the all-time award for halfwitted foolishness."

"*Hush.* The fire told me that we would be six, and it also said that we must take Hari for sure. Naturally I assumed Valdur was the sixth, but it appears Valdur had other ideas."

"So now you think this—this blubbering idiot is the sixth?"

"Yes." Dillah tossed Valdur's pack to Cadon, and nodded towards the newcomer. "In fact, I'm starting to wonder if he's the reason we came to the city."

"To find this helpless fool? To take him with us?"

"We're wasting time, Furin Fox."

"But he couldn't even climb up here on his own! He's more handless even than Hari!"

"Thank you very much," Hari mumbled, stirring. Cadon was relieved. It was Hari's first sign of life in some time.

"And what if he doesn't *want* to come with us?" Furin went on, ignoring Hari's interruption. "Have you thought of that? Are you going to be the one who knocks him out and carries him, Dillah?"

"No," Dillah said sweetly, "since I'm already the one carrying Sashah. But I'm sure that won't be necessary, and I'm sure he'll have no trouble keeping up, with your gracious assistance. Hari, tell our new best friend that he's coming with us and it's time to go, will you?"

Hari sat up, groaning, and squinted through the darkness at the newcomer. He froze. After a moment, he slid himself closer on his bum, and thrust his face nearly nose-to-nose with the other. Then he collapsed gently onto the tiles again, and covered his eyes with one forearm. "O dear Lords in Heaven," he breathed.

"Is there a problem?" asked Dillah.

"I think there might be."

"Never mind, just get on with it. Tell him he's coming with us."

Obediently, and without uncovering his eyes, Hari spoke to the newcomer in oddly flat Balim. He said only a short phrase or two, Cadon noticed, yet the stranger responded with a spring-flood torrent of words in a passionate whisper. He stopped only when another shriek from the garden cut hideously through the night.

"He says yes," Hari translated.

***

Filkamos accepted his burden with surprise and hefted it curiously on his back. So this was what it felt like to carry something. Interesting, he thought, though he could already tell it was the sort of experience that would quickly pall on him. And where were the meat and fruit he had ordered? Plus the three concubines, the masseur, and the large draft of his very special wine? The little man had said something about him accompanying his worshipful servants, and he had agreed, for it certainly did not please him to stay where he was, nor to return to where he had been. Still, he did expect to have his commandments carried out first. The tall one, however, was already striking out along the rooftop in a willowy version of a scramble, and the others were rising to follow. Intrigued, Filkamos rose with them.

***

Two small armies confronted each other beside the empty expanse of the god-king's bed.

"We could start killing each other now," said the Recorder mildly from the centre of his phalanx of guards, "or we could talk first. Myself, I think we should talk."

Calviram's eyes were fixed on his sister, woodenly upright between two Dreeve toughs on the other side of the chamber. "Then talk," he said bitterly. It was too late now for him to kill the little slut himself, and there was no chance the Dreeves would oblige—what better proof could they produce that they were falsely accused of her murder? Beside him, one of Sallik's men growled and raised his sword, and Calviram reached out and pushed the sword down. "Talk, damn you," he repeated, "and start by telling me what you've done with the mortal shell of the Lord in Earth."

"You're asking if we stole the god-king's corpse? Not so far as I know, Prefect. I thought maybe *you* did. No? So it appears we are all witnesses to yet another wonder."

"What are you talking about, Dreeve?"

The Recorder shook back his long sleeve and counted off the miracles on his long, bejeweled fingers. "First, the resurrection of the Consort, as you can plainly see. Second, the ascension of the Electa and the Shield. Third, the vanishment of the Lord in Earth."

Calviram felt exactly as if the floor had shifted under his feet. "What was the second one?"

"The ascension of the Electa? Have you not heard? It appears the Electa and her entire faction rose into the air and wafted themselves back to Heaven."

"I suppose that means you had them murdered."

"Murdered? Nothing of the sort, Prefect, I assure you. Truly I do. Here, ask the one who stayed behind."

The Dreeve troops parted, and Valdur Il Jinoon was pushed forward. He smiled warmly at Calviram.

"Valdur?"

The Lazooner raised his hands and eyes elegantly towards the ceiling. "Up," he said. "Up to heaven. Farewell them all." And then, with casual grace, he eluded the trooper clutching his shoulder and seated himself on the edge of the god-king's conjugal bed. The Dreeve commander, horrified at this blasphemy, lunged forward to drag him away, but the Recorder put out a restraining hand.

"I do believe that might be construed as a sign," he said, gazing significantly at Valdur. "Don't you agree, Prefect?"

Calviram opened his mouth, fully intending to tell the Dreeve bastard where to stuff his accursed signs, his hostages, and the entire Dreeve clan; but he stopped abruptly and stared at the little Lazooner taking his ease on the glittering counterpane of the Lord in Earth. "Why, yes," he said slowly, "you're quite right, Grandis, that's a sign. In fact, it's about as clear a sign as I've ever seen. Shall we talk this over, you and I?"

***

Chanithel blessed her stars that she was wearing the light and relatively comfortable garb of a bodymaid. In her own clothes, she doubted she could stand such a long time on her own feet, with her knees alternately melting and stiffening with terror. It was bad enough being a captive of the Dreeves, but it was worse staring across the chamber into her own full brother's eyes and seeing nothing there but a cold murderous anger. And now the two of them, Dreeve and Hithe, were conferring in low voices by the gallery door, and she knew with perfect certainty that her personal fate was being decided along with the corporate fate of Balimhavar.

Her eyes fell on the golden emissary from Heaven—for now she was quite sure that he was that—comfortably seated on the conjugal bed of the Lord in Heaven. He looked up and smiled at her, and on impulse she stepped out from between her guards and sat down beside him on the bed. There was a loud enough murmur at that to catch the attention of the Recorder and her brother.

"The signs are coming down like spring rain tonight," the Recorder remarked. Defiantly, Chanithel reached out and took Valdur's hand—let them bury her alive for that, she thought, but she was tired of being afraid—and to her surprise, the lords of the two great houses nodded as if in approval and returned to their low-voiced conference.

***

"Trusting you—*you*—how odd that feels, Grandis Dreeve. Well, if I must, I must."

"We must indeed trust each other, my very dear Calviram." The Recorder's long-toothed smile reminded Calviram of an elderly but still dangerous rat-prince. "You do not want the other houses scrutinizing your crimes committed this night."

"*My* crimes, Grandis?"

"Our crimes, then. Much better that we ally ourselves than have all the others allied against us. The last thing we want is a bloodbath from which neither of our houses can profit."

"Agreed."

"Very wise. So let us run through it one more time." Again, the Recorder counted off on his fingers. "We jointly attest to the miracles wrought tonight by the Lords in Heaven, who sent the Electa and the Shield down to gather Filkamos to themselves—"

"—and to carry him up to heaven in clouds of glory," Calviram finished. "We shall need to arrange witnesses."

"That is not a problem. In return, the emissaries from the Lords in Heaven have left behind one of their own ineffable kinsmen to assume the burden of being the Lord in Earth."

"I assure you," said Calviram, "that Valdur will play his part beautifully. He's a talented lad. And then there's Chanithel."

"Of course, my dear Prefect—that is, my dear Palace Master. The blessed Consort, struck dead by the nearness of the Lords in Heaven as they lifted up the Lord in Earth, has been resurrected in this world as a token of their special favour and their desire that she should continue in that role. And in return—"

"—Damissel becomes the new Electa. You continue as Recorder, I become Palace Master. I think that's a fair distribution. The Electa and Shield go to you, the Consort and Lord in Earth to me."

"That is not how we'll present it to the other houses."

"The other houses," Calviram said, "must surely see how Balimhavar will benefit from such a fine balance of the powers." He smiled at the Recorder, thinking how much better the old sod would look with a slash across his throat. Then he let his smile fade. "Shall we—" he paused tactfully, "—require a new Domo of the Shield Guard?"

"Yes, my dear Palace Master, I rather think we will." The Recorder spread his hands in a gesture of grief. "Alas, what a good man he was. I'd suggest one of the Kilves, perhaps. I think we could both trust a Kilve to take his oath seriously."

"I was thinking of my cousin, Sallik Hithe."

"My *dear* friend. How can you jest, when I shall soon be in mourning for my own beloved cousin, the late Palace Master."

Calviram conceded the point gracefully. "One of the Kilves, then. And that's the end of it, I think. Shall we?"

The great lords embraced. Their kiss, the seal of a new pact, sounded like a slap in the hushed chamber.

***

Valdur, calmly stroking the lustrous silken counterpane with his free hand, looked up in time to see the Prefect and the unpleasant old man coming out of a close embrace. It seemed to him, as a performer adept at hiding his thoughts and revulsions, that the Prefect's diplomatically blank expression was concealing a frantic desire to wipe his lips. Instead, Calviram began to issue orders to both factions of the troopers, while the old man nodded approvingly in the background. Valdur caught many of the words: temple, great household, spread word, bring priests, stop killing. In moments the room was almost empty of troopers.

When only a few remained, Calviram bowed politely to the old man and strode across to the god-king's bedside. He picked up a bundle of clothing from the floor—sumptuous stuffs, thought Valdur, rainbow silks worked in gems and pearl-picked embroideries—and thrust them at his sister with a few sharp words. Then he turned to Valdur and pointed to a couple of equally beautiful robes lying abandoned in the middle of the bed.

"Put on you," he said in halting Lazooner, "and after then—"

Words seemed to fail the Prefect at that point, since he paused to think for a moment and then resorted to some unambiguous and highly explicit gestures, while nodding towards Chanithel. Chanithel gasped. When Valdur looked from Calviram's face to hers, he saw her eyes were wide and shining, and her lips were parted in happy disbelief. Valdur shrugged and reached for her.

"Not now," said the Prefect hastily. "Later." He pointed to the viewing stands that filled much of the bedchamber.

Valdur understood at once, and in that instant saw gleaming vistas of wonder and luxury stretching unbroken before him to an impossibly distant horizon. And better yet—unending prospects of rapt audiences, of thousands of eyes fixed admiringly upon him, of glory and worship and lovely costumes and many, many people to listen to his poetry. He drew the robes towards himself and pulled them one by one over his head. In his heart, he prepared himself to deliver, with the help of the Prefect's obliging sister, the performance of his life, a masterpiece to astonish and delight—*all night long.*

***

The official death toll was gratifyingly low, only two or three hundred once all bodies had been collected from alleys, gardens, and the sites of small massacres in the marketplaces and down by the waterfront. The last victim to be counted was also the most eminent, the Palace Master Villamar Dreeve, found mysteriously strangled in an obscure corner of the temple. His obsequies and the mass burial of his women were the only sombre notes in what was otherwise a time of rejoicing, a week heavily freighted with auspicious omens. There were no obsequies for the god-king Filkamos, for he was not dead, but gloriously translated to Heaven. Many reported having witnessed the glowing cloud that carried him to the stars, or having watched him mount a luminous stairway to the sky in the company of the other emissaries from Heaven.

The new Lord in Earth, so graciously gifted to the people of Balimhavar, was greeted with mass outpourings of thanksgiving. When an extraordinary Day of the Electa was celebrated ten days after that night of marvels, and the new Lord in Earth reached out with a flourish to touch the hand of

Damissel Dreeve, the very foundations of Balimhavar shook with joy.

Epilogue

Calviram Hithe, Palace Master of Balimhavar at the centre of the world, saw good sense in nurturing an official version of the late god-king's ascension. His sister the Consort, when gently quizzed on what she herself had seen in the Electa's preserve, was a little vague until prompted by her new husband. Then she remembered with perfect clarity: it was a cloud she saw, somewhat in the shape of a glowing flight of stairs, which the god-king and the emissaries from Heaven seemed to mount without going to the trouble of moving their feet, almost as if they were floating straight up. Thereafter, both of the dominant folk-visions, cloud and staircase, were deemed to be acceptable renderings of the miracle. This saved Calviram a great deal of trouble.

But there were still a few heresies to suppress in those busy first days of the new dispensation. The most troublesome was a report circulating among certain farmer folk to the north of the city, in the farmlands bordering the useless and largely untamed mountains that fringed one edge of the Balim delta. Five separate witnesses claimed to have seen a small band of travelers striding at superhuman speed though the fields in the hours before dawn on that fateful morning, led by a tall and divinely handsome youth who sang lustily as he strode, as if in the happiest of moods.

"And then, my lord Palace Master," breathed the elderly farmer who had become the chief prophet of this gospel, "came the most wondrous thing of all. Two men were walking side by side at the end of the procession, and I followed them behind the thorn-hedge for some time, and heard the divine words they spoke to each other. And most assuredly, great lord, they were speaking of Heaven."

Calviram kept his face blank and his voice level. "What were their words, my good man?"

"Well, great lord, one of them kept asking if they were there yet. And the other kept saying no, not yet; but that when they arrived, there would be all the food they could eat, and divine drink by the barrelful, and more concubines than even the Lord in Earth could count. So who else could it have been, but the Lord in Earth and his companions on their way to the glories of Heaven?"

"Who indeed? Anything else?"

"Yes, lord, one thing more. The Lord in Earth asked the other if they'd be going back to the city soon, because he was hungry and his feet were getting sore; and the other assured him they would return in a while, but first they had to see about the food and all those concubines. And so they walked on, great lord, and vanished into the wilds at the edge of the mountains."

The prophet beamed, and the Palace Master beamed back at him, thanked him most kindly for the illumination, and sent him off with the Prefect Sallik Hithe to receive the standard reward given to prophets of inconvenient revelations. Stamping out the rest of the movement would not be a difficult matter, the work of a few days for a troop commanded by the efficient new prefect. But forgetting the prophet's words would not be so easily done.

When the Prefect Sallik returned, he found the Palace Master at the north-facing window, gazing towards the mountains as they caught the last of the sunset. Sallik joined his cousin there.

"Do you want me to go after them, Calviram?" he asked bluntly. "Do you want me to make sure they never come back?"

"No," said the Palace Master, smiling. "I think we can trust the Lords in Heaven to take care of that." But he stood by the window for some time after Sallik left, as if watching for a shaft of glory to lance from the mountaintops to the sky, before he turned back to the pile of tablets on his desk.